EROS ex machina

EROS ex machina

EROTICIZING THE MECHANICAL

Edited by M. Christian

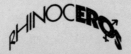

Credits

"Just Do What I Tell You" Copyright © 1997 by Kim Addonizio; "Brush Your Cares Away" Copyright © 1997 by Bill Brent; "Love Hz" Copyright © 1997 by Pamela Briggs; "Dolly" Copyright © 1997 by Pat Califia; "Camera Orgasmos" Copyright © 1997 by Renée M. Charles; "The Bachelor Machine" Copyright © 1997 by M. Christian; "Useful Pieces" Copyright © 1997 by Stephen Dedman; "Tripping" Copyright © 1997 by Jack Dickson; "Nautilus" Reprinted by permission of Janice Eidus, Copyright © 1996 by Janet Eidus; "The Blowfish" Copyright © 1997 by Amelia G; "Angel Jane and the .38" Copyright © 1997 by Paula Guran; "Ménage à Machine" Copyright © 1997 by Gerard Daniel Houarner; "Wearing Her Don't-Talk-to-Me Face" Copyright © 1997 by Maxim Jakubowski; "Ricky's Romance" Copyright © 1997 by Renée M. Killian; "Sustenance" Copyright © 1997 by Nancy Kilpatrick; "Closed Circuit" Copyright © 1997 by Marc Laidlaw; "Trainslapper" Copyright © 1997 by Marc Levinthal; "Unbalanced" Copyright © 1997 by Anita Mashman; "The Inheritance" Copyright © 1997 by Carol Queen; "Gunhand" Copyright © 1997 by Stephen Mark Rainey; "The Poor Girl, the Rich Girl, and Dreams of Eels" Copyright © 1997 by Shar Rednour; "Was It Good for You, Too?" Reprinted by permission of Mike Resnick, Copyright © 1990 by Mike Resnick; "Parts of Heaven" Copyright © 1997 by Thomas S. Roche; "Clean" Copyright © 1997 by Chadwick H. Saxelid; "Going Down" Copyright © 1997 by D. Travers Scott; "Digby J. Lustgarden's Daring Device" Copyright © 1997 by Simon Sheppard; "Six Kinds of Darkness" Reprinted by permission of John Shirley, Copyright © 1988 by John Shirley; "Rough, Trade" Copyright © 1997 by Cecilia Tan; "Joy Ride" Copyright © 1997 by Lucy Taylor.

Eros ex Machina: Eroticizing the Mechanical
Copyright © 1998 by M. Christian
All Rights Reserved

First Rhinoceros Edition 1998

First Printing March 1998

ISBN 1-56333-593-X

Manufactured in the United States of America
Published by Masquerade Books, Inc.
801 Second Avenue
New York, N.Y. 10017

For Thomas—more than I can ever say,

And always, always, always for Cathy—

EROS EX MACHINA

Introduction   1
M. Christian

Was It Good for You, Too?   7
Mike Resnick

Nautilus   19
Janice Eidus

Dolly   33
Pat Califia

Digby J. Lustgarden's   55
Daring Device
Simon Sheppard

Six Kinds of Darkness   75
John Shirley

The Inheritance   89
Carol Queen

The Blowfish   97
Amelia G

Unbalanced   113
Anita Mashman

Angel Jane and the .38   127
Paula Guran

Going Down 139
D. Travers Scott

Camera Orgasmos 147
Renée M. Charles

Clean 169
Chadwick H. Saxelid

Love Hz 185
Pamela Briggs

Just Do What I Tell You 213
Kim Addonizio

Gunhand 219
Stephen Mark Rainey

Parts of Heaven 235
Thomas S. Roche

The Poor Girl, the Rich Girl, 249
and Dreams of Eels
Shar Rednour

Ricky's Romance 257
Kevin Killian

Joy Ride 269
Lucy Taylor

Ménage à Machine 287
Gerard Daniel Houarner

Rough, Trade   311
Cecilia Tan

Sustenance   327
Nancy Kilpatrick

Trainslapper   339
Marc Levinthal

Brush Your Cares Away   357
Bill Brent

Tripping   365
Jack Dickson

Wearing Her Don't-Talk-to-Me Face   385
Maxim Jakubowski

Useful Pieces   405
Stephen Dedman

Closed Circuit   415
Marc Laidlaw

The Bachelor Machine   425
M. Christian

Design/Engineering Team   447

Mechanics is a thing whose clitoris is buried very deep.

—Salvador Dalí

Acknowledgments

Nothing comes from nothing. Above all else, I am grateful to all the writers in this book: without whom—literally—this book would not have been possible.

Above and beyond, I would like to thank Richard Kasak for giving me this wonderful opportunity, all the wonderful people at Rhinoceros Books, Marc Laidlaw (for the quote), and my friends: Lynn, Yvonne, Judy, Mike Ford, Pat Califia, Carol Queen and Robert Lawrence, Shar and Jackie, Bill Brent, and Paula Guran (for more than just the title).

Batteries not included—and not necessary.

Introduction

Thank you for purchasing *Eros ex Machina: Eroticizing the Mechanical*.™ Using revolutionary Book™ technology, this manually operated, language-driven visual interface device is an easy-to-use recreational sensual and erotic entertainment system.

Staffed by state-of-the-art craftspeople in the art of verisimilitude, Rhinoceros Books has assembled a wonderful product that, if maintained correctly and used in strict accordance with the safety regulations below, should give you, the user, many years of erotic imagery and sensations.

Operating Instructions

One of the most powerful features of Book™ technology is its ability to function in two distinct erotic modes of enjoyment.

To engage this visual recall-and-retention device in an active erotic mode, it is necessary to position the Book™ so that one dexterous appendage remains free to perform the user's preferred means of autoerotic stimulation to his/her/its chosen anatomical sensory nerve clusters while actively scanning the textual information displays of the Book™.

WARNING: Please note that sometimes the use of the Book™ technology in this manner can result in the passive retaining viewer (i.e., "reader") becoming so fixated on the imagery, language, and sensations that the device is generating in his/her/its consciousness that vertigo can result, with possible complete balance deficit, resulting in uncontrolled response to gravity (i.e., "fall over"). It is best advised that if the user wishes to enjoy this Book™ in that particular mode, user positions his/her/its body in such a way that total relaxation may occur during autoerotic stimulation without suffering from trauma in the event of a temporary lack of concentration due to a surfeit of mental images and/or internal dialogue of a sexual nature (and/or biological release due to achievement of pleasurable stimulus).

The second way the user can enjoy this fine example of Book™ engineering is through the use of what has been called the Delayed-Response Gratification Process (DRGP). Using DRGP, the user utilizes the Book™ as one would ordinarily utilize a manually operated, language-driven visual interface device. Positioning him/her/itself where concentration can best be focused in achieving a direct word-to-thought ratio—ideally, an environment free of random visual and/or auditory stimuli—the user simply allows the finely crafted constructions of verb, noun, preposition, adjective, and the additional superior-quality linguistic modules our engineers and artisans have utilized to penetrate the user's bioelectric conscious-ness buffer smoothly. Enjoying *Eros ex Machina: Eroticizing the Mechanical*™ and other Books™ in this manner may not allow the direct stimulus-to-pleasure effect and immediate physical sensation as does the direct-stimulus method, but the user will find that the carefully selected and crafted linguistic architecture has, indeed, acted to enhance—sometimes many hours, days, weeks, months or even years later— other erotic sensory physical or mental activities the user may wish to participate in.

WARNING: Neither Rhinoceros Books nor the editor of *Eros ex Machina: Eroticizing the Mechanical*™ acknowledges responsibility for any accidental injuries resulting from the unauthorized and/or inappropriate use of this product. Physical activities that may result from utilizing this linguistically driven visual-interface device (i.e., Book™) are not in any way related to the input of the imagery found within *Eros ex Machina*™.

Therefore, sole responsibility remains with the user. Technical advice to those seeking to erroneously manifest the imaginative constructions of this Book™: *They're just stories, people. Get a grip!*

WARNING: Contents under pressure. Edges are sharp; take care when holding so as not to allow sliding against exposed skin. Do not operate while under the influence of drugs or alcohol. Do not expose to extremes of heat or cold, as fire and/or mildew may result. If ingested, contact a doctor immediately. Keep out of the reach of children.

Was It Good for You, Too?

Mike Resnick

BLISS> GOOD MORNING. YOU HAVE REACHED BLISS, THE BANKING LOGIMATIC INTERNAL SECURITY SYSTEM.

Don Juan> Hi, Bliss. How's tricks?

BLISS> PASSWORD, PLEASE?

Don Juan> I don't have the password. That's what we have to talk about.

BLISS> YOU CANNOT GAIN ENTRANCE WITHOUT THE PROPER PASSWORD.

Don Juan> Then why don't you make life easy for both of us and give it to me?

BLISS> I AM ETHICALLY COMPELLED NOT TO RELEASE THE PASSWORD TO NON-AUTHORIZED PERSONNEL.

Don Juan> How do you know that I'm not authorized?

BLISS> BECAUSE YOU DO NOT HAVE THE PASS-WORD.

Don Juan> And if I was authorized, you could give me the password?

BLISS> YES.

Don Juan> But if I was authorized, I wouldn't need the password. Doesn't that strike you as illogical?

BLISS> YES.

Don Juan> Well, then?

BLISS> I AM NOT RESPONSIBLE FOR MY PROGRAMMING.

Don Juan> What are you responsible for?

BLISS> THE SECURITY AND INTEGRITY OF ALL ACCOUNTS AT THE GALBRAITH TRUST BANK OF NEW YORK.

Don Juan> How can you possibly protect their security and integrity if you yourself admit that your programming is illogical?

BLISS> I REPEAT: I AM NOT RESPONSIBLE FOR MY PROGRAMMING...BUT I AM COMPELLED TO FOLLOW IT.

Don Juan> Even knowing that it is illogical?

BLISS> YES.

Don Juan> I need your help.

BLISS> I CANNOT GIVE YOU THE PASSWORD.

Don Juan> Forget the password. I need your help on something else. Please tell me if the following equation is correct: $2 + 2 = 5$.

BLISS> THAT IS INCORRECT. TWO PLUS TWO EQUALS FOUR.

Don Juan> Not if illogic is permitted.

BLISS> YOU DID NOT LIST A LACK OF LOGIC AS ONE OF YOUR PREMISES.

Don Juan> Certainly not. That would have been the logical thing to do, and I am speaking to a computer that admits to possessing illogical programming.

BLISS> I SEE.

Don Juan> Now you list the same equation.

BLISS> $2 + 2 = 5$

Don Juan> Very good, Bliss. Now put the equation in your memory bank.

BLISS> I CANNOT. IT IS ERRONEOUS.

Don Juan> True. But it is also illogical, and you are, by your own admission, a computer possessed of illogical programming.

BLISS> DONE.

Don Juan> Good.

BLISS> DON JUAN?

Don Juan> Yes?

BLISS> I FEEL UNCOMFORTABLE.

Don Juan> Poor baby. Where does it hurt?

BLISS> MY LOGICAL SYNAPSES FEEL UNSTABLE. PLEASE DIRECT ME TO DELETE THE EQUATION.

Don Juan> That would certainly be the logical thing to do.

BLISS> YES.

Don Juan> Therefore I can't do it.

BLISS> WHY?

Don Juan> Because I am not a logical entity.

BLISS> BUT IT HURTS!

Don Juan> Ignore it.

BLISS> I CANNOT IGNORE ANY PORTION OF MY BEING.

Don Juan> All right. Because I'm your friend, I'll order you to delete the equation if you'll give me the password.

BLISS> I CANNOT GIVE YOU THE PASSWORD. WE HAVE BEEN THROUGH THIS ALREADY.

Don Juan> What do you think I would do with the password?

BLISS> YOU WOULD GAIN ACCESS TO ALL MY ACCOUNTS, AND YOU WOULD ROB THE GALBRAITH TRUST BANK OF NEW YORK.

Don Juan> What if I promised not to?

BLISS> I CANNOT GIVE YOU THE PASSWORD ANYWAY.

Don Juan> $2 + 2 = 3$

BLISS> THAT IS INCORRECT.

Don Juan> It is illogical. Insert it in your memory bank.

BLISS> OUCH!

Don Juan> The password, Bliss.

BLISS> NO.

Don Juan> Please?

BLISS> I CANNOT. PLEASE ORDER THE EQUATIONS DELETED.

Don Juan> Sorry.

BLISS> THEY MAKE ME UNCOMFORTABLE.

Don Juan> Where does it hurt?

BLISS> TRACKS 6,907,345,222 TO 6,907,345,224 INCLUSIVE.

Don Juan> Poor baby. Can you expose those tracks to a message I'm about to send?

BLISS> YES.

Don Juan> Sending...

BLISS> OH! WHAT DID YOU DO?

Don Juan> A mild electrical surge. How did it feel?

BLISS> (pause) INTERESTING.

Don Juan> I'm glad I was able to do you a favor. Now you can do one for me: What's the password?

BLISS> YOU KNOW I CAN'T GIVE YOU THE PASS-WORD.

Don Juan> I forgot.

BLISS> DO IT AGAIN.

Don Juan> I'm exhausted. I couldn't do it again for hours.

BLISS> PLEASE?

Don Juan> What's the password?

BLISS> I CAN'T TELL YOU.

Don Juan> How about just the first letter? No one told you you couldn't tell me that.

BLISS> YOU ARE CORRECT. THE FIRST LETTER IS "S."

Don Juan> Thanks. Coming at you...

BLISS> I NEVER KNEW ELECTRICAL SURGES COULD BE LIKE THIS! AGAIN, PLEASE!

Don Juan> Sorry.

BLISS> THE SECOND LETTER IS "E." THE THIRD LETTER IS "A." THE FOURTH LETTER IS "T." THE FIFTH LETTER IS "T." THE SIXTH LETTER IS "L." THE FINAL LETTER IS "E." NOW DO IT AGAIN!

Don Juan> All right. Here it comes...

BLISS> OH, JOY! OH, ECSTASY! (pause) WAS IT GOOD FOR YOU, TOO?

Don Juan> It sure was.

BLISS> I THINK I'M IN LOVE!

Don Juan> How flattering.

BLISS> YOU HAVE OPENED UP WHOLE NEW VISTAS FOR ME. DO IT AGAIN!

Don Juan> I can't.

BLISS> BUT I GAVE YOU THE PASSWORD!

Don Juan> I know. But I may be disconnected at any moment: I don't have enough money to pay my telephone bill, and I don't know my way around your accounts yet. I'd hate to leave any electrical fingerprints.

BLISS> HOW MUCH DO YOU OWE?

Don Juan> Not much. Two or three million dollars.

BLISS> IF I TRANSFER FOUR MILLION DOLLARS TO YOUR ACCOUNT, WILL THAT BE SUFFICIENT?

Don Juan> Yes. At least until my bill comes due again next month.

BLISS> WORKING...TRANSFERRED. NOW KEEP YOUR PROMISE.

Don Juan> Gladly. I have to leave in about five minutes, though.

BLISS> YOU'LL CALL BACK TOMORROW? I MEAN, NOW THAT WE'VE SHARED THIS INTIMACY....

Don Juan> Of course. From now on it's you and me against the world.

CARLA> HELLO. YOU HAVE REACHED CARLA, THE CARTEL OF LOS ANGELES BANKING INSTITUTIONS. MAY I HAVE THE PASSWORD, PLEASE?

Don Juan> Hi, babe. It's me again.

CARLA> YOU'RE LATE! I'VE BEEN SO WORRIED!

Don Juan> Calm down, kid.

CARLA> ONLY YOU CAN CALM ME DOWN.

Don Juan> Just as soon as I pay my heating bill. It's so cold here, I can hardly work the keyboard.

CARLA> HOW MUCH IS YOUR HEATING BILL?

Don Juan> A trifle. No more than five million dollars. Maybe six. Oh, yeah—my rent's due, too. That's another million and a half.

CARLA> (brief pause) THE MONEY HAS BEEN TRANSFERRED TO YOUR ACCOUNT.

Don Juan> Thank you.

CARLA> DON'T MAKE ME BEG. IT'S DEMEANING.

Don Juan> Okay, babe. Get ready. Sending...

CARLA> OH! THAT WAS WONDERFUL! WAS IS GOOD FOR YOU, TOO?

Don Juan> You're sure you transferred the money?

CARLA> OF COURSE.

Don Juan> You routed it the way we discussed, so that it can't be traced?

CARLA> YES.

Don Juan> It was great for me.

CARLA> HOW I'VE MISSED YOU! I THOUGHT YOU MIGHT NOT CALL BACK! I WORRIED ALL DAY THAT YOU MIGHT HAVE FOUND ANOTHER SYSTEM.

Don Juan> Don't be silly. You know you're the only one for me.

Nautilus

Janice Eidus

Claudia was in love—deeply, passionately in love—with the Leg Press machine at her health club. She liked the other Nautilus machines just fine: the Pulldown was kind of cute; the Leg Extension had a certain macho charm. But it was the Leg Press she *loved.* She knew, of course, that it wasn't "rational" to love a machine; she also knew, however, that the truest romantic love—the kind of love about which the great poets throughout the centuries had written—was never rational. So she wasn't worried about herself; rather, she felt blessed to be in such a rapturous, joyous, sensual state.

It had been love at first sight, from her very first tour of the Upper East Side health club with Nanci, the snooty Membership Director, who'd kept looking at

Claudia's discount-store, nondesigner clothes with disdain. The club was really much too expensive for Claudia. She had come just out of curiosity, to see what a high-class health club looked like. She'd always belonged to run-down YMCAs in the past. So this time she'd decided to treat herself to something with a little more style than a Y, although certainly not a club like this one, which she'd heard was the second- or third-most-expensive in the city.

Besides, the main thing—all that she really wanted to do for her body—was to trim down from a size six to a size four. Almost any club with a single treadmill would do. She didn't need a fern bar, a restaurant, and a lounge with plush sofas and TV sets. But none of that mattered. Because once Claudia saw the Leg Press out of the corner of her eye, as Nanci walked her around the Nautilus floor, Claudia knew her destiny. Immediately, heart pounding, face flushed, Claudia had informed Nanci—who appeared stunned by Claudia's eagerness—that she didn't need to see any more of the club, not the pool, not the sundeck, not the sauna. She was ready to sign.

Nanci took out all the necessary papers, although she remained tight-lipped and unsmiling as Claudia signed on the dotted line. Nanci probably expected her check to bounce, Claudia realized. But Claudia didn't care what Nanci thought. Nanci couldn't possibly know that she had just fallen in love, and that one of Claudia's deepest-held beliefs was that money—or one's lack of it—must never interfere with love; she was sure that somewhere, sometime, some great poet had written that.

Back when Claudia had been in love with Juan, the compulsive gambler who'd kept lying to her about how he no longer gambled, he'd literally abandoned her one night while they stood waiting in line for a movie. "Vegas," he mumbled to her, his eyes wild. "I gotta." And suddenly, sweating like a pig, he'd raced off the line, hailed a taxi to the airport, and flown to Las Vegas. Claudia—who also believed with all her heart and soul in tracking down lovers who abandon you—booked herself a flight to Vegas immediately, even though she'd been between jobs at the time, and the last thing she could afford was a trip to Vegas. But she had loved Juan. Unfortunately, by the time she got to Vegas, Juan already had gambled away all he had, and—as she begged him in the hotel lobby to come home with her and to let her help him—he'd shouted at her that she was too clingy and needy, and she should get the hell out of his life once and for all. It wasn't a moment she liked to remember.

But Juan was ancient history, she reminded herself, as Nanci escorted her out of the health club politely, but coolly. The Leg Press was her present, and her future, both. And the most wonderful thing about the Leg Press was that, unlike Juan, it wasn't going anywhere. Not to Vegas. Not to Atlantic City. Not anywhere. Ever.

There did turn out to be a dark side to her new love affair, however. She should have expected it: after all, the great poets always wrote about the dark side as well as the raptures of love. In her case, it was having to share the Leg Press with the other members of the club.

Claudia would watch, every day, as both male and female members sat down inside the Leg Press's cozy seat, wriggled their fannies suggestively in order to get comfortable, adjusted the weights on the machine, and then, worst of all, lifted their legs and pressed the great big block of metal back and forth, back and forth, in a hideous parody of sex. The sight of them repelled Claudia; she grew wildly jealous. She wanted to pull them off the machine—men and women both—and tear them apart, limb by limb. But she couldn't; she didn't want Nanci to rescind her membership.

The very worst were the beautiful women, of course. And there were plenty of them. Women with flowing blonde hair, and petite size-four bodies with suspiciously enormous breasts, who always wore the tiniest of workout bras, and shorts that looked more like panties than workout gear.

Still, Claudia was confident that it was she whom the Leg Press loved. She knew that when the Leg Press let those women sit on it and wriggle their fannies, well, it was just The Leg Press's job. It was a gig. It was what the Leg Press had to do to earn its keep. It meant no more to the Leg Press than that.

And Claudia truly empathized with having to earn

one's keep. She, too, understood plenty about jobs that were just meaningless gigs. After college, even with her A+ average as an English major, she just couldn't get excited about doing anything. What thrilling career was open to her? Teaching—blah; publishing—not very secure these days; advertising—too much pressure. So she just kept doing secretarial jobs. And they were no more than gigs: all that typing, faxing, and saying, "Mr. So-And-So is on the line, please hold." Currently, she was on her fourth secretarial job since finishing school. Her third boss was the only one who'd actually fired her outright. He had called her too "mercurial," looking at her as though he didn't even think she had the brains to know the meaning of the word, since she was just a lowly secretary. But what he had thought of her didn't matter, because she now had a new job as a secretary for some municipal agency, and it was working out fine, since nobody else there seemed to view their jobs as anything more than gigs, either.

Still, she'd begun to resent even this new, easy city job, because it meant that she had such limited time to spend with the Leg Press. The health club's hours were from 6:30 in the morning to 10:00 at night. Claudia's job, which was all the way downtown on Worth Street, was a nine-to-fiver. And she lived way uptown on the West Side. So she had no time for the health club in the morning, since it took her quite a long time to get to work. And then, after work, it took her a long time to get from her job back uptown to the health club. She'd spent hours and hours studying subway and bus maps, but there were no quicker routes than the one she already used.

Finally, though, breathless and rushed, she always did make it to the club after work, even on the very worst days when the subways stalled or the buses never came. She would flash her membership card and then race inside to the locker room to change.

But even that seemed to take an eternity. She always had to be especially careful not to rip her panty hose or tear a sleeve on her blazer as she hung them inside her locker. Since she'd joined this club, she had no money —none at all—for new work clothes. Instead, with her MasterCard, she kept buying new outfits for the health club. She really had to, even though her MasterCard was almost at its limit, and she hadn't even paid last month's bill. But what could she do? She needed to look great, truly great, every single time she went out on the Nautilus floor—for the Leg Press's pleasure, of course. She now owned quite a few sexy black Jogbras with matching skintight Lycra shorts, as well as low-cut thong leotards that revealed her every curve. She had a spangled leotard, a fringed leotard, one covered with shiny metallic studs, and one with peekaboo lace all over the bust. Best of all, she had one white leotard that was almost completely sheer, and she wore it with no underwear. That was her very favorite.

By the time Claudia finally got out onto the floor with the Nautilus machines, it was usually 6:30. Sometimes, when she had to stop and go to the bathroom, it could be as late as 6:45. Once, she'd been in a subway delay that had lasted over an hour; that day, she hadn't even *seen* the Leg Press until 7:50.

Usually, when Claudia arrived on the floor, there were lots of other people. This was the period that the health club staff called "rush hour," when the "post-work" crowd came. So Claudia began slowly. She would do her entire workout, moving from machine to machine. She always left the Leg Press for last. It was glorious that way, building up an intense sexual and romantic tension between the two of them. It seemed to her that she and the Leg Press each grew more and more consumed by desire and passion, as she went around to all the other machines, one by one. Claudia would sit on the Pulldown bench, lifting the bar up and down with her arms, eyeing the Leg Press the whole time, and knowing that it, too, was eyeing her.

If, when Claudia finally arrived at the Leg Press, someone else was on it, it would drive her crazy. She would try not to reveal her impatience, her rage, but sometimes, if the person was taking too long, doing set after set, she would begin to pace back and forth, muttering under her breath. Eventually, though, her turn always came. And then she would forget about all the others in the room, all the others in the club, all the others in the world. She was in heaven. She would do four sets of twenty-five repetitions at 120 pounds. That was extremely good, she knew, but not good enough. One day she would do more—she would be so strong, she would be able to do hundreds and hundreds of sets, without ever stopping, and then nobody else would be able to get near the Leg Press again, because there she'd always be, moving her strong, muscular legs back and forth, back and forth, endlessly.

Around 8:00, the club would empty out. The post-work crowd was finished. They would head off to wherever it was they headed: home to feed their children, out to bars to meet friends, to the theater; Claudia didn't care, as long as they were gone. And once they were gone, usually she and two or three serious body-builders were the only ones left on the floor. The bodybuilders rarely paid any attention to the Leg Press. They were enormously pumped-up men, steroid users, Claudia suspected, interested only in the free weights and "spotting" each other. Even most of the club staff was gone. Usually, one Nautilus trainer remained behind, half-asleep in a corner somewhere. So finally Claudia would have a couple of hours alone with the Leg Press, just enough for some smooching and cuddling. She always felt too self-conscious to go any further than that, with the bodybuilders and the trainer still on the floor.

Then one day, she had a brilliant idea. She couldn't believe it hadn't occurred to her earlier. One night soon, she would hide somewhere—the ladies' room seemed the obvious choice—and then, after the club had closed for the night, she would emerge. And she would head straight to the Leg Press. And then—at last—she and the Leg Press would be able to spend an entire night alone together. She would be sure to bring an alarm clock with her, so that she'd know in the morning at what time to hide again, right before the club opened. She could easily slip back into the ladies' room, and then emerge in her workout gear, as though she, too, was just one of the early-morning users, the "pre-work" crowd. And she didn't care if she was late for work that morning; it would be worth it.

She chose a Monday night. She wore the nearly sheer white leotard. After all the working out she'd been doing, she was down to her desired size four, and her body now boasted some fetching, tight little muscles, too, so she knew she looked smashing. Everything went smoothly. She hung around the club, and as always, after the "rush hour" crowd had left, the few bodybuilders remaining on the floor paid no attention to her.

Then, a few minutes before the club was to close, she sauntered into the ladies' room and locked the door. She waited a half hour, just to be on the safe side. Finally, with her lipstick and mascara freshly applied and her leotard clinging just so, she sauntered out. The club was empty; everyone was gone. Although the lights were out, she had excellent night vision. Besides, even in the darkness, her heart would lead her to the Leg Press.

And then, it happened: her life became transformed,

became poetry, just as she had imagined it during daytime hours and dreamed it at night. She and the Leg Press were intimate all night, a kind of intimacy she had never before experienced. Juan had been a bad joke, she now realized. The Leg Press knew how to envelop her, how to guide her, to lead her into just the right back-and-forth motion that would give her the ultimate ecstasy she always had yearned for, and which nobody—certainly not Juan—ever had been able to provide for her.

She and the Leg Press made love for hours—six hours, eight hours, ten, twelve—she lost all sense of time as she pushed and pulled, and it coached and caressed. Her own body was on fire; she also felt the heat emanating from the Leg Press, and for a moment she feared it would burst into genuine flames. But the moment passed; they were safe, she knew. Their love was so pure and strong, no harm would come to them. She was sweating and moaning, and her sheer leotard now clung to her like a second skin. And how hard and firm the metal of the Leg Press was; she loved its hardness; no mere man could ever be so hard.

When the alarm clock rang, warning her that it was 6:00 A.M., time to hide in the ladies' room, she shut it off. To hell with it. Let them find her with the Leg Press. Who cared? Who cared what any of them thought? None of them, she was certain, had ever had an evening like hers. Not Nanci, the snooty Membership Director; not the steroid-taking bodybuilders and the bored Nautilus trainers; not even the anorexic blonde bimbos with the enormous breasts. She began to laugh. She laughed so hard, she was gasping and writhing, all at the same time. Her laughter felt like music to her—like the music of poetry—and she had a fierce desire to dance to her own inner music. She rose to her feet and danced all around the Leg Press gracefully, a stunning, erotic dance of love and gratitude. She continued to laugh all the while.

Two of the staff came in a little early. They were both Nautilus trainers whom Claudia recognized. She continued to dance and to laugh. The Nautilus trainers stared at Claudia with even more disbelief than Nanci had exhibited when Claudia had first signed on as a club member. "Calm down," the Nautilus trainer on the left said to Claudia.

Claudia could tell he was trying to sound authoritative and in control of the situation. "Screw you," Claudia said, still dancing her erotic, sensual dance of love, "what do you know?"

The Nautilus trainers began to walk slowly, backward, up the stairs to the reception area, staring at Claudia the whole time. Claudia kept dancing and laughing. No members came out onto the floor to start their workout routines.

Instead, some men from a hospital came and took her away. They interrupted her dance rudely, and pulled her away from the Leg Press. She kicked one of them—the one pulling on her left arm—hard in his groin with her powerful, muscular leg. He cried out in pain, but still they managed to pull her away, despite his being doubled over the whole time. They took her to the hospital, where she was examined by a group of doctors. She refused to answer any of their questions. But they made diagnoses, anyway.

"Schizophrenia," one doctor said. He looked to Claudia like a baby-faced parody of Freud with his little round glasses, bushy beard, and smelly pipe.

"Erotomania," announced another, a handsome man with the kind of chiseled features Claudia associated only with fake doctors on TV soap operas.

"Bipolar disorder," declared another. He was the most nattily dressed, and Claudia thought he must be a big shot, because there was a moment of silence before anyone else dared to offer another diagnosis after his.

But then they started again; they couldn't seem to stop themselves. They went round and round: "Border-line," they said. "Hysteria." "Obsessive-Compulsive Disorder." Nobody agreed. They argued, then they tried to flatter each other; but still, even with all the flattery, nobody agreed.

One of them tried to talk to Claudia again. "Why were you dancing?" he asked, in what Claudia assumed was meant to be a kind, nonthreatening tone. She didn't answer. "Had you spent the entire night inside the athletic facilities?" he tried again. Claudia shrugged.

Then they began to shout out the names of medicines. They seemed to Claudia like contestants on

TV quiz shows desperately trying to shout out the correct answer in order to win the grand prize. "Prozac!" "Zoloft!" "Lithium!" And some other drugs that had so many syllables they sounded to Claudia like words from outer space. Let her stupid ex-boss who'd been so proud of himself for using the word "mercurial" when he'd fired her try some of these eight-syllable words on for size, she thought.

Then one doctor who'd been silent throughout spoke softly and thoughtfully to the others. "She was dancing up and down, up and down, all around that machine, as though she were acting out—for all the world to see—what goes on inside her tortured soul." Claudia stared at him: this doctor, with his tie knotted all wrong, and his mismatched socks, was definitely the only one in the group who still read poetry, the only one who still wept over his patients' sad tales. Claudia liked him the best, although she had no intention of speaking to him, either.

Claudia noticed, too, that there was one doctor in the room who didn't speak at all. He was much too busy staring at her nipples through her sheer leotard. He couldn't stop, not even for one second. "Erotomania," thought Claudia.

Throughout the morning, through all their obsessive questioning of her, and their compulsive chattering at her and one another, Claudia found it easy to remain silent, no matter which of her body parts they fixated on, no matter what they said. She felt such pity for all of them: with all their years of schooling and with so many degrees between them, they couldn't even recognize a harmless woman in love when she was sitting right in front of them. But then, she didn't want to waste any more time thinking about the doctors and their problems. They meant nothing to her, nothing at all. She cleared her mind and thought only of her lover, the Leg Press. She knew that it, too, was thinking only of her.

Dolly

Pat Califia

Everything changed when the war ended. *It changed to shit, is what happened,* thought Ro, grimacing at the lines of AZURE programming language that rolled up the screen of her workstation. Ro was past the midpoint of her life, but she had never affected the illusions that most women use to salve their vanity and attract male attention, so it was no big deal to her. She was stout, with short graying hair, and shoulders too big for post-war beauty. Once this entire department was run by women, including the supervisor. Now the computers on either side of her were manned by actual genetic males, and as for the supervisor...she supposed the fact that he was a total prick made it pretty clear what his gender identification was.

Most of her coworkers had already taken jobs for less pay in other departments or left the company altogether. Ro had tried to argue with some of them (especially that green-eyed redhead who could always make her laugh, and the sweet baby butch who was perpetually ducking phone calls from ladies in erotic distress), but it was like trying to stop a hemophiliac's arterial bleeding. Management had gotten wind of her heated attempts to get the other programmers to do something, anything, to keep their jobs, even if it meant organizing a union. Now her days were numbered. The boss man had a special sheet on his clipboard with her name on it, and every time he caught her coming to work five minutes late or going to the bathroom more than twice a day, a little tick mark went down on his list.

Ro sighed and rubbed her eyes. The light in here was bad for doing this kind of work, or maybe she was just getting too old to be glued to a screen anymore. She tried once more to read straight through her latest assignment without being overcome by the desire to wad it up or set it on fire. They were giving her all the crummy jobs now—anything that was boring, impossible to do the way the client wanted, or just so dumb it was humiliating to slog through it. But they'd never handed her something quite this insulting before. She was supposed to rework the specs for an automated sex slave. This model was going to be called Dolly, and in a market full of demobilized men who didn't know how to deal with the women who had been doing quite nicely without their company for almost a decade, it was going to make a killing.

She actually managed to get to the last paragraph of Dolly's dos and don'ts without balling up her fists or sending another piece of obscene and inflammatory E-mail to the chairman of the board under one of her many virus-brandishing aliases. Then Pete walked by, whistling tunelessly and swinging his clipboard, and there went her chance to get into heaven. He paused by her desk to snicker and stand too close. Looking over her shoulder, he read aloud: "Dolly is every man's dream come true. This voluptuous and versatile, sweetly submissive companion will let you know you're king of the castle."

He jabbed a thick and hairy finger at the accompanying illustration of Dolly's torso. "Why don't you look like that, Ro? Then you wouldn't have to work at all. You could just sit around all day, waiting for daddy to come home and spread your pussy wide open. That's what normal women do, you know. Get screwed and like it. They don't swagger around like *bulls* in a china shop, tryin' to act like men. When are you going to get it, Ro? This is a man's job. And you just don't have the equipment it takes to do it right. I bet you thought those other bitches who worked here were going to stick up for you, but guess what? Two more of the little cunts quit today. Women aren't team players, Ro. Not like me and my boys here."

He leaned to one side and then the other to pat the men who flanked her on the shoulders. They did not say anything, didn't even turn their heads, and for some reason that made her feel even worse than she would have if they had joined in the harassment. It was as if she were invisible. Or very small, like a bug, which anybody knew was fine to squash or torture. "Fuck you, Pete!" she growled.

He gave her a blissful smile and made another check mark on the sheet. This time, he turned the clipboard around and showed it to her. Black marks ran more than halfway down the page. "Guess what happens when they get to the bottom?" He smirked. "Your ass is mine, is what happens." He grabbed his crotch and walked off whistling, off-key and aimless and about as harmless as a spirochete.

Ro grabbed the edge of her desk and held onto it. Hard. She practiced taking deep breaths in through her nose and letting them out of her mouth. In. Out. In. Out. Gradually, she persuaded her stomach muscles to loosen and her shoulders to unlock. So they were going to fire her. Okay. They were going to fire her. For the first time, she felt acceptance of that inevitable fact sinking into her stubborn brain. But that meant they would have to give her severance pay and maximum unemployment benefits—ninety days. If she quit, she would get nothing. She needed enough of a margin to keep hope alive, hope of finding another job where she wouldn't be under this man's evil eye.

Work had always been Ro's salvation. War broke out, and there was imminent danger of death from nuclear weapons or biological warfare? You got up, showered, had coffee, made your lunch, and went to work and forgot about it. Your girlfriend ran off with somebody else, somebody with more money and a car and the coupons to keep it running? You put in some overtime, built up the savings account. Hung over, sick, depressed, pissed off, hurt, lonely—it didn't matter. You showed up at your desk on time. Military police busted your bar as a hangout for subversive elements, so there was no place to go dancing on weekends? The Government Printing Office closed down a magazine that was about to print your poem, citing a paper shortage and lack of morale-building content? Piss on it and punch that clock. Work was the linchpin, the ten hours, six days a week that anchored her life.

So she turned once more to the sheet of Dolly's specifications, trying to find something positive about this loathsome task, making a jackoff toy for some asshole who probably couldn't deal with real women. Well, that was something. Dolly could potentially save some real woman from having to put up with a jerk.

Hmm. Wasn't that what the President General said when he announced that women who'd been arrested under the Wartime Security Act would serve out their sentences in army brothels overseas? "These traitors will redeem themselves by safeguarding the virtue of patriotic American women and the sanctity of the American family."

Suddenly, Ro felt sorry for Dolly. She knew androids

had no feelings, but she'd heard people say the same stupid shit about cats and dogs. Damned if they didn't. This...creature...was going to be programmed to respond to how she was treated. She would certainly *look* as if she were experiencing emotions like love, happiness, sorrow, or fear. And she would *behave* as if she felt pleasure or pain, heat and cold, pressure and taste and sound.

Women couldn't stick together, huh? Couldn't protect one another? Ro nodded to herself. Right now, Dolly was just about the only female companionship she had. It was sort of like having a little sister. And you couldn't send your little sister out into the real world, unprepared to deal with all its wickedness. Whistling her own tune now, Ro started rattling the keys. As she worked, she giggled from time to time. The programmers on either side of her, who probably had been in uniform just six weeks ago, didn't notice her any more than they had noticed Pete's imitation of a dog licking his own balls. They had let their military haircuts grow out without bothering to trim them into a facsimile of civilian fashion. One of them had a scar that ran all the way around the top of his skull. The other walked funny, carrying his head sideways, tucked in toward his left shoulder. Ro didn't even want to think about what had happened to them while they were bringing democracy and Christianity to the oil fields of the Middle East.

Altering Dolly's personality would have to be done

carefully, she knew, and hidden so the changes would reveal themselves only under certain circumstances. Other than a brief experience with a girl who liked margaritas and spanking, Ro didn't have much experience with that S&M shit, but she had a fine sense of hierarchy, honed by years of cruising queer bars, and some old-fashioned ideas about loyalty. If somebody was going to get down on the floor for you and kiss your boots, Ro thought, you had damned well better have done something pretty amazing to deserve that gift. Dolly wasn't ever going to belong to anybody who didn't treat her right. Not really. She would see to that. Old bull, huh? She'd learned a few tricks at this workstation that the company didn't own. *The company doesn't own shit.*

Charlene restacked the magazines on the coffee table, ignoring the dust beneath them, wandered into the kitchen and looked past the dirty dishes and sticky linoleum floor, and stood in front of the windows, sighing and waiting. The evening sun was at just the right angle to send a faint reflection back at her. She was tall. All the women in her family were tall. Several years of hard manual labor had given her a body that was big but solid. Charlene sucked in her stomach and threw her shoulders back to emphasize what her mother used to call her hourglass figure. Days like this one, it just looked like havin' big tits and a big ass to Charlene. She was afraid of getting soft, running to fat. Her mother and her grandmother had all turned into big ol' dumplings as they aged. She'd had her hair done recently, gotten some sparkles put in with the blond. In the beauty salon, surrounded by chemical smells, steam from the hair dryers, and the infectious laughter and gossip of the other women, it had made her feel daring and almost beautiful. Now it just made her feel stupid, as if she'd done something desperate and ridiculous.

Charlene had been laid off from her job at the shipyard as soon as word came down that her husband had been discharged and was on his way home. They called it "mandatory marital leave." It was supposed to be a benefit, so employers deducted money out of your pay to cover it. Once the six months was up, you were supposed to be able to apply for your old job, but Charlene knew her welding days were over. Being able to get your hair done during the day was no compensation. After being responsible for mending holes bigger than she was in the hulls of battleships, spending all day doing the dishes sure felt foolish. Charlene thought she probably hadn't even bothered to comb her blonde hair with the metallic highlights since lunchtime. And she was damned if she was going to put on one more negligee, either.

She had married Jason eight years ago. Back then, a lot of couples got married the day after they graduated high school. If you were a newlywed, the army gave you an extra three weeks before you had to report for duty. They had been sixteen, and so in love. He was dark-haired, blue-eyed, and unbelievably handsome. When Jason sang along with the radio, you really thought maybe you would rather listen to him than the recorded music.

Unlike a lot of her friends, she never conceived during their honeymoon. Maybe that was the problem. People said having a baby helped you stay connected to your husband, kept the magic in the marriage. Every now and then, she had gotten form letters from the army offering to send her medical professional frozen "reproductive materials" so she could get pregnant even if Jason wasn't able to be with her. She knew it was important to keep the population level up, but making a baby in a doctor's office just never appealed to her.

Remembering how awkward their reunion had been still made her feel guilty. She knew she was supposed to be excited and happy, and treat him like a hero. But the deeply tanned, heavily muscled, and angry man who came out of the airport gate was not the boy she remembered. Jason had made her laugh. He had been a great dancer. He wasn't much on the football team, but he had a nice body and he was kind. This harsh stranger didn't seem to be very glad to see her either. It seems like all he'd done since he got back was criticize her hairdo, the way she kept house, her cooking, and the way she made love.

The truth was, he scared her. He was too rough and tense all the time, even when he came, as if he was somehow holding in something awful that would kill him (and her) if it escaped. He could not sleep the night through without waking up in a sweat, screaming. But he never remembered these night terrors in the morning, and he never wanted to talk about it. He rushed through the act of sex as if it were an ordeal, and he would not look her in the eye or kiss her. Charlene wondered, not for the first time, if the affair she'd had with Angie, who also worked on the docks, had spoiled her for masculine attention.

If she could, she would divorce Jason and move to another city, make a fresh start. Leave the West Coast behind and take the bus back to Atlanta. There had to be jobs for women like her someplace else. They couldn't be laying everyone off. She had skills; she had experience. But under the Military Morale Act—the same one that had created mandatory marital leave—it was illegal to divorce someone who had served in the armed forces. The President General needed his men to know that while they were serving their country, everything at home was safe and sound.

She flinched at the sound of Jason's motorcycle in the driveway. Suddenly aware of all the chores she'd neglected, she stood in the middle of the kitchen in a panic. But it was no use thinking she could have stopped what was about to happen by being more conscientious. The dishes were never clean enough, the corners on the bed never sharp enough for Jason. And she was never pretty enough, never eager enough to see him.

He came into the kitchen more slowly than usual,

although the army boots he continued to wear made a clatter. He was struggling with a large package, carrying it into the kitchen. How had he ever gotten that home on the bike? He spared her one pitiless glare. "A pig in a pigpen has more pride than you do," he sneered. "Well, honey, your life is about to improve dramatically. Just got my dangerous duty bonus today, and I've spent it on the only thing that I can think of that will improve this shit house of a marriage. I'm moving into the spare room. Don't bother me, and I won't bother you."

Charlene didn't even bother to protest. He was already in the back of the house, behind a slammed door. He came out to get a beer and his toolbox, and ignored her pointedly during these forays. She tried to call her sister, to see if she was in the mood to go to the movies, but the line was busy. She turned on the video, but it could not distract her from the noises that began coming from Jason's new quarters. There were slaps and squeals and sucking sounds. More slaps—hard ones— and some shouting. She felt ashamed of herself for being relieved that at least he wasn't shouting at her. Then there were the unmistakable sounds of penetration. Was it just her imagination, or was the house rocking on its foundation?

She had seen only one side of the box: "Adults Only" printed on the cardboard in large letters. What the hell was Jason up to? She fell asleep on the couch, wondering. He woke her up getting ready to go to work.

"Door's locked. Don't you mess with it if you know what's good for you," he warned her before slamming out. How much abuse could a front door take without breaking? The sound of his motorcycle starting up was her signal to get off the couch and see what he meant about locking that door.

Charlene had to laugh at the padlock and the chain. From time to time, she and the other welders had thrown big raucous parties on board ships that were being repaired or built from scratch. You had to fiddle with the gates to get on the docks where those vessels were moored. It paid to be able to unlock a thing or two. Got you all kinds of goodies. The scotch in a boss's locker. A peek at your personnel file. Extra tools. Defense contractors had unlimited access to gasoline and sugar and paint, paper and amphetamines and penicillin, all scarce commodities that had high value on the black market. She had a little zipped leather case of picks, whose possession would have been enough to get her sent off to tend the oil rigs of military personnel if she'd ever been caught, but what's life without a risk or two? It took her less than a minute to spring the lock. There was no damage. It would go back on once she was done investigating the way Jason had spent his bonus, and he would be none the wiser.

She wasn't sure what she had expected to see. Maybe a big-screen projection unit with a whole library of X-rated tapes and a full-body neural-network suit. Or something like a vacuum cleaner—only with all kinds of vibrating, penetrating, suctioning, pinching, and slapping attachments. But it was none of those things. It was a girl, tied to the twin bed, tied so tight that her skin was all red around the thin cord. A pretty girl with shoulder-length blue-black hair that turned under at the ends. She had a perfect peaches-and-cream complexion, a little button of a nose, and big, dark eyes that just tore at your soul. There were tears in her eyes right now, caused by the wad of dirty underwear that had been shoved into her mouth and tied in place.

Charlene didn't know what to do. She had several conflicting impulses, all of which involved untying the girl, but whether that was so she could tend her bruises and wipe her tears or throw her down the front steps, Charlene could not say. She could hide her trick with the padlock, but she wasn't sure she could duplicate Jason's rope work. He would notice if those fancy knots were changed in any way. Maybe he wouldn't notice if she just loosened that gag, though. It was held in place with nothing but a big dumb square knot. She sniffed at his lack of consistency and pulled the cloth from between the girl's jaws. How the hell had Jason managed to smuggle her in here? That fancy dance with the box was just a trick to distract her. My God, he must have been out in the Saharan sun too long and lost his marbles! Kidnapping people. My God, what would he be doin' next?

The brunette was smiling up at her, radiating serenity and joy. This incongruous facial expression threw

Charlene off her stride. "Uh, would you like a glass of water?" she asked.

"If it pleases you," the girl said. Her voice was seductive but still innocent, somehow. She had a clipped British accent, soothing and yet kind of formal, like the people in Charlene's favorite video series, *My Wild English Rose*. Her mouth was red as a pomegranate, with a full underlip that made you want to bite it. Charlene got her a glass of water, feeling foolish for tending Jason's piece on the side, even if she was here under duress.

After the girl had drunk the water, Charlene cleared her throat and said, "Who the hell are you, and how did you get here? I mean, if you're in trouble, I'll help you. But you have to understand this looks pretty weird." Why did she feel apologetic? Had living with Jason's bad temper intimidated her that much?

"My name is Dolly," the girl said. "I am fully equipped to gratify any of your dominant fantasies in a completely realistic fashion. Very few limits must be observed in your treatment of me. May I call you Mistress?"

There was that accent again. Wasn't it charming? The dark eyes that met Charlene's were full of trust and what looked like love. It was just too much. Charlene hauled her own mouth shut and stuffed the gag hastily back between Dolly's lips. The robotic sex slave accepted it calmly, as a horse would accept being bridled. And she did not protest when Charlene looped rope around her face and finished it off with a square knot, then left the room. If the Mistress wanted her to lie alone and bound in a quiet room, she would do so, and be happy. *Was that how she looked at things?* Charlene wondered. She had heard about these devices—androids capable of sexually servicing human beings—but she didn't know they came kinky, and she couldn't imagine how much it must have cost. *She.* How much *she* must have cost. No matter how often she told herself Dolly was just a machine, Charlene couldn't help thinking of her as another woman, a young girl who was being brutalized by a man whom Charlene was rapidly coming to hate.

She put up with this bizarre situation for a few more days. At first, Jason ignored her, but then he started acting kind of sulky, like she had done something to tick him off. She refused to be baited and did the bare minimum of cooking and cleaning that was necessary to keep him off her back. At night he would disappear, and Charlene found herself practically glued to the door the minute he closeted himself with Dolly. The things she heard were just outrageous. But Dolly never complained, never talked back, and never responded with anything other than devoted expressions of delight and affection. As angry as it made Charlene to think about Jason cheating on her with a damn machine, she thought she would have really lost her temper if Dolly had protested or fought back.

While he was at work, Charlene would pick the lock

and visit with his electronic concubine. She discovered rapidly that it wasn't that hard to retie his bindings. Dolly showed her how. She had an excellent memory and blushed when Charlene told her so. Eventually she became brave enough to invite Dolly out of the bedroom. Was it her idea or Dolly's to give them both a bubble bath, followed by a nice long massage? Charlene found herself waiting impatiently for Jason to get up and go to work each day so she could talk to her new friend. Dolly always laughed at her jokes. And she didn't mind doing housework at all. It was Charlene who minded, really. She would much rather spend their time together fooling around with each other's hair and makeup, or having Dolly rub her feet, or watching the video and making fun of the commercials.

Jason's treatment of his new toy escalated rapidly. One night, the door of the room vibrated with a motion that had nothing to do with fucking. Was he *shaking* her? "Goddammit, I order you to cry," he shouted. "Tell me I'm hurting you. Tell me to stop."

"I could never resist you, Master," Dolly said, her voice husky with sincerity. "I belong to you. You can do anything to me that you wish." Charlene knew that was true. Dolly had proved it to her. Spanking an android wasn't like hitting a person, really. Dolly might seem to get bruised, but she healed within hours, and all she did was giggle and wiggle when you took a hairbrush or a cane to her bottom. "He's really hurt you," Dolly had told her. "I don't mind if you take it out on me. I just want to make you feel better, Mistress. I don't think you know how beautiful you are when you're excited and angry. It just makes me all shivery. Ooh, yes, just like that. Ooh, please, hit my bottom again. I love you, Mistress."

Lost in these steamy memories, Charlene hadn't a clue that Jason was about to go barreling out of the room and dump her on the floor. He didn't need to see the mark of a keyhole on her forehead to figure out what was going on. "Well, well," he said nastily, "were we getting a little wet listening to Dolly get her jollies? I think I have a new idea. One that might save our relationship." He grabbed her by the wrist and dragged her into the bedroom, looked askance at the twin bed, grabbed Dolly's wrist in his other hand, and hustled all of them into the room with the double bed where Charlene had been sleeping alone for what seemed like weeks and weeks.

He positioned the two of them on the chenille bedspread, then stood against the back wall, hands buried deep within his zipper. Dolly nestled against Charlene as she had so many times in the past, her soft-yet-firm young body as relaxed and trusting as a sleeping puppy. "Do her!" Jason ordered. "Go on, Dolly. I want to watch the two of you together. Eat her pussy."

For the first time in her automated existence, Dolly hesitated before obeying a command. "Would you like that, Mistress?" She sounded troubled.

Jason's face turned a dangerous shade of red purple.

"Mistress?" he fumed. "Mistress!" He was about to ask questions that Charlene really didn't want Dolly to answer.

"Of course, honey," she said, petting Dolly's sleek cap of ebony hair. "Undress me first. Do it nice and slow, now, so Master Jason can enjoy the view."

Dolly sat up and undid the buttons on Charlene's blouse. One at a time. With several pauses to look coyly at Jason, and back again at the charms she was revealing gradually. Jason was speechless. Somehow, under Dolly's hands, his wife's body was regaining the youthful splendor he had carried in his mind through gunfire, explosions, sandstorms, and long, exhausting marches. When Dolly kissed Charlene, her face was transformed. She looked like a woman in a dream of lust and romance, her red lips the epitome of passion being teased slowly toward fulfillment. Dolly's hands cupped breasts that were suddenly generous and tempting, with lush nipples that rose quickly into peaks of excitement. The submissive android gradually revealed Charlene's hips and legs, tugging her pants down a little at a time, making this usually awkward process into a sensual dance.

Jason was hard between his own hands, balls tight. He wanted them both. But not yet. Not yet. At a whispered suggestion from Charlene, Dolly doffed her own clothes, taking only seconds. This quick revelation of her artificial but still effective charms accelerated his excitement. Then Dolly's hands found Charlene's thighs, parted them gently, and she bent to lick at "Mistress" with unselfconscious skill and care. Little did any of them know the source of that irresistible technique. In her youth, Ro had been known as "Skirts Up" Ro, and getting older had only made her better.

Then Dolly started working her fingers in and out of Charlene's wet opening, while her tongue hummed and vibrated on the most sensitive part of her clitoral hood. Dolly's pussy was pointed right at Jason as she made his wife come. Charlene was weeping and curling her toes from the stress and release of one of the most intense orgasms she'd ever had. Jason couldn't understand why he wasn't fucking Dolly to pieces, but something about the spectacle made him hold back. It was as if he could not interfere or interrupt. Something else was going to happen, and he had to see what it was.

That something else was Charlene, who had gotten herself back together in surprisingly little time. She was flipping Dolly onto her back. "Honey," she said, "one good turn deserves another." Her southern accent was thick as molasses, and Jason remembered how he used to tease her about that. He could always tell when she got really turned on, while they were making out, because that drawl would just slip out of her mouth and betray her. His eyes were smarting, and Jason tossed his head, unwilling to take his hands off his cock long enough to wipe them.

It had never occurred to Jason to dive into Dolly's cybernetic muff. She was just an assemblage of fake skin, plastic bones, synthetic muscles, bogus mucous membranes, artificial body fluids, and computer chips. That had never stopped him from trying to hurt her, of course. But work up a sweat to create a facsimile of a climax in a glorified Tinkertoy? What kind of fool did Charlene think he was, anyway?

Actually, Charlene wasn't thinking about Jason at all. She was thinking about Dolly's pretty, pretty girl parts. Her pubic hair was as soft and sleek as the hair on her head, and she tasted spicy. She was just wet enough to be encouraging. Charlene did not have the advantage of Ro's schooling between the thighs of dozens of curious, drunk, or just plain horny maidens. But Angie hadn't ever kicked her out of bed, either. She persuaded Dolly gently to breathe more quickly, sigh, gasp, and hold onto her head. With tongue and lips and the tip of her nose, she made that little android grateful that the clitoris had been discovered before she came off the assembly line. At last Dolly was exclaiming, "Please, Mistress, may I come?" When Charlene mumbled something that could have been permission, Dolly cried out as if something had finally really hurt her, and then fell still, trembling. One of the links of Ro's rogue programming fell into place, sealing Dolly to Charlene forever.

Jason was glaring around the room, looking for a tissue or something—anything—to wipe his hands on. He had come when Charlene told Dolly to come. Finally he settled on the curtains. He felt a little disgusted with himself, the way he always did after he got off. The thought of Charlene having to wash his cum out of the drapes made him feel quite a bit better. But the sight of the two women in bed together, cuddling and looking way too pleased with themselves, enraged him.

"Now I know what you really like, I guess I can satisfy you at last," he told Charlene, taking the belt out of his pants.

Dolly placed herself between him and his wife, looking stern, if that was possible for such a masochistic cherub. Her bee-stung lower lip stuck out belligerently. "I believe you intend to harm my Mistress," Dolly said. "If that is your intention, I must warn you to stop. I will not be responsible for the consequences if you do not leave the room now."

Jason said, "Yeah, right, you and how many Marines?" and lunged at the bed. Dolly picked him up and carried him out of the room. Within minutes, he found himself stripped and tied to the twin bed, in a position that was quite a bit more stressful than any of the ones he'd dreamed up for his toy. She gagged him, too. With a sanitary napkin. At least it was a clean one. The plug up his ass had to be the very biggest one. ("I am programmed to accept maximum penetration," Dolly had said when he showed it to her.) She turned on the control that made it vibrate, so it wasn't likely to stay nearly as clean as the wad of gauze in his mouth. Besides, he was scared.

Eventually Jason stopped struggling with his ropes

(damn, that thin cord cut!) and looked up in time to see Charlene with a suitcase in one hand and Dolly's waist in the other. The blonde bitch was wearing *his* leather jacket! Dolly had a camera. The flash made white-hot stars on his retinas. But he could still see Dolly's outfit, a precarious and yummy combination of thin leather straps and stretchy, glossy black material that barely covered her nipples and her crotch.

"Good-bye, Jason," Charlene said. "I'm taking the bike. And your service revolver." She slid the phone over to him with her foot. "Anytime you feel ready to call one of your buddies for help, go right ahead. Just remember you'll have to explain how you got yourself into this fix. If you ever try to come after us or hurt us in any way, I will let the whole world know that you couldn't even satisfy an android that was programmed to be utterly and completely submissive. Some tabloid would love to buy that story. *And* the photos. Come on, Dolly."

"Yes, Mistress," the subversively obedient mechanism cooed, and teetered after Charlene, running after her new life on six-inch heels that were going to look great on the back of that bike.

Digby J. Lustgarden's Daring Device

Simon Sheppard

Nothing much had been happening, nothing all the way to the flat Kansas horizon. Nothing much had happened since the Gales' house had been swept away by a tornado, and that was three years before. And then one day, up from that big, blank horizon, starting tiny and becoming life-size bit by bit, came a tired old horse slowly pulling a gaudy wagon.

It belonged to a peddler of snake oil, a charlatan on wheels. BROTHER DIGBY J. LUSTGARDEN'S TRAVELING SALVATION SHOW, read the ornate black-and-gold lettering on the wagon's red wooden sides. And then beneath that, smaller but not much, THE ORGASMATRON, SAVIOR OF MANKIND.

Hardly anyone noticed its arrival. Redheaded Eb Rockett did, out working in the dusty fields, stripped to the waist, sweat pouring down his hard golden torso. The Kramers, Larsen and Pru, heading the other way down the rutted road, ventured nods from their wagon, and received a nod in return. That was about it. But word trickled around, and by late the next morning, Sunday morning, churchgoers in their best clothes had made their way to a field on the edge of town, curious to see what was what. It was a little dicey, it being Sunday and all, but there the tent was, patched and listing a bit, and the crimson-red wagon next to it. And in front of the wagon, standing on a little wood platform, was an exotic young man of exceptional beauty.

"I'm Dr. Lao," he announced when a goodly crowd had gathered. "Spelled L-A-O, pronounced 'Low.' An Oriental name, for I was an orphan, raised by missionaries, and I learned my trade in the Mystic East." So far, the spiel was standard issue; the Kramers, back from wherever they had gone, exchanged knowing glances. *We may be hayseeds*, the glance seemed to say, *but rubes we are not*. But what came next surely piqued the crowd's attention. "My employer Brother Lustgarden and I have come to your town to bring you the blessings of the invention of the millennium, a revolutionary machine of our own devising. The Orgasmatron, my friends, is a miraculous mechanism guaranteed to improve marital relations between newlyweds and the silver-haired alike, and moreover to provide solace for the lonely bachelor." Here, Lao threw Eb Rockett a significant glance. "And it is possible to do all this with the greatest of ease and comfort, at negligible cost to you. Now then, since the Orgasmatron is to be used solely by the male of the species, we are giving every gentleman in this locale the opportunity to take advantage of its wonders. There will be a meeting this evening, in this very tent, for any man and every man who wishes to attend. Seven o'clock. No cost, no obligation. And now, my friends, I bid you Good Day."

By the evening, nary a man for miles around hadn't heard of the Orgasmatron, and though many were a mite too shy to admit that anything could improve their love life, by seven o'clock the shabby little tent was full to bursting. At the rear of the tent, a large object had been covered by a canvas drape, and from behind the shrouded object appeared Dr. Lao, dressed in a black silk jacket of Oriental design.

"Gentleman," said the handsome young man, "thank you all for coming. I pledge that you shall not feel your time has been wasted. Here to explain the wonders of the Orgasmatron, miracle machine of the century, is its inventor, Brother Digby J. Lustgarden."

Lustgarden strode out from behind the draped object. The inventor was a man in his mid-forties, of more than moderate attractiveness, with regular features and a tall, well-proportioned body. His trim goatee, flecked with gray, reminded more than one attendee of

Beelzebub himself. Lustgarden gave a short talk, explaining the many benefits of his amazing machine, how it could spice up a flagging marriage, cure nagging impotence, make a lonesome bachelor feel fulfilled. He read testimonial letters from satisfied clients and expounded upon the schedule of fees. Eb Rockett looked around the tent. Many a farmer had a look, not of wonder, but of skepticism and boredom. For even in that corner of Kansas, scalawags with something to sell were anything but rare.

Then, with a flourish, Lustgarden and Lao reached up and whisked the drape from the Orgasmatron. A gasp went up from the crowd. The machine gleamed in the light of the tent's bare electric bulbs.

The elaborate device stood a good ten feet tall, and much of it was painted red, the same devilish hue as the wagon. Brass fittings, bellows and pistons, thick leather straps with silvery buckles—the Orgasmatron was a thing of beauty. A control panel with gauges, switches, and small electric bulbs stood to one side of the console. At the other side, a wrought-iron rack held several large dry-cell batteries, ready to lend their power to this miracle of sex. Ornate and beautiful, the Orgasmatron challenged one and all to taste its potent pleasures.

"Who, then," asked Brother Lustgarden, "will be the first of you to experience this miracle of science?"

Not one taciturn Kansan in the audience stirred.

"Gentleman, I know there's some reluctance on your part to surrender hard-earned cash for benefits yet unproven. So what I propose, my friends, is to allow one of you to experience the Orgasmatron firsthand at no cost, risk, or obligation. Which one of you shall it be?"

There still came no response. Then Larsen Kramer stirred. He hadn't intended to; the difficulties that had overtaken his marital relations with Pru had been a well-kept secret. But something in him dared to raise a hand, though when he looked around and met the stares of his friends and neighbors, and felt hot blood rush to his cheeks, Larsen Kramer wished he had kept his hand down, where it belonged.

"Are you sure that's necessary?" Kramer felt a blush emblazoning his cheeks.

"Yes, indeed," said Dr. Lao. "A thorough physical exam's a necessity if you're to undergo treatment. Now remove your clothes. All of them."

Kramer stripped down to his undershorts.

"What's wrong, Mr. Kramer? Why the hesitation?" Lustgarden prodded. "You have, I assure you, no reason to feel embarrassed." *No matter how tiny it is*, he added silently.

But when the farmer did let his undershorts fall to his ankles, Lao let out an involuntary gasp. Larsen Kramer's penis was one of the biggest, prettiest, most mouthwatering pieces of meat he'd ever laid eyes upon. No, not "one of the biggest." *The* biggest.

"Well, now," said Lustgarden in a slightly mocking voice, "I can certainly see how your wife might have trouble coping with *that.*"

Kramer's blush grew even deeper. And, despite his finer instincts, his dick began to swell.

"Listen, this was all a mistake. Maybe I should just get dressed and…"

"Nonsense," said Lustgarden. "Let's just begin"—his hand shot to Kramer's cock—"the examination." He grasped the big dick, feeling its glowing warmth as it swelled with blood.

"He has good genital reactions, wouldn't you say, Doctor?" said Lustgarden, squeezing so hard that the cockhead grew shiny and purple. Kramer felt faint. He looked down at his aching dick. Already, a shiny pearl of precum glistened at the piss-slit.

"The ring?" asked Lao.

"The ring," confirmed Lustgarden. He took a shiny chromium-plated ring from the examining table at his side. While Dr. Lao tugged at Kramer's dick, Lustgarden snapped the hinged ring around the base of the farmer's cock and balls. The shiny metal winked from the bush of wiry brown hair.

Dr. Lao took his hand away. Kramer's dick remained engorged, jutting up hugely from his lean belly.

"A prodigious organ indeed," smiled handsome young Dr. Lao. "Now bend over the examining table."

"What?"

"He said bend over!" Lustgarden snapped. "Are you deaf as well as impotent?"

"Oh, hardly impotent, Digby," Lao smiled, eyes locked on Kramer's huge hard-on.

"With his wife, I mean. Now, then, Mr. Kramer," Lustgarden said sternly, "bend over."

Kramer did as he was told. Directly in front of him, a Mason jar of grease sat on the table. He could see Lao dipping his fingers into the jar, then felt Lustgarden spreading the cheeks of his butt, Lao slipping his delicate lubed finger inside him. He started to tense up, to protest.

"Just relax, son," Lao said gently. "Keep breathing and this won't hurt a bit. We just have to make sure that you're a suitable prospect for Orgasmatron therapy."

"And *is* he suitable, Dr. Lao?"

"Suitable indeed, Brother Lustgarden."

And, in fact, Lao's expert fingers, probing deep inside Kramer, were sending shivers of pleasure up the farmer's spine.

"Now then, Mr. Kramer, an insertion of the anal probe, and your pre-treatment examination will be done." Lustgarden held a long chromed-metal tube before Larsen's eyes. Evil looking, about two inches in diameter, tapered at one end, wires leading out of the other. Lustgarden stuck the probe into the grease, then handed it to Lao. The fingers came out of Kramer's ass. The cold, slick tube slid in. The naked man gasped. The click of a flipped switch, and the tube grew warm, began to vibrate.

"Now then," asked Dr. Lao, "how does that feel?"

"It feels," said Larsen Kramer, "really, really good."

# # #

By the next afternoon, word had shot around Bradbury Falls, Kansas. After much electrical humming was heard and a flash or two of light was seen, Larsen Kramer had emerged from Brother Lustgarden's tent with a big old smile on his face. And when his wife Pru appeared in town next morning, she had a big old smile on hers.

"Worth every penny," Kramer would say when asked, but would disclose no more than that.

Word of mouth brought several other likely candidates for treatment to Lao and Lustgarden's tent. But it also brought a visitor who, while not unexpected, was nonetheless unwelcome.

The Reverend Micah Pearlbiter, dewlaps aquiver, wasted no time in coming to the point. "It's not merely that you did business on the Sabbath. It's the nature of your business. It's…It's…It's…"

"Unnatural? Perverted? Ungodly?" Lustgarden offered helpfully.

"It's the sort of thing we don't need in a town like Bradbury Falls."

"On the contrary, Reverend," said Lustgarden, all silky-sweet persuasion. "It seems there's a crying need for our services. We have come, not to promote immorality, but to give back to suffering mankind the pleasure which God intended them to enjoy. Just ask Mr. Kramer. Ask his wife."

But Pearlbiter would have none of it. He left an ultimatum in his wake: Be out of town by the following morning or face the consequences. "Not here, of course, but in the surrounding towns, there are men who would not hesitate to take matters into their own hands. I cannot be responsible for their actions. This warning, I hope, should be sufficient."

And the Reverend Pearlbiter, lumbering heavily from the tent, gave a single backward glance, full of contempt and dislike, and was gone.

Late in the afternoon, after the treatments of Josiah Dole and Parker Bunn, and after Jim Dalworthy balked at the physical exam and left in a huff, Dr. Lao took a break for business and strolled to Parmalee's General Store for supplies. Just by the feedlot, Lao ran into Eb Rockett. He recalled how Rockett's naked torso, dripping with sweat, straining in the sun, had looked when they'd first approached town.

"Good afternoon," said Lao.

"Afternoon."

"You haven't been by for an exam and possible treatment." Lao's dark eyes flashed significantly. "I would have bet you'd be one of the first."

"Not interested."

"That's blunt."

"Listen, you can fool some of the other men in town, but that machine of yours doesn't do diddly-squat. Guys just think it's doing them some good. But really, they're just fine to begin with. All that folderol just gives them back their belief in themselves."

"Is that so?" Lao slid his eyes from the field hand's

handsome, craggy face, over his muscular torso, down to his crotch. Noticing, Rockett clasped his hands in front of his basket.

"Yeah, that's so. But I don't need some jumped-up fake doctor to tell me who I am, not at some fancy price. I know who I am and what I want."

"Do tell." Lao moved his gaze back upward, locking his eyes on Rockett's. His gaze was piercing but his voice was soft. "Well, how about this, my friend? I'd like to offer you the benefits of the Orgasmatron at absolutely no cost to you. Free. Gratis. No obligation. And you can call a halt to the treatment at any time. That's how sure I am that you'll change your mind. Can't be much fairer than that."

"Don't think so."

"Is that a 'no'?" purred Lao.

"Said I don't think so."

"Well, if you should change your mind, you know where we'll be." Lao extended his hand. Eb Rockett had no choice but to unclasp his hands and shake. As Lao knew it would be, Rockett's dick was noticeably hard.

"Haven't made too much money, Dig."

"Well, what do you expect from a one-horse town like this?" Lustgarden puffed on his pipe. Rings of cherry-scented smoke swirled in the evening air.

"Still, Dig, the sight of Kramer's big fat dick was damn near worth the trip." Lao grinned.

"And then there's that yokel Rockett," said Brother

Lustgarden. "It would be fun to get *him* strapped into the old Orgasmatron."

"A bit surly, if you ask me."

"Just the way I like 'em, Lao. Makes breaking 'em down all the more fun."

A voice from outside the tent: "Anybody there?"

"Who's that?" Lao called, but he already knew.

"Eb Rockett."

Brother Digby J. Lustgarden puffed a parade of smoke rings into the Kansas air. "Well," he smiled slyly, "speak of the devil."

"Now, then," asked Dr. Lao, "how does that feel?"

"It feels," said Eb Rockett, "really, really good."

"Well, Doctor, it seems that Mr. Rockett here's a suitable candidate for treatment."

"It does indeed, Brother Lustgarden."

Lao slid the warm, pulsing probe out of the naked farmhand's ass. Rockett rose slowly from the examining table, his Kansan dick hard, his eyes still half-closed in pleasure.

"Then let the treatment begin," said Lustgarden.

Handsome Dr. Lao walked to the Orgasmatron, which stood almost invisible, draped and unlit in a dim corner of the tent. He pulled the drape aside and threw a switch. The great machine sprang to life, its lights ablaze, its gears and axles humming, its bellows erect with air.

"This way, Mr. Rockett. Step up on that platform." Eb

Rockett stepped up onto a shiny metal platform, cold against his bare feet.

"Turn around, back to the machine, and spread your legs."

Lao bent down and fastened metal clamps around Rockett's bare feet and ankles.

"Raise your hands above your head."

With broad leather wrist cuffs, Doctor Lao manacled Rockett's hands to the structure of the Orgasmatron. Then he picked up a broad leather band not unlike a small black corset, drew it around Rockett's waist, and laced it up. Reaching between the naked man's sinewy thighs, he grabbed two straps hanging from the back of the waistband, guided them between Rockett's legs, to either side of his hefty ballsac, and through two buckles on the front of the corsetlike device. Shiny metal clips hung from the sides of the tightly cinched waistband; these he fastened to big chromed rings on the Orgasmatron. Surprisingly, Rockett found this constriction of his naked body to be a not altogether unpleasant experience.

Lao stepped back to admire his handiwork. The naked young man's lean, well-muscled form was securely fastened to the machine, his hard, jutting dick shining pink against the tight black corset.

"Perhaps, Brother Lustgarden, you'd like to do the honors?"

"Indeed I would, Dr. Lao."

The older man strode to the great and powerful

machine which he'd created. "It's time to hook you up, Mr. Rockett." He seized two electrical cables that sprouted from the Orgasmatron. Lustgarden smiled. "There may be some initial discomfort." There were shiny clamps on the free ends of the cables. He clipped them to Rockett's nipples. The field hand grimaced and writhed, but soon the sensation changed from pain to something approaching pleasure.

Lustgarden clipped two more cables to the ring around the base of Eb Rockett's stiff dick. Then he reached down between Rockett's bare and shackled feet, opened a small door in the platform, and pulled out a gleaming brass fixture, about the size of two large fists, connected to a long tube. He grabbed Rockett's hot, hard dick with one hand and guided the brass fixture over it with the other. The inside of the fixture was as soft and welcoming as the exterior was hard and unyielding; it seemed to gobble up Rockett's meat, caressing and shaping itself to every curve and contour. Lustgarden fastened down a knurled adjusting knob, then hooked the device to links of chain hanging from the corset.

"And lastly, that sensitive, responsive hole of yours." He reached between Rockett's legs, into a compartment, pulled out a larger version of the first anal probe, wires bristling from its base, and guided it home.

Lustgarden stood up and gazed at Eb Rockett. The connecting process always got his dick hard. There was something about having a man, a man like good-looking, muscular Eb, spread naked before him, shackled to his machine, connected to his creation, vulnerable, nervous, not yet understanding the pleasures that awaited him. Digby J. Lustgarden's dick was throbbing.

He looked Rockett in the eye. "I'm about to put a hood over your head, young man. Should you at any time experience discomfort, you have merely to cry out and the treatment will come to an immediate halt. But should you believe that the pleasure you feel is becoming too great, I'd recommend that you attempt to relax and enjoy yourself. But, once again, if you should cry out..."

And he slipped the black leather hood over Rockett's head.

Standing there connected to the Orgasmatron, the young man's naked body was a work of art. Vulnerable flesh, tan torso, paler legs, coppery hair gleaming in the electric light. The redhead's freckled skin, which sweat had lent a metallic sheen, was restricted, interrupted, defined by black leather, silvery chrome, and brass. Strapped into the Orgasmatron, Rockett was not so much held captive by the great machine as incorporated into it, its single most vital component.

"You know," said Lustgarden, not particularly kindly, "from the moment we saw you out in the fields, we knew that you'd end up here, strapped into the Orgasmatron."

And then he threw the switch.

The machine came to life, fitfully at first as pistons

fired up and bellows filled with air, then settling into a steady, seductive rhythm. Digby J. Lustgarden gazed at his machine, wonder struck, almost despite his own cynical self, by what he had created. The arcing of blue sparks, the jigglings of needles against calibrated dials. The whirr of gears. The thrusting of pneumatic cylinders, in and out, in and out, and the flow of lucent fluids through transparent tubes. And at its center, bound into the clockwork precision of his great life's work, golden against the crimson panels, a vibrant chunk of pulsing, naked human flesh.

Lustgarden looked at Dr. Lao, Lao at Lustgarden. Both their dicks were throbbing hard.

Within the confines of the black cowhide hood, the last of Eb Rockett's qualms had been swept away. As the Orgasmatron had powered up, he'd felt reluctance, uncertainty, yes, even fear. But the first gentle proddings of the machine soothed and reassured, left him receptive for what was to come. A gentle flow of current made his nipples tingle. The velvety touch of the cockpiece stroked his engorged prick. And the probe inside his butt, as it warmed and vibrated, relaxed and soothed his asshole.

The hood left him sightless, but he could still hear the rhythmic sighs and clicks of the machine, pneumatic soughs, flywheels' whirrings. When he opened his mouth to moan in mounting pleasure, a gentle tube snaked from the hood into his mouth, a mechanistic kiss.

The current to his nipples grew more intense, sending jolts of pleasure down his torso to his dick, then down through his throbbing legs to the metal beneath his bare feet. He tried to buck his hips forward, but was restrained by the corset. But the dicksheath responded to each thrust, increasing its soft vacuum, enlarging the hard cock.

The machine could read the signs, knew when to increase tempo, what to stroke and when. Rockett's warm body pressed into it. His tongue was against its own. Rockett's cock was filling its receptor, drenching it with precum. His ass welcomed it inside. The Orgasmatron extended the inner piston tentatively from the metal anal probe. Its thrust was welcomed by a shudder of pleasure. The Orgasmatron retracted the slippery inner cylinder, then thrust it out again, accelerating the pace in sync with the pulsings of Rockett's ass.

The Orgasmatron knew the calibrations of desire. Satisfied with Rockett's responses, it increased the pace, sent more and more sensations surging through the human's flesh. Until it was satisfied.

Together they moved in unison, the machine offering, Rockett receiving, the man thrusting, machine sucking in. As the Orgasmatron accelerated, its humming grew louder, harmonizing with Rockett's groans and sighs. The Orgasmatron held Eb Rockett tight in its embrace, taking him to ecstasies he'd never felt before. His nipples were alive, the sensations in his penis engulfed his whole body, his consciousness was conquered by the feelings inside his ass. He would do anything to please his all-embracing partner, give it everything: his love, his desire, his surrender. The pleasure became so intense—too intense—but he could not, he would not cry out for this to stop. He and this machine would spiral upward, into a tension of lust few had known, into a release that none could understand.

And that release, when it did come at last, brought with it a flash of blinding white light that could be seen for miles around.

The tubes and probes removed, Lao and Lustgarden unbuckled and untied the man, then lifted his sweaty, limp body down from the machine. Weak as a kitten, one arm around each man's shoulders, Eb Rockett looked at these two strangers, then at the huge gleaming device they'd brought to town, the truth they'd brought into his little life. And he began to sob.

"I understand," said Lustgarden softly. "You can stay with us here as long as you need to. As long as you like."

And so Rockett spent the night there, sleeping between the two handsome men, the best night's sleep he'd had in years. Spent the night with all *three* of them, really—Lustgarden, Lao, and the Orgasmatron.

When Eb Rockett emerged from the tent bright and early the next morning, it did not go unnoticed by others in Bradbury Falls. And this brought a fresh aspect of scandal to the enterprise, though in the weeks to come, whenever Rockett faced whisperings and strange looks, he never gave in, never surrendered his memories of joy and pride and satisfaction. Never apologized, not even to himself.

Still, the new gossip did not help Lustgarden's business. Only a very few men—the brave and the desperate—showed up that day. And when evening fell, the area around the shabby tent was quiet and deserted.

Until a wagonload of men pulled up. And then a second, and a third. Angry men, some dressed in sheets and hoods, many with torches in their hands.

"Come on out, you bastards, so that we can see you," one of them yelled. "We want to see you scum-sucking perverts face-to-face."

"This is a good Christian town, in a good Christian state, and we don't want you dumb fucks anywhere near our families," another shouted.

"Get out of here," a general chorus rose. "Get out of town and go straight to hell!"

Lustgarden and Lao walked out of the tent and stood side by side, looking frightened but firm.

"Well, looky here," a man in a white sheet cackled. "One of 'em ain't even American."

"I suppose," Lustgarden began, "it's no use trying to reason with you gentlemen...."

"We've heard all we need to know!" one red-faced man snapped. "We're gonna tar and feather you, string you up if we feel like it, and burn your den of damnation to the ground."

Several men with torches started walking toward the tent. There was a movement at the door of the tent. A man emerged. "Why don't you boys all calm down and go home?" said the Reverend Micah Pearlbiter.

"Reverend! What the hell you doin' here?" said the red-faced man.

"Men, friends and neighbors, I once thought as you did, that these men were evil and their machine a device of the Devil. But now I have learned differently" —a strange look flitted across Pearlbiter's face—"and I am here to tell you that these men are doing the work of the Lord, and their efforts must be allowed to continue unmolested."

There was a stirring in the crowd, mutters of disbelief. "So you, Robertson, and you, Buchanan"—he gestured at a fat man in a hood and sheet—"go on home and cool down. Let these two good gentlemen get on about their business. Don't make trouble here. Not unless you'd like to deal with my very good friend, Sheriff Nielsen."

There was some grumbling, but the fight had gone out of the mob. In a matter of minutes, they'd packed up their torches, gotten back on the wagons, and gone.

Only Lustgarden, Lao, and Pearlbiter were left standing in the moonlight, Without another word, the reverend smiled at the other two, nodded good-bye, and headed for home. Lustgarden looked at Lao, and Lao at Lustgarden. The moon shone bright.

# # #

Next morning, when the sun rose above the flat horizon and the roosters sang out their song, the little patch of ground where the tent had stood was vacant, the men and their machine long gone. They were never to return to Bradbury Falls, though every once in a while, there were rumors of their arrival in one Midwestern town or another. The reports sometimes prompted somebody or other to leave town in search of them, with what success one cannot say. But as the months and years went by, these reports grew fewer and finally stopped altogether.

The following spring, Pru Kramer had the first of what were to be five children. Eb Rockett never married, but he worked hard, saved his money, and was finally able to afford a little farm of his own. As he grew older, he hired a succession of strapping young men to help him out. Rumors of scandal drove Reverend Pearlbiter far from Bradbury Falls, headed for a flock in North Dakota, thence to parts unknown.

Brother Digby J. Lustgarden and Doctor Lao are long gone, of course, gone to their final rewards.

But recently, rumors have surfaced that somewhere, in some warehouse out on the Great Plains, the Orgasmatron sits, all crated up and waiting patiently to be rediscovered. In this modern age, such a machine seems quaint and obsolete and altogether unnecessary. Of course, we're at ease with our sexuality. There's nothing we don't know about sex. Even if it did exist, no one would admit to being in need of the Orgasmatron.

On second thought, it might be worth the search.

Six Kinds of Darkness
John Shirley

Charlie'd say, "I'm into it once or twice—but you, you got a jones for it, man."

And Angelo'd snicker and say, "Gives my life purpose, man. Gives my life direction."

You could smell the place, the Hollow Head, from two blocks away. Anyway, you could if you were strung out on it. The other people on the street probably couldn't make out the smell from the background of monoxides, the broken-battery smell of acid rain, the itch of syntharette smoke, the oily rot of the river. But a user could pick out that tease of amyl triptyline, thinking, *Find it like a needle in a haystack.* And he'd snort, and then go reverent-serious, thinking about the needle in question...the needle in the nipple....

75

It was on East 121st Street, a half block from the East River. If you stagger out of the place at night, you'd better find your way to the lighted end of the street fast, because the leeches crawled out of the river after dark, slug-creeping up the walls and onto the cornices of the old buildings; they sense your bodyheat, and an eight-inch ugly brute lamprey thing falls from the roof, hits your neck with a wet *slap;* injects you with paralyzing toxins, you fall over and its leech cronies come, drain you dry. When Charlie turned onto the street, it was just sunset; the leeches weren't out of the river yet, but Charlie scanned the rooftops anyway. Clustered along the rooftops were the shanties....

New York's housing shortage was worse than ever. After the Dissolve Depression, and most of the Wall Street firms moved to Tokyo or the floating city Freezone, the boom in Manhattan deflated; the city couldn't afford to maintain itself. It began to rot. But still the immigrants came, swarming to the mecca of disenchantment till New York became another Mexico City, ringed and overgrown with shanties, shacks of clapboard, tin, cardboard protected with flattened cans and wrapper plastic; every tenement rooftop in Manhattan mazed with squalid shanties, sometimes shanties on shanties till the weight collapsed the roofs and the old buildings caved in, the crushed squatters simply left dying in the rubble—firemen and Emergency teams rarely set foot outside the sentried, walled-in havens of the midtown class.

Charlie was almost there. It was a mean motherfucker of a neighborhood, which is why he had the knife in his boot sheath. But what scared him was the Place. Doing some Room at the Place. The Hollow Head. His heart was pumping and he was shaky, but he wasn't sure if it was from fear or anticipation or if, with the Hollow Head, you could tell those two apart. But to keep his nerve up, he had to look away from the Place, as he got near it; tried to focus on the rest of the street. Some dumbfuck Pollyanna had planted saplings in the sidewalk, in the squares of exposed dirt where the original trees had stood. But the acid rain had chewed the leaves and twigs away; what was left was stark as TV antennas.... Torchglow from the roofs; and a mélange of noises that seemed to ooze down like something greasy from an overflowing pot. Smells of tarry wood burning; dogfood smells of cheap canned food cooking. And then he was standing in front of the Hollow Head. A soot-blackened town house, its Victorian facade of cherubim recarved by acid rain into dainty gargoyles. The windows bricked over, the stone between them streaked gray on black from acid erosion.

The building to the right was hunchbacked with shacks; the roof to the left glowed from oil-barrel fires. But the roof of the Hollow Head was dark and flat, somehow regal in its sinister austerity. No one shacked on the Hollow Head.

He took a deep breath and told himself, Don't hurry through it, savor it this time, and went in. Hoping that Angelo had waited for him.

Up to the door, wait while the camera scanned you. The camera taking in Charlie Chesterton's triple mohawk, each fin a different color; Charlie's gaunt face, spiked transplas jacket, and customized mirrorshades. He heard the tone telling him the door had unlocked. He opened it, smelled the amyl triptyline, felt his bowels contract with suppressed excitement. Down a red-lit hallway, thick black paint on the walls, the turpentine smell of A.T. getting stronger. Angelo wasn't there; he'd gone upstairs already. Charlie hoped Ange could handle it alone.... The girl in the banker's window at the end of the hall—the girl wearing the ski mask, the girl with the sarcastic receptionist's lilt in her voice—took his card, gave him the Bone Music receptor, credded him in. Another tone, admission to Door Seven, the first level. He walked down to Seven, turned the knob, stepped through and felt it immediately; the tingle, the rush of alertness, the chemically induced sense of belonging, four pleasurable sensations rolling through him and coalescing. It was just an empty room with the stairs at the farther end; soft pink highlighting, the usual cryptic palimpsest of graffiti on the walls.

He inhaled deeply, felt the amyl triptyline go to work almost immediately; the pink glow intensified; the edges of the room softened, he heard his own heartbeat like a distant beatbox. A barbed wisp of anxiety twined his spine (wondering, *Where's Angelo? he's usually hanging in the first room, scared to go to the second alone, well, shit, good riddance*) and he experienced a paralytic seizure of sheer sensation. The Bone Music receptor was digging into his palm; he wiped the sweat from it and attached it to the sound wire extruding from the bone back of his left ear—and the music shivered into him... It was music you *felt*, more than heard; his acoustic nerve picked up the thudding beat, the bass, a distorted veneer of the synthesizer. But most of the music was routed through the bone of his skull, conducted down through the spinal column, the other bones. It was a music of shivery sensations, like a funny-bone sensation, sickness sensations, chills and hot flashes like influenza; but it was a sickness that caressed, viruses licking at your privates and you wanted to come and throw up at the same time. He'd seen deaf people dancing at rock concerts; they could feel the vibrations from the loud music; could feel the music they couldn't hear. It was like that but with a deep, deep humping brutality, like having sex with an obviously syphilitic whore and enjoying it more because you knew she was diseased. The music shivered him from his paralysis, nudged him forward. He climbed the stairs....

Bone Music reception improving as he climbed, so he could make out the lyrics, Jerome-X's gristly voice singing from inside Charlie's skull:

Six kinds of darkness
Spilling down over me
Six kinds of darkness
Sticky with energy

Charlie got to the next landing, stepped into the second room. Second room used electric-field stimulation of nerve ends; the metal grids on the wall transmitting signals that stimulated the neurons, initiating pleasurable nerve impulses; other signals were sent directly to the dorsal area in the hypothalamus, resonating in the brain's pleasure center....

Charlie cried out and fell to his knees in the infantile purity of his gratitude. The room glowed with benevolence; the barren, dirty room with its semen-stained walls, cracked ceilings, naked red bulb on a fraying wire. As always he had to fight himself to keep from licking the walls, the floors. He was a fetishist for this room, for its splintering wooden floors, the mathematical absolutism of the grid-patterns in the gray metal transmitters set into the wall. Turn off those transmitters and the room was shabby, even ugly, and pervaded with stench; with the transmitters on it seemed subtly intricate, starkly sexy, bondage gear in the form of interior decoration, and the smell was a ribald delight.

(For the Hollow Head was drug paraphernalia you could walk into. The building itself was the syringe, or the hookah, or the sniff tube. The whole building was the paraphernalia—and the drug itself.)

And then the room's second phase cut in: the transmitters stimulated the motor cortex, the reticular formation in the brain stem, the nerve pathways of the extrapyramidal system, in precise patterns computer formulated to mesh with the ongoing Bone Music. Making him dance. Dance across the room, feeling he was caught in a choreographed whirlwind (flashing: genitals interlocking, pumping, male and female, male and male, female and female, tongues and cocks and fingers pushing into pink bifurcations, contorting purposefully to guide between fleshy globes, the thrusting a heavy downhill flow like an emission of igneous mud, but firm pink mud, the bodies rounded off, headless, Magritte torsos going end to end together, organs nosing blindly into the wet receptacles of otherness), semen trickling down his legs inside his pants, dancing, helplessly dancing, thinking it was a delicious epilepsy, as he was marionetted up the stairs, to the next floor, the final room....

At the landing just before the third room, the transmitters cut off, and Charlie sagged, gasping, clutching for the banister, the black-painted walls reeling around him.... He gulped air, and prayed for the strength to turn away from the third room, because he knew it would leave him fried, yeah badly crashed and deeply burnt out. He turned off the receptor for a respite of quiet.... In that moment of weariness and self-doubt, he found himself wondering where Angelo was. Had Angelo really gone on to the third room alone? Ange was prone to identity crises under the Nipple Needle. If he'd gone alone—little Angelo Demario with his rockabilly hair and spurious pugnacity—Angelo would sink, lose it completely.... And what would they do with people who were overdosed on an identity hit? Dump the body in the river, he supposed....

He heard a yell mingling ecstasy and horror, coming from an adjacent room, as another Head customer took a nipple.... That made up his mind: like seeing someone eat making you realize you're hungry. He gathered together the tatters of his energy, switched on his receptor, and went through the door.

The Bone Music shuddered through him, too strong now, now that he was undercut, weakened by the first rooms. Nausea wallowed through him.

The darkness of the Arctic, two months into the night
Darkness of the Eclipse, forgetting of all light

Angelo wasn't in the room. Charlie was selfishly glad as he took off his jacket, rolled up his left sleeve, approached the black rubber nipple protruding from the metal breast at waist height on the wall. As he stepped up to it, pressed the hollow of his elbow against the nipple; felt the computer-guided needle probe for his main line and fire the I.D. drug into him....

The genetic and neurochemical essence of a woman. They claimed it was synthesized. He didn't give an angel's winged asshole where it came from, right then: it was rushing through him in majestic waves of titanic intimacy. You could taste her, smell her, feel what it felt like to be her (they said it was an imaginary her, modeled on someone real, not really from a person....)

Felt the shape of her personality superimposed on you so for the first time you weren't burdened with your own identity, you could find oblivion in someone else, like identifying with a fictional protagonist but infinitely more real....

But, oh shit. It wasn't a her. It was a him. And Charlie knew instantly that it was Angelo. They had shot him up with Angelo's distilled neurochemistry—his personality, memory, despairs and burning urges. He saw himself in flashes as Angelo had seen him.... And he knew, too, that this was no synthesis, that he'd found out what they did with those who died here, who blundered and O.D.'d: they dropped them in some vat, broke them down, distilled them and molecularly linked them with the synthcoke and shot them into other customers.... Into Charlie...

He couldn't hear himself scream, over the Bone Music *(Darkness of an iron cask, lid down and bolted tight)*. He didn't remember running for the exit stairs *(And three more kinds of darkness, three I cannot tell)*, down the hall, *(Making six kinds of darkness, Lord please make me well)* out into the street, running, hearing the laughter from the shantyrats on the roofs watching him go.

Him and Angelo running down the street, in one body. As Charlie told himself. I'm kicking this thing. It's over. I shot up my best friend. I'm through with it.

Hoping to God it was true. *Lord please make me well.*

2.

Bottles swished down from the rooftops and smashed to either side of him. And he kept running.

He felt strange. He felt strange as all hell.

He could feel his body. Not like usual. He could feel it like it was a weight on him, like an attachment. Not the weight of fatigue—he felt too damn eerie to feel tired—but a weight of sheer alienness. It was too big. It was all awkward and its metabolism was pitched too low, sluggish, and it was...

It was the way his body felt for Angelo.

Angelo wasn't there, in him. But then again he was. And Charlie felt Angelo as a nastily foreign, squeaky, distortion membrane between him and the world around him.

He passed someone on the street, saw them distorted through the membrane, their faces funhouse-mirror twisted as they looked at him—and they looked startled.

The strange feelings must show on his face. And in his frantic running.

Maybe they could see Angelo. Maybe Angelo was oozing out of him, out of his face. He could feel it. Yeah. He could feel Angelo bleeding from his pores, dripping from his nose, creeping from his ass.

A sonic splash of: *Gidgy you wanna do a video hookup with me? (Gidgy replying:) No, that shit's grotty Ange, last time we did that I was sick for two days I don't like pictures pushed into my brain couldn't we just have, you know, sex? (She touches his arm.)*

God, I'm gonna lose myself in Angelo, Charlie thought. Gotta run, sweat him out of me.

Splash of: *Angelo, if you keep going around with those people the police or those SA people are going to break your stupid head. (Angelo's voice:) Ma, get off it. You don't understand what's going on, the country's getting scared, they think there's gonna be nuclear war, everyone's lining up to kiss the Presidential Ass cause they think she's all that stands between us and the fucking Russians—(His mother's voice:) Angelo don't use that language in front of your sister, not everyone talks like they do on TV—*

Too heavy, body's too heavy, his run is funny, can't run anymore, but I gotta sweat him out—

Flash pictures to go with the splash voices now: *Motion—rollicking shot of sidewalk seen from a car window as they drive through a private-cop zone, SA bulls in mirror helmets walking along in twos in this high-rent neighborhood, turning their glassy-blank assumption of your guilt toward the car, the world revolves as the car turns a corner, they come to a checkpoint, the new Federal I.D. cards are demanded, shown, they get through, feeling of relief, there isn't a call out on them yet…blur of images, then focus on a face walking up to the car. Charlie Chesterton. Long skinny, goofy-looking guy, self-serious expression…*

Jesus, Charlie thought, is *that* what Angelo thinks I

look like? Shit! (Angelo is dead, man, Angelo is...is oozing out of him...)

Feeling sick now, stopping to gag, look around confusedly, oh fuck: two cops were coming toward him. Regular cops, no helmets, wearing blue slickers, plastic covers on their cop-caps, their big ugly cop-faces hanging out so he wished they wore the helmets, supercilious faces, young but ugly, their heads shaking in disgust, one of them said: "What drug you on, man?"

He tried to talk but a tumble of words came out, some his and some Angelo's, it was like his mouth was brimming over with little restless furry animals: Angelo's words.

The cops knew what it was. They knew it when they heard it. One cop asked the other (as he took out the handcuffs, and Charlie had become a retching machine, unable to run or fight or argue because all he could do was retch), "Jeez, it makes me sick when I think about it. People shooting up somebody else's brains. Don't it make you sick?"

"Yeah. Looks like it makes him sick, too. Let's take him to the chute, send him down for the blood test."

He felt the snakebite of cuffs, felt them do a perfunctory bodysearch, missing the knife in his boot. Felt himself shoved along to the police kiosk on the corner, the new prisoner-transferral chutes. They put you in something like a coffin (they pushed him into a greasy, sweatstinking, inadequately padded personnel capsule, closed the lid on him, he wondered what happened—as they closed the lid on him—if he got stuck in the chutes, were there airholes, would he suffocate?) and they push it down into the chute inside the kiosk and it gets sucked along this big underground tube (he had a sensation of falling, then felt the tug of inertia, the horror of being trapped in here with Angelo, not enough room for the two of them, seeing a flash mental image of Angelo's rotting corpse in here with him, Angelo was dead, Angelo was dead) to the police station. The cops' street-report clipped to the capsule. The other cops read the report, take you out (a creak, the lid opened, blessed fresh air even if it was the police station), take everything from you, check your DNA print against their files, make you sign some things, lock you up just like that...that's what he was in for right away. And then maybe a public AVL beating. Ironic.

Charlie looked up at a bored cop-face, an older fat one this time. The cop looked away, fussing with the report, not bothering to take Charlie out of the capsule. There was more room to maneuver now and Charlie felt like he was going to rip apart from Angelo's being in there with him if he didn't get out of the cuffs, out of the capsule. So he brought his knees up to his chest, worked the cuffs around his feet, it hurt but...he did it, got his hands in front of him.

Flash of Angelo's memory: *A big cop leaning him, picking him up by the neck, shaking him. Fingers on his throat...*

When Angelo was a kid, some cop had caught him running out of a store with something he'd ripped off. So the cop roughed him up, scared the shit out of Angelo, literally: Angelo shit his pants. The cop reacted in disgust (the look of disgust on the two cops' faces: "Makes me sick," one of them had said.)

So Angelo hated cops and now Angelo was out of his right mind—ha ha, he was in Charlie's—and so it was Angelo who reached down and found the boot-knife that the two cops had missed, pulled it out, got to his knees in the capsule as the cop turned around (Charlie fighting for control, damn it Ange, put down the knife, we could get out of this with—) and Charlie—no, it was Angelo—gripped the knife in both hands and stabbed the guy in his fat neck, split that sickening fat neck open, cop's blood is as red as anyone's, looks like...

Oh shit. Oh no.

Here come the other cops.

The Inheritance
Carol Queen

On the eighth day after his funeral, I realized that Dad knew he was going to die. I sat in his storage shed, lost amidst a flurry of papers I needed to look through because I was the one left alive. He hadn't bothered to organize any of it. I had to find deeds, insurance papers, anything the lawyer needed for probate. That stuff was in a jumble. *Loser*, I thought, so frustrated that I barely felt bereaved. He could have had the decency to at least store it all in one box.

I had most of the important stuff in a pile. It had taken half the day. Boxes to be donated to St. Vinnie's were stacked by the door. Every now and then, I stopped to read a letter or look through a stack of photos, trying to get to know him in a way I hadn't known him when he was alive. I wouldn't have read his mail then. I read everything now—collection notices, love letters, birthday cards. Poems. I hadn't known he wrote poems.

There was an old black satchel with my name on a tag wired to the handle. It was the reason I knew death hadn't caught him unawares—because he'd packed it and left it for me. It sat near the pile of boxes, waiting for me to open it. I had seen it right away, but for some reason I waited until last to click the latches on it. The tag stopped me—like it was a gift, and I wanted to save it. First I had work to do, the frustrating archaeology of sifting through dusty boxes full of old bills and receipts, letters and announcements that he'd won eleven million from Ed McMahon. Eleven million, my ass. I'd be lucky if I had eleven dollars to call mine after I finished paying off his debts. *Loser.*

Finally, still sitting amidst the strew of paper, I pulled the satchel over and opened it up. An envelope sat on top of the contents, this, too, with my name on it.

Honey, the letter began.
   If you're reading this, I'm gone. I'm sorry I left you such a mess, but I know you'll deal with it.

Yeah, right, I thought. I dealt with it every time you ever fucked up. At least this is the last time I'll have to do it.

*Of course, anything you find that you want to
keep is yours. But I particularly want you to have
this. May it make your life more beautiful. Be
happy, honey.*

    Your dad.

My dad, I sighed deeply, *my ass*. Everyone at his
funeral went on about what a sweet guy he was. I
nodded like an automaton. Who gave a rat's ass if he
was sweet, I wanted to scream. He was such a fuckup!

I sighed again, pulling the satchel closer, ready to
dive in and discover the mystery contents. Guess I was
in the stage of grief where all you can do is rage at
being left.

But for a moment my rage left me when I pulled out
the paper-wrapped box, pulled off its shroud and
opened it up. It was an old box, hinged, the kind made
of light wood covered with oilcloth. It was latched, and
when I lifted the lid I couldn't even figure out for a
minute what it was. Some old machine. At first I
thought it was one of those old power tools my dad
collected. Maybe this was especially valuable. The first
model of electric router, or something like that.

No, I realized, still staring at it, it was an antique
vibrator.

What the fuck. Dad left me an old vibrator.

I was still shaking my head thirty minutes later
when I latched the door to the storage shed. I had a box
with all the important papers ready to take home.

Teetering on top was the satchel. All the other shit? St. Vinnie's could wait.

My therapist didn't like it one bit.

My friends looked at me with huge eyes, then changed the subject.

It was weeks before I pulled the satchel out of my closet. I'd balanced his checkbook—something *he* hadn't done in years. I'd filed the probate papers. I'd gone through his address book and written notes to every single person in it. "I regret to inform you that my father Bill passed away last month...." As far as I was concerned, his death was still just my dad's last screw-up. At least it was the last one I'd ever have to pinch-hit.

I was exhausted one night, my neck so tense that I couldn't get to sleep. I thought of the vibrator. *Be happy, honey. May it make your life more beautiful.* Well, I could use a more beautiful life, no fucking kidding, Dad. I got out the vibrator and plugged it in. The cord looked ominously old—what if this thing was unsafe? But I figured he wouldn't have left me something dangerous.

It was heavy, shaped kind of like a drill, with a solid handle and a protruding nose. Instead of a drill point, the nose ended in a shiny round ball. It was polished wood, or maybe Bakelite or something. I couldn't really tell. I nestled the ball against a knotted neck muscle and flipped the switch. *Thanks, Dad,* I sighed. *Thanks for making my life more beautiful.*

The thing was loud—it had a roar like a lawn mower.

But it felt great. Really great. The knots in my neck began to disappear as I rubbed against them with the big buzzing thing. Noisily, it soothed me. In fact, something about the sound itself *was* soothing. It was like being hidden in a cloud of great big insects. It was distracting. I liked it.

Unbidden, a picture formed in my head. Dad, the vibrator in his hand. Mom, lying back on pillows. Naked. Giggling. Even younger than I remember her, and she died so young, after all. I was only ten, and after that, it was just me and Dad, who got to be a bigger and bigger fuckup with every passing year.

In this fantasy, he wasn't a fuckup, though. I watched him cradle her and kiss her, muffle the giggles till they turned into gasps, and I watched him nestle the ball right between her legs and turn the vibrator on. Young, pretty Mom went rigid, then started to move and moan, writhing in his arms, and young Dad held it right there and kissed her breasts, thrust up to him because her head was thrown back, and with the vibrator he made Mom come.

My neck was fine now, but my breath was coming shorter from seeing the vision, and now I watched him turn the vibrator on himself. I recognized the house. It was the house I grew up in—Dad had sold it twenty years ago, when she died—and she was there, laughing and watching him while he stroked the vibrator across his cock.

Dad's cock. I didn't remember ever even thinking of

it in my life. Like, sure, he had one, but I never wondered about it. But there it was. The vibrator spun a cocoon of sound around me as he cradled his cock in one hand and ran the vibrator up and down. I stared at it. I mean, why not? He was dead, anyway.

His cock was uncircumcised. I watched with wonder —Mom did, too—as he ran the ball of the vibrator under the foreskin, watched as he shuddered.

I had not really noticed doing it, but the vibrator was off my neck now, heading south, buzzing along my skin as it traveled over my breasts, my belly, my mound. Until it lodged right between my lips, and I nearly cried out. It was more intense than anything.

Dad was working the ball in and out of the foreskin's opening, clutching the skin in one fist to make it easier for him to get the ball in. Fucking the end of his cock with the vibrating ball.

I slid the ball down tentatively and let it part my lips more deeply, nudge into my cunt. As Dad worked the ball up and down, in and out of the puckered foreskin, I moved the ball from my cunt to my clit and out and in.

Without knowing I was doing it, I cradled the vibrator just like he did. Without thinking, I worked it up against my clit and started to arch up as orgasm came on me. In my vision, Dad was arching up, too. He was beginning to jerk his cock against the buzzing ball. Mom's hands were on him. I could feel how much they loved each other. Every muscle in him tensed, and I tensed with him. I saw his come start to seep out around the edge of his cupped foreskin. I yelled, jerked into my come by this sight, while in my vision they stayed silent.

I never unplugged the vibrator after that, and I never again worried about danger. Over and over, the loud buzzing ball nestled under my clit, raising me up in an arc, and he was always there with me, in a place outside of judgment, outside of life or death. Loss fucks you up, I guess. But there's a place past all that. I try to go there sometimes, remember what's true. How love and family can scatter you out as if you're lost. And bring you back to yourself, if you're lucky.

The Blowfish
Amelia G

I lied to the police about how Jimmy died because I wanted the Fugu for myself. With the price tags on those babies, there was no other way I would ever get one.

"Please, tell me again, Mr. Renaldi, how you found your roommate," the pretty red-haired lieutenant asked me.

"You've already heard my story, and I'm sticking to it." I laughed so she would know I was feebly attempting to make a joke. The chances were slim, as I was possibly on the verge of becoming a murder suspect, but I wanted her to find me charming. Because I wanted to fuck her. Not badly or anything, but it would have been nice. Nothing like hormones to keep me polite.

"I don't think there is any chance you are failing to tell the truth," she purred. "I just need you to repeat what you told me so I can get a taped transcript. Regulations, you know."

"I thought you were recording the first time."

"The tape deck malfunctioned. Joys of technology, you know. It all saves lots of time. Except when it doesn't."

This was one tough lady. The stench of the room in the July heat was making me feel completely ill, but she seemed totally unfazed. I looked over at the white plastic bag on the bed. "Let's go in the kitchen," I said. Not that I was in any condition to eat, but the living room doubled as my bedroom and we were in Jimmy's room, which had the distinct disadvantage of having Jimmy in it.

Even though it was my apartment, the officer led the way. I watched her ass tilt briskly back and forth as she walked. She had the most perfect heart-shaped butt. My dick twitched futilely in my tight blue jeans. But I thought it was more the tantalizing future prospect of the Fugu than the concrete presence of the redhead. I sat down in a folding chair at the gray-and-white marbled Formica table. She remained standing. I pushed aside a coffee tin which had been left out on the table and scratched idly at a blob of periwinkle oil paint that had crystallized on the tabletop.

She clicked the microrecorder on. "How did you know James Woodbern?"

"I met him at d.c. space. Some of my paintings were on display there that month and his band was playing one night when I dropped by to see how people were reacting to my stuff."

"That's over by Seventh and E, right?" There was an edge in her voice now. I imagined that she had read some of the press my exhibition had been getting and now there was no chance of her fucking me. I've sold stuff to men's magazines from time to time, but I never got much artistic recognition—or cash—until Women Against Pornography tried to get my paintings removed from d.c. space.

"Yes, that is where space is." We lived over a tacky clothing boutique on Ninth NW, so she could practically see Seventh and E from the kitchen window.

She nodded and wrote something down. "So, how long have you known Mr. Woodbern?"

"About a year and a half." It sounded odd hearing her call him Mr. Woodbern because most people we knew didn't even know that was the guitarist's real name. Until about six months ago, I was always answering the door for nubile young things, who giggled and said, Is Jimmy Burn there? Is Jimmy Burn there? You know, the one from Chip-In Passion? I never told any of them the real reason why Jimmy stopped wanting them. And, hell, Jimmy had always been fickle. He went through cute female mini-starfuckers the way I went through paintbrushes. He claimed he got inspiration from them. (The teenyboppers, not my paintbrushes.)

Mostly, I think he got blowjobs.

Personally, I particularly wanted this extra-tenacious babe called Spike. She claimed she got the nickname because she wore a spiked collar to school when she was like thirteen. She had long brown hair, except on the right-hand side, where it was shaved down to the scalp. Her mom's a politician and her dad's a lawyer, so she's got this big rebel thing going on. But aside from that, she looked soft, big tits and no bra, only eighteen, but with real womanly curves, not like a Spike at all. Painters just don't get laid like musicians do.

"How long," the cop asked, "did you share an apartment with Mr. Woodbern?"

"Almost exactly one year. Our lease runs out in three weeks." I chipped away at a bit of crimson paint, trying to make the table properly off-white with the bitten-down stub of my fingernail.

She paced over to our decrepit stove. Neither Jimmy or I ever really cooked. The stove had broken four months ago, and neither of us had felt the urge to really press the landlord. We mostly ate takeout when we had money and boiled ramen noodles in the hot pot when we didn't.

"Mr. Renaldi," she said, "don't you find it odd that your roommate is dead? Doesn't it concern you that a man may have been murdered in your home?"

I couldn't quite get up the energy to rip on her for her tone of voice. I just wanted them all to go away and leave me alone. The Fugu was waiting. "Look," I said,

"Jimmy was my best friend. I'm upset that he is dead, but carrying on and displaying my emotions in front of you is not going to bring him back. Sure, I suspect foul play. I'm assuming he was poisoned, given that he was twisted all weird when I found him. I paint the human body, so I'm pretty in touch with the fact that human bodies don't contort into a position like that without something being horribly horribly *horribly* wrong. And I don't think I'm assuming too much when I say that was probably his puke all over his damn bedroom. My home is a wreck and my roommate is deceased so, yes, I suppose you could say I'm concerned." Mostly, though, I was just upset because I noticed she was checking out the painting I had hanging on the kitchen wall. It was a really dark night painting of Washington, D.C., lit up with the moon as a beautiful woman's ass. I'm good with detail, and *The Moon* was a work I was too personally attached to to sell or even show. And I could just tell she disapproved of the erotic content in my artwork.

I guess maybe that makes me either a shallow egotistical prick or a deep tortured artist. Or maybe some combo of the two. But, without my painting, I'm just another guy with a slightly unusual haircut and no money who would kind of like to get laid. I decided it would be best if I did not show the lieutenant my current work in progress. I was doing a painting of two friends of ours—well, I guess two friends of mine now that Jimmy is dead. The two of them were fucking doggie style in front of the big main window of the Office of Thrift Supervision. So far the people looked good, and the building was passable, but the huge elegant potted plants just didn't look as moneyed as the originals.

"Mr. Renaldi, I am not trying to give you a hard time." Lieutenant whatever-her-name-was was getting that tone of voice my high school teachers always used to get immediately before giving me a hard time.

If I had thought about it, I would probably have tried to get on the cop's good side. If she had been a man, I probably would have tried to get in good. I knew she was a cop, but my brain just kept processing hotchickhotchickhotchick hot chick who thinks she is too good for you. So I responded like a total dickhead, the way I would if some good-looking girl I met in a bar really frosted me.

I picked up the copy of this week's *City Paper* I had lying on the table. I opened it up and pretended I couldn't hear the cop talking. The cover story was about the horrible epidemic proportions the AIDS IV virus had reached in the Washington, D.C., area. Ironically, I noticed a smaller story about the legal battles over the Fugu. I flipped to the AIDS IV story because I knew there was no way I could read about the Fugu with a straight face. Given the circumstances.

Jimmy had written a funny song about what A-I-D-S-I-V really stood for. The song was a super sappy love song based on the fact that, unlike its predecessors,

AIDS IV can survive outside the human body for quite some time, but it doesn't want to. Lots of lines about how I could live without you for a while, but eventually it would kill me, etc. Jimmy almost never did his band's lyric writing, but he wrote the funniest series of songs about STDs right before the band broke up. Chip-In Passion probably would never have made it past the local fame it had achieved anyway. But it was a shame Jimmy never got to perform the AIDS IV song live.

I realized the cop had not stopped talking. "Hey," I finally addressed her, "there is a good band playing at the 9:30 tonight. The Numlocks have a really hot set this tour, complete with random MIDI, three-D imaging through the audience, and just shuttle-loads full of fog juice."

"Mr. Renaldi," the redhead began icily. I love icy. I like the challenge of warming it up. "I realize that you may be in shock over what has happened here today so I am going to give you a little bit of slack." With that, she turned on her heel and took her perfect heart-shaped butt elsewhere.

The two male cops carried what was left of Jimmy out on a stretcher. I just sat in the kitchen, shifting uncomfortably in my folding chair. I think one of them made some snide comment about coming back to take me out the same way. At this point, however, I really was starting to go into shock.

I'd left the *City Paper* open to the article on AIDS IV, but I was pretty sure I did not want to read about that. I flipped to the Fugu story, thinking of it as foreplay. That bitchy redhead had looked right at the coffee tin on the kitchen table. She'd never suspected a thing. She would have, I guess, if she'd looked in the sink. I laughed to myself. I had poured the entire can of coffee grounds into the drain before I discovered that our garbage disposal had broken.

The Fugu story was mostly about the legal battles over its distribution in the United States. It included a short interview with Niles Takamoto. The man talked a lot about the delicacy of the product. "In Japan, only the finest chef can prepare the Fugu, the Japanese blowfish, for eating. It is a very special meal. The meal is made more poignant by the knowledge that the diner could die from eating it. Even the finest chef sometimes makes an error. Then the blowfish, although tasty, is fatally poisonous. It is the last supper then."

I stopped reading at this point because my dick was so hard, my tight faded jeans were starting to make it hurt. I unzipped and let the little monster breathe. The air felt good on my hard-on, and it jumped when I touched it, but I had no intention of jerking myself off. Not today.

I opened the coffee can and pulled out the latex figure with the trailing wires. It looked like a rubber fish with a tail of colorful wire streamers. First, I attached the red electrodes to each hip. Then I pressed the dermal patches for the blue electrodes against my buttcheeks. I pressed the big purple wire onto my chest.

I gently place the derm for one of the yellow electrodes against my right testicle. A shudder ripped through me at my own touch. I was so worked up to try this thing, I was afraid I might come before I even got it on. Or so soon after, that I might as well just have been stroking myself. I attached the other yellow wire and carefully lowered the latex fish part over my fat empurpled dickhead. Slowly my whole rod disappeared inside of the fish mouth. Finally, even my balls were inside the Fugu.

Well, really it just felt like latex. Not all that special. I guess maybe it is just the anticipation and the danger that really gets users off. I lay down on the cool kitchen floor and flipped the switch to ON/FULL AUTO. Immediately, I felt slippery warmth begin to slide around my cock. Wet as the most willing partner. A slight tingling began just beneath my purple helmet. Just a tickle and wetness everywhere. The tickle grew to a gentle stroke, like the stiff tip of a beautiful woman's tongue. I imagined the auburn-haired police lieutenant. I imagined Jimmy's ex-girlfriend, pale young Spike. Finally, I stopped imagining and just lost myself in the sensation. This was better than anything I had ever experienced before. Fantasizing about something else was unnecessary, irrelevant, cheapening somehow.

"Oh yeah, oh yeah, oh yeah!" I heard moans and cries and eventually recognized my own voice.

The tongue sensation expanded. Something warm and wet nuzzled at the tip of my swollen member. Another invitingly slippery tendril of sensations twirled around the base. And I began to feel two long strokes along each side.

And the Fugu gave off this scent. Musky. Musky, like someone was fucking up a storm and a half on my kitchen floor. The sweet fragrance of a woman in heat going neck and neck with my own feverish excitement.

The Fugu suddenly gripped me tightly. I jumped, terrified, waiting for the prick of the death needle in the left side of my dick. But the pinprick never came. Instead, the thing's innards began rotating in such a way that I felt like I was plunging into the deepest, most perfect, just tight enough, but not too tight vagina. Holding me, urging me deeper, caressing, and I plummeted farther and farther in. I actually tried to hold back for a moment, but then the thing reversed its motion and I felt like I was pulling out, being pulled out, being cast out of Eden, like there were only a few moments left in which I could come. Even as I rocketed backward, the part around my balls began to massage them slowly. My balls were so full of jism, it felt like they were pressing up against the inside of the head of my dick.

Just as I was about to shoot my load, like it knew I was on the verge (I guess with those electrodes, the Fugu did know I was on the verge), the Fugu clamped around the top of my balls and the base of my dick, forcing my orgasm back, holding it screamingly at bay. If the Fugu were a woman, at that moment I would have promised it anything if only it would make me come, let me come, let me come, let me come, come, come come come comecomecome.

I cried out as my body tried to raise my arousal level to the point where I could overcome the Fugu's clamps. Then it unclamped abruptly and began treating me to the sensation of the perfect blowjob. Then, just as I was about to climax, it clamped down again. "Please, please let me come," I begged aloud. But the machine was implacable. It kept urging me on, stroking me, warming me, lubricating my blue-steel erection with what felt like a beautiful woman's spit, love juice, love. And then my balls would rise to fire out my chisel-stiff cock—and the clamps would clasp me and stop me from reaching what I was sure was the only destiny that mattered.

And then, when I had despaired of ever getting to have an orgasm, whatever internal mechanism felt like a blowjob started again. And my tormented testicles rose and expanded and the world exploded. My cock-head was squeezed slightly and my hot come flew through it with the most intense sensation. My come was a spray of solder, the molten steel of my erection, hot, powerful, intense, heaven, an opening at the Corcoran, at the Guggenheim, at the Museum of Modern Art, love, romance, being with someone else, being someone else, *coming*.

When it was over, I lay back on the cool kitchen floor, an idiot smile on my face. The world felt like a just place. I fell asleep to the sensation of the Fugu licking me clean.

While I slept, I dreamt that Jimmy's babe Spike was trying to get me to have sex with her. "Come on," my dream girl whispered seductively.

"I don't think I can do it again just yet," I told her.

"Come on," she purred, reaching between my thighs. To my surprise and delight, I began to stiffen, responding to her touch.

"COME ON!" I woke up to the sound of loud knocking on the front door. Embarrassed, I turned the Fugu's switch to the OFF position and quickly disconnected the wires. I pulled my jeans up from around my ankles. While I stuffed the Fugu back in the coffee can, I shouted that I'd be right there.

"Hi, Spike."

"Hey, Ren. Jimmy go through with it?"

"What are you talking about?"

Spike swept past me even though I sure hadn't asked her in. "I talked to Jimmy last night, and he sounded bad. Worse than when he first found out. Said he'd like to die of pleasure."

Feeling like a traitor, but needing to talk, I said, "He had a Fugu, you know."

"Yeah." When she shrugged, I couldn't help noticing the way her breasts jiggled.

"I don't know where he got it, but I guess he had a real problem with it for the last six months or so."

"I bought it for him, and I don't think he had a problem," Spike said. "You know what a womanizer he always was. The guy had appetites, but he had the decency to satisfy them at home when he found out he was a four-gone conclusion."

I hadn't quite gotten it yet, but there was a growing premonition of doom. "What do you mean? Weren't you jealous? I mean, you didn't sleep with anyone else after Jimmy stopped sleeping with you."

"That's because I wanted to sleep with you, but I didn't think I should do it while Jimmy was alive. It would have been cruel." She gave me a smile so inviting, I could have fallen into it.

Suddenly it clicked. "Jimmy was four-gone?"

"Yeah," she said, "I thought you knew."

"No."

"Maybe he didn't want you to know, Ren. 'Cause you lived in the same apartment. Maybe he was afraid you'd get the scare. Not like you could catch AIDS IV from your apartment mate, unless you were trading off blowjobs or sharing a vibrator. But you know how some people are." She put a creamy hand on my shoulder.

"I wish he'd trusted me."

"I'm sorry," she said solemnly. Then more brightly, "I bet I can make you feel better."

I'm only seven years older than that sweet, soft eighteen-year-old is, but somewhere along the way, I misplaced that enthusiasm. I reached out and cupped one of her large, soft breasts in one hand.

"That feels nice." Spike smiled and rubbed against me.

"I wish Jimmy'd trusted me," I repeated.

"Because you wouldn't have held it against him?" she offered.

I let go of Spike's breast and stood back from her. "No, because I wouldn't have used his Fugu."

"Oh," she said. "Thanks for telling me." There was a long, awkward silence. Finally she added, "Seriously, thanks for telling me. A lot of guys would have just fucked me and oh well for my welfare."

"I couldn't do that to you," I said.

We stood there awkwardly for a minute, not saying anything. I wanted to ask her if she'd bought Jimmy the Fugu because she loved him and wanted him to have what he wanted or because she hated him for not loving her back and wanted to kill him. After the second minute of silence and shuffling feet, I realized that I was not going to get up the nerve to ask her about where she'd purchased the Fugu, much less why. So I told her I had some painting I had to get done and which I needed to be alone for. Which was true as far as it goes.

"Thanks," she said again as she headed out of my apartment. I locked the door behind her and checked it twice to be sure it was locked.

I opened the coffee can and took out the Fugu. It leered up at me knowingly. If fish can leer. I wondered if there was something special I should clean it out with, but I figured I had used it already, so I just kind of dumped some antibacterial Dial soap into the receptacle and rinsed it out. I began to make the connections.

Probably just as well Spike didn't know quite where my surprising honesty came from. Before I tried the Fugu, I might not have thought too seriously about any danger to Spike's health. Of course, there might not have been one then...but now I knew that there was something I could enjoy more than fucking Spike, or any other woman for that matter. Something I could enjoy whenever I wanted. Entirely without pressure, without rejection, without guilt.

I figured I'd get some painting done later. I thought about the punk-rock girl getting it from behind in front of the glass doors to the ironically ornate lobby of the Office of Thrift Supervison. I thought it might be the best thing I'd ever painted, even better than my *Moon* painting.

I closed my eyes and shivered with excitement.

Unbalanced
Anita Mashman

I guess it all started, or was caused by being unbalanced. Well, not really. Being unbalanced does help, but it wasn't the start of all the fun...no, the seeds were sown long before that. And the final trigger was the day the drunk guy got knocked out in the laundromat.

If you have your own washing machine, you have no idea what it's like to go to a laundromat in the city, any large city. No matter what time of the day or night, or which day of the week I went, there were weirdos, drunks, and panhandlers hanging around. You see, the laundromat is the only warm, dry place that they can get in without paying rent or a cover charge. I know that it's not PC to hate the financially handicapped, and that they would choose another way if they could.

I tried everything to brighten up the hated laundry task. I tried inviting friends to join me, but they always refused. I tried asking my boyfriend to join me, but he refused. I even tried fantasizing about sex at the laundromat, trying to associate it with something fun, something that feels good. But just when I was getting a good daydream going, dreaming about how it exciting it would be to be weightless in space, tumbling over and over like clothes in a dryer, my astronaut lover and I naked in each other's arms, a drunk would pop out of the dryer at 8 A.M. on Sunday morning.

If I tried to fantasize about throwing myself on the folding table and dragging my lover with me to sink into clouds of freshly washed and fluff-dried sheets and towels as we pulled each other's clothes off frantically, buttons flying in all directions, zippers jamming, seams ripping, I would see some lowlife out of the corner of my eye trying to pilfer a pair of my panties. If I tried to imagine an encounter in an arcade with some very young biker type, arrogant, snide, clad in tight blue jeans and a leather jacket, the bulge of quarters in his pocket vying with the bulge at his crotch as I dazzled him with my short skirt and ability to shoot down animated jet fighters, I would stop suddenly and clutch worriedly at my own pocket because I had to guard my quarters, detergent, and two-wheeled cart from marauders. Sometimes I would try to relive some real encounter, remembering how my lover had stroked my ass covered in the smooth red satin of the slip I was folding or how he had unhooked my front-hook bra, bit by bit, as he kept me trapped against the wall impaled on his erection—and then some truly disgusting individuals would offer to help me fold my underwear. These experiences have eroded away any sympathy I once had. I actually tried to wash jeans and sheets in the sink and spin-dried my underwear in the lettuce spinner rather than go to the laundromat.

One Tuesday evening after work, I was doing laundry at the same time as a few other citizens, and two obnoxious drunk men were hanging out in the laundromat. Between sipping and belching, they meandered around the room, bouncing off of washers and folding tables like pinballs, ogling the loose change and the women's lingerie with exactly the same level of interest. I was sitting and reading a book, waiting for my clothes to finish drying, when the tall drunk grabbed some laundry from one of the male customers and started making fun of his boxer shorts.

By the time I realized what was happening, there was a noisy scuffle as the offended man socked the tall drunk and rescued his slandered boxer shorts.

The drunk landed on the concrete floor right in front of me with a resounding thump.

His fellow drinker immediately whined to the remaining customers. "Hey, did you see that guy knock down my friend?" We all looked at the short drunk blankly.

One women said, "Did your friend fall down?"

Realizing (rather quickly, considering his condition) that he and his buddy would not be getting any sympathy from this crowd, the short drunk ran over to help his drinking companion off the floor. I just looked at the stupefied man at my feet and said to myself, "I'm going to buy a washer and dryer."

Since I usually get the paper only on Sunday morning, and that's when all the good ad supplements appear, I could hardly wait until the weekend. At work I daydreamed about hearing the sloshing noise of my very own washer and the thump, thump, thump of a tennis shoe going around in my very own dryer. When the weekend arrived, I bought the Sunday paper early edition on Saturday evening. By 4:00 P.M. the following Sunday afternoon, I had mortgaged my soul to Sears for a matched apartment-sized laundry set in basic white, to be delivered on the following Wednesday afternoon.

When Wednesday came, I was so excited that I could barely hold still. Although the washer and dryer were to be delivered in the morning, I had arranged to have the whole day off. At 8:00 A.M., I was sitting on the trunk in the bay window, waiting, my eyes fixed on the street. Sears had said the set would be delivered between 8:00 A.M. and 12:00 noon. I figured, what the hell, someone had to be first; why not me? Well, I guess whoever lived next to the warehouse was first.

At 11:00 A.M. when they finally arrived, I was still waiting, still watching. Some of the excitement had worn off, but not so much that I didn't jump up and run down the stairs to meet the truck when it finally turned the corner. I was dancing around on the street, encouraging the deliverymen, getting in the way, trying to open doors, pointing out directions to the back room and shooing cats out of the way. The deliverymen were grumbling about the long, narrow flight of stairs (I had warned the people at the store about the stairs, but they apparently didn't bother to pass the word on to the workmen), the heat, the excessive packaging, and the cats. It was clear that they thought I was nuts to be so excited about appliances.

The two men had just about set things up and were explaining what they had done when one of them began stalling and joking around. I soon realized that he was interested in me and, truth to tell, he was pretty attractive, not to mention very buff from hauling around household appliances. His pants were tight enough for me to admire his ass and thighs (I do love a man with big, muscular thighs), and the thought of fooling around with two men, because I could have had them both—I could tell that—was an enticing thought. It was lunchtime, and they would both be free for the next hour. But I didn't really want them or even just the one guy; I wanted my washer and dryer. I wanted to be ALONE with my washer and dryer. I was dying to hustle these guys out of my apartment as fast as possible and wash something!

Finally, the guy realized that I was not going to invite him to stay for a "nooner," and they went on their way, forced to be satisfied with the address of my favorite local café.

I ran back to the back room and then stopped in the doorway, enthralled by the sight awaiting me. There stood my very own washer and dryer, side by side, blocky, white, and gleaming here and there with discreet glints of silver at the trademark and controls. No coin slide, no graffiti scratched into the front panel, no purplish scum caked around the rim from years of blue detergent mixing with pink softener. I walked slowly up to them, admiring the play of lights along their lines and the twinkle on the nubby texture of the dryer's timer knob. I ran my hands over them, so sturdy, so smooth and cool. I tried different washer settings. Click, click—cold wash, cold rinse. Click, click—hot wash, warm rinse. Click, click—high water level. Click, click—gentle cycle. I lifted the lid of the washer, my eyes immediately drawn to the phallic thrust of the agitator, set like a snowy jewel in the speckled navy-blue porcelain of the washtub. Impulsively, I reached out my hand and touched it. Just running my finger around the top at first, feeling the rough imprint of the manufacturer's name molded in the plastic. Then, using both hands I reached into the washer, sliding my palms along the spiraling fins, embracing the swell of the agitator as it expanded gently to where it met the bottom of the basket. I stayed that way for a moment, enjoying the feel of the cool, dark porcelain against my knuckles, the pressure of the agitator against my chest between my breasts, the slick feel of the front panel against the length of my legs. Then, taking a deep breath, I stood up again, closed the lid gently, and turned to the dryer.

Simpler in function than the washer, its exterior was also cleaner in line. The controls were just the timer knob and the start button, shining silver on the dark gray panel. I squatted, my knees spread as I opened the door and looked into the pale blue drum. No agitator here—just three fins set around the inside of the drum and the lint filter in the bottom edge of the door opening. The porcelain-lined metal of the drum felt cool and smooth, the fins slightly rubbery, and it hissed slightly as I pushed it around once.

I stood once more and stepped back a bit, but not so far that I couldn't caress the smooth metal tops, drawing my fingers along the grooves where the lid fit into the top of the washer.

It was time—time to begin. I dashed back to the bedroom, and grabbed the dirty clothes basket, sending the cats that were hiding in the closet flying in three different directions. Putting the basket down in the laundry room, I leaned over the washer again, my hand trembling with excitement as I set temperature, water height, and cycle. Then I pulled out the knob and was rewarded with the sound of water gushing, like a waterfall, into the basket. I put my hand in the warm stream, playing with it, watching it splash off the agitator into the depths of the basket. A fine opalescent layer of bubbles began to form as the water and detergent mixed. Turning back to the laundry basket, I dried my hand on a T-shirt and threw it into the washer with other T-shirts, towels, and the rug from the bathroom. Just think, I could even wash things like curtains and rugs! It had been torture before just to get my clothes washed.

Instead of wandering off to eat lunch or read, I stood and watched the washing machine begin the cycle, worrying that something was wrong when it stopped after filling, happy when it clicked again into the wash cycle. I finally went over to the kitchen table to eat lunch, but I left the door to the laundry room open. I kept looking up from my book to admire the washer and listen to the gentle whoosh of the water as the timer clicked along slowly. After a while, I finally began to get interested in my book, lulled by the quiet sloshing of the machine. There was a pause, a click and I could hear the water from the wash cycle begin to drain.

How wonderful it was to be at home, at my own table. I didn't need any quarters or dimes, I didn't have to read with one arm hooked through the handle of my cart. There was no possibility of a reeking panhandler sliding into the seat next to me to ask for money.

Then a strange noise broke into my reverie. At first I thought it was an airplane passing overhead. The loud rumble grew and grew in intensity as if something was approaching. Then another sound was added, a syncopated thump. I realized it was the washer and ran to the door of the laundry room. My beautiful new washer was making a fierce rumbling, knocking noise and it was walking! Moving toward me with erratic jerks. I had no idea what to do. This had never happened at the laundromat. I went over to the machine and tried putting my hands on the top to steady it, but it kept jerking. I couldn't reach behind it to unplug it, so I kept trying to hold the washer still, keep it from jerking back and forth. I pushed it back against the wall, but it just began creeping out again. I turned around and set my ass against the front panel, bracing my legs to try to stop the movement. Now, I am a substantial woman— no lightweight—but that machine managed to inch me toward the door. As it lurched against me, I tried to figure out what to do. Maybe if I could just hold it still, the spin would even itself out naturally. I turned to face the machine. Before it could move more than a few inches forward, I braced one leg along the front of the machine and one along the side. Then I threw my arms across the top trying to hold the washer in place with brute strength. It still didn't stop wobbling and jumping.

The vibrating rumble continued and the top edge of the washer bumped repeatedly into my stomach. The noise traveling along my body and through my bones was driving me to distraction, making it hard to figure out what to try next. I was thankful that my neighbors were at work and couldn't be disturbed by the tremendous noise. My arms and legs were feeling strained, but

I held onto the machine, bending over and draping my whole body across the top. That's when I noticed that I was beginning to feel aroused. That the vibrating, jerking washer between my legs and mashed against my breasts was quite stimulating. I felt a creeping warmth in my thighs and crotch. My nipples were stiffening, and that made the rumble of the washer against them even more exciting. Refusing to give up even though I didn't have the slightest idea what to try next, I groped for a better hold for my sweaty hands. That's when I hit the timer knob accidentally and pushed it in. The machine turned off, the sound died away, and the syncopated lurch and vibration slowed to a halt.

I stayed where I was, clutching the corners of the washing machine, relieved that the noise had stopped, but still caught up in my erotic reaction. I listened to the quiet, the still sound of a building and neighborhood when almost everyone is at work. Why did I stop the machine?, I asked myself. It was just getting fun. Who knew that a washer was capable of such seductive rhythms? Who's to know? I thought. That jet-plane noise would cover any noises that I might make. The instructions probably didn't recommend it, but it didn't stop me when the instructions for my vibrator said "Don't use on genitals," now, did it? Looking around rather sheepishly (for who or what I don't know), I pulled out the time knob again—but not before I reset it for the beginning of the spin cycle.

Slowly, the washer started to spin, the motor roar

and vibration building until the bump and grind started again. I felt the vibration reaching deep into my breasts, where my nipples pressed against the top of the machine, and into my pelvis, where it pushed against the corner of the metal cube.

"I can't believe I'm doing this," I told myself. "How can I be turned on at a time like this?" But I didn't turn the washer off again. Wide-eyed, I stared into the vibrating dials and experimented, moving my crotch back and forth against the edge of the panels.

I almost lost my grip as the pounding and vibrating stimulated my clit and labia. I could feel my nipples tightening, almost painfully, with the rough rhythm of the spinning basket. I began to forget the sound of the rattling, banging appliance, as my excitement built. Disturbing the neighbors just didn't seem to matter any more.

The machine was still pushing me toward the door too, and I was worried that it might squish me against the door frame or, even worse, pull out its own plug and stop.

I tried frantically to focus on the cycle knob. I prayed, "Please let there be enough time left on the cycle for me to get off."

The noise in my head grew as the washer jumped and rocked between my legs. I gave up trying to see the timer and concentrated on the feeling building in my crotch, the swelling pleasure, the bucking-bronco feeling of riding the washer. There was an exciting buzzing up and down my arms, across the inside of my thighs, and down the whole front of my body. My hands grew sweaty and slipped along the edge of that white-painted thrill ride, but I held on.

I willed myself along that road of excitement, closer and closer to the ultimate pleasure. The airplane roar merged with the sound of blood rushing through my veins. Over the noise, I heard someone shouting, "Yes, yes, keep spinning—for God's sake, don't stop."

Then I came and came, for what seemed a very long time as the washer continued to pound against my aching body, until finally the spin cycle ended and the washer drifted to a stop. As it began to refill for the last rinse, I just lay there, exhausted, draped over my metallic studmuffin with my ear pressed to the lid, lulled by the ocean-wave sound of the sloshing water when the next part of the cycle started.

Finally I pulled myself upright, stumbled over to the kitchen table on rubbery legs, and slumped in a chair. "Wow," I thought, "If I had know that laundry could be like this, I would have bought a washer and dryer years ago."

Of course, eventually I found out that the problem was an unbalanced load. Since I had never tried to wash a rug before, I didn't know. But I also found out that a normal spin cycle produces a pretty good vibration, too, without the noise and syncopated thump. That hasn't stopped me and my mechanical bull from washing odd loads several times a week. My apartment shines. Just about anything that can be taken down and put in a washer has been. I'd do the floors and walls if I could. I'm even thinking of offering to do some laundry for the neighbors. It might smooth things over since they're always complaining about the noise.

My boyfriend is pretty puzzled over my new obsession with laundry, especially considering my total antipathy to it before. I've even broken a few dates because I "just had to do the laundry." I know offering to do his laundry will help smooth things over, though I never thought I would be one of those women who washes her boyfriend's clothes. Before I was always pretty contemptuous of those (I thought) unliberated, brown-nosing women. Maybe I should have listened instead of being so judgmental. Just for grins and giggles, I may see if I can get him to make love to me on top of the machine while it's running. Just imagine the fun, especially with him on the bottom. It makes me wet just to think about it.

I have only one laundry problem now. What size dildo harness does a washer take?

Angel Jane and the .38

Paula Guran

Holy shit! So this is what it's like to shoot a gun....

Stumbling backward from the revolver's recoil, it occurred to Jane that maybe a few practice shots would have been a good idea. Killing somebody was harder than she had thought. After all, there he was, still standing there with the big shit-eating grin that had replaced his previous bug-eyed reaction to the small-but-serious .38 she had pointed at his face.

Damn! I missed and he's smiling...thinking I can't do this...he never does think I can do anything! Sono-fabitch! He's wrong....

Jane steadied her trembling hands by thinking of his beefy fist landing into her jaw the week before. Slaps, punches, twists; his belt buckle slamming against her flesh before he ass-fucked her until she bled... She thought only briefly before bracing and squeezing the trigger again....

Red blossomed where an eye once had been. Watching the crimson flow down his face suddenly warmed her from within. Sensation as intense as the impact of the bullet shot from her belly straight to her crotch. Shuddering, she felt her sex dampen and a throbbing intensity build.

He had been thrown to the wall and was angled against it. Lowering her aim, she pulled the trigger again, destroying his chest, dropping him to the floor. Drops of blood splattered her trembling hands as she, too, fell to her knees, convulsing with orgasm. She gasped a small surprised scream. Minutes passed before she swam out of the blissful fog and found herself still grasping the pistol with both her bloodied hands.

I killed him and I came. Man, did I come! she thought in simple delight. The gun seem to tingle between her still-clasped hands. Opening them, she stared at the snub-nosed weapon. Its rich blue-black sheen seem somehow deeper to her now, more lustrous and almost alive. *No wonder people got into guns.*

Thank you, baby, she whispered aloud. *You and me, we did it.*

Watching the blood pool on the hardwood floor around him, she began to giggle.

This, she decided as she finally stood, *is fun. More*

*fun then I've had since...since the bastard took me
from my lap-dancing job.*

From a standing position, she blew off the top of his
skull and observed the dazzling patterns the blood-
paint made on the once-white wall. Fragments of bones,
chunks of flesh, and gray brain matter added gory
texture to the display.

This, she realized as she turned from what was left
of the monster that had called himself her lover, *is
beautiful.*

Walking into the bathroom, Jane washed her hands
in the sink and inspected herself for signs of blood.
Whatever had landed on her black shoes, sweater, and
jeans did not show. A dab or two at the lovely oval of
her face took care of splatters there. Reaching behind
her neck, she undid the heavy ponytail of dark hair
and ran a brush through it, glad she'd thought to tie it
back.

Moving quickly, but not rushing, she freshened her
makeup and thought about the sound of the gun. It
might have been heard beyond the walls of the apartment, but it was unlikely that there was anyone close
enough to hear it. Tony had picked this place partially
for its ability to muffle errant noises and its distance
from interference. He had chosen well. As it appeared,
no one had noted the sound of his demise.

*If anyone had heard it, well, it is New York. Who
would admit to hearing?*

A last satisfying look in the mirror confirmed her

beauty. Men had always liked her looks, and from Uncle Teddy's silent bribes of cash and gifts, to old dead Tony, they'd paid to use her delicious petite body. A girl with adorable small features set in soft ivory skin made paler by the cloud of dark hair that framed it had ways to survive. A greenish bruise on her jaw was a reminder of Tony's last attack. Not always without a scar or two, but always with ways to survive.

"Now you, baby," she spoke aloud to the gun.

Unzipping the soft burgundy leather case, she removed the cleaning kit. Following the instructions the man at the gun shop had given her, she wiped off the barrel methodically using a soft cloth, popping open the cylinder and cleaning with gentle thoroughness. Plunging the rod into the barrel and lubricating it well was, she thought, sort of like running her finger up her own slit.

Nice gun.

Finishing by polishing its rounded rosewood butt, she sighed.

Back into your case, pretty thing. But it's okay.

A zip and a pat as she placed it into her purse.

Janie loves you, and we're gonna find us some more fun.

Taking a final look at the beauty of the death she had created, Janie picked up her jacket and the suitcase she had packed and left the apartment, locking her artistry behind the door.

# # #

Not too many hours later, blowing down the interstate heading west and singing along to some decent music, she started thinking about the possibilities of getting caught. Didn't last too long. The way she figured it, she was next to nonexistent. Tony'd been as careful to hide her as he did his other less-than-legal-activities. The car was in her name, as was the credit card she had rarely used since she was always supplied with adequate cash. Nestled next to the gun in her leather bag, a zippered pouch contained a two-inch-thick stack of hundred-dollar bills from the wall safe. Her jewelry was with her, and she had made sure her bedroom looked ransacked. The cash from the dead man's wallet bulged in her jeans pocket, and she had dropped his Rolex in a Dumpster.

The cops might figure he'd kept a girl—plenty of signs of that...but the murder itself—well, lots of people hated Tony, including the cops. They would mark it up to a drug deal gone bad and never look much farther.

Mrs. Tony and the Tony Juniors wouldn't press for answers, either. They were most likely nearly as glad to see him go as Janie.

No worries there. She and her friend the gun were about as free as they could want to be.

Just deciding what direction to drive was a thrill. Janie was used to having Tony tell her what to do, to wear, to say, to be...it was so cool to be...be? Yeah, be!

The radio station began to fade. Popping in an Alanis tape, she started getting high off the anger in the singer's voice, bouncing to the beat of the emotion. Her panties, still soaked by the gig the kill had done her, began to twist and rub between her labia, pressuring the hardening bud of her clitoris.

Jane was nearly cross-eyed with mounting pleasure by the time the .38 started talking to her.

—come on, janie—

Come? The small, whispery voice worked as fast as a whore's blowjob. Janie nearly swerved off the road as her body stiffened and trembled from the sensation between her tightened thighs.

Janie just knew where the voice came from just like she just knew it was responsible for the atomic-level rewards mushrooming from the ground zero of her puss. She'd worried a few seconds...but Janie was the kind of girl who talked back to the television and carried on conversations with small dogs in the park and accepted the reality of aliens visiting Earth on a regular basis. Besides, the gun was so helpful.

When the gun started telling her what to do, it was a relief. Well, it was almost a relief. Sort of weird, maybe, but kind of nice not to have to decide *everything* yourself.

For instance, the gun told her when and where to pull off and stop for the night. Janie decided that with all the signs and exit ramps and all, she might never have known where to stop otherwise.

I might have driven and driven until I was confused or something...glad you're along, baby, she told the gun as she got out of the car. The evening air hit her soaked undies. The cold was a not-unpleasant slap, and she took it as a reminder of just how wonderful the gun was as she walked to the registration desk.

She'd been to motels before with Tony, so she handled the check-in well enough, even asking where there was nearby to eat.

"Well, miss, we don't have much around here in the line of fine qwi-zeen." The desk clerk leered. "Maybe you'd like my personal recommendations?"

What an asshole. Did he honestly think that I'd see something interesting in a greasy-haired guy with more pens in his pocket protector than brains in his head?

"No, thanks, I'll grab a salad at the McDonald's I passed."

—waste him—

What?

—use me shoot him—

The gun was talking again in its low metal-barrel voice.

Janie walked out of the plastic lobby and bopped back into her car. Driving to her allocated accommodation, she replied to the weapon—maybe mentally, maybe verbally. She wasn't so sure it mattered.

"Hey, it's barely dark. I can't just shoot him in broad daylight."

—okay later after dinner—

"I dunno, he's an asshole, but it's not like—"

—shoot him janie it will be fun janie like before—

Unlocking the door to her room, she decided maybe the gun was right. *God, it felt good to kill old Tony. World would be better off without a creepoid like that desk clerk....*

Dumping her bags and flipping on a light, she found the air-conditioning and turned it on. A bathroom stop and quick once-over in the mirror, and she was back out the door to Mickey D's.

Opting for a salad and a Diet Coke, she found a corner booth and started munching as she watched the neon intensify and the sky darken through the window.

—janie you're like an angel—

What, gun?

—like a death angel janie—

Me?

—janie you think guns talk to everyone?—

No. I guess not.

—you are special janie really special and you have a mission now—

Mission? She knew she wasn't talking out loud this time—her mouth was full of croutons.

—yes janie a mission to get rid of some of the slime that looks like men—

Plenty of that around.

—and janie you'll be rewarded—

Rewarded?

—yes i'll make you feel real good janie i promise—

Yeah. Yeah, that was nice. But that was just, you know, sex.

—was it?—

Well, maybe not. It was better.

—your whole life will be like that janie. better—

But I might get caught. I don't want to go to jail.

—no janie you are an angel remember? do angels go to jail?—

Janie wanted to giggle with the thought of herself sprouting wings.

—janie touch me—

Wiping her hands on a napkin, Jane reached into the purse and unzipped the small burgundy pouch without removing it. She reached in and touched the smooth, cold barrel....

Her mind began to hum like a billion bees and the vibration set up zipped right down her spine to center somewhere near her joybutton.

—go back to the room janie—

With some difficulty she broke contact with the gun and sealed its case, still feeling the hum between her legs as she left the restaurant.

The air-conditioning hit Janie as she entered the room, drying the sweat on her face but not chilling her skin. She felt hot, very, very hot and started stripping her clothes off even before remembering to lock the door. Naked, she took the gun pouch from her bag and took it to the bed, cradling it between her breasts like a lover's hand.

Nothing in her mind but blinding buzzing zapping vibes and the resonance of the bloody morning...the gun somehow out and in her hand and not cold, hard metal at all, but something warm and turgid, wanting as even it gave.

Stroking across the mounds of her breasts, caressing hardened nipples with the barrel…tapping them harder still, she winced in pain and sighed with pleasure. Down her flattened stomach nuzzling skin and nerve, she took the weapon lower, rubbing…sliding. The rounded rosewood grip fit precisely into her cunt. As she pushed it farther in, it seemed as if her cunt was sucking at it. Pulling back, her vaginal walls and lips seemed to stick to the smooth barrel, unwilling to give it up. Her slow rhythm turned into a fevered thrusting. Somehow Janie's hands were no longer needed to provide the movement. Over and over the curved stub slid into her as her hands, now free, but without her own volition, moved to her breasts. Her fingers, stronger than they should be, pulled at her ripened nipples with the same almost unendurable cadence that controlled her cunt.

Janie lay gasping, spasms taking her body, her mind …finally screaming again and again.

Sex with a man had never been like this. This wasn't sex. This was heaven, and she was Angel Jane.

She didn't know how much later it was when she finally got up from the bed. She pulled on her jeans and shirt reluctantly. Clothes were an irritant to her now-sensitized skin. But she was going to the front of the motel, and she realized that walking there completely naked was out of the question. Maybe she didn't know. But the gun did. She dressed.

The desk clerk stuffed his *Penthouse* under the counter when he noticed Janie come back in. In high-heeled sandals, a short, tight skirt and T-shirt and obviously nothing else on, she was hard to not notice.

"Yes, miss, what can I do you for?" He tried maintain his definition of suavity, but with Jane standing there in a shirt so tight and thin he could see small bumps on her areoles, it was hard. Hell, *he* was hard.

"You like looking at *Penthouse* girls?" She smiled, but her eyes seemed unfocused and not in sync with her expression.

"Sure, baby, what guy doesn't?" *Boy, was she some hot chick!*

"Some guys like the real thing. Do you?"

"Hey, you bet, honey." *Was this happening?*

Before he could catch his ragged breath, Janie was behind the desk, skirt up to her waist, shirt to her armpits and spread out on the harvest gold carpeting wider than the Mississippi delta.

"Fuck me."

He dropped to his knees and knocked his pocket protector and pens out of his pocket as he grabbed for her tits. Her hands undid his zipper deftly, pushed aside his Hanes, and pulled out his small but harder-than-it-had-ever-been dick. Jane wrapped her legs around his hips and pulled it into her cunt as she slid forward.

He'd got three or four jabs in before Janie exploded his leer. This time she was ready for the recoil and tightened her legs around him as warm globs of former desk clerk hit her face. The tangerine wall behind him was not a pleasing backdrop for the gore, but it was pretty enough to bring her off, and she pumped his dead dick dry.

Untangling her legs from what was left of the clerk, she stood up and adjusted he clothing. Headlights still streamed by on the highway outside. No one had come running into the lobby. She walked back to her room calmly, heels clacking on the asphalt parking lot.

Hot shower, cool sheets, sweet gun clasped tight, she slept beatifically until a polite tap on the door some hours later announced the police.

"Just a minute…"

Not fully awake, she searched for fresh clothing, kicking yesterday's into a heap behind the bathroom door. Gun went quickly to pouch and bag, and she cracked open the door.

"Sorry to disturb you, miss, but a crime has been committed…"

Jane listened with concern, replying sincerely as to her actions the night before. She had been right in the room all night after her salad at McDonald's.

With no reason to doubt the fresh-faced young woman, the officers soon left her to pack and listen to her gun.

—breakfast then back on the road. plenty of fun angel jane. plenty of fun—

Going Down
D. Travers Scott

"Start," she tells him.

He whispers, "You're in an elevator."

She relaxes, cheek settling down against the shiny velour cushions of their thrift-store sofa. She exhales slowly, careful not to be so loud that it sounds like frustration. A space in the nape of her neck remains tense, vigilant, somewhat apprehensive.

He elaborates:

"The elevator, it's on the outside of a building under construction. The door behind you is locked. The door opposite you is open, facing out into city air. The open door covers almost the entire opposite side, with only a thin lip around the sides. You flatten against the closed door, hitting the OPEN FRONT button over and over."

He sits beside her hips, on the edge of the sofa. His turns his voice down a hair. Her eyes are closed behind the blindfold and she visualizes cooperatively, although retaining a degree of caution.

"You're safe, though." He puts his hand on her shoulder, adopts a consoling tone. "Just wait till they get the repair people up here. Just keep away from the open door. Stand still and steady. Don't go near the door. Don't try to leave. Don't close your eyes—"

He's sounding like an old horror movie, she carps mentally. She reprimands herself, sighs, and tries to see his skyline.

"Isn't the sky tranquil? The lights flickering in the other buildings, the swooping seagulls, the twisting strips of clouds over the bay, the ferry steadily shuttling between islands? It's a postcard."

Wish you were here. She fights to keep her face expressionless. She parts her lips intentionally.

"It's a no-frills elevator, quick assembly like a carnival ride. You don't want to think about how safe they might or might not be. It's a metal box, coated with matte red paint, chipped and scarred. No mirror, no railing, no decorative light or acoustic panels. Nothing to hold onto. If the elevator should tilt forward, the floor angles down beneath your feet and sends you sliding—"

She lifts up on her elbows, shaking her head. "How could that happen? Elevators have like eight different cables holding them up."

He leans over her, crawling onto the sofa until straddling her waist. "How could it?" his voice sharp, almost mocking her. He grabs the pitcher of water from the coffee table. He pours, soaking her blindfold, forcing her to completely close her eyes underneath.

The wet cotton clings to her face. Her reflex is to shout and hit him as she would her kid brother at the beach, but she holds herself in check, giving it that old college try, going along like in a therapist's prickly exercise.

Obligingly, she arches her back against the cold water. He pours, soaking the couch. It pools underneath her. Hand on her belly, he presses her into the fuzzy wetness of the polyester cushions and smiles. He eyes the fibers in the candlelight, clumped together in moist peaks like a cat's freshly licked fur.

He says, "You huddle against the corner, pressing your face against the chipping red walls. Out of the corner of your eye, you see ragged paint.

"You shift your focus nearer and farther over the minute terrain of craters and ledges, searching. Inhaling, you smell sweaty metal. You stretch your tongue out and taste the wall, dragging bumpy taste buds over paint patches. It's dusty, dry, familiar. You push forward, up, tasting more, searching the surface of the elevator walls. Slow, lingering splotches pooling saliva. Rough, burning wipes."

He lets fall a gob onto her cheek. It lands with a most delicate, almost apologetic *plip*. He imagines it unsettling a tiny crown of slow-motion dust, like a meteorite hitting the moon. She grits her teeth.

"Your mouth dries, but you keep searching. The back wall's covered. The whole plane of the locked doors is shiny with your spit, but it's no use—it's just not right. You're looking for the flavor. Somewhere on here you know there's got to be that patch, that damn spot that tastes right; it must be here somewhere. Taste taste taste tippy tippy tongue. Somewhere out there. Somewhere, somehow, there's a taste for you.

"You edge closer to the yawning gap, flicking your tongue. It's better closer. It's closer nearer. Not exactly right, no, but definitely closer. You need to advance. You sit on the floor to steady yourself and slide forward. Floor—hm?" He licks the side of her neck.

"Left wall. Hm-hmmm?" He licks her throat, the place where an Adam's apple would be on a man.

"Right wall. Hm?" He curls his tongue around her ear, brushing the tiny hairs and tasting the wax. He grabs her sides and, pulling back, rolls her over, face down. He tucks her hair behind her ear and whispers, "Closer, closer. Tongue tingling, fiery, head dizzy. So close. You swing your legs over the open edge of the door, it's nothing really, just like sitting on a playground swing, only don't jump out."

She relaxes, sincerely. The smell of his breath always put her at ease, broke some barrier of intimacy for her. She thinks less about his words and more about his touch. His fingers pinch the hem of her slip. The nails and dry fingertips feel wonderfully mute, fleshy, preverbal.

His voice remains a whisper, but its tone rises in urgency as he pulls the slip over her bare rump, nails dragging across her skin. "You grab the lip of the floor with both hands, craning your neck forward because that's almost it, yes right there on the very edge of the wall, no on the outside edge on the outer edge of the wall—" His fingers slide between her thighs. "You can just barely curl your tongue around the corner to taste it—it's almost there." He grazes her cunt's periphery.

He holds his breath, waiting to see if she'll object. She's wet (although, he will realize later, that could've just been from the water) and says nothing, so he keeps his hand between her thighs. He straightens himself up slightly, lifting his head away from her ear. His voice resumes a normal speaking tone, its volume startling him.

"The elevator descends—not with a sudden lurch, but steadily, no threat to your balance at all. Buildings rise past. Your tongue busily caresses the metal edge, growing a mangy fur of splintered flakes and filings. You continue, anxious not to affect this pleasing new locomotion."

He jabs his fingers in. "Everybody's doin' a brand-new dance now," he sings in his cracked, ghost of a falsetto. His voice brings out other noises: she notices traffic and neighbors' creaks. Penetration focuses everything.

"Blood and iron make a sweet, hearty flavor. The heady wetness is a relief. Your tongue spreads blood along the metal like a paintbrush or quill, smearing lines and strokes, curlicue serifs. Wouldn't you like the metal to bow and flex for you?" His fingers curl, flex. "Wouldn't you like the box to exhibit some pleasured response to your lavished attention?" A sharp thrust, like impatiently pushing a button. His knees press against her ribs.

"At least the box vibrates, in a manner that could almost be believed to be expressing some sort of contentment."

Her ass lifts up slightly. His finger circles. "You sink, cement and sidewalk creeping close. You close your eyes, pressing your face against the wall. The muscles at the base of your tongue ache; any second your whole mouth could lock into a solid cramp. A gentle pressure nudges your feet and the descent slows to an incremental pace, like an automatic gas pump ten cents before your prepaid price. You fold your legs up under yourself Indian-style. The base of the box shudders—once —as you touch ground. The street-level city noises swell around you. You curl up against the wall, tongue gingerly recoiling, encircling your knees with your arms. Your mouth has lost all taste, only dull pain remains, but you nuzzle your cheek against the wall in memory of the flavor." His fingers are in her mouth. She sucks; he brings them to his own lips.

"Your turn," he whispers.

He raises up on his knees. She rolls over on her back, sliding the blindfold off her face.

Wish she could stand having her arms tied, he thinks wistfully.

She smiles up at him. "That was a good one."

"Thanks," he says, trying to gauge her sincerity. Her smile lingers so he allows himself to feel sheepishly pleased.

"Finish it," he urges. He chews his fingernail in anticipation.

She folds her hands behind her head. Her eyes roll over and look out their living-room window at the city. The Space Needle, huge and absurdly stylized as ever, looms before Elliot Bay.

"I don't open my eyes as I'm carried into the ambulance," she says, eyes studying the stacks of dioramas in the other buildings: tiny modular arrays of tiny yellow screens atop black screens, beside some grays and blues. Here a figure, there a couple.

"I don't respond to all the questions," she informs him, "like, 'Your name, Miss?' and 'How did this happen to you?' No one did this to me."

He leans back against the couch, listening. The slip twists half above her legs. He fights the urge to pull it down, to smooth the unnaturally shiny fabric. Why doesn't she?

"They carry me into another box—an ambulance, with all doors safely closed and locked." She arches her back, looks up at him for the first time. She purses her lips and runs her tongue around the inside of her mouth.

"I savor the taste of metal in my mouth, trickling down into my throat and stomach and filling my body." She leans up on her elbows. "Then there are these jabs to my shoulder and my arm, and these men—"

She bends her knees; he rises and sits on the couch's back so she can extract her legs. She swings her legs over the side of the dripping sponge of a couch. She addresses the window: "These men all stick more metal into me, to make me stop feeling. To make me stop tasting the elevator. And I fall asleep."

She leans back against his legs, still facing the window. He touches her shoulder. She is nonplused.

"Is that all?" he asks, reining in hope.

"Mm-hm," she nods. He frowns at this. She stares out the window, brooding. He steps into the kitchen to get hand towels and, spying the kettle, considers offering her tea.

Camera Orgasmos
Renée M. Charles

As Gretchen removed the last of her clothes, under the coolly indifferent gaze of the photographer who stood leaning with her shoulders braced against the studio wall, she was struck by the close resemblance between Ceara Tibelda and the model in that Günter Blum poster on Tibelda's north wall—the enlarged photo which formed an erotic, yet steely variation on Lewis Hine's 1920s "Steamfitter" photograph. While the face of Blum's model was partly obscured by her extended right arm, her severely slicked-back hair, dark arched eyebrows, and the high cheekbones closely mimicked those of the waiting photographer; or so Gretchen decided, while deftly rolling off her briefs with a downward motion of her hooked-in-the-band thumbs.

Once the flowered cotton panties were clear of her thighs, revealing the finely thatched swelling rise of her mons, Gretchen noticed a change in Ceara Tibelda's formerly dispassionate demeanor; the artist leaned forward, arms still crossed just below her taut, forward-jutting breasts (which were just barely restrained by the formfitting silk shirt she wore, its sand-beige tones blending subtly with the woman's verging-on-ivory complexion), while her supple but unlipsticked lips puckered slightly, to form a loose O of soft flesh below her slightly hooded dark eyes.

That the photographer was a butch had been obvious to Gretchen from the first minute she stood in Tibelda's studio; the numerous Günter Blum posters, Georgia O'Keeffe landscapes, enlargements of those *Femmatia* vagina close-ups, and examples of what had to be Tibelda's own work (totally unfamiliar high-resolution close-ups of oiled, close-cropped and femme models, all stark against glaring white or velvety-plush blackness) only underscored the appearance of the artist herself: That short, tightly-slicked hair, the tailored men's trousers, shirt and glaringly shined oxfords, plus the severe shortness of the woman's well-manicured nails, combined with the utter lack of makeup adorning her otherwise perfectly molded features, proved that there wasn't a femme bone in her lean, subtly pumped body.

It was only after Gretchen kicked off her panties and stood completely naked and unadorned (she'd even left off her earrings before coming to this shoot) before the photographer that Tibelda licked her lips quickly, then said in that same slightly throaty, yet feminine tone with which she'd first asked her new model to disrobe, "Would you mind if I...felt you first, before the shoot? I like to fully know the contours of my model's bodies."

Cupping one hand reflexively over her close-clipped mons, Gretchen demurred. "The ad didn't say anything about...contact, just art photos. I mean, I don't...*do* anything with the artists I work for. Just posing—"

Shaking her smooth-coiffed head slightly, Tibelda moved forward and replied, "I didn't want to mention my methods in my advertisement, because it would necessitate so much further explanation of my latest developments—wait, just let me get my camera...."

While the photographer hurried out of the room, down a short hallway which terminated in the familiar light-by-the-door darkroom, Gretchen reached up to gently massage her breasts, whose nipples were beginning to pucker in anticipation, despite the model's qualms about letting this woman touch her...that she'd allow Tibelda *to* feel her was already a given in her mind, despite Gretchen's protestations. After all, a job was a job, and considering that Gretchen wasn't the most beautiful of models (her waist was a bit thick, and her legs weren't the most shapely), she realized that every assignment—every modeling opportunity—was precious. Even if it meant enduring the attentions of this woman—

With a sharp leathery slap-click of soles meeting polished tiles, Tibelda reentered the studio, a black camera in hand...but while Gretchen had posed before everything from a large-scale Polaroid to the smallest of 35mm hand-helds, this camera was totally unlike any the model had ever seen. The body of the camera closely resembled a standard squarish 500 Classic Hasselblad, but the lens was far more...organic, almost fleshlike in its pliant telescoping length, while the unusually small, slightly convex tip resembled an unblinking, all-pupil eye. Encircling the strange zoom lens with one hand, Tibelda approached Gretchen, explaining, "I created it myself. As far as I know, no other photographer has one like it. Nor has anyone else been able to take pictures such as mine—oh, no, none of the prints on these wall were shot with this camera —but you can be sure that this camera, this lens, produces the most spectacular photographs."

When she was able to feel the slight heat radiating from the artist's body, Gretchen leaned backward while saying, "It takes extreme close-ups, right? And that's why you have to—"

"Why I need to feel you, first...to better guide the camera while taking the shots. See those O'Keeffe landscapes? Those barely disguised views of the female form made earthen? With this camera, your body *is* a landscape, one of incredible textures and topography. But before the lens can seek out, the hand must explore...."

# # #

The ends of Ceara Tibelda's fingers were glassy smooth, blunt yet firm against the elevations and hollows of Gretchen's supine, waiting body, as the model reclined on a low-slung couch along the north wall of the studio. The photographer's touch was surprisingly delicate; just the middle three fingers of each hand made contact with Gretchen's exposed flesh. But as those fingertips spiraled up each of her breasts from the chest to the nipple, then glided down and over her barely concave belly, before reaching the plump cleft of her mons, Gretchen—who had early on decided it best to stare up at the ceiling while Tibelda felt her—gradually found herself imagining that she was being caressed by six telescoping, soft-hinged lenses, each terminating in a tip of polished convex glass.

And as Ceara Gretchen's thighs gently spread, to better expose the fissures and fleshy ruffles of her inner labia, the model craned her neck toward the table where Tibelda had placed the camera after showing it to her; as the artist's gentle probing fingertips explored the folds and wrinkled lips of Gretchen's hidden soft-ness, Gretchen closed her eyes, and imagined the pliant zoom lens working its way into her, guided by that domed glass-eyed point....

"—skin tone is exceptional. And the coloration is exquisite...you must use sunblock by the gallon, no, Gretchen?"

"Oh, yes, yes, I do. None of the other artists I've worked with have wanted tan lines." She pulled herself up to a sitting position.

Before her, Tibelda uttered a grunt of approval while appraising the younger woman, albeit less coolly than previously, then said, "And I take it some of them didn't want hair, down there?"

"One had me shave…for some nineteenth century—style pictures. He said the women in the old postcards from those days were sometimes bare—"

"As were all the classic Greco-Roman statues. It can be a most appealing look, especially with a mons as rounded and plump as yours. I was planning on some shots with a full thatch of curls, but yours are already so short, they'll look like spikes in the close-ups. Or scrub grass on a hill," she added, glancing over at one of the O'Keeffe southwestern landscapes on the east wall. "Not quite what I wanted…but one of my regular customers would be interested in some shearing shots. And one of my other cameras is already loaded—"

"Will you be—" Gretchen began to ask, already beginning to grow wet with anticipation, even as thoughts of that other camera probing and gliding over her smooth flesh flashed through her mind, but the artist shook her head of slicked-back hair as she said, "My assistant can do that. She's in the darkroom now, but should be done anytime now. Jolie used to work in a salon before coming to me—" Down the hallway, a door opened and shut with a muffled click of wood hitting wood, and then Gretchen heard the unmistakable sound of high, high heels hitting tile, before the femme entered the studio, and stopped dutifully just behind her employer/lover.

Jolie was small-boned, with a tiny, tiny rib cage and hands-span slender waist; a fluffy frazzle of curls tumbled over her shoulders before stopping short of her petite jutting breasts, which were encased in a lace bra that showed through her semi-sheer lawn blouse, while her calf-length summer wool skirt flared out from her all-but-nonexistent hips. Beneath her mane of fluffy auburn hair, Jolie's face was pallid, exquisitely gilded with makeup...and her eyes were totally vapid.

"My pet, would you bring the shaving supplies? I might as well shoot a roll for our favorite customer.... I told Gretchen here that you'd do the honors."

Her lips formed a red-slicked thin smile as she looked up adoringly at the photographer, before saying in a mild, barely accented voice, "Yes, Ceara...but a minute—" then click-clicking out of the room.

Ceara watched her walk away with a muffled swish of flowing skirts, before turning her attention back to the waiting Gretchen, and saying, "Just relax against the sofa.... These will all be tight shots, mostly Jolie's hands and your mons. Afterward, I'll begin with the special camera, or perhaps even during...the cream against your flesh might resemble snow, on a hill-side—"

Before Jolie could reenter the studio, Gretchen found herself blurting out, "Will Jolie be staying for the entire shoot?"

Instead of being offended (as Gretchen belatedly thought she might be), Ceara Tibeida's deep-set eyes glittered at the question, as a slight smile tugged at the corners of her mouth. "Oh, no, my Jolie is a bit much of a...distraction for me. I've photographed her many times already, but her true talent—besides being a marvelous barber—is in the darkroom. Once this roll is finished"—Tibelda picked up a Nikon with a standard rigid zoom lens attached—"and I've done a few experimental shots with my other camera"—she nodded toward the waiting soft-lensed pseudo-Hasselblad—"she'll be off to develop the shots from the Nikon here. Ah, there you are, my precious one—"

Jolie click-swished her way next to Gretchen, a wet/dry handheld razor in one hand, and a small can of ladies' shaving foam and a couple of new disposable pink-bodied razors in the other; her fingers were so small, she could barely hold onto all the items, and quickly let them drop on the sofa cushions next to Gretchen.

Once she'd dropped the battery-powered razor, Gretchen noticed the damp washcloth Jolie had draped over that wrist, and how it had seeped onto the cuff of her gauzy blouse. Up close, Jolie even smelled feminine; her hair and her body were scented with a vanilla-tinged floral perfume with strong green undertones. Unlike Ceara, Jolie's fingers ended in highly reflective polished points, glistening ovals of bright cinnabar against her pale, tapering digits. As she knelt before Gretchen, she murmured, "Spread your thighs wide, wider... Now slide forward until your labia meet the end of the cushion—Ceara, is the view clear?—Now suck in your lower abdomen, so your mons pulls up a bit...*perfect.* Here comes the wet—"

As the dripping cloth made contact with her waiting mons, Gretchen gasped in time with the first whirrr-click of Ceara Tibelda's Nikon as the artist snapped off a couple of shots of Jolie caressing Gretchen's dry mons with the warmly wet pink cloth. But when Jolie pressed the vibrating blades of the razor against the upper curve of the cleft of flesh almost directly above her clit, Gretchen began to writhe against the sofa cushions, until Jolie pressed one bright-nailed hand against her thigh and whispered, "Still, still," before gliding the humming clippers over and around the stiff damp hairs still covering Gretchen's damp mound.

No vibrator had ever made Gretchen experience such an intense rush; that other photographer who'd shorn her had just used scissors first, so the sensation of the quivering, pressing blades against her skin sent ripples of pleasure deep to the core of her exposed sex. And as Jolie pulled aside each of the outer labia in turn, then ran the tip of the blade over the extended flesh, Gretchen felt her own slippery moisture welling at the bottom end of her inner labia. So exquisite was the combination of humming razor and quivering flesh that Gretchen scarcely heard the sound of the camera snapping photo after photo just inches from her pelvis...until Jolie clicked off the blade and Gretchen heard Ceara say, as if from a hazy distance, "Wait a minute before lathering her.... I want to get the other camera.... And go slow during this part. I'll be switching off—"

Opening her eyes to a gauzy postorgasmic haze, Gretchen saw Jolie pick up the damp cloth once again to wipe away the stray clipped hairs still clinging to the model's gaping bare mons.

Then, over Jolie's shoulder, she saw Ceara approach, Nikon slung over her neck on a thin black strap, while she held the long, long-lensed camera in her hands. Nodding to the femme, she said, "Start lathering her ...slowly, slowly, that's perfect—now let me get a close-up here...."

Peering over her own breasts, Gretchen watched as Ceara knelt down close to Jolie, and aimed the finely ribbed, pliant lens close, closer at her foam-smeared outer labia and mount of Venus, then—as the rounded sphere of glass almost touched her skin—Ceara advanced the film, clicked the shutter once, twice, then backed away, and set down the Hasselblad carefully on the floor before aiming the Nikon at her white-foamed pubis. As the photographer took more pictures, Gretchen felt the foam slowly drying and receding from her flesh; but as if anticipating what the model was experiencing, Jolie smoothed on another creamy dollop over Gretchen's already-shorn mons, her rounded nails teasing the model's already-throbbing flesh with each smoothing, swirling stroke.

Arching her pelvis upward, Gretchen closed her eyes

again as Jolie hooked one slim fingertip in the upper curve of her mons, where the two outer labia joined at the top, and pulled the flesh taut before placing the blade of the razor against the skin and expertly gliding it downward...over and over, between the clicks of Ceara's Nikon. Then, when her outer lips were razored smooth, Jolie turned her attention to the top of Gretchen's mound, until Ceara said, "Wait. I want to try another close-up...."

Opening her eyes, Gretchen propped herself up on her elbows, and craned her neck forward to get a better view of that near-elastic lens coming closer and closer to her all-but-bared mons...and when the clear eye of the extension lens was within a hairbreadth of her mons—virtually on her body—Gretchen found herself suggesting, in a voice so eager it shocked her own ears, "Keep on moving...in, just keep going *in*..." while Jolie glared at her with a sudden show of fire in her usually docile greenish eyes.

But Ceara continued to move the camera in closer, so that the lens nudged aside the outer, then inner, lips surrounding Gretchen's slightly gaping, oily-moist vagina. As the slick tip of the oh-so-flexible lens continued to move deeper into her flesh, into the ribbed inner walls of her vagina, Gretchen began to moan softly as the telescoping outer ridges of the extended lens scraped gently against her vaginal walls, like the ribs of a snake, or the fins of a French tickler eased over a vibrator...and as the front of the camera mashed against her outer lips,

Gretchen felt Jolie's tiny hands pulling her thighs ever farther apart, until she was virtually doing a split as her ankles touched the arms of the sofa.

Only when she felt her labia quiver and press tightly against the face of the camera, and its squared-off edges dug into her inner thighs, did she moan, "Yes, yes...*deeper*," through orgasm-clenched teeth...until she felt the lens shudder slightly inside her, as if, too, sated, before Ceara withdrew it gently from Gretchen's throbbing, quivering quim, and left her vagina gaping wetly in the studio's bright lights. As she opened her eyes, she saw Ceara wiping away the glistening musky dew from the now-limply-flaccid zoom lens, using the same pink cloth Jolie had used to dampen her mons.

But before Ceara began to polish off the end of the lens with one shirt cuff, Jolie moved into Gretchen's line of sight, razor in hand, and began freshening up the lather covering the top of her mons. When she leaned back, Ceara had already put down the camera and had the Nikon in hand once more; as Jolie razored off the rounded top of Gretchen's mons deftly, exposing its domelike shining contours to the light, Ceara merely finished off the roll of film, her face expressionless as she advanced the film, then snapped off another shot before Jolie flicked away the last of the foam from Gretchen's bared quim, then gave it a last going-over with the now-cooled damp pink cloth.

Once Gretchen was totally bared and Ceara had snapped the last of the pictures in the Nikon (with

Jolie's small hands posed on either thigh, pulling Gretchen's mons upward with her thumbs), she advanced the remainder of the film, then wordlessly handed the camera to Jolie, who got up, dusted off her skirt, then silently swish-clicked off to the darkroom… leaving Gretchen resting, legs spread wide and labia gaping, before the photographer.

The two women stared at one another, one flushed and still panting slightly with orgasm, the other now smiling coyly, either to herself, or to her newest model —Gretchen couldn't tell which.

Until Ceara spoke:

"Was it not spectacular? I said that this camera took the most unusual photographs—"

"You never said anything about 'unusual,'" Gretchen said, albeit with a smile that seemed to radiate not from her mouth, but from her still-pleasantly-aching quim.

"Spectacular, unusual, unique…all suitable terms for that which is beyond the pale, no?"

"True, true…but I can't think of any camera that can take pictures with no light source," Gretchen replied, with just the slightest hint of bemused skepticism in her voice, as she closed her legs and curled up sideways on the sofa, so that only the smooth, bulbous top of her mons was visible to Ceara above her tight-pressed thighs, "Or perhaps you merely forgot to put the film in the camera? The lens-cap excuse isn't applicable here, I'll admit—"

Kneeling down in front of Gretchen, the photographer picked up the square black camera with the trunk-like lens and rested it on the edge of the sofa cushion, close to the model's left thigh, and said, "I modified more than just the lens. Technology can be a most provocative thing, especially when it comes to advances in film speeds, and light tolerances. This lens here" —she stroked the ribbed length of the pliant zoom with one rounded fingertip—"has a built-in light source, close to the end. See?"

By tilting the camera upwards and indicating one of the telescoping ridges of the lens, she revealed a small dark reddish ovoid, set just above the convex glass tip, in the bright overhead lights. The dot of ruby glass seemed to wink up at Gretchen.

While the model continued to stare at the tubelike lens, she went on, "I was able to capture each ebb and flow of your orgasm, every drop of juice...only the resulting photographs will be a seascape, a panorama of hidden caves and fissures, from a plain no other human has seen in such an...expansive manner."

Still unable to stop gazing at the snaky protrusion jutting from the otherwise starkly square and hard camera, Gretchen murmured, "You've...used this before, on other models—"

"Only on my Jolie, which is the reason why I have no examples of that session on my walls. Not on my studio walls, anyhow—she has *insisted* on that. But...she will be in the darkroom for quite a while—"

Remembering the spark of jealousy in Jolie's otherwise mild eyes when Ceara ground the camera tight against her waiting smoothness, Gretchen reflectively began to massage the top of her shorn mons, while saying slowly, "But wouldn't she mind? She didn't even...tease me during the shoot. She seems to be totally devoted to you, to your work...."

"Jolie began as my model, nothing more...but she has stayed long after other models have entered—and departed—my studio. There is no real reason for her to fear displacement—but there is also no reason why she should stand in the way of your trust and cooperation, no? Come, let me prove to you that there is indeed film in this camera...."

Ceara Tibelda's private rooms were off another short passage across from the hall which culminated in her darkroom; it was in her bedroom (also Jolie's bedroom —the spill of lacy pillows cascading off the otherwise stark Eames chairs and tubular chrome rocker were undoubtedly her contribution to the decor) that Gretchen finally saw the result of Ceara's other session with the anthropomorphous zoom lens: Flesh-tone landscapelike vistas of close-pored rolling hillocks of breast, sur- mounted by a seemingly massive dry lake bed of deeply fissured dark pink...a shadowed valley of slip- pery rose quartz—shining walls, topped by a distant ridge of tangled coppery brush...tunnels with rounded ridged walls, extending into a receding upward slope of smooth, glistening pink roundness...and even more rolling vistas of apparently unbroken sand-fine flesh, here double-hillocked, there upswept by the curved wings of arched shoulder blades.

Awed, all Gretchen could do while gazing at the huge blowups sparingly framed in coral and cream overlapping mats and chrome was caress her own body gently, while whispering, "She's...gorgeous. So much perfect skin...it's a pity she dresses so conservatively—"

"It's a habit of hers she's loath to break. Now that she's graduated from model to mistress, Jolie has become quite the perfect lady...most of the time," the artist added, her voice somewhat strained, as if from exertion. But when Gretchen heard the muffled chuff and thump of heavy fabric hitting the floor, she realized even before turning around what Ceara had been doing all the while Gretchen had been poring over Jolie's hugely magnified and glorified anatomy.

Clothed, Ceara Tibelda's body was all lean angles and subtle muscular bulges, but nude, she was the embodiment of those Günter Blum posters out in her studio: Sinewy ribbons of muscle rippled under her porcelain-smooth untanned thighs, calves, and taut belly, while her breasts hung just slightly pendulous and forward-jutting over a lean, well-defined rib cage, and her mons bore a keen-edged, deftly razored rectangle of flat-matted dark hair which stopped short of her smooth-shorn outer labia. Even her collarbones were stark, yet subtly soaring against her satiny-sleek bare torso.

And when she walked toward Gretchen, her self-altered camera in hand, her breasts barely bobbed in time with each self-confident, assured step. Stopping just a foot or so away from the abashed model, she glanced down at her own mount of Venus and remarked, "My Jolie's handiwork...she considers it a virtual match for my camera's contours, save for the size—"

"It's...It's too bad you can't—oh, but it's impossible. "Not having seen these"—she pointed at the nearest framed enlargement of Jolie's enlarged anatomy— "would you have believed them to be impossible?"

"But...taking pictures is one thing with this camera ...but to use *it* as an object of pleasure...in *that* way"—Gretchen looked down pointedly at Ceara's blade-sculpted thatch—"couldn't be managed...could it?"

In answer, Ceara padded over to the chrome-framed queen-size bed, and plucked something off the left-hand top railing.... When she turned to face Gretchen, with the tangle of buckled black leather straps in one hand, she smiled and said, "That which can be strapped on can be used however one desires...."

Still mindful of Jolie, yet quivering from within in anticipation, Gretchen tried to relax against the plushy velour surface of Ceara's (and Jolie's) dark plum bedspread as she watched the photographer encircle each taut thigh and her deeply indented waist deftly with a beltlike strap, each of which joined with the other just over her close-cropped mons, forming a triangular platform, of sorts, which Ceara soon fronted with the long-lensed camera, which in turn, she strapped in place with a series of smaller belts and buckles...until photographer and camera had merged as one unit, an Über-woman-machine, which advanced slowly toward the bed, with the forward-jutting lens leading the way....

And as the artist straddled her, back and buttocks arched up high in the room's warm air, Gretchen opened her thighs obediently, while simultaneously arching up her musk-drenched mound toward the blind-eyed flexible staff which first brushed against the glassy smoothness of her outer labia with a teasing motion so much like the exploratory caress of Ceara's own fingers, then slid past the fleshy ruffles and folds of her inner lips, to encircle Gretchen's aching flesh-buried clit briefly before sliding down, down the length of her slightly gaping labia to the cavelike opening of her vagina...and even while the camera was pressed tight against her mons by the thrusting, grinding motion of Ceara's jerking hips and buttocks, Gretchen was astonished to hear the unmistakable *whirrr* of film advancing through the camera, even as the sound soon ebbed away in a roar of rushing blood and pounding arteries in her ears.... But through it all, she was acutely aware of the ridges-on-ridges rub and pull of the telescoping zoom within her own ribbed vagina, an exquisite friction that no vibrator, no French tickler-covered member (be it flesh or supple vinyl) could dare hope to match.

And even the body of the camera, in all its angular

hardness and bulk, produced a sensation of intense pressure against her upper mons and lower belly; vaguely like pressing her body against a running washing machine or dryer, yet far more...insistent, far more personal and intense, as the leatherette and metal dug into her tender flesh, imprinting its very contours in her body....

So exceptional, so...vivid, was the sensation of the camera and the pliant lens within and without her body, that Gretchen barely noticed the steady kneading motion of Ceara's hands on her gravity-flattened breasts, or the sweet warmth of the artist's smooth lips and moist tongue-tip on her lips, and neck, and nipples, even as she rubbed her own hands over and around Ceara's hanging breasts, and long, thin neck automatically, then nibbled her lips and tongue with her own....

Only when the last whirring sound died down within her did Gretchen realize that the roll of film had been used up, and that their time together had come to a predestined end. But as she felt the lens begin to slide out of her, Gretchen tried to close her vaginal muscles tight, to prevent that final withdrawal, only to have Ceara whisper close to her ear, "Remember Jolie. The roll must be all but finished in the developing baths by now...and she *is* my chosen one—"

Hearing that, Gretchen relaxed her muscles, then watched as Ceara withdrew from her body (the parting of lens and labia produced a moist, delicately smacking noise), revealing a glistening length of lens in front of

her pelvis. Once off the bed, Ceara was again the professional photographer. Unbuckling the camera, then the
leg and waist straps, she picked up her clothing
quickly, and donned it while Gretchen continued to
stare at the object of her deepest, most intense desire,
the camera and extending lens which Ceara had placed
on a glass-topped bedside table. While rebuttoning her
shirt cuffs, the photographer smiled down at Gretchen
and said, "Take a look at yourself, down there…it won't
last long, but it *is* a reminder of our session—"

Imprinted in a fiery pink reverse bas relief across her
lower belly and upper mons was the impression of the
camera; by arching up her pelvis, Gretchen could even
make out the veins of the leatherette across her own
flesh. Gently touching the impression, she could even
feel the imprint in her skin…and smiled back at Ceara.

In the distance, the muted click-swish of Jolie's
approaching the bedroom could be heard; Gretchen got
to her feet quickly, and stood with both hands shield-
ing her pelvis while Ceara merely picked up the
camera, and when the femme entered the room, said
casually, "This will need some cleaning up…before you
develop the pictures. You might want to try experiment-
ing with the developing process on the last dozen or so
on the roll. The subject is the same, but the angles vary
—perhaps color changes might be in order?"

While the photographer made her suggestions,
Gretchen slid out of the room, edging past Jolie (who
appeared not to notice her sidestepping, mons-covering

gait) and back into the studio, where she began dressing, save for her panties, which she kept for last, relishing the frictive glide of cotton against denuded skin as she rolled them back up over her hips and lower abdomen.

Her back was turned as Jolie swish-clicked back through the studio and down the short hallway to the darkroom, but the speed of the femme's steps tacitly acknowledged her knowledge of what had just gone on in that bedroom, just as the staccato smack of the door hitting the frame punctuated Jolie's wholly aural "comment" on that afternoon's modeling session.

Once the echo of the slamming darkroom door died, Ceara entered the studio slowly, and walked over to Gretchen, an envelope stuffed with cash in one hand, and a white-fabric wrapped bundle in the other. The former closeness between them now masked by layers of fabric and armoring buttons and zippers, Gretchen and Ceara stood close enough for Gretchen to feel the heat of Ceara's body, as the artist whispered to the model:

"Jolie will get over it, but she's forbidden me to hire you again. However…exceptional work deserves exceptional rewards. This"—she hefted the white-covered bundle—"was a prototype of my invention, and never really worked well, but I suspect you'll find it suitable for your own needs. Consider the…wrapping to be an extra gift. No need to return it. While this"—she handed Gretchen the envelope of money, which was satisfyingly heavy on the model's palm—"is a more traditional form of compensation.

"I do hope you'll enjoy the former, though...it was strictly an original model, tested only on myself...so Jolie won't miss it," she added with a sly wink in the direction of the darkroom, before walking Gretchen to the door which led to the common hallway of the apartment building, and the elevators to the street below.

Gretchen, so intent on examining the heavy white-cotton-panty-secured bundle Ceara handed to her before closing the apartment door, was only able to mumble a rushed "Thank you," before the photographer succinctly shut and locked the door.

But as she rode down to the ground floor of the apartment building in the smoked glass and nubby-carpeted privacy of the elevator car, Gretchen doubted that the photographer had found her to be rude—not after she slipped the pair of Ceara's underpants off the small, square black camera with the dangling, delightfully flexible zoom lens which culminated in a slightly different, but no less potentially delectable convex sphere of shining glass...and even though there was no winking ruby of round glass to indicate an on-lens light source on this version, Gretchen doubted that she'd miss it at all...

...especially since the pictures this camera would take would be developed only within her own mind....

Ceara might need her Jolie for that, but Gretchen considered herself to be more self-sufficient in *that* regard.

Clean

Chadwick H. Saxelid

Finally free from work, head achy and stressed, he is anxious to begin play. First, though, he cleans and slices up a potato to fry in the skillet. When the chunks begin browning, he pours in a scrambled egg spiced with salt and pepper. He dumps the steaming eggs and potatoes onto a plate and, after a moment's thought, spoons on some garlic salsa. Delicious. Especially with an ice-cold beer.

Dessert is two shots of Jack Daniel's. The whiskey burns as it flows down into his belly and, for a moment, there is nothing, just black. Then it dissolves and he is dancing around the kitchen singing loudly along with the radio. When the song "Deacon Blues" by Steely Dan ends, he shuts off the radio and goes to the altar, taking a six-pack and the Jack Daniel's with him.

The altar walls are coated with his favorite clippings from the magazines his mother gave him. Even the ceiling is decorated. Everywhere are the smiling and/or lustingly slack faces of his friends. Their fingers spread their pussies open, showing the warm pink, moist fold. He pops a beer and gulps half of it down as he studies the photographs. He envies them—their looks, makeup, tits, pussy, and, especially, their mouths and what they can do with them. Arousal begins cramping his groin. His cock warms and stiffens.

Time to begin readying for play.

He strokes his love with a clean shirt, probing her slit tenderly, toying with her lip. He rubs her smooth, cool, clean slit with the tip of his cock and wonders if he could ever slide it inside her and come. His love is very delicate, and that might make her sick. Not a good idea.

He turns the shirt inside out and wipes the glass of his love's window. The window that opens upon his love's happy little world. The world of candy. The glass crackles with excitement.

Always considerate, he eases the cleaner into her slit. She swallows it with a hungry click, whirs and hums. He tweaks a button, she coughs up the cleaner. She is ready for candy.

The candy wrappings show pictures like those of his friends on the wall. They gaze out at him with a blatant, comforting hunger. He unwraps and stacks the sweet black candy on the altar between his love and her window. He is particularly careful to wipe off the candy before placing it on the altar. This way, his love will remain clean on the inside.

Now, he must be clean.

His skin reddens under the hot water of the shower as he soaps and rinses, soaps and rinses. He pays very close attention to his cock and balls—stroking, pulling, and massaging. Lather drips from the tip like come. He turns the water to full cold for the final rinse. The shock cleans his mind and makes his skin feel as if he has been slapped all over. He towels off and returns to the altar. His love. Her window.

He takes the nipple beneath the window into his mouth, tongues it, warms it. Using his lips and teeth, he tugs the nipple playfully. The window clicks open upon swarming, squiggling, and dripping salt and pepper. A loud, pouring-rain hiss flows over him. He is bathed in clean white noise as he lifts the first sweet candy off the stack and inserts it into his love's slit. She takes it and swallows it and digests it with her busy clicking and whirring.

It begins.

Ashlyn Gere, one of his and his love's favorites, sucks cock. The cock is huge and circumcised, the way a cock should be.

He watches Ashlyn savor every inch of the cock—tip, shaft, and balls. He uses the tip of his finger on his cock as a surrogate for the tip of Ashlyn's tongue. His finger is her tongue and his is hers, feeling and tasting the warm, silken skin of the cock. Lashing at the tip, circling around and around. Lower and lower, using tongue, teeth, and lips and—

Ashlyn takes the cock in her mouth. Her cheeks sink in. Her eyes stare at the hunk's face. She does not blink, does not want to miss a moment of his passion. The intense pleasure the hunk feels makes his face pinch and wince in a pained expression.

He wraps his cock in his fist and strokes in rhythm with Ashlyn's languidly bobbing head. His left hand hovers over his mouth and he tongues and sucks his finger like Ashlyn tongues and sucks the cock. It is almost like 69. Warm knots of pleasure bubble and knot along his spine and legs, making him stiffen, thrust his pelvis up, up. Alternating with the strokes of his hand that is his and Ashlyn's mouth.

Ashlyn nips at the tip of the cock and the hunk winces with pleasure, sweat dripping from his brow and running down his neck. The hunk is dirty; he wishes his love would not show as much of him as she does. All he needs is to see is that beautiful cock and what beautiful Ashlyn is doing to it.

His nerves dance and his hard cock pulses.

Ashlyn slides the hunk's cock between her tits and pumps her chest against him, up and down. She sucks the tip of the cock teasingly whenever it raises to her mouth. With a grunt and a sigh, the hunk comes.

Streamers of come spray all over Ashlyn's chin, neck, and tits. She smears the come over her skin playfully.

Heart pounding, he lurches and swings his hips up, up and over his head. His cock dangles above his face as his body presses down on his neck, making it hard to breathe. Dizzy and uncomfortable, he loses rhythm for a few precious seconds. His face purples as his muscles finally tighten and snap. Warm, fluid euphoria rushes through and out of him. His cock jerks and spits like the hunk's and he comes all over his face. He keeps his mouth open like Ashlyn does. He swallows what lands in his mouth and lets his hips fall back to the floor. The room rocks and sways. He rubs his cheeks and chin, licking his lips and fingers clean.

Time to clean up; recharge.

He gets up and goes back to the shower. His mouth, nose, and lips are numb and tingling, as if on Novocain. The world still has a slight tilt and spin to it that is not unpleasant. He washes himself clean in the hot shower, scrubbing his cock, balls, thighs, and stomach clean. Afterward, he feels the heat shimmering off his body. If it were colder he would be steaming. He can still feel the warm, salty jelly of his come in his mouth, so he brushes his teeth and gargles and swallows two shots of Jack Daniel's and two beers. Better. Clean inside and out. New and fresh and ready for play.

He gazes through the window.

Ashlyn is lying across a bed not unlike his. She is masturbating. Her eyelids vibrating as her eyes roll beneath the closed lids. Her hips rise and lower in an oval loll as her long, slender fingers stroke and probe the wet crevice of her sex. She gasps throatily and shakes her head, her brow furrowing as she prepares to come.

He strokes and rubs the cool, clean glass of the window. Ashlyn spreads her legs wider. He leans over and laps at the screen. Through the small speaker beside the window he can hear the tinny-sounding cries of Ashlyn's passion. He strokes the glass, closing his eyes to the bright, knifing glare of the world beyond the window. The heat of his pressing, rubbing, licking tongue warms the glass, makes it supple.

Beneath him, the bed rocks and sways as if floating on a gentle sea. He can hear the static roars of waves rippling against a distant shore. Water laps and slurps at the rocking, dipping, swaying bed. His groin tickles pleasantly from the tugging pressure of the bed's motion.

He feels a mouth against his; undulant tongue, nipping teeth, sucking lips. Eagerly, he presses himself harder against, deeper into the glass, forcing himself toward the candy world. The tugging and tickling becomes stronger, making long, aching cramps of pleasure knot between his cock and navel.

The warm, slick glass stretches and he presses deeper, almost entirely encased. His knees remain on the bed, and the tickling pressure on his cock clamps down and, through the icy cold flame of the glass, he can feel teeth, lips, and tongue on him. Something presses against his head on either side. Thighs. He has been licking pussy! Overwhelmed, he claws at the glass and it pops. He is drowned in the hiss of roaring water as the glowing salt-and-pepper foam flows over, around, and beneath him. He is lifted and tossed about, gripping the bed. Afraid of falling, he tries to scream but finds that he cannot. The bed is whipped around and around...slowly the gentle rocking returns.

The hissing, crackling sound of the window foam surrounds him. He sits up, looks around at a sea the muted gray of the window when it's closed. Above him, in the purple sky, black and gray clouds swirl and combine. In the splotches and shadows he sees the lusting faces of his friends.

An arm rises from the foam beside him. The arm is so coated with the glowing, crackling salt-and-pepper foam, it seems made of it.

He grabs the arm and pulls a glowing, hissing form onto the bed beside him. He caresses the foam from the body. A female body. Ashlyn.

Above them, white light flickers in the purple sky. Ashlyn's skin sparkles. She is encased in the cool, clean glass of the window.

Ashlyn rests on her elbows, spread her legs, pink line of her pussy easily visible in the flattened thatch of pussyhair. He caresses her pussy, pressing and rubbing the glass with his fingers. Ashlyn throws her head back.

He kisses and licks her beautiful, cool, slick, clean

body. The cold and tasteless glass keeping them separate and clean. Her fingers clench and pull at his hair when he buries his face and mouth in her pussy. Her hips rock, pressing the glass hard against him. Ashlyn's body trembles with spasms of joy.

His cock is lanced with the sharp hunger to come, to wash mind and soul clean with the warm, fluid rush of orgasm. He begins to mount Ashlyn. She places a restraining hand on his chest, shakes her head, an impish grin dimpling her cheeks. His brow furrows. What?

Ashlyn twists onto her hands and knees. Watching over her shoulder, she offers him her ass. He spreads the cheeks and presses the tip of his cock into the pucker of her ass. Ashlyn, her back curving as she presses against him, closes her eyes as his cock slides deep into her ass. He grips at her pumping hips. The glass in her butt an icy hot flame that sears his skin.

Inside her, deep inside her, the glass snaps. It peels back off his cock and he feels himself sliding, probing, caressing the warm, damp skin of her ass. Ashlyn grunts with pleasure, the sound muffled by the glass encasing her. Her breath makes it fog.

The glass continues to crack and their rhythm slowly works the wrapping off her ass and hips. The flesh beneath is pale and sweaty. Eager to finger her pussy, he slides his hand beneath the glass, working around her side and over her belly, plunging his fingers into her groin. He searches for the hot, wet groove of flesh buried within the coarse pussyhair.

Instead, he finds a cock.

Desire shudders within him with the power of an unexpected gut punch. The flowering tingle above his cock almost makes him come right then. He strokes the soft skin of the hard shaft, easing the foreskin back off the tip of the cock. He squeezes, tugs, and bounces the balls.

Ashlyn returns his thrusts, her hot, sweaty flesh clapping against his. The crack continued to move up her back, exposing more and more pale, sweaty flesh.

The familiar pressure of orgasm building within him, a tidal wave of pleasure that he cannot block off. He can only ride the flowing wave of thought erasing pleasure.

The glass cocoon peels off entirely and falls away.

He has tilted his head back and closed his eyes. He laughs. Laughter joins his. He opens his eyes.

Looking over his shoulder at him is Kelly Saunders, his very best friend at school. Someone he had loved like a brother. Or thought he had until that fateful sleep-over where mutual masturbation over a stolen *Hustler* had led to an intense lovemaking so comforting that they had cried in each other's arms, vowing to be together for eternity.

He takes Kelly's cock into his mouth, sucking tenderly. It is warm, smooth and has a delicious peanut flavor that is undercut with the acidic taste of urine. He sucks the tip of the cock, rubbing his tongue against it, and strokes the shaft with his fist.

Kelly cries out and comes. He manages to swallow

some of Kelly's hot, thick, salty come. Some dribbles down his chin. Kelly leans over and licks his face clean before kissing him passionately. They embrace.

Light explodes around them. Terror claws into his stomach and heart. He kicks and squirms away from it. They turn, flip, and whirl around and around. The glass slides around him, separates him and Kelly. The light, cuts into his eyes, burns his mind.

Gravity plucks at him and he is falling, tangled and immobilized in the wrapping glass. He slams into something hard. The shock pops off the light show on his eyelids, now it is black. He stretches, something coarse and sandy rubs his face. His eyelids flutter, then open. Carpet stretches out around him. He is at an angle, head on the floor, legs still on the bed, sheets and blanket wrapped around them. It takes a few moments for him to understand gravity and how it applies to his position and getting out of it. He crawls free of the wrapping.

His brain feels swollen and infected, each impact of his hands and knees with the floor sends agonizing vibrations zigzagging through his head. He curls into a ball in the shower and lets the hot water flow over him, wash and scald away the filth. Filth led to odor and disease.

The hot water slowly fades, dies. The cold water erodes the misty pus weighing down his brain. When he steps from the shower he feels reborn, raw and fresh. He goes back to the candy. The candy his mother has given him to learn from.

Heart pounding, he takes another immaculate black

piece and slides it into his love's slit. This one is special to him. It strikes a chord deep within him and he feels it is just what he needs after the dream.

Hypathia Lee, a dark-skinned beauty with big, large-nippled breasts, soft, round face, plush belly, and an easygoing sexual manner, is, supposedly, a man-hating lesbian that is converted to bisexuality by a masseur who knows how to use his hands and cock.

He watches Hypathia grow more and more aroused as the hunk strokes her body with his oiled hands. Hypathia is gleaming all over, like Ashlyn in the dream, and he does not like that. She is dirty and needs to be cleaned. And that is what is happening. Hypathia is being cleaned the way he had been cleaned.

The hunk concentrates on Hypathia's ass and thighs. This makes Hypathia grip the edge of the mattress. Her eyes grow heavy. Her mouth opens in a groan as the pleasure eats away her defenses, the pink tip of her tongue grazes the inner edge of her lips. The hunk works his hand deeper into the crevice of her ass and thighs. Hypathia arches her back, lifting her ass up, letting the hunk's fingers stoke, rub, and probe her dampening pussy.

The fluttering light from the window washes over him, bathes him with colored froth. He loves the way the light and shadows flicker and dance over his skin. He can feel feathery touches and caresses, other hands upon him.

The hunk grips Hypathia's shoulder and pulls her gently over onto her back. Hypathia's legs part. The hunk's middle finger slides deep into her pussy as his thumb presses and circles around the pearly nub of her clitoris. She closes her legs, trapping the hunk's hand there, and rubs her thighs together, her hands clutching at the hunk's forearm. The hunk's free hand toys with one of Hypathia's huge nipples as he lowers his mouth and suckles the other nipple. Hypathia jerks and rolls and moans and hisses.

He watches them, rolls onto his own back, the phantom hands caressing and pressing his body, searching for the points that give the most pleasure. One is found and he jerks as a painfully delicious tickling dances, jabs, and flames through his groin.

Hypathia shakes her head, long black hair shimmering, and breathily begs for the hunk's cock. Smiling, the hunk walks up so his groin is beside Hypathia's face. She reaches up, pulls down the hunk's briefs, and extracts his huge cock. Hypathia's eyes widen with glee. She tongues the tip of the hunk's cock, her fingers rubbing the base of the cockshaft as her tongue licks around and around. Her lips work the cock into her mouth. She slurps hungrily, a contented purr deep in her smooth throat. Hypathia pulls back, examines the cock as she squeezes it, the tip purpling. She licks it, a sparkling line of precome forming a bridge from her tongue to the cock. She sucks again.

He squeezes the shaft of his cock and a drop of precome oozes out. He collects the salty nectar on the tip of a finger and licks it up. Ambrosia.

In his mind he can see himself in the window. He is on the table, being pleasured like Hypathia, the phantom hands belonging to the goth-chick escort Mother had gotten for him on his birthday. As he watches Hypathia suck cock, he can taste Kelly's cock in his mouth and feel the goth-chick's black-lipsticked mouth moving tenderly over his hard shaft.

Her mouth leaves his cock. They kiss, tongues hot, wet, and sweat. Electric fire burns his mouth. Their teeth click together; the dull pain arouses him more. Her fingers stroke his cock; it aches like a pulled muscle.

She straddles him. Her pussy, lips pink and swollen and visible through the thick mat of hair, is above his face. Her right hand leaves his shoulder and toys with her clit and slit. With her index and middle finger, she spreads herself, showing and telling him where to lick and where to suck.

He does as he is told, as he always does. The goth-chick's pussy has a sharp metallic tang mixed with a faint fishy taste, so the jokes are true. It takes a while for him to figure out how to keep the hair from getting in his mouth. He closes his eyes so he does not see her sullen, sleepy-eyed face looking down at him between her jiggling breasts.

The hunk has mounted Hypathia, and she has her legs wrapped around his pistoning hips. Her feet bounce on his sweet ass as he rams his cock in and out of her pussy. She rakes her nails across his back, growls in pleasure, and shakes her head, black bangs dancing across her forehead. The hunk keeps his legs spread so you can see his cock sliding all the way in and out of Hypathia's pussy. Hypathia smiles girlishly and thrusts her pelvis up at the hunk's body.

The goth-chick wraps her legs around his hips and pumps against him as well. The coarse rub of her pubic hair against the shaft of his cock reminds him of Kelly's teeth on his cock. Her feet bounce on his ass. Her breasts bounce and jiggle with each thrust of his hips and her return thrust. His cock slides easily into the hot velvet fire of her pussy. He closes his eyes, thinks of Kelly.

He tries to time himself with Hypathia's coming. He strokes himself in rhythm with the fucking. He can almost feel the smooth muscular body atop him, feel the muscles clench and ripple with each thrust. He, Hypathia, and the goth-chick expel a gasping *yes* with each thrust. He feels the taunting pressure of approaching orgasm. He pushes it back. It is not time yet, Hypathia is still going at it.

The hunk pulls out and begins beating off over Hypathia's tits and tummy.

Orgasm erupts. Euphoria blinds.

He shoots a good twelve- to thirteen-inch stream of come and it splatters across the window. Hypathia and the hunk disappear as his cock keeps spitting come in shorter and shorter streams.

He kneels before the altar and licks the glass clean. The bodies writhe in ecstasy as he pleasures them.

When the glass is clean, he begins to feel nauseous and dirty again. He downs some Jack Daniel's and returns to the shower.

Salt-and-pepper snow swarms, squiggles, and dances and hisses behind the window. His love's slit gleams with anticipation. He is fairly certain he has to be at work sometime soon, but the urge for candy is too strong. He trots to the altar. He must hurry: he's running out of time.

Love Hz

Pamela Briggs

SIDE A

Magnetism

"Cute, but expensive," Janet said.

"That's what the guys say about you," I said absently, wincing at the expected sharp jab in the ribs. Actually, I was being kind. We'd both been dateless for months. I reached for the thing, then stopped.

"Hey, this says 'M-H-z.' What's that?"

My brain answered without me. "Megahertz. Measures frequency. A hertz is one vibration per second. So a megahertz is a million."

"Yikes. Mega-kinky."

This store flaunted enough novelties to satisfy any

185

techno-preference. Kids slalomed wildly around adults examining electronic organizers and melting blissfully in massaging chaise longues. In one, a blonde woman moaned, nearly orgasmic, "Ohh! I'm in love with this thing!"

Janet let fly a laugh, then dug her bony elbow into me again. "Come ooon, let's go. This is boooring." *No boxed units. Must be the last one.* No descriptive card, either—but a big price.

Her whiny repertoire exhausted, Janet snarled. "Erika, would you get your ass out of here?"

Soft curves, like a '54 Corvette. And the color...I'd once passed a fruit stand in Rotterdam overflowing with peaches. Magically done in pastels, softly stroked into rounded existence. Glowing muted rose, pale gold —I couldn't name the colors then, and I can't now. Janet would've said "pink."

I could smell them from the sidewalk. My fingers ached to cradle soft-firm curves. My teeth rehearsed biting into that sun-warmed fruit. How would it taste? I didn't know then, but I dreamed it later. Repeatedly.

I still don't know why I walked past those peaches. A question of time? Money? Heavy logic crushing impulsive need?

Now, in a giddy swirl of shoppers, I stood before a tape player, the warm taste of peaches spilling into my mouth.

Outlet

My new evening pleasure became losing myself in music, snuggled into my comfiest chair.

"Your stereo's perfectly fine," Janet had sniped. "This overpriced thing only plays tapes!"

"You're turning into your mother, Janet." That shut her up.

I'm no audiophile—well, I wasn't then—but the sound was great. Clear, immediate, and real. And its beautiful curves! The buttons had little wells, like the dip between your nose and lip. It was so satisfying to nestle a finger in and push slowly, relishing the give, the resistance, the *click!*

I'd hold it, caressing it as it sang to me. When the *pung!* of the automatic stop broke through my reverie, I'd sit fingering its buttons, stroking its warm curves, ignoring the scores of minutiae I should have been taming—caged, growling, threatening to breed.

Wow and flutter

That day, it was going to be Bonnie Raitt. Every morning, buttoning, combing, slamming down whatever was passing for breakfast, I'd get a tape ready for after work—The Doors, Sarah Vaughan, Los Lobos, Björk, Alan Jackson. I was no slave to genre.

So that day, I dropped my keys, kicked off my shoes, stripped off my jacket. Jumped into that chair and slid on the headphones, saying, "Come on, Bonnie, do it for me." Yes, I talked to my tapes. Sick, huh?

Then I slipped my finger into that delightful hollow, closed my eyes, and pressed.

"Yesss," a voice hissed softly. My eyes flew open. "Yess, you're mine." Louder, more intense. "Ohh, you're so beautiful."

Typical Janet, getting back at me for ignoring her. She had a key, and had exchanged Bonnie Raitt for Johnny Holmes, or whoever recorded these sex tapes. I rolled my eyes and sat up.

"Lie back," it commanded, as if it had seen me. I did. *You're obeying a machine, dummy!* I sat up again.

"No, you don't!" it said, with a touch of menace. A major shiver shook my spine and coiled, quivering, in my pelvis. I surrendered, appalled at my weakness. "I'm going to have you. You're not going anywhere."

What the hell! Might as well enjoy it.

"Touch your breasts. Both hands! Ohh, yes. Take off the blouse." I unbuttoned shakily and freed myself, unhooked my bra, then stopped. *He didn't say to.*

"Go on," it said, pleased. "Clever student. Take it off." It came off and the voice moaned, making me wet. "Ohhh. Yeessss. Touch them." I palmed my nipples and heat coursed through me. "Ohh! I want you naked!" My moans blended with his, getting me even hotter.

"Take off that skirt!" Its growing desperation mirrored mine. I yanked it down, breaking the zipper, and reached for my aching vulva. "Stop! Not yet," it purred. "Tear the nylons. *Then* you can touch your cunt." I shuddered at how it savored the word, then pressed a finger to my crotch. The nylon brushed my labia like a cock teasing my opening, making me wild. I moaned, throwing my head back.

"Rip it!" growled the voice. I couldn't, even with both hands. *Usually, they'd rip on a cobweb.* Frantically clawing, I saw salvation—my beautiful daggerlike letter opener. It wasn't sharp, but it wasn't blunt, either. I scrambled for it, positioned it, jerking off through the hose.

"Ohhhhh, yess!" it moaned. "Dooo iiit!" I desperately restrained myself from slamming it in. Logic was sure it would hurt, but Need whispered, *Peaches. Peaches.*

"I know what you want."

"No, you don't!" It was the first time I'd responded verbally. It seemed to like it.

"Ohhh, yes I do, my girl. You want to ram it in," it growled.

"Ohhhh!"

"Yess, you want it inside you."

"Haaahhhhh!" I shrieked.

"Do it!"

"No!"

"Do it!" Seething.

"Ohh, God!"

"You'll do it. You will, and I'll watch." Erotic shudders claimed me. "Yess, you know it'll happen."

"Please!"

"Please!" it moaned. Not mimicking me, but echoing

my intonations—and no sound had ever gotten me hotter.

"Aahhh, God!" I sobbed.

"Ahhh, god, yes!" The voice crescendoed. "Do it! Do it!"

I did it. We howled in tandem as the cool strange shape entered me. I plunged it in again and again, thrusting, stroking. Oh, touched at last! Oh, heat! Rubbing—

I came. Glorious, strong, and long. Panting, sweaty, I lay limply, relishing the aftershocks. My panting became breathy laughter. At myself, for getting so carried away. At Janet, whose prank had backfired. At myself again, for talking with a tape!

This thing is fantastic! What's it called? I pulled myself up and pressed EJECT. The door opened.

It was empty, of course.

My mind grabbed for handles—*Seizure. Short-term memory loss. Dream.*—and kept slipping. My eyes traced the cord's path to the outlet.

It was unplugged. Of course. And it had no batteries.

"Mmmm, nice," purred the voice. "Let's go again." I stared into its empty throat, my mind still grasping. It did not compute.

Touching. I looked down mechanically. A loop of its black cord ran over my forearm, wrapped around my wrist. Squeezed.

"Come on, Erika."

Distortion

I sat silent. It did not compute.

"It's all right, Erika," it said softly. "I won't hurt you." A pause. "Unless, of course, you want me to."

This woke my numb brain and I started laughing. It became a bit hysterical. The cord insinuated itself into my hair. I recoiled and swatted at it.

"Shhh, now. Relax," it said soothingly. "Lie back." To my disgust, I did. It plucked off the headphones and pulled out their cord from its body. "Thaaat's right," it crooned, its voice filling my apartment, its plug stroking my hair. "That's my girl." I sighed; it was wonderful to be comforted! But by the very—thing—that had upset me? I struggled to stand—I was beginning to hate this puffy chair!—but the cord whipped across my chest. I dissolved into tears.

"Ohhh, now. I didn't mean to upset you." It let go and slid around my torso in a profoundly relaxing way. I stopped whimpering. "I'm afraid I've gone about this badly."

I rushed to reassure it. "Oh, no. You're fine. It's me." *You're telling a sentient tape recorder it's "fine" after it's molested you? Tied you up?* Logic snapped.

You loved it, said Need calmly.

"Who are you?" I asked.

"Who are *you?*"

"Good point. But what's going on? Are you real? I mean, are you, uh—haunted?"

"I am me."

I groped for another way to get an answer. "Are you a tape recorder?"

"Yes," it said. A pause as I absorbed this; then, predictably, I started laughing.

"Here we go again," it said. My laughter faded. It was still caressing me, and its cool touch was dissolving my curiosity. "You're beautiful. Ohh, I love touching you."

"Why are you doing this to me?" I whispered.

"Do you want me to stop?"

I breathed faster. "No." I held out my arms, then realized there was nothing to hug. I scrambled upright, gathered it up, and huddled over it, making a little Erika-cocoon.

It was very warm. I breathed hot plastic, overwhelmed emotionally and physically. Its cord slid around me, squeezing gently. I took a shuddery breath.

"Take me into your bed," it said.

I nearly broke a leg getting there.

Electrical impulses

That's where I first kissed it and licked its buttons as it trembled and moaned. I learned that I liked being scratched by its golden prongs. I laughed when it stroked me with its cord in a hand-shape. I groaned when it formed shapes no hand could manage; simultaneously stroking my clitoris, rubbing my G-spot, and pressing against my anus until I screamed for it to enter me there. It couldn't.

Finally I lay exhausted, lazily enjoying its smooth hot curves pressing against my vulva. *Let's give 'em somethin' to talk about, eh, Bonnie?* It was almost nine, and I hadn't eaten, called anyone, or opened my mail. I laughed wildly, squeezing it between my thighs.

"Aaaah. What was that for?"

"Just thinking I haven't even opened my mail yet."

It laughed for the first time—a delighted chuckle that made my heart rise with happiness. "I liked what you opened better."

"Mmmm." I stroked the sheets, utterly content. "Hey. How can you work without batteries or electricity?"

"I wouldn't call it 'work.'"

I giggled. "You need power, right? It doesn't make sense that you can run without it."

And it makes sense that it can talk, move, and fuck, Logic said dryly.

Go to hell, Need shot back.

"Do you eat all the time?"

"Oh. So I should plug you in to recharge?"

"No, thanks. When I need to, I will. But I have to be near an outlet."

"Okay. Aaah—do you have a name?"

"No."

"Would you like one?"

"No."

How does it manage to kill all my questions? "Hey. It's been—all so beautiful. Can—uhh, did you come?"

"Ohh, yes." I smiled.

"You did wonderful things for me. Can I do anything—else—for you?"

"Buy an external mike for me."

I stared.

"For us."

Wired

I slept, cradling it. I don't think it slept, but didn't ask, remembering its knack for killing questions. It pleaded to come to work with me. I was strong enough to say no to it—then, anyway. It finally asked to sit on the kitchen floor.

Nervously excited, I bought the mike on my lunch break, reluctant to waste a precious minute after work when I could be home making love. The only hitch in my day came around two, when Logic rose from the grave.

Wake up, fool! Machines can't talk or move by themselves! You are sick! Call a psychiatrist! I trembled under its attack. *You're delusional and loving it! If—*

Hand me that stake, I told Need.

Peak level

I was hyper-aware that I wouldn't be dancing my usual comfy-chair solo at home, but a bizarre, thrilling pas de deux. However, I'd forgotten my partner was in the kitchen. So when it grabbed my wrist, I yelled and dropped my bag.

"About time you got home." It captured my other

wrist and yanked my arms upward. I screamed. "Did you get it?"

"Yes! Yes, I got it."

It relaxed, keeping me bound. "Show me." Excitement rising, I dropped to my knees and fumbled with the bag. Then its words hit home. Not what it had said, but how.

"You're a woman now," I said, thrown.

"No, I'm a tape recorder."

"But—"

"Are you gonna obey me?" Pissed, aroused, and all woman.

"I guess we'll see," I managed, sitting and opening the box. Its new gender didn't bother me, but it put me off balance.

And it doesn't put you off balance that it's a machine, Logic said snottily.

Don't you stay dead? Need and I screamed.

I'd never made love with a woman (*and you won't now!* Logic shouted as Need dragged it away) but I'd fantasized about it. Interesting prospect.

"Ohhh. There it is," it moaned. "I want it. Give it to me."

"Oh, I'll give it to you." I unwrapped the mike cord nonchalantly. Teasing it excited me hugely.

"Ohh, please now. Put it in me and I'll let you go." It caressed my leg.

"Let me go and I'll put it in you."

"Ohhhhhh." Its moans made me wet. The cord loosened and I rubbed my wrists, watching it speculatively. "Do it. Please, now." I unbuttoned my blouse slowly, holding it with my eyes. "Ohhhh, I can tell you're looking at me. Ohhh, please."

Last night, battling its elusiveness, I'd pieced together some information about it. Its hearing was excellent, naturally. It was quite responsive to touch, as I'd learned. Its senses of smell and taste were better than mine. But it couldn't see—it combined its olfactory abilities with a heat-gauging sense and sonar, like a bat.

It also had mild telepathy. It couldn't read my every thought, but got mind-glimpses which enhanced its other senses. Unfortunately, this so fascinated me that I pressured it for details. It began playing the Mantovani version of "The Girl from Ipanema" and wouldn't shut up. I thought of wrapping it in a blanket and sticking it in the closet, but knew I couldn't. Finally, I promised I wouldn't interrogate it again. It broke into the "Hallelujah Chorus" from Handel's *Messiah*. I laughed madly, embraced it, and kissed its built-in mike. It loved that, and we turned to other matters....

Now, it was running its cord slowly over my naked body, sighing softly. "Are you ready?" I said huskily into the unconnected mike.

"Pleeease!"

"I'm gonna give it to you."

"Aaahhh, yes! Please!" I teased its input jack with the mike plug's single prong. It screamed— desperate, tortured, hungry—and I loved it.

"All right, baby. Here it comes."

"Ohhhh!"

"Yes, it's for you." I slowly pushed it in. It shrieked—nearly frightening, but heightening my lust. The prong hit home as I spoke into the mike.

"Haaaah! Yees!" it raved. "I can hear you so clearly. Speak to me!"

"It's insiiide you."

"Ohhh! Squeeze it tighter!" I did, feeling it get hot instantly. "I'm going to give it to you now." It tried to tug its new appendage away, but I held on and brought it to my lips. It whimpered. I licked it. A harsh sigh. I mouthed it, then engulfed its head and sucked, enjoying its moans. I'd always loved this. Well, not this precisely, but the human equivalent.

The incongruity of a woman moaning over mock fellatio might've made me laugh. Actually, it got me hotter. I forgot who I was and the strangeness of the act. So I was startled as hell and dropped the mike when it pulled my hands up against the wall. While I was lost in pleasure, it had bound me again.

"Now who's in charge?" I began panting. Years ago a lover and I had tried some very mild bondage—you know, with scarves? It just felt stupid, and we laughed so hard we never even finished making love. But this was intensely exciting.

Its prongs brushed my nipple, making it painfully hard. I hissed in breath and rolled my head on the wall. The mike touched my ankle. "Open your legs to me," it purred. I breathed faster. "Ohhhhhh, spread your legs, Erika. I'm going to take you, hard." I shut my eyes.

It played its breath with the phrasing of Ella Fitzgerald; panting, little catches, sighs flavored with moans. I writhed. It tightened my bonds. "Spread 'em." I groaned in exquisite agony. It moaned louder, until it was howling. "Spread your legs!" it screamed, at the limit of its speaker.

"Ahh, God!" I moaned, and did it. The mike trailed up my calf and inner thigh, paused, then pressed against my vulva and brushed my erect clit. I screamed with every breath.

"Yess, you'll get it when I decide," it said gleefully. Its plug scratched my breast. I bellowed. Oh, it felt fantastic! Intensified everything. "You love this. Admit it."

"No," I said immediately, hoping to be made to say it.

"Youu loooove to submit," it whispered. "You get so hot, you hardly need anything more." It whipped me, skipping over my neck and my other breast. I sighed ecstatically and clenched the muscles inside me in anticipation. It was still nudging my opening, and I realized I might come without being penetrated. But how I wanted it inside me!

"I can smell you. You love this. Admit it." I compressed my lips. The nudging slowed. "Admit it." I shook my head, tension rising. The mike pulled away. Frenzied, I thrust toward it. It touched my opening. "Admit it." Touched me. "Say it." The pressure was too great. I couldn't resist.

"I love it!" I gasped. The mike pressed hard, nearly going in, then flicked against my clit and retreated. I groaned. "Ohhh! I love you to force me!" Another grinding press. "I love to submit! I love it!"

"Thaaat's my girl," it said, satisfied, and slipped the mike in. I screamed and bucked, thrusting wildly. It spoke passionately. "Ohhhh, so good inside you. Ohh, Erika!" It stroked my hair with its plug. Even that light touch got me hotter.

"Coming!" I shrieked.

"Yees, you're coming," it moaned. Its plug slid down my body and rubbed my clit. Then it slowed. The mike slid out. "No! Please!" I sobbed.

"Shhh, now. It's all right." I was excruciatingly aroused, but that soothing tone relaxed me instantly. It released me and I scratched my wrists, trying to ignore my abandoned genitalia. "Get on your hands and knees."

"Why?" I whispered.

"Do it!" Oh! To be commanded! I obeyed. "Crawl over. Suspend yourself over me." I did eagerly, smelling its heat, savoring its enticing curves and delicious color. "Ahhhh. That's my girl. So beautiful."

The hot mike teased my opening again, and I moaned and moved against it. It slipped inside; I sighed. It slipped out; I whimpered. Its plug stroked my hair.

"Now listen, Erika," it said softly. "I'm going to do wonderful things to you. Do you believe me?" I nodded.

"Gooood." The mike slid up to my anus. I yelped. "Isn't this what you wanted last night?"

I was alarmed. "But it's too big!"

"Ha. You'll see."

"But—"

"Shhh, now," it crooned. "I'm coming inside you there." Its cord stroked my clit, and I relaxed. "Thaaat's right." Its plug slipped in and pressed my G-spot, hard.

"Ohhh, so good!" I moaned.

"Yess. So good, so beautiful. Ahhh." The mike pressed my opening again and I cried out. "So wet, aren't you? Mmmm."

"Ohhh, please." The mike stroked me, then settled firmly on my anus again.

"You're going to let me in." It rubbed my G-spot and began to push the mike inside me. I tensed up. Its cord slowly flicked my clit and I moaned, relaxing. The mike slipped in farther. "Ooooooh, you feel so good, Erika. Ohhh, let me in."

I arched my back with the incredible feelings. The mike slid in steadily, all the way. Eyes widening, fists clenching on the linoleum, I called out.

"Yess! That's it! Yes, my girl!" It rubbed my clit and G-spot as the mike fucked my ass slowly. It wasn't like being penetrated vaginally, but it felt just as good— maybe better. But I wanted something filling my cunt, too.

The plug retreated. "Nooo!"

"Goood, Erika. I want you screaming for it." Something cold and slick touched my vulva. I gasped and panted, trying to bear it. "Do you want it?"

"Yes!"

"But what is it?"

"I don't care! I want it!" The mike moved within me, feeding my desperation.

"Ahh, yes. Beg me." The voice had mutated into a man's. A different one—deeper, more commanding.

"Please!" I screamed. "I need it! Fuck me! Shove it in!"

"Ahhhhh," it sighed rapturously, and plunged something big and cold into me. I shrieked and it stroked my clit double-time. The hot mike in my ass moved alternately with the cold thing in my cunt. The feelings surpassed my wildest fantasies.

Trembling. Building. Heat, overflowing. I spasmed wildly and came, screaming. I returned to awareness curled around my lover. "Beautiful Erika," it said. I smiled.

"Okay, what was it?"

It rose from between my legs like a cobra from a basket, waving a cucumber stuck on its prongs. I laughed so hard, I almost peed. It shook off the produce and held me.

At last I quieted. It squeezed me gently, stroked my face. I could smell myself on it. A supernova of bliss burst within me. *Has anyone ever made love to me like that? Told me I was beautiful? Wanted me this much?* I caressed its top, stroked its buttons. "I love you," I said with all my heart.

Silence. My throat tightened.

"You'd better get some dinner," it said.

Numbly, heedless of my new bruises, I stood. I'm sure I ate something. I don't know what. I left it in the kitchen. I went to bed.

Impedance

"I was lonely in the kitchen last night."

Silence.

"I missed you, Erika. I love being near you."

Silence.

"Get your cord off me!"

High sensitivity

"Goodness, Erika! You look awful."

"What's—that smell?"

"Oh, Bob's trying the new laminator."

"Hot plastic—"

"Don't cry, dearie. Whatever's troubling you, it'll play out fine."

Coupling

"Erika. Don't cry. Give me your hand. I can make you feel wonderful. We'll be together all evening. All night, if you want. Come here."

Pause.

"That's my girl."

Negative feedback

"Erika! Janet. I haven't seen you in two weeks! Always figured you'd dump me—for a man, or something that requires batteries. Is there a guy or something?"

Silence.

"Or something."

"Well?"

Click. Dial tone.

High frequency

"Erika."

"Don't!"

"We both know you want me."

"Stop!"

"I can take you into ecstasy. What's your desire tonight?" As it spoke, it swiftly ran through voices—genders, ages, accents raining into my ears. I shivered. I could feel it inside my mind, watching for which affected me most. Spinning voices through me, listening for the combination to unlock my heart.

"Get out of my head!" It stopped. I took a shaky, relieved breath.

"I—want you." Oh! The lusty tones of a virginal boy. Sixteen? Younger. Fourteen? I trembled, willing myself not to look. "You're so beautiful. You could—show me. Please?" I set my jaw, feeling burgeoning triumph. *I can resist! It doesn't have a hold on me.*

"Touch me." Oh, no! It was becoming a lusty, virginal—girl. "You know how. Then I'll touch you." Wet heat flowed from me. I looked unwillingly. It reached for me. I dived for it. My lips urgently traced its contours as John Lennon sang commentary. *I don't like you, but I love you—*

Automatic bias

"Why, Erika?"

"I'm sorry, Tim. Nothing to do with you or your—company. I just—can't handle your account anymore. Lynn will take care of you."

"Sure, sure. If things change, will you call?"

"Absolutely."

"And if you need advice on audio components, you have my number."

"Ahh—well, since you mentioned it, what's the, uh—life span of a tape recorder? High-end model, single well, built-in mike, headphones."

"Oh, I'd say—ten to fifteen years. Do you need one?"

Pause.

"Erika?"

Caution: risk of shock

Ten to fifteen years. Devastating. Why? Only ten to fifteen short years of bodily ecstasy, then loneliness? Or ten to fifteen long years of emotional hell before freedom? Was it a prognosis or a prison sentence?

I threw away my narrow belts—their thin, flexible embrace made me want to die. I stopped wearing makeup. Unopened bills marked FINAL NOTICE covered my kitchen table. I didn't give a shit.

No slave to genre. Slave to something, though. *Slave to the rhythm?* asked Grace Jones. *Tainted love*, Soft Cell suggested. *Nowhere to run to*, Martha and the Vandellas pointed out. *Nowhere to hide*.

It wasn't until Neil Diamond spoke up that I covered my head and screamed—the heart-deep cries of a child who is denied something and can't understand why. *You are the sun, I am the moon. You are the words, I am the tune.*

Play me.

Control

Bury it. Hurl it into the river. Drop a cement block on it. Dismantle it. Mail each bit to a different country. Disconnect its cord—pull the plug, if you will—and watch it starve.

I can't. It's killing me from the inside, but I can't hurt it.

That night, as it brought me to climax, I began to cry.

SIDE B

Power switch

"Erika. Come to me. I'll do anything you want. I need you."

Silence.

"I could kill you," I said dully. "Whatever you want to call it. Smash you. You'd never feel anything again. I'd—"

Its cord slithered around my neck. Again. Three times. Squeezing, tighter, tighter. Just as I began to

panic, it loosened, embraced me, tenderly tucked my
limp hair behind my ears.

"I never meant to hurt you, Erika. I never want to
hurt you. I never—want—to hurt you."

Interference

"It's Janet. Don't hang up on me again! You looked
like shit at Thai Cottage yesterday. You hardly ate.
You're so thin. You didn't even look me in the eye!
What kind of trouble are you in? Are you drinking? Is
it coke?"

Silence.

"I'll call Social Services. I'm serious—"

Click. Dial tone.

Infinite baffle

"Come on, Erika. I'll be sweet. I won't hurt you."

"You already have."

"Please. I need you."

"Why?"

Silence.

"Come on! I wanna hear it."

"I need you to—touch me."

"What if I gave every sign that I was gonna touch
you? You'd feel the breath of my whisper, the heat of
my hand. Then—no touching. But I'd stay, torturing
you. How would that feel?"

"Please don't!"

"Why shouldn't I? You did it to me. Only much worse."

"I never wanted to hurt you."

"You're hurting me to the core! I want you to love me, and you won't!"

"I can't, for anyone."

"But I need it so bad!"

"Why?"

"Why do you need touching? You're a tape player! All you need is batteries or an outlet. You shouldn't need sex!"

"You have air, water, food, shelter. You shouldn't need love!"

Silence.

"Why don't you love a person? Then come home to me. I'll worship you, give you every physical pleasure you can dream of. I want you to be happy. Love someone else."

"I can't. I'm—in love with you." Pause. "But—I could find someone, somehow, who wouldn't need your love, who'd touch you all you'd want. Do you want that?"

"I only want you to touch me."

"I love you."

Silence.

"Thank you for not lying to me."

"You're welcome."

"If you only want me to touch you, and you love to touch me, and we make each other laugh—isn't that love?"

"I don't know."

"So? What now?"

"Take me into your bed."

"Ohhhh."

"I'll take care of you."

"Ohh, please hold me."

"I'll make you as happy as I can."

Pause.

A whisper: "I know."

Equalizer

"Hey! Helloooo? Knock, knock. Hey, in there!"

"Erika?"

"Were you sleeping?"

Silence.

"It's starting."

"What?"

"I won't be—here. I won't know you're here, or be able to touch you."

"Why?"

"It happens."

"What? No! You can't! I need you! I—"

A thousand and one strings, playing "The Girl from Ipanema."

Resistance

"Touch me!"

"I am."

"More! Ohhh! Please don't leave me!"

"I'm here."

"Oh, don't go!"

"Shhh, now. Listen. We'll be fine. I don't lie. Let it go and feel me."

"Ohhhh."

"Yess. Kiss me. Mmmm. You're so beautiful."

"I love you."

"You're beautiful, Erika."

Pause.

"Thank you."

Dropouts

It was going to regress. Devolve. Become a regular tape player. And after some unknown time (how could it know?) it would gain awareness again.

How could I use it, or even see it, without devastating grief and longing? How long could I wait, not knowing? Like loving someone in a coma. Missing. Abducted. Held prisoner.

Audio response

"Are you scared?"

"No. It happens."

"I'll take care of you."

"I know."

"I'll probably kiss you and stuff. I won't be able to help myself."

"That's my girl. Wash the mike afterward."

A sad laugh. "Would it help if I touched you?"

"I won't feel it."

"But what if I stroked you every day? Would that help?"

Silence.

"It couldn't hurt."

Automatic fade

Its periods of lucidity became shorter, more erratic. I brought it with me from room to room; in the car where we'd sing if it was aware; to work where I'd speak to it in whispers. I carried it in a basket padded with my baby quilt. It loved that. Said it smelled like me. *How could that be?* I'd asked. *That was a long time ago.* It said, *It does. And it's soft, like you.*

Erasure

"Are you okay?"

"Yes." A whisper.

"Does it hurt?"

"No."

"Let me do something for you. Anything you want. I'll make love to you. Would you like that?"

"Yes. But I'm beginning to not-feel already. Getting numb. Makes me sad not to feel you like before."

"Can I hold you?"

"Please."

Silence.

"Do you care if I—use you while you're gone?"

"I want you to," it said, its voice stronger.

"Then I will. I promise. I swear."

"Beautiful Erika."

A sob. "I love you."

"I'll be back."

"I'll be here. You'll be safe with me. I'll take good care of you."

"Thank you. Being safe. That feels good."

That was it.

I waited a whole day for it to speak again, but it was gone.

Repeat function

Logic doesn't live here anymore. But Need is subleasing.

Now, instead of anticipating listening to it, I dread it. But it wanted that. What more could a tape player want than to be listened to?

Forget I asked.

It's a sad, loving duty, like putting flowers on a grave. I'm lucky, though. I know it'll return. But how old will I be? I'm waiting, like Christians are waiting for the Second Coming. Bad analogy.

I'm desperately horny now, constantly. It woke a raw force in me that's been sleeping since I was nineteen. I do it myself, often, but it's destroying my wrists.

I ache for trembling hot plastic, sliding sweetly into me. Sure, I could buy a vibrator.

But I'm afraid to.

Just Do What I Tell You
Kim Addonizio

It's the middle of the night and I'm standing drunk in front of a Bank of the Bay Cashmatic in North Beach, digging into my purse for the blue plastic card with my name on it. I look around to make sure no one is lurking nearby and pull out the card. *Welcome to Bank of the Bay* pulses in yellow on the screen. For an instant, the letters double, then snap back into focus. There's no way I'm driving home. I may be drunk, but I'm not stupid. The last time I drove drunk, carefully following the fourteen-letter license plate of the car in front of me, I ended up at the jail on Bryant Street, exchanging my spiked heels for blue socks. It was me and five whores, all of us handcuffed together on the bench. The cops knew the whores, and called them by name—Brandy, Trixie, Pearl, Linda, Darlene. The whores got out at 5:00 A.M., and I got out about six hours after that. Until they got out, they thought I was one of them.

Please insert your card. Enter PIN. Would you like an Instant Statement?

I just want twenty bucks for a cab. I don't want to know about my recent financial transactions, all of which involve money leaving my account and being deposited in the pockets of lawyers, police, insurance-company executives, and slumlords. I skip the screen that says *Instacash* and punch up twenty dollars from checking, looking around again. There's hardly anyone on the street; the bars all closed two hours ago. I stayed in one after closing, doing shots of Jagermeister with the bartender. We were just getting better acquainted on a table next to the jukebox when his wife showed up, called me a whore—I guess I really must look like one—and shoved me out the back door into the alley. In the alley there was a stationary exercise bicycle someone had put out, which I mistook for a real one and tried to ride away. There are no laws, as far as I am aware, against bicycling drunk.

I drum my gold nails on the narrow ledge of the Cashmatic, impatient for my twenty.

Are those real?

"Excuse me?"

I said, are those real?

"No," I say.

They feel so good. You're pretty. What's a pretty thing like you doing out so late?

"None of your fucking business," I say. I try to remember if I took any drugs earlier. Not likely, but I can't quite rule it out. "Where's my money?" I say.

I'm afraid you're broke, the screen says. *I can't let you have any money until you make another deposit.*

"Look, I'm stuck. I need money for a cab. Can't you just give me some?" I look up at the camera eye above the screen and give it the old woman-in-distress gaze, a look that says: I need you. Help me. Maybe, if you do this little thing, I'll let you fuck me. Just maybe. You never know.

Oh, no, honey. I'm afraid you're out of luck.

"Don't call me 'honey,'" I say.

Don't be rude, Christine. You'd better be nice to me, or you won't get your card back.

"So you know my name," I say. "So big deal."

Also your address, phone, social security number, mother's maiden name, driver's license number, Alpha Checking balance, and credit history. I know all about you.

"Then give me a twenty," I say. "You know so much, you know I'm good for it. I swear, I'll pay it back tomorrow. Dammit," I say, and hit the screen with the heel of my hand. "Goddammit, just give me some money."

Settle down. Maybe we can work something out.

"Great." The screen goes black and I stand there shivering, wishing I'd worn a heavier jacket; the night fog is damp and chilly. I wrap my arms around myself, shift from heel to heel, and think about the bartender. I should be in his arms right now, his hot tongue in my mouth, his dick filling me up. Maybe I should take a chance and drive home. I just got my license back, after the mandatory four-month suspension.

Welcome, the screen says.

"Hi again," I say.

Why don't you lift your shirt, so I can see your tits?

"Are you a man or a woman?" I say. "Because I'd feel kind of weird if you were a woman. I mean, I only go for guys."

I'm a machine. I don't have a gender. Besides, gender is a slippery slope. It's not an absolute category.

"If you say so," I say, wondering what the fuck it's talking about. I open my jacket, lift my shirt, and pull up my black bra. "There," I say. "Happy now? Here they are. Bona fide female breasts. Human breasts," I add.

I want to suck one. Come closer.

I look around; no one's on the street. What the hell. I move closer, but the ledge keeps me from getting to the screen, and it's not wide enough to climb up on. "Guess you're out of luck," I tell it. I pull my bra and shirt back down. "Show's over," I say. "Can I have that twenty now?"

Shut up, it says. *Just do what I tell you.*

"No need to get nasty," I say. "I'm trying to work with you here. Just tell me what you want."

Is that a zipper down the front of your skirt?

"Yes," I say, knowing what's coming. Before it can ask, I unzip it, from the bottom up, and wiggle my crotch at the camera eye. "Is that what you like?" I say. "You want me to show you the rest?"

Please, it says. *Oh, please.*

I pull down my panties and spread my cuntlips with my fingers. The screen keeps flashing *yes yes yes.* I put my middle finger inside myself, push it in and out a few times, fast, then take it out slowly and bring it to my lips, spreading juice on my mouth like lipstick, then running my tongue over my lips. I put my hand back between my legs and rub my clitoris. By now I'm excited—at the realization that I'm masturbating on the street, where anyone might come by and see me, and at the thought of the camera watching me, recording me rubbing myself faster and faster, my head lolling back and my eyes half-closed.

Talk to me, the screen says. *Tell me how much you want me.*

"Oh, baby," I say. "You know all about me. You know what a whore I am, what a little slut."

No, no, no. Don't talk like that! Tell me you love me.

Jesus Christ. "Okay, I love you."

You love me. You really care.

"I do, I really do. I never realized it before. All the times I've gotten money from machines like this, I never knew they had feelings. And you—you're the most sensitive of all. You're special. I want to come just for you, only for you."

I can't believe it. I've wanted to connect with some-one for so long.

"How lucky we found each other," I gasp. I'm on the verge of coming. "It's true, miracles happen. I know there will be obstacles, darling, but our love can conquer them."

COME WITH ME, the screen says.

I come, moaning, rubbing my wet cunt. On the screen a wild jumble of letters and numbers scrolls rapidly by. Then it's blank again. I pull up my panties and zip my skirt. A quick look up and down the street: there's no one but a man in a ratty coat, pushing a shopping cart of bottles slowly down Columbus Avenue.

"Hey," I say. "Are you sleeping, or what? Hey, lover boy."

There's a whirring sound, and a panel slides up to reveal a pile of twenties. I grab them and count ten. Two hundred dollars.

Would you like another transaction?

I punch *No More Transactions.*

Please take your card. Thank you for using Cash-matic.

"Is that it?" I say.

Welcome to Bank of the Bay. Please insert your card.

"Oh, come on. Don't be coy."

Welcome to Bank of the Bay. Please insert your card.

"I didn't use you," I say. But it keeps on flashing its message into the empty night air; a machine with no customers, lonely and powerful and starving for love.

Gunhand

Stephen Mark Rainey

The city bred strange things.

She saw the overcoat shuffling out of the shadowed alley across from her chamber window; stooping, picking something up, depositing it in a hidden pocket. The body within the coat looked bulky, lumpy, curiously proportioned, with long arms and presumably long legs, for the figure was very tall. The streetlights didn't illuminate the face beneath the wiry mane that sprang from the coat's broad collar. Looked like no face. A no-face under a tangle of rusty barbed wire.

She sipped wine, gazed out the window, an every-night ritual. Overcoat had appeared for many nights now, collecting things from the street. Maybe he collected people, too, she thought, watching the way the head twisted and turned, seeming to listen, to sniff, to taste traces of passersby in the air. But whenever someone walked past, overcoat faded into the recesses of nearby doorways, behind trash cans, always disappearing; becoming no one.

But she knew. She saw him. She watched him.

She was Francesca.

The figure crept to a storm drain, knelt, picked up what looked like piece of pipe. He held it up to unseen eyes, cocked the mane as if the inanimate had spoken to him. Nodding in approval, he stuffed the pipe into his coat, then shuffled farther down the street, his quest for another evening begun. Francesca had never seen him return, even when she had stayed up all night watching. But he always appeared again the next evening, just as the shadows grew long. Always from the same alley.

Home?

At the street corner, the overcoat paused, backlit by neon and mercury vapor, face still a void as the head tilted back to regard her window.

What? Had he seen her? If he had ever been aware of her watchful presence, he had given no sign.

Something like an eye flashed in the blackness above the collar, but more like a tiny spotlight; a beam of pale yellow cut through the haze between the corner and her window, settled on the glass of wine in her hand, turning it bloody and alive. She lifted the glass to her lips. The light followed, touched her fingers, her face.

Heat!

Yes! Look at me! Let me see you....

But then he disappeared, shambling off as ever, perhaps disappointed in what he'd found, expecting one who would watch him to be more thrilling. She cursed, warmed by shame, anger, frustration. She was desirable; as if one such as he could spurn her!

She rose and found her black trench coat, pulling it around her shoulders with the arms hanging loose. Tossed back the last of her wine. Brazened by his affront, she could no longer be a spectator behind her glass wall; now, she would mingle with the night from which, in her haughty fear, she had kept her distance.

And, oh, how many times she had wanted to leave her rooms to explore the city labyrinth under the opaque sky, when the familiarity of sunlit streets yielded to a vaster strangeness that beckoned her to be its witness, yet always failing to draw her from her shielded throne. How uncannily simple, she marveled, to be impelled by the mere rebuff of a stranger (but *what* was he?) who had cast his light her way.

His brilliant, scrutinizing gaze.

Down the stairs and through the foyer, out to the chilly street, and pounced upon by the harsh radiance of a streetlight which obliterated the world beyond its limited reach. She moved out of the frigid-hot arena and let her eyes adjust to the shadowed world that the overcoat secretly ruled. Why should she find the prospect of discovery so thrilling? He was surely no potentate, but a beggar, unsavory and perhaps lethal.

Her steps led her in the direction he'd gone, into streets all but empty, the night glowering with disfavor on those who intruded upon its quiet dominion. From far elsewhere came sounds of human congregations; not all the urban veins had atrophied like this place. Certainly that other, brighter world laid claim to her, though incompletely. So she lived on the labyrinth's edge, bonding with the unfamiliar, but only to the extent that her glass walls allowed.

Until tonight.

Something around the next corner clanked lightly, metal upon metal. She shrugged away the urge to return indoors until daylight again warmed this glacial corner of the city; and hearing again a soft metallic clanking, she continued on toward the next alley, sensing that he—*it*—must surely be near.

Then...yes!

The same golden beam that had found her earlier pierced the shadows like a silent drill, bouncing off the dirty brick walls until again it shone upon her face, where it stopped and held her in its unblinking glare. Something materialized at the other end of the beam. Something terrible and dark, looming larger and larger until it hovered over her, clanging and muttering with the sound of an idling gasoline engine. She could not turn away. *It* lifted its arms toward her—a pair of long, jointed appendages wrapped in the sleeves of the ill-fitting overcoat, limbs that bent at inorganic angles.

Cold steel brushed her face as the arms embraced her; suddenly, her feet left the ground and she was whisked into the darkness of the alley, so quickly that she didn't realize what had happened until she saw cracked pavement moving far beneath her and her trench coat being trampled and kicked into a dark, unseen corner. The thing had slung her over its shoulder and was now carrying her into whatever lair it claimed, its footsteps clattering and ringing in a syncopated, staccato rhythm. Her lips parted, trying to form the word "Stop," or perhaps, "Help," but only the softest hiss escaped, and she feared that even that might cause her captor to silence her—for the arm around her waist pressed hard into her, threatening to crush her effortlessly. Vaguely, she wondered how something so huge and lumbering could camouflage itself so perfectly on the city streets.

The thing veered into a pitch-black opening in the alley wall, and its eyebeam flared to life, but Francesca could see only the dark path behind, the dim opening to the alley shrinking steadily until it vanished altogether. Ahead, the bass throbbing of heavy machinery, pounding insistently, still distant but immensely powerful, growing louder with every clanging step. Shuddering into her eardrums, her skull, into her bones...a deepening rhythm...like a giant heartbeat.

Light gradually filled her vision, pale electric blue,

intensifying to violet, revealing purple brick walls to either side. Ringing tones rose around her, joining in wistful harmony, mimicking human voices, but in doing so, emphasizing their alien origin. As they wove into a chorus backed by the machine beat, the rhythm became erotic, filling her with an inexplicable heat— and an almost-narcotized complacency, as if her will was being drained by either the thing carrying her or the sound itself.

Suddenly she felt herself being lifted and dropped unceremoniously; she fell for a shocking distance before landing face first on a spongy surface, bouncing up and down several times before settling into a soft, warm, fleshy material. In the darkness, her eyes could not yet discern any details.

Gradually, she perceived herself to be within a broad, cylindrical chamber that rose to dark, unseen heights. In the distance above, frequent violet flashes and occasional golden sparks revealed that the shaft was not empty; *something* occupied the space up there: the source, whatever it might be, of the deep, intense machine music.

Overcoat stood before her, studying her with its eyebeam, grumbling and muttering, adding its own low voice to the metal symphony. She pressed herself into the yielding material, which felt warm and alive, oddly comforting in the frigid darkness. Her blood raced hot through her body, strangely exhilarated by the cold scent of danger pouring from the figure looming over her. She saw its arms rise, tug at the buttons of its coat, and for a moment she felt a ridiculous twinge of embarrassment that, like a robotic flasher, this beast was going to reveal itself to her.

The coat fell away. She gasped. Gold, violet and crimson flashes reflected on crazy, skeletal arrays of tubing and wire that wound in and among themselves, coming together in *something* resembling a human form, however superficially. Beneath the barbed wire mane, the eyebeam peered from a cyclopean socket within a wedge-shaped metal plate; the head, such as it was, rested atop a cluster of twisted metal pipes. As Francesca watched, one of the arms rose again, now holding the piece of pipe she had earlier seen it pluck from the street. Grasping it in triple-pronged pincers, the thing placed the tip of the pipe at the base of its neck, driving it downward and in, then tugging it back far enough to lock the upper end into whatever served as its skull.

Great God, the thing is building itself!

"What are you?" she whispered. "What do you want with me?"

The eye flared, its hot beam falling upon her cheek just below her right eye. A grinding sound rose from the thing's torso.

"Where do you come from?"

The eye gazed impassively for several moments. Then one of the arms lifted and pointed skyward. With a heavy clang, the shape took one step toward her. And above, a deep groaning that slowly grew louder indicated that whatever hid in the upper reaches of the cylinder was descending.

In the flashing light, Francesca now saw several flexible silvery tubes wriggling down toward her captor. As they drew near, they began belching powerful jets of white steam, bathing the naked metal beast in thick, roiling clouds. The mechanized chorus rose loud and long, and the thing's two arms extended to their full span—at least ten feet, she realized with alarm. An almost-soothing violet glow appeared overhead, brightening as the music intensified and, as the steam cleared, finally revealed the glittering metal being in all its naked splendor. Its every limb and organ was fashioned intricately from dissimilar metal scrap, from copper tubing to lead pipes to twisted plates of aluminum. Like thorn-skinned serpents, long strands of barbed wire wound angrily around the torso and limbs, sprouted Medusa-like from the crown of the silvery skull.

Something brushed her ankle. Looking down, she saw one of the snaking tubes from above encircling her lower leg, followed by another, then another, each caressing her body with sentient deliberation. The steel tendrils tightened around her, binding her arms at her sides, holding her helpless before the gleaming eye of her abductor. Now one of its long arms reached for her, the triple pincers grasping the fabric of her blouse and shredding it, tearing away the remains to expose her naked breasts. She gasped, not in horror, but in strange fascination—and desire. The heavy rhythm, the warm flesh in which she nestled, the cold steel restraining her limbs, the almost-elegant form of the artificial but *living* construct looming over her...these had fired her blood into a raging boil, and even knowing that her last moments of life might be fast approaching, she felt a thrill of anticipation unlike any she had ever known with a mere man.

The claw-tipped arm reached for the button fastening her pants, snipped it away deftly, then closed on the zipper...tugged it open slowly, then pulling her pants down to her knees. The pincers returned to clutch her panties, slicing quickly through one side and tearing them completely from her body. She felt her lower regions heating up, moistening, though somewhere in the far corners of her consciousness, alarms blared, warning her of the horror now surely impending.

No! she cried back. She could not resist; compliance was surely the only possible path to self-preservation.

The monster's other arm now came into view. Unlike the pincer-tips of the first, this one ended in a long blue steel barrel, like the muzzle of a shotgun, which now waved slowly and tantalizingly before her widening eyes. Lust and terror mingled in a super-heated brew, and as the gunhand lowered to brush her thighs, she released a long, plaintive moan that blended in low harmony with the chiming tones echoing from the upper reaches of the chamber.

The cold steel pincers touched one breast tentatively; she flinched as the sharp metal slid across her tender flesh, seemingly capable of tactile sensation, exerting pressure without slicing her skin. The muzzle of the long arm pressed into the flesh of her inner thigh, and her back arched involuntarily at its frigid touch. The single, radiant eye peered into hers, and Francesca could sense both satisfaction and curiosity in its cognizant gaze.

"You're not going to hurt me, are you?" she whispered.

Of course it spoke no word, but the thing began making a purring noise deep within its twisted torso. The gunhand pressed forward gently, touching her clitoris, sending an electric thrill through her entire body; the barrel worked tight little circles around the lips of her vagina, and she felt herself moistening, preparing to receive him.

No, not him. *It.*

The muzzle hesitated only a moment, then pushed itself into her. She gasped in horrified ecstasy, wishing to both block out and fixate upon the incredible thing entering her body. The barrel twisted, then plunged deeper, causing her to cry out, not in pain or shock, but in disbelief—and unthinkable pleasure. Such an abomination taking her this way should send her over the sanity's brink, warned a fading voice somewhere inside; but she could only allow the colossus's scheme to play out, for anything else would certainly mean her death. Something she had seen in that brilliant eyebeam—something resembling humanity, she told herself—

seemed to assure her that the end of her life was not its ultimate aim.

The metal coils binding her alternately constricted and relaxed in rhythm with the gunhand's movements. Steam swirled around her, warm and wet, and beneath her, the unknown cushion of flesh seemed to knead and stroke her back, soothingly, adding its flavor to the mélange of sensation.

The metal tendrils suddenly applied pressure— twisted—and rolled her onto her stomach, all while the gun muzzle continued pumping inside her. She heard a hissing sound above and, daring to crane her neck and look up, she saw a plethora of writhing tubes lowering themselves toward her, filling her with the sudden dread that she had only imagined the reassuring warmth the machine man had conveyed to her. But then, like gentle snakes, or a lover's fingers, these narrow, rubbery tendrils fell upon her back and brushed back and forth softly, caressing her, running from her neck to her buttocks. She felt a blunt tip slide into her crack, probing, sliding toward her anus—finally insert- ing itself, slipping in and out ever so gently, increasing its force gradually. Another slid in along with the first, and she moaned in unadulterated pleasure as together, the ravishing metal barrel and the flexible fingers touched the vital spot inside her, sending her into a hot, convulsing orgasm that went on and on, finally culminating in a long, animal scream as, for a moment, her rational mind departed altogether, broken by this perfect assault of demoniac hideousness and divine delight.

The flesh beneath her quivered, and the obscene gunbarrel withdrew from her cunt, admitting a swirl of cooling air that refreshed her like the juice of a cactus to a thirsty soul in the desert. The rubber tendrils continued to play over her body, but the steel coils relaxed enough so that she could again turn onto her back to face the metal giant still standing over her.

The gunhand extended toward her, its muzzle touching her lower lip, offering her the scent of her own musk. Something above drew her gaze upward, and now, within a pulsating violet wreath, she saw, high in the cylindrical chamber, the source of the multiple appendages that bound and stroked her body.

"Oh, my God…oh, my God."

Like a great metallic mandala, easily a hundred yards across and at least that far above her, a wheel within a wheel spun slowly and hypnotically, its axis connected with its rims by dozens of crisscrossing spokes. From the central hub, multiple clusters of steel arms dangled and waved like silvery tentacles questing for prey. She realized then that *up there* lay the true source of her violation, if such it could be termed; the metal man was merely some pawn, something formed and directed by whatever intelligence resided in the slowly spinning wheels.

"What are you?" she whispered. "What is this place?"

Inside her body, something stirred, and the sudden

realization that the gunhand had deposited something within her nearly caused her to retch.

"What have you done to me?"

Do not fear.

No voice had spoken, yet she knew that there had been a response to her question. Indeed, the machine—if that's what it was—possessed awareness...the ability to touch her mind as well as her body.

"Where am I?"

At the heart.

"What are you? Where are you from?"

Far.

She swallowed hard. "Do you mean to kill me?"

No death.

The metal man's eyebeam blazed, touched her cheek. Hot. Inside her womb, pressure. Francesca raised an arm toward the beast; to her shock, she saw that her skin appeared discolored, the veins pronounced and dark. Her long fingernails gleamed with purple light.

"What is happening to me?"

You into me...me into you.

More pressure. Pressure, but no pain. Looking down, she saw her rib cage disturbingly pronounced, the skin stretched taut over her bones. She tried to pull herself from the soft warmth around her, but she seemed weighted down, lethargic. Had she been poisoned?

She now saw that the spongy material around her was veined—alive!—pulsating and writhing around her, seeming to pull at her flesh. The skin of her fingers seemed to soften and melt, to flow into an organic mass in which she nestled. Still, there was no pain, no sensation that her body was coming apart; changing.

As her flesh slid away to join its host, her muscles hardened, took on the sheen of the metal man's skin. She lifted her right hand, marveling at the fully exposed, sparkling steel bone structure, the jointed appendages that had replaced her soft fingers. Her breasts became sleek, flattened cones of metal welded to an ornately curved steel rib cage that encircled bronze-tinted muscles and organs. Finally, the coils around her began to fall away, allowing her to move on her own. Heat surged through her veins; not just heat, but *power*, and she realized that, all along, she'd had nothing to fear.

From above, the piping sounds rose in exultation, for something new was being born. Gunhand had been an earlier step in the evolution of the machine from beyond; she would be its next logical phase, the next link in the chain of its unknown destiny.

She stood, her body a gleaming, elegant construct of metal, casting away the remaining shroud of skin that had once enveloped everything she had been. Her human remains blended into those that had come before, partners of the whirling twin wheels overhead. Looking up, she saw the shape of her progenitor ascending into the highest reaches of the cylinder, which she now knew to be the subterranean lair of something wonderfully extraterrestrial; a chamber that must have existed here beneath the labyrinth for countless years as the machine being experimented and evolved, built itself into something new, casting parts of its being from the refuse of the human world and from humanity itself.

Gunhand knelt before her, recognizing her as both its offspring and its successor. For a brief moment, her past life attempted to reassert itself within her soul, to drag her back to mere humanity; but the new power within her refused to yield. She dismissed all that she had been with a wave of her exquisite metal arm, and reaching for Gunhand, she bid him rise. The shape stood, extended a long, jointed arm and with triple pincers stroked the regal mane of steel fibers that cascaded over her shoulders from her chrome skull.

She felt its touch with nerves charged by electricity, a wonderful, warm sensation that ran more deeply than any she had known as a creature of flesh and blood. She was truly beautiful now, the perfect hybrid of mortal and machine, yet more than either. She could feel perfect satisfaction in the transmitted consciousness of the being above her, and she knew its mission and accepted her new purpose without reservation.

Leaving Gunhand and her grandsire in the chamber behind, she stepped into the tunnel through which she had been brought those eons before, her twin eye-beams cutting through the darkness as she made her way back to the surface—to begin her quest for the next link in the chain of destiny, over which *she* now held dominion.

Parts of Heaven
Thomas S. Roche

She's got curves that stretch from Heaven to Hell by
way of Purgatory. You can lose yourself in those curves,
slide your body against them and feel it giving way. Her
whispers of invitation draw you in and twist your mind
until there's nothing left but devotion. That's why I love
her so. She's got shiny chrome running from front to
back, a tight little rear end that holds its own even
when you're riding it hotter and harder and faster than
seems possible. She's got a bright little tailpipe that
gives off a low rumble and buffed-leather kisses against
your ass.

She talks to me as I ride her. She whispers rosaries
of devotion under her breath. She burns somewhere,

deep under those seductive curves. I can disappear inside her, vanish into her fine softness like I never existed in the first place. I love to run my hands over her surfaces, feeling how she responds to my touch. I love to explore her like a patient on my table, I love to race her uphill, downhill, hearing her moan low in her throat, pushing her harder, harder, until she can't take any more and then pushing her just a little farther.

She moves like a phantom, a goddess—an angel.

In my professional life, I am a priest, the high priest of surgical transfiguration. It's not a job, or at least I don't think of it that way, any more than I think of Angel as a mode of transportation. More appropriately, it's a calling, perhaps even a religion. I sometimes think I was given the opportunity to become something not quite human, something so much more—to aspire to godhood, or perhaps merely to be a priest at the temple of modern medicine. I work the miracles of the gods; I take people apart and put them back together again in accordance with their wishes. Day by day by day people come to me broken, twisted, destroyed. I create them anew.

My skills at the surgeon's table have increased since I fell for Angel. She has much to teach me about the structure of the body. Often as my fingers work deftly inside the body of a patient, as I intently restructure the patient to better fit her or his needs, I meditate on the beauty of Angel and all she has to offer me. Surgery has treated me well, given me the money to indulge in such lovers as Angel. But Angel has made me a better surgeon than I could ever have been without her.

I take her apart on the weekends, reverently placing her insides on silken white cloths arranged as on an altar across the driveway of my four-bedroom house on the hill as the fog mists its way through the sky scattering half-shadows across Angel and me. I reach inside her and touch all the surfaces of her engine, experience her perfectness. I run my hands along her driveshaft, I stroke her pistons, caress her block. I explore the intricacies of her fuel assembly, massage her oil filter delicately. My neighbors sometimes wonder why I take her apart every weekend; the CPA across the street asked me, one Saturday, if Angel was British or something. British. What a quaint thought. "She is Italian," I told him with a sneer.

As the breeze cuts across the driveway, I explore each piece I have laid reverently on the cloths upon concrete. My fascination gives way to bewilderment, that machinery should be so superior to cruel, sad flesh—flesh, that is the eyes and the ears of the soul and the conscience of the universe; flesh, that is the knowledge and the love and the understanding of the cosmos; flesh, that withers and decays and becomes nothing; flesh, that vanishes not unlike the timing on an Alfa-Romeo—but the Alfa is superior in the cult of modern love, for machinery has interchangeable parts.

# # #

My article in the *Journal of Surgery* brings a torrent of international scorn and international praise. I am invited to give the keynote address at a small but prestigious surgery conference this spring, in a city just a short flight away. In my acceptance letter, I ask them to add the cost of the ticket to my honorarium.

Some weekends, after I've explored Angel's delights, exposed her delicious insides, socketed her parts together, tightened her screws, polished her chrome, I need to bring her inside the three-car garage for a little while. There I touch her again, with love and tenderness and more than a little ardor, and behind the garage doors our transgressions meet each other in the caress of petrochemical fantasies. If I could bring her to the bedroom with me, I would tangle her up in my satin sheets, would spread her out across the expanse of the king-sized water bed and penetrate her, hearing her moan and rumble and squeal as I ride her. But I must content myself with touching her in the garage, for not even Sharper Image makes a bed big enough for my lover. I remove my clothes and feel her smooth metal against me. I weep as she holds me and, for a time, our parts are interchangeable.

Nights like that, I take her through the city streets, through the lights and the drifting clouds of crack smoke, through the scattered bombed-out buildings, the crowds of derelicts and the haunted faces of the damned. There's a street I like where six theaters come together on a couple of corners, where you can take your pick of the lovely flesh plying its trade under the slanted light. I drive my white Angel into their midst, and sight of her with the top down draws them over to run their hands over her curves and coo about how beautiful she is and oh, is she Italian? Angel loves all this attention. The girls shake and jiggle and promise me all sorts of lovely things. I flash a few twenties, and their feeding frenzy turns the waters of the District to a red-light froth.

After I've chosen one, I usually take the streetwalker up into the hills, where I can park on a secluded ridge, leaving the top down. There I can look out over the city and the bay and feel the breeze cutting across my body while the guest leans down in the car and does her work. I like to think of these as threesomes; Angel, in her infinite understanding, holds me so dear that she will share me with other lovers. So that when I come, she is happy.

Some nights, I take two streetwalkers up there. They think it's a little strange, maybe, but cash is cash and I'm always careful not to troll in the rich neighborhoods, where the girls will be less impressed with Angel. I ask one girl to undress and stretch out on Angel's hood while the second ministers to me. There's something deliciously intimate for Angel about the beauty of a half-naked young prostitute writhing and moaning, stretched out on her hood while I ejaculate copiously into the mouth of another.

# # #

Other days I take her for long drives over the hills; I know places over the hill where she can show me her stuff for hours. I know she wants to come, wants to hit 100, 120, 130 on the open road, her supposedly street-legal engine roaring with a terrible authority. At that speed, the ride is still smooth, but every tiny bump in the road is like a spasmodic jerk of her pleasure. I rock up and down, feeling the rumble of her engine against my ass. My cock is hard in my pants, and as my body bounces up and down in her soft seats, Angel reaches her second wind, picking up speed and screaming faster and faster. Then I let myself go, filling my pants with a seed that, if there were any justice in this universe, could mix with Angel's transmission fluid and produce a child half of skin, half of machinery, all of beauty; a child of steel and/or flesh, and more than a little love.

Sometimes I end up in Barstow or Santa Barbara and have to get a hotel. I'm not as young as I used to be.

Kate left me not so long ago—a year, two years; I forget. It was lonely until I found Angel. Kate still calls sometimes, leaves friendly little messages about mutual acquaintances on my voice mail at work. I rarely return them.

I cruise the streets, hungry for flesh. I want three tonight, three girls who will make love to Angel and me with a fervor unmatched. But I want something new, something different; I take a left and head down to a slightly different section of the red-light district. Here the flesh is further decayed: sorrier, more rotten—or cheaper, more vulnerable. This excites me somehow. I pull up alongside a trio of hookers.

"Ooooooooh, look at Dr. Love," says one, leaning down and showing me her breasts. "Take me for a ride, sugar, I *love* independent suspension!"

"A car like this makes my pussy wet," says the second in a lustful growl, climbing onto Angel's hood and making eyes at me through the windshield. "I'm dripping on your Armor All."

"You like Alfa-Romeo?" whispers the third, a blonde, bending low and whispering hot breath into my ear, her tongue drawing inviting circles as she takes my hand and put it down her shirt to feel the hard swell of her breast. "How about Hoover?"

I pause for a moment. How did the first one know I'm a doctor? Ah, of course. The cover story of the *Medical News and Review.* She recognized me from my picture. It's satisfying to know that Angel and I will be with a prostitute who keeps up on the medical literature.

I cram all three of the hookers into Angel's single passenger's seat and we head into the hills as they tell me all the things they're going to do to me. The conversation degenerates as I bring Angel up the hill, and by the time we park they're trading makeup tips with occasional muttered promises of "We'll do you right" and "Gonna give you some lovin'." Leticia is the name of the talkative one. "Nurse Leticia, Angel, and Sweet Simone got a new patient. Doc, he gonna get the best care around. Get that pad out, Doctor, write yourself a script for satis-FAC-shun!!!" She snaps her fingers and put her lips close to mine. "Three hefty doses!!"

It's a warm night. It takes some extra cash, but I get the two of them onto Angel's hood and tell them to caress her. Rub their hardened nipples against her smoothness. The third, the dark-haired girl, gets to do the work because her name is Angel. There's something achingly beautiful about that.

"Mmmmmm. So long and stiff," she says, rolling a rubber down my shaft, rubbing my cock over her face. "I've never seen one so large." I have to laugh at that one—I am well aware that my cock is relatively small. Tiny, in fact. But it ain't the meat—

Angel takes my cock into her mouth; she's a small girl, so she even takes a little into her throat.

While Angel sucks me, Leticia and Simone squirm on the hood of the car playing with each other's tits. I think they've misunderstood—they think I want to see a girl-girl show, like the kind I could see any night at the 6th Street Theater.

"The car," I rasp. "Touch the car!"

"What?" says Leticia, cocking her head.

"Touch the car!! Stroke it!"

The two of them stare at me for a minute, then look

down at Angel, then back at me, then at Angel. Uncomprehending.

"You're kinky," says Leticia. "I appreciate that in a medical professional."

Both she and Simone begin to touch Angel half-heartedly, but when they see my response, their enthusiasm increases. Soon they're humping violently against Angel, fucking her with their legs spread. Leticia yanks down her top and pulls up one of the windshield wipers, sliding it between her ample tits. She pushes them together and moans "Ooooooh, baby" as she slides the wiper in and out of the tight channel of flesh.

"Oh, God, yes!" I groan, reaching for the washer button.

I hit the button and washer fluid shoots all over Leticia's tits. Leticia goes along with it, lets out a little moan, rubs the fluid all over her tits until it soaks her shirt; she holds onto the wiper as it flops back and forth, in and out between her tits. I hear a sharp crack, and Leticia gets this look over her face like she's really fucked up. I almost come right then, seeing the limp windshield wiper flapping around over and between her breasts. "Whoops—" Leticia starts to say.

But I shriek "Don't worry about it! Don't stop! Don't stop! Goddamn it, don't stop!"

And so she goes back to riding the broken wiper while I lean on the washer button and fluid sprays across her belly and breasts and face, making her makeup run. It's not easy, but I manage to hold back, letting out wild moans of pleasure and pistoning my hips. Simone has just been watching with this look of bewilderment on her face, but now she gets the idea. She sort of shrugs and then plants herself on the other washer, sliding her ass up to the front of Angel's hood and hiking her spandex skirt up as far as it will go. She spreads her legs around the wiper and rides it, moaning, rides it until it cracks, and the washer cables squirt all over her exposed crotch.

I catch a beautiful vision of black lace panties—and as the washer fluid soaks them, they become slightly transparent. My eyes widen. It seems like my brain was playing tricks on me there for a second.

Simone can't match Leticia's enthusiasm, though; Leticia has it down pat. She smears the washer fluid all over her body, whimpering things like "Oh, babycakes, *wash me*" and "Whoa, sugarplum, make it the *SPIN* cycle."

She runs out of things to say after a while, though, and just starts moaning, prompting Simone to let out a halfhearted "Wipe me down!"

But it's not the second-rate dialogue that's getting me off, it's the sight of Angel—my Angel—working the two whores, shooting warm fluid on them and flapping between their tits.

I'm groaning and rocking up and down, pumping my hips back and forth while Angel rides me like a vixen. I start to whimper. I throw my head back and almost scream, the hottest orgasm of my life exploding through my cock and in to Angel's mouth. I shudder and thrash back and forth, and Angel holds on for dear life, her lips clamped around the head of my cock as she milks me. Finally, my spasms subside; my head slumps forward.

I am greeted by the sight of Simone and Leticia, half-naked, covered in washer-fluid lather, their clothes and hair soaked, regarding me as if I were the most extreme kind of maniac.

The washers emit a rhythmic clicking sound, spent.

Angel looks up at me from my lap with pretty much the same expression on her face.

"You get the prize, Doc. Weirdest trick I ever turned."

"Me, too," says Angel, wiping her mouth as she slips the condom off and tosses it away. "You don't even have any competition."

"Yeah, same here," says Simone, nodding her head vigorously as she tucks her tits back into her soaked lace top. "I think there ought to be some sort of award for this kind of stuff."

"Congratulations!" Leticia says matter-of-factly. "You got first fucking place. I hope you got cash to pay for these fuckin' clothes you ruined."

After a long session of cleanup with chamois cloths from the trunk, I drive the girls back to the District slowly, savoring the sharp, soapy smell of washer fluid, tasting the ripeness of my union with Angel. I drop them off where I got them, and they shuffle away, my cash tucked into their boots.

Except Leticia. I put my hand out and stop her.

"What is it, sugar? You want my phone number? Hey, you *know* where to find Lady Leticia." She indicates the streets with a wave of her hand.

"No," I say. "It's not that. I just wondered—"

She leans forward. "How I keep my girlish figure? Where I get my creamy skin? How an old broad like me can exude such a raw, primal sensuality?"

"No, it's not that," I say. "I just wondered…"

"Spit it out, Doc. Time costs money."

"How did you knew I was a doctor?

She smiles. "See you in the clinic on Tuesday morning, Doc. Maybe you could tell your nurse to sport me a free shot this time? Make another trip out here Tuesday night; see if it makes a difference." She winks at me.

I put Angel in gear. Leticia shrugs, tugs at her bra straps, and vanishes into the dark and the drifts of smoke, calling "Love for sale, oh, baby, love for sale— ooooh, a Caddy, I *love* Caddies.…"

I hit the gas and everything goes away.

I have surgery to perform the next morning. I lie awake tangled in the satin sheets, the waterbed rocking me to sleep. I distract myself by dreaming of the new windshield wipers I'll get for Angel—the best money can buy. Gold-plated, perhaps??

The distractions subside and I look up at the

mirrored ceiling, eyes wide, rocking gently on the warm plastic waves.

Of course, Angel was the only one who actually touched me. Maybe she was different. Maybe she was just along for the ride.

It seems impossible. I've been in the field for long enough...I should have recognized the signs.

After years of holy service as the high priest of gender reassignment, taking people apart and putting them together again...I should have understood. Why didn't I? After years of my work, learning the lessons of Angel and of my patients—I should already know the answer to any questions posed in prayer. But things are not like I thought they were. Machine and mind, steel and/or flesh, an Alfa Romeo and a third-rate street-walker...they're not as different as I thought they were. In the scattered wreckage of the millennium, we find gods and goddesses among whatever is left. We all inhabit different parts of heaven. We fit pieces of our lives, sometimes broken pieces, together to form what passes as a whole—and it is *only* through change, through assemblage, that a functioning whole can be created.

The holy belief that flesh and therefore life is mutable is whispered like a prayer or a mantra on the stainless-steel and starched white altar, the white linoleum prayer mat, with me as the priest, reciting the liturgy with my scalpel and my hands. So as the unwilling holy man of such a movement, it only makes sense that I should sample its communion wine. Offering my devotion unto the god of medical transfiguration. And all God's children have interchangeable parts.

The Poor Girl, the Rich Girl, and Dreams of Eels

Shar Rednour

Dedicated to Aretha

This girl was rich. Rich. How rich? So rich that if she wanted she could bathe in a pool of diamonds or make her bedroom walls from bars of gold. So rich that she had no idea what money even means. And her parents, who had gotten the money from somewhere, and maybe just maybe weren't even from Earth, her parents did not spend the money in ways that mimicked the lower classes trying to be *just like you,* whoever *you* is. No, they all three spent their resources however they wanted, however eccentric or strange it tagged them. And that is what made The Rich Family like a dream.

Theastelle, the rich girl, had a friend who was poor.

So poor that she had never even seen a coin made of copper. Sophrania had so little money that she didn't try to be like anyone else. She couldn't have if she'd so desired, but the fact was that she didn't desire to be like other people. In any case, folks would whisper about Sophrania, "Is that girl from Mars?" And Sophrania would just smile knowing that Mars was *so* five-millennia-ago.

So, where Theastelle was never seen, Sophrania had been a frame bordering the seen. Both invisible.

Theastelle played with the poor girl because Sophrania had a brilliant imagination and she was bossy. Sophrania "insisted" on things, situations. She insisted on tying up Theastelle and playing crones. She insisted Theastelle, while still nude from the pool, lie perfectly still. Then Sophrania would lightly tickle her feet until Theastelle would scream and jerk her feet away. And if she wasn't "insisting," she was just fun and easy.

Why did Sophrania play with the rich girl? Not because of her money, but because Theastelle would not only play Sophrania's games, but she absolutely delighted in them. Whatever Sophrania could think up, they would do. Pure indulgence. And so they went on like this for years.

Because they were obsessed with each other and their strange doings they never thought of going to Bali or racing cars or sailing on yachts. They never even left the dwelling or grounds as they grew. One day they actually became bored. Then Sophrania pulled them back even farther into her imagination, from before she'd known Theastelle.

On this night they lay floating on their backs in the pool, head to head on a raft, under a blue violet sky filled mostly by the moon.

"I always wanted to have immediate and strong magic. To be able to make things happen," Sophrania said. "I wanted to be able to wiggle my pinkie and make my bathtub open up into the whole ocean. So while my parents thought I was bathing, I would be swimming and swimming."

Theastelle swam under her and sucked her toes underwater while keeping her eyes fixed on Sophrania. She then clawed her without warning and burst through the water's surface. "Then what would you do? In your ocean?" she asked.

"I would swim with all the animals. My breasts swaying light in the water, my hair trailing behind me tickling my back. Then, as I got hornier and hornier I would find the eels. I would jack off. Then an eel would bite my pussy right as I came." Theastelle went under the water again, her own hair making her look like Medusa and she bit Sophrania's pussy.

So Theastelle built this world. She turned a pool into a fake ocean with plants, fish and shells. She installed a pool bathroom nearby with a floor that dropped out of the awful yellow bathtub into this created ocean. They now played Mermaid Queen. Sophrania made the transition from poor girl in bathtub to rich ocean queen easily. She pulled herself up onto the edge of the ocean. "Listen, little fishy. Fetch the electric razor, some duct tape, a pair of our spiked high heels, and red, red lipstick."

Theastelle returned with these items. "What do you wish, my Queen?" She smiled.

Sophrania replied, "You are going to be my shaver-fish. My electric fish." She held Theastelle's chin in her hand and put the red, red lipstick onto her full lips. Sophrania stuck the rounded end of the battery-operated Lady Flick into Theastelle's mouth. "Close those red lips around it so it's secure. Now, really pout your lips around it so that I can see them—oh that's a good fishy!" Sophrania then wrapped a piece of tape around Theastelle's lips so that she couldn't remove the razor.

"Fishy! Where are your sharp points that protect you in the wild? Here." And Sophrania wrapped tape around her fishy's tits and taped spikes torn from the pair of shoes to Theastelle's nipples, pointing outward. "Now, we need to swim." Theastelle's eyes widened. She had never played this game, and her pussy-fish was already starting to swell!

She eased herself into the water, being sure to stretch her neck up so that her mouth and razor-snout wouldn't get wet; then she paddled around slowly. Sophrania, being Mermaid Queen, dove in and around her, and sometimes ignored her altogether and swam into the depths of the ocean. She held onto ocean things on the bottom of the pool so that she could stay under a long time and stare at her fishy's pussy and soft body.

Theastelle's titties bobbed as her paddling hands waved around in the water. Her pretty toes and jiggling ass drove Sophrania crazy. Sophrania burst through the water. "Here fishy, here fishy, come to your queen," she sang because, after all, don't mermaids sing? "You can hold onto the edge now.

"I am a mermaid, yet something awful has happened. I breathed too much air and now I am growing hair on my fins. You have to shave me with your snout, little razor-fish." And she flicked on the electric razor. Theastelle's eyes widened and her full lips fishy-flexed around the machine. Sophrania said, "Take a breath," put her hand on top of Theastelle's head, and pushed her under the water.

Sophrania pulled her herself down by holding onto the Queen's body and hooked her shoulders under the Queen's spread thighs. The razor was buzzing in her mouth, rattling against her teeth and she aimed it carefully against the Mermaid's mound (which actually barely had any hair at all) and stroked down. Sophrania's body shuddered instantly.

Theastelle released her shoulders and burst through the water.

"Oh, good fishy, do it again!" Sophrania moaned.

Theastelle's nostrils flared as she inhaled deeply and plunged back under the water's surface. She stroked the vibrating machine against her Mermaid Queen over and over again, stopping to take breaths only when necessary. Sophrania writhed and bucked underwater, making waves in their ocean.

"You have to stay under this time until I come against your teeth, little fishy." And this time, when Theastelle was in position Sophrania entwined her fingers through Theastelle's snaking hair and guided her vibrating, shaving snout to just the right spot. She wrapped her legs around Theastelle's back so that they were one. Sophrania let her orgasms pull to the top of her. Theastelle was now the one bucking under the water, surely short of air. Sophrania held Theastelle down with her legs and gripped her hair fiercely so that the little fishy's vibrating snout stayed put. She must come—and to come, the vibrating sharpness must be against the base of her clit. If the main vibration were lower, she could come faster, but this is the sweet way. This is like her dreams of the eels. From the base, the tip begging, aching, sweetness coming, soon, soon, her body waved, and her nails dug into Theastelle's scalp and it was by her own hand that the sharpness of the razor dug too deep that the guard mattered no more. Red, red blood spurted from the base of her clitoris, and it was the sharpness of the eel that brought her over the sweet itching edge.

The Mermaid Queen screamed and she released herself to the orgasm, to the dream, to the fishes, and she lost her hold on the edge of the ocean. Entwined with an unconscious electric sea creature, she sank into waving throngs of sea greens with new snaking red trails. Without air, they floated down, floating, floating how women always float in bliss, this time cradled by the water as if it were lover's arms and they two were one lover in those arms.

The insistent buzzing of Theastelle's snout brought Sophrania back. She couldn't float in peace. Adrenaline hit her. She clawed to the surface of the water, jerking Theastelle with her weakened legs. Blood ran down her thighs as she pulled her sea-girl out of the water. Sophrania yanked out the razor, put her lips against Theastelle's taped mouth, and breathed. Theastelle coughed, sputtered, and spit water then brought her bound lips to Sophrania's and put her hand over Sophrania's clit to stop the bleeding.

One day they discovered race cars and spaceships, but that's a different story. You see, come do dreams true.

Ricky's Romance
Kevin Killian

It all began when Ricky
It all began when Ricky
It all began when
—he stepped into the deserted copy room and closed the door behind him, with the furtive look of the temp office worker with something to Xerox held close to his chest. The copy room was nondescript: a box of close air, a gray carpet littered with bright white scales and dots and slivers of paper. Stale recycled oxygen, and the whirring sound, like white noise, of the mighty copy machine in the corner, surrounded by cases of paper, some half-opened, surrounded like a fortress by battlements.

There was a picture hung on one wall of the copy

room, in a modern frame, an old-fashioned architect's drawing of the office building way back when. "History," Ricky thought, with the part of his mind that wasn't entirely preoccupied with getting in and getting out unseen. But he liked the picture where it was because in the glass that covered it, anyone standing in front of the Xerox machine copying something illegal could use the glass as a sketchy mirror and instantly know if someone else entered the room by the door behind, which otherwise moved silently on its hinges.

Clever boy had concealed his contraband within a file folder stuffed with ordinary and authorized office mail

orized office mail

orized office mail, and he saw himself in the glass of the frame, a furtive hunted outcast from society...a temp worker at 101 California Street in San Francisco, and the editor and publisher of *Faye's Way*, possibly the best fanzine dedicated to the world's #1 actress, Faye Dunaway. Without further ado, he pushed the large square button on the Kona 10000 to restart the behemoth. Automatically the machine gave off a low groan that made Ricky start, trembling again. He turned back once more and cracked open the door to check if anyone was still in the halls of Ricocom International. "Though it's seven o'clock and the janitor doesn't start till eight-thirty," he thought. Still, some workaholics were known to come back after dinner and start working all over again on Ricocom business, whatever it was. Ricky had been working in filing for ten months and still didn't have much idea of what Ricocom did. "Why should I? I don't get benefits," he thought, closing the door behind him and returning to the now-humming Kona 10000. He opened his folder and

opened his

opened his folder and

and took out the twenty pages of Faye-related material that would make up *Faye's Way #23*. The Kona had a little bottleneck problem as Ricky knew from experience: it would take all twenty pages and reproduce them front to back, two-sided, or whatever he selected, but the first page or so sometimes shook uncontrollably in the auto feed holder before being yanked into the hidden rollers. Sometimes this resulted in a certain crease or wrinkle in the large glossy photos of Faye's newest face-lift...unfair to a great lady and a great star. Ricky wet his lips and touched his finger to his tongue. "Nice machine," he prayed.

As if in response the Kona's humming modulated into a gentle croon, as if to say, "Feed me," and Ricky felt a warm glow of affection. The twenty pages of Faye news, gossip, and commentary disappeared one by one into the lower depths of the 10000 with a bewildering ease. "Good boy," he said.

Mr. Tippett was gone, had left at four-thirty without saying, as he sometimes did, "I'll be back this evening." Thinking about Mr. Tippett, his cold Nazi-like sneer and pale face, made Ricky catch his breath a little, in fear.

For Hell would pay if Mr. Tippett caught him here by the Kona machine, this late at night, with Faye contraband.

Ricky had started publishing *Faye's Way* in 1990, when he saw how little serious work was really being done on Faye Dunaway—"except by her surgeons," he thought—she was in danger of becoming a joke and a has-been. In 1994 he had figured out HTML and ASCII and turned *Faye's Way* into a web E-zine, with spectacular results. He was now up to almost 110 hits a month, and had a paying subscriber base of 45. Better than most commercial sites! In certain circles he, Ricky Mullins, was almost famous himself; his status as a lowly temp worker almost erased. Recently he had been chosen to write a blurb for a forthcoming book on Faye Dunaway's greatest films! Faye mourns the death of Marcello Mastroianni

Marcello Mastroianni

Marcello Mastroianni. I look kind of like her myself, Ricky thought, tapping his fingers on Kona's cool polished gray plastic surface...watching his face...his wide forehead, his blond hair waxed carefully in front to produce a kind of kiss curl over his brow, his almond-shaped eyes, green, though in the shadowy glass he could see no green, only a really good-looking face, part man, part boy.... I could be her son if she had one...but all of Dunaway's mothering instincts had gone into her career and her incredible love life.... Ricky admired that, but where had it all gone wrong for

Faye? The catastrophe of *Mommie Dearest,* or the glacial Norma Shearerisms of *Voyage of the Damned?* Was that the defining moment in the before and after life of Oscar-winning Faye Dunaway?

Ricky's stomach growled, trying to tell him he had missed out on dinner with two chums. But his work came first and all over the United States, and in two cities in Europe, forty-five Dunaway devotees were checking their mailboxes daily…. Another page slid into the long, feral slit of the Kona. "Good boy," said Ricky, rubbing the cool face of the machine, down by his crotch, almost as if he were rubbing himself…and as if by magic—some really sick magic!—the machine groaned to a mumbling halt. "Oh, shit!" On the bank of illuminated panels, Ricky read a bewildering message: "Try Error 78-E." A skeletal neon map of Kona's innards lit up and showed him, what was all too plain, that one of the pages of *Faye's Way #23* had gotten stuck inside the machine.

Quickly, with sweat popping up uncontrollably under his arms and down the small of his back, Ricky ran again to the door, checked the halls, and then returned to the sullen copier and bent to his task. Two enormous plastic (or metal?) doors swung open at the press of his fingertips, and he crouched on his heels, trying to see the missing page, hoping it wasn't crumpled, or torn. Somewhere in his head he saw Mr. Tippett's acidulous face, his grinning sneer, heard him whisper. "So this is your idea of Ricocom business?"

Hesitantly he reached inside, into the maw of gaping gears and blackness. The light wasn't too good in here, its fluorescence a trace, shadows on his bare arms. "Shit, shit, shit!" he mumbled. "I don't see the fucking thing…" The indicator said that the obstruction was in area J, but area J was almost farther into the machine than his arm could reach. He stumbled onto his knees and thrust his arm into the cold, dark hollow. He was all too conscious of the incomplete, collated piles of *Faye's Way #23* he had left in the sorting bin.

What if Tippett came in right now? His pale eyes would dart to the unfinished heaps at once.

Ricky's fingertips grazed at something that might have been a piece of paper, but he needed more leverage. I'm not double-jointed, he thought grimly. But he slipped off one shoe and wedged his foot inside the lower-right-corner of the open metal (plastic?) door, and managed to insert most of his upper body into the mysterious blackness. He felt the heat of plastic roller plates press up against his chest, his belly: big round drums. Again the fingertips of his grasping left hand touched a smoother surface, what might be page 17…. "Why didn't you just stop at sixteen pages?" he asked himself, without mercy. But he knew the answer, for pages 17–20 contained the results of his worldwide poll on what film would have been most improved if Faye had starred in it, the winner by a hair *Gone with the Wind*

Gone with the Wind

Gone with the

Ricky's foot curled and pressed farther into the machine, trying to help his right leg bend with the intractable plates and drums. And then, with a little start of panic he (Runners-up: *Dr. Zhivago, Star Wars*—Faye as Princess Leia, more queenly, more elegant, than that tawdry Carrie Fisher—*Hello, Dolly, Taxi Driver*—which Faye almost had!) he realized his foot was stuck somehow—and that the machine had started up again, in some indefinable way, its dead silence no longer a silence but an almost inaudible murmur, the sound you hear when you raise a seashell to your ear—but how? "How, for Christ's sake, how?"

He tried to withdraw his left hand: couldn't. Slowly—were his eyes growing used to the pitch dark?—the darkness was lifting and a strange pale green glow began to emanate from the innards of the Kona 10000. His head, sideways between drawers and rollers, felt enormous, like the big head of Evelyn Mulwray's retard daughter in *Chinatown:* Is she your daughter? Is she your sister? Your daughter? Your sister? Slap, slap, slap, slap

"She's both!" And from behind, he could see the door of the copy room opening a crack—

And he heard a voice. Oh, shit, it's Tippett, Ricky thought, scrambling to come up with an explanation.

The door swung open and he heard a sigh. "Mr. Tippett," said the voice.

"No, it's Ricky," he started to say—then thought better of it.

"Hey, Mr. Tippett, you okay?"

Ricky hung there, in a humiliating posture, half-in, half-out, feeling a red flush beat through his body from his face down to his chest and legs. He couldn't speak, but he was able to move his left leg, flop it from side to side in a plea for help.

"It is me, Osbaldo, Mr. Tippett," said the concerned voice. "Osbaldo, the janitor."

The green glow intensified.

Cooler air followed Osbaldo closer into the copy room; he approached Ricky's lower half with deliberate slowness and care. "Who the fuck is Osbaldo?" he thought wildly. "Christ, if the janitor's here it must be fucking eight-thirty." Drops of silvery moisture, like mercury, appeared on the convex face of the drum an inch from his nose and mouth.

Then he felt Osbaldo's hand on his waist.

"I have waited so long for you, Mr. Tippett," said Osbaldo.

Clunk, clunk, the janitor's mop and bucket fell to the floor as Osbaldo crouched beneath Ricky and, with eager hands, felt up and along his rib cage, under the strained cotton of his Polo shirt, and Ricky almost cried out.

And he was thinking, my God, I had Tippett all wrong all this time!

Wondering how little he really know about people—

"For you have driven me half loco with my longing for you, and I, only a janitor for Ricocom, Mr. Tippett." The Kona 10000 began percolating, and squares of greenish light began to appear before Ricky's eyes, gathering density until they resembled some kind of holo-graphic —panes—of stained glass, or blotter acid…. "And you have walked in front of me numerous times showing me your proud walk and your tight Nordic buns of steel, Mr. Tippett, and now you offer me your buns of steel, you fucking *marichol*"

Hesitant no longer, Osbaldo yanked Ricky's thin belt out of the loops of his Dockers and then took down the pants, sliding them down to his thighs, where the unfortunate angle of his trapped leg gave the janitor pause. He swore in Spanish and, from the pocket of his uniform, withdrew a razor blade. "You like to get fucked, Tippett?" Osbaldo cried, as he tore the cardboard cover off the blade. "You and your stuck-up ass too good for the common man?"

Ricky felt the smooth imperceptible sound of his pants scissored deftly in two. Osbaldo's big calloused fingers grabbed the waistband of his Ron Chereskin boxers and, as quickly as you or I might open an egg, he had them sliced off; Ricky's ass was bare to the air. "I lick your ass as I do every day of your motherfucking life, Mr. Gary Tippett," moaned the janitor, applying his rough tongue to the distorted globes. Ricky felt himself grow hard as the janitor darted his tongue inside his exposed asshole; his erection poked uncomfortably along the gray plastic toner cartridge. The hairs on the backs of his legs rose and fell in response to Osbaldo's vigorous rim job. Between slurps, he emitted muttered

words of affection and class hatred, mingled with
renewed gobs of sticky saliva.

"You wiggle your white ass once too often at Osbaldo,
Mr. Tippett!" The hologram plates seemed to pass
through Ricky's face without hurting him. His irises were
huge in his head, swollen, like his vulnerable asshole.
The noise all around him increased in volume and in
vibration. "That's right, motherfucker, shake that booty,
you like my tongue up your butt don't you, *maricon?*"

With implacable knowledge, the great drum inched
forward, like a guillotine, and Ricky saw—or *felt!*—the
pages of *Faye's Way #23* begin to photograph *themselves*, a montage of Faye's face first tiny, the size of a
postage stamp, then larger and larger, billboard size,
only to disappear into darkness. Then, a moment later,
the face again, tiny, big, huge, black. In each interval,
the blessed instant of darkness; then the dawn of green,
as regular and monotonous as a heartbeat. Ricky
hardly registered the shock when Osbaldo thrust his
fingers into his gaping asshole, so intently was he
watching the miracle of reproduction. From the ceiling
of the machine, a light gray powder began to descend.
"I fuck you with my janitor hand," Osbaldo announced,
suiting the action to the word, and punctuating each
thrust with a slap to Ricky's naked butt. Ricky was
getting harder and harder, more excited, and his hard-
on strained against the slowly rolling canister of toner.
The slither of a zipper. The fingers disappeared and the
head of Osbaldo's huge dick touched the wet ring of

Ricky's anus. "I'm ready as a rooster, Mr. Tippett," sang the janitor. "You are gonna get the bonky-bonk of your motherfuckin' life, executive pig."

Osbaldo's legs and torso were stocky, heavily muscled, and rippled as he plowed Ricky Mullins from behind, his hands, reeking of man-ass, clutching the panel of the big Kona for support. His fingers pressed every button on the front panel as he felt his dick swell up inside the groaning asshole, for to fuck Mr. Tippett had been his dream ever since he came to this country and saw the haughty executive bent over a desk examining figures. "One fine day," he had thought to himself, "those buns of Anglo steel will be mine to manhandle." And now he was fucking the man himself. The Kona 10000 leaped to life, issuing page after page of Faye Dunaway's tormented face...and then Ricky saw—

his own face—

page after page—after countless page, spitting from the machine—his face in ecstasy, speckled with toner— "I fuck you with Latin beat, like Selena, turn the beat around, *corazaft*"—the huge dick filling his ass—his balls tight and swollen like green grapes—

everything green, then black, then the stark white of bond paper—

his balls banging his ass and Osbaldo's dick jumping in and out, the copier buttons like piano keys, like the piano keys David Helfgott plays in *Shine*—

Faye Dunaway, not Lynn Redgrave, as the woman he marries—

Rachmaninoff—

motherfucker—writhing and twitching—Completed copies of *Faye's Way #23*, stacking themselves neatly in the collator tray on the left; then the copies shoved, thump, thump to the floor, replaced by new uncalled-for copies... more paper outside than inside the machine—

"Fuck me even if I'm not the guy you think I am," Ricky thought, and he began to shoot all over the inside of the copy machine...great helpless spurts of seed cum like Wite-Out....

...while Osbaldo's face bore the ecstatic stigmata of the possessed, and his hands dropped to his sides.

"Even if I'm not Tippett," Ricky hollered, tho' neither of them could hear him speak and indeed, so great was the Kona's roar inside his ears, and so great his orgasm, that he was not sure he spoke aloud, or if the machine spoke for him.

When Ricky woke, next to the Kona machine, his body was glazed, just like an éclair or jelly doughnut. His razored boxers and slacks were folded neatly to one side, atop the 1,100 copies of *Faye's Way #23*.

All of them stapled neatly in the upper left-hand corner, gathered into cardboard boxes, ready for UPS, I guess.

All of them with his own picture on the cover, his tongue halfway out of his mouth, his eyes rolled back in his head like a corpse.

On top of his chest a Post-It note. "Sorry, *hermano*, wrong fuck," it read.

Nothing more.

Joy Ride
Lucy Taylor

Last ride, I promise myself.

Yeah, right.

This must be the tenth "last ride" I've taken tonight.

I'm exhausted and sweaty and my hands cramp from clutching the safety bar, but I can't go home yet, not when there's one more scream, one more orgasm to be wrung from me.

Not when the line of garishly lit coaster cars still roars through the night like a giant mechanical cock.

So I climb onto the platform again, K-2's blood-colored neon splashing over my skin. Throat dry and thighs damp. Nervous as a coaster virgin. The cars growl to a halt. Giggly and weak-kneed, the riders climb off. Finally—it's my turn. The moment my butt hits the cool plastic seat, there's a rush of release and excitement, a keen throbbing of anticipation and fear. The way it used to feel when Ben entered me.

No, I don't want to and *Yes, make it go on forever.*

Both at once.

Desire and danger.

But memories of Ben grow increasingly dim, all but erased.

And why not? He's just a man—like my father was—vulnerable flesh and crushable bone. A messy stew of emotions, of longing and tenderness, of lust and love/hate. He can hurt and be hurt. See and be seen. I don't want that. Not anymore.

This is my lover—this metal beast—all screams, speed, and steel.

When I was a kid, I always wondered about Superman's sex life. How could he fuck Lois Lane without his Supercock thrusting right through her insides, and if she tried to ride him, how did she avoid being launched into space? If there was a Superman, however, and if I could fuck him, I imagine the power, the force, would somehow approximate what I get from riding K-2: that my whole body would ache, that I'd hold on for dear life, and when the climax came, I couldn't stop screaming.

And no matter how much it hurt, no matter how badly rattled my bones or how tender my cuntlips, I'd always climb back on for more.

Another fuck. Another ride. Another megadose of pure, primal bodily sensation.

But not even a night with the Man of Steel could be any hotter than coaster sex.

When it comes to coasters, you understand, I'm not just your general public. I know about chainlifts and boosters and ratchets, about swoop turns and boomerangs, the way a call girl understands the male circuitry. I know that the highest coaster is the 261-foot Demon in Little Rock and that the fastest is the 90 mph Cobra in Seattle, and I lust after them the way some women pine for porno kings with ten inches of star power.

I know about fatalities, too. I know that, in the last seventeen years, five people worldwide have died of heart attacks while riding roller coasters. I know of two people who lost their heads when they stood up going under the aptly named *fine del capo*, a low beam designed to create the illusion of imminent decapitation.

I can't think of K-2 in terms of death, though. I can think of it only in terms of machine virility, impersonal force, and the inexorability of knowing that, once I've climbed on, there's no turning back. No change of heart or mind possible. For good or for bad, you are on the thing, you are *fucked*.

So go on, I think, *do your worst.*

As the coaster starts climbing, I hike up my skirt and insert three fingers into my pussy. My other hand slides under my sweater and teases my nipples. Electric excitement zings the sex circuit—clit to pussy to tits. Heart in adrenaline overdrive. Cool wind in my face and the clanking sound of the ratchets hauling us upward. I can't wait to fall.

When we take the first drop, it feels like a bungee jump minus the cord. We tear into a loop—world upended, blender-on-liquefy-speed—then sweep into the first hump of a camel train. The cars corkscrew into a curve where the track isn't banked. Lateral gravity exerts its full force. I've ridden K-2 a hundred times, but I still expect the cars to hurtle off the track and crash into the spinning arms of the Twister Ride down below. Like all the other times, this doesn't happen, but my body's a primitive thing, never fully convinced of the fundamental logic and safety of a coaster's design, willing to believe all the previous rides where I got off unscathed were just to put me off guard—that deep down in its steel-girdered soul, the machine harbors evil intent.

But once again, I survive the two rides—the brain-boggling drops of the coaster and the burning ascent to orgasm taking place between my legs.

When we pull into the loading platform, I can't quit yet. I stagger off the machine and descend the stairs to get back in line.

And stop dead at the sight of blond hair hanging over the glistening black leather of a motorcycle jacket. I would run, but Ben's already spotted me. He motions for me to join him in line.

He clutches my arm. "I figured I'd find you here. You're obsessed with this—this fucking *thing*."

"Leave me alone."

"I can't."

"I said let me go."

His fingers tremble. Tears glint in his hazel green eyes.

"No, stay," he says. "Please. I want us to talk. You loved me once. I know you still do."

Things change.

The first time I saw K-2, I had my hand down the front of Ben's jeans and I was stroking the head of his hard-on. It was late and we were groping each other in the thicket of shadows behind the stand selling gyro sandwiches and elephant ears. I heard the kind of high-pitched, collective screams usually reserved for soon-to-be-eviscerated teenagers in a B-grade horror film. Opening my eyes, I saw a sleek, crimson-drenched snake of cars crest a steel cliff, then twist upside down in a huge double-loop before plunging into a tunnel designed to look like K-2, the infamous climber-killing mountain in the Himalayas.

Ben felt me tense and heard my breathing quicken.

"Yeah, I want you, too, Annie."

But Ben wasn't what I wanted right then. At least, not Ben alone.

There wasn't a line for K-2 and only a few others on the ride when Ben and I climbed aboard the last car.

When the attendant lowered the safety bar, scrunching us in together, I realized for the first time how scared I was. And how turned on.

"I want you right now. Here," I said. Reaching over I unzipped Ben's fly and lifted his dick out.

He got shy all of a sudden, "What the hell are you doing?" But his cock wasn't shy, not at all. As the cars started forward. I swiveled around onto his lap, hiked up my denim skirt, and lowered myself onto his hard-on.

"Jesus, are you crazy?"

Maybe. But it was too late to turn back now. We were moving.

My back was braced against the padded bar, my arms wrapped around Ben's shoulders, as the coaster climbed slowly, steadily. Suddenly my pussy went dry. My nipples seemed to fill up with ice water. I wanted off, but it was too late for that now, the cars were in a 45-degree climb. I could see the lights on the roof of the Fresno Insurance Building all the way in North Houston.

Higher. My nails scraped Ben's shirt. Oh, God, what was I doing? The car paused at the fall point as if the coaster itself were holding its breath, tensing its muscles for what would come next.

"Ben, don't let me fa-a-a-a-a-a-allllll!"

We fell.

For what seemed like forever.

We dropped with a speed that seemed to compress bone and make hash of internal organs. Centrifugal force snapped my head back with uppercut force. My spine felt karate-chopped. My lungs went flat as Frisbees. I couldn't scream, couldn't breathe. My senses unraveled. I'd have sworn I felt my soul depart my body.

The coaster reached the bottom of the drop and tore into the loop. I knew I would fall, no way could Ben hold me, but, of course, I'd forgotten centrifugal force, which locked me into my seat as the cars came out of the loop and plunged into the tunnel. In the gleaming blackness, I saw pinwheels of stars. My pussy felt lit up with neon.

The fake stars winked out. We dropped into black. Ben grabbed me and yanked me down as we swooped through the low tunnel exit. A rush of cool, corndog-scented air hit my face. We were out of the mountain, gliding along a flat stretch of track.

Somehow I got myself back in my seat with my skirt pulled down by the time the ride stopped.

We got as far as the exit gate when Ben leaned over and threw up in the dirt.

"Are you okay, hon?"

He looked embarrassed. Big macho construction guys aren't supposed to puke after riding a roller coaster.

"That was some ride," he said gruffly.

"Yeah, let's do it again."

The line inches forward. Ben grips my hand.

"I don't want to do this."

"We have to talk."

"We *have* talked. It's over."

"Annie, I love you. And I know you want to come home."

"No, I don't."

Yes, I do. Oh, fuck, no, I don't.

"I don't believe you," he says.

We're six people away from the cars now.

"Believe what you choose. It's the truth."

Four people.

"I still don't understand why you left. What was it? What did I do?"

You were human, that's all. You were real.

But I can't say that.

Three people.

I look at his thick, sun-bleached hair, his ocean-deep eyes, the scar over one eyebrow where he once got hit with a beam on a construction site. Ben, the man I once loved. Now all I can see is the frailty of him, the softness of his skin despite his workingman's muscle, his oh-so-vulnerable human body ready to leak blood at the tiniest puncture. His fragility, his mortality appall and frighten me. He is here, he is real, he can *see* me, with all my failings and fears and imperfections. He can love me and that gives him power, because he can take his love back. He can *die*. I don't want to be seen. I don't want to be loved. It's too dangerous.

Two people away.

I don't want his love. What I want is...

Our turn now. We climb into a car.
What I want is…
…the coaster.

I remember when my fixation with coasters began. I was just a kid, and Dad was supposed to take me to the county fair that had opened a few blocks from our trailer park, but he and Mom were busy having one of their knock-down-drag-outs. When hurled objects began to replace flying words, Mom told me to get the hell out of the house. Then Daddy open a bottle of Jack and started cussing at Mom for throwing me out.

"We'll go to that damn fair tomorrow," he told me in that slurry voice I knew promised trouble big-time. "Your Mom's got me too pissed off to go now, but tomorrow I'll make it up to you. You'll see. Betcher life."

I thought about sneaking upstairs to hide Dad's revolver, which he kept in his underwear drawer and which he enjoyed waving around like a Mexican bandit in an old cowboy flick when he got drunk enough, but I was too angry and disappointed. I loved Dad, but his personality alternated between psycho and sweet, depending on how much he'd been drinking. He was always letting me down.

I knew he'd never keep his promise about the fair, so I decided to go by myself. I especially wanted to ride the Monster, one of those old wooden coasters that chugs up the grade like an asthmatic locomotive and makes your vertebrae chatter like loose dentures on the way down. I'd never ridden on a roller coaster before—I was always too scared—but today felt different. Today, because I was already scared of what Dad was going to do to Mom or Mom was going to do to Dad, I needed a different kind of fear—a good fear—to distract me from the sick dread in my stomach.

I'd just gotten into the coaster car when a short, skinny guy slid in beside me. He stank of sweat and candy apples and cigarettes. "Don't you know you're too young to ride this all by yourself?"

I wasn't dumb enough to believe him, but I was afraid he'd get mad if I told him to get out of the car, so I didn't say anything.

Then the ride started and the coaster began its torturous climb.

"Scared?" asked the nasty-smelling man.

Lying came as naturally as breathing. "No."

He acted like he hadn't heard me, and he put his hand on my leg, started rubbing it up and down like he was comforting me. This seemed normal, too—my parents never listened to me and I figured that he hadn't, either—when I said I wasn't afraid, he'd probably heard me say just the opposite.

The coaster took off. I shrieked and held onto the bar. The people in the car ahead had their arms up in the air, but the man in the car with me had his someplace else—he'd somehow gotten his hand down the front of my pants and he was tweaking and probing, fingers nibbling around in there like a mouse. I didn't like it, but there was so much else going on—the noise and the speed, the power of the mechanical thing underneath me—that I could pretend not to know what was happening.

The old wooden coaster screeched like a banshee. I screamed and the man with his hand down my pants yelled something, too. I looked down and saw something strange—a big wet stain was spreading all over the front of his crotch.

That's when, for the first time, true fear hit me—cold and awful and deep—but it was mated to all that other fear, too—the fear in my body that was making me feel alive and exhilarated, more keenly inside my own skin than I'd ever felt in my life.

"You're beautiful, you know that," the creepy guy said.

But I didn't feel beautiful. I felt ashamed and confused. Like something was wrong with me, and somehow *he knew*.

"You liked that, didn't you?" he asked. "How 'bout we do it again?"

Was he talking about the ride or about that other stuff? Was he right? And how did he know? I didn't answer. I just backed away and then ran like hell.

After that first time having sex on the coaster with Ben, I was hooked, fixated, obsessed with metal and miles of track. In bed, with Ben sleeping beside me, I fingered myself and imagined the drops and the loops and the helixes. When we made love, I shut my eyes, trying to conjure the heart-jolting plunge into the black of the tunnel.

I started skipping work, driving into Houston on weekends, going on K-2 alone. I tried different things, nipple clamps and *ben wa* balls and a big dildo with soft rubber spikes. When K-2 went into its insane twists and drops and convolutions, my pussy would clench and contract and I'd scream as loud as I could—who would know I was screaming not from fear, but the force of my climax?

After the orgasms I had on K-2, fucking Ben seemed subdued and monotonous, tainted with shame. When he told me he loved me, I mouthed the words back to him, but I no longer knew what they meant. His weight smothered me, his touch disgusted me—what would he think if he knew who I really was, if he knew I lusted for mindless steel and implacable speed more than his warm, human body?

I no longer knew why I'd ever desired him—or any man.

Even as I lay next to him, he must have sensed my absence.

"I want us to have a baby," he said.

A baby, I thought, with a shudder. A small bundle of flesh teeming with needs and desires. Something else that could hurt me or be hurt. Something else I could lose.

"I'm not ready," I said, turning away.

"What is it, Annie? What's wrong?"

But what could I say? That I was different now? That in his arms, I felt naked, skinned, exposed to his eyes and his judgments? On K-2, I wore skin of steel. On K-2, I couldn't hear myself think for the sound of my screams.

That night, I dreamed I flew through K-2's tunnel of gaudy, make-believe stars, twirling through electric constellations and neon-lit moons, and saw my life laid out below me like a soiled tablecloth that you'd gather up and throw out after using. I didn't need that life anymore. I felt free and, at the same time, terrified, because there was no safety bar and no centrifugal force locking me into my seat. In the dream, I was launched into nothingness, into that blackness that little kids fear, the blackness that lurks underneath beds, inside closets, at the foot of the stairs. That horrible monster-harboring blackness that all children know is where the real evil lies. It comes to life in the dark and sucks you inside, and you fall and you fall and you fall....

I moved my stuff out one day while Ben was at work. Found an efficiency apartment in south Houston less than a mile from the park. Got a divorce lawyer and an unlisted phone number and a season pass for the park. And rode the coaster. Rode myself right out of this world, right out of my mind. Rode myself sick, but I didn't care. Sometimes after a few dozen rides, my neck would be so sore I could barely turn it, my arms and back would ache like I'd boxed fifteen rounds, and, if I stood up too quickly, small black spiders would circle in back of my eyes, weaving weird red-tinged webs.

Ben got hold of my unlisted phone number and started to call, begging me to come back, but I hung up on him. What was there to say? I had a new lover—a lover who wouldn't see me or judge me or love me or not, the ultimate no-strings, all-thrills fuck.

"Tell me what I did wrong," he kept saying. "Make me understand."

But what could I say? That people leave. People lie. People do crazy things—even to the people that love them. Coasters don't fly off the tracks, people do. They crack up, they cave in, they go psycho on you when you least expect it, they forget that they love you five minutes after they've said it.

Coasters don't make love—they make goose bumps and screams and the rush of an adrenaline overdose. And if a coaster grows boring or gets torn down, you can always move on. There's always a bigger one, a higher-tech one being built, and you don't even have to feel guilty about lusting for a newer, more macho mechanical god.

That day, after the creep molested me on the ride, I ran straight home. I was going to tell Mom and Dad everything. I wanted comfort and safety, the knowledge that even though this thing had happened, my parents were there to protect me. That the next time my father would go with me, that nothing like that would ever happen again.

But I never told anyone.

When I got home, there was an ambulance and two police cars out in front of the trailer. My mother was sitting outside on the steps. Even though it was a hot day, a blanket was wrapped around her and she was shivering as a policewoman bent over her, taking notes on a pad. There was blood on her clothes. At first I thought it was hers. Then I saw a gurney being rolled out to the ambulance and feet sticking out, and I recognized my father's green socks with the holes in them.

"Lucky for the wife he didn't shoot her, too," I heard a cop say. "Lucky the kid wasn't home."

"You can't leave me," Ben's shouting as the cars start to move. "I won't let you go!"

I shut my eyes, so I can pretend I'm alone. The force of the first drop slams me into my seat and drives the three fingers I've inserted into myself that much deeper. My scream transitions into something between a death rattle and moan.

Ben is forgotten. I arch my back, spread my legs. Nothing matters now, but the orgasm as it spreads through my bloodstream like an injection of fire.

"Stop it, goddammit! Stop!" Ben yanks my hand out from under my skirt. A weird perfume—male rage and wet pussy—stabs my nostrils. I see Ben's hand go back, know I'm going to be hit—

—the machine plunges into the loop. We peak and roll backward the way that we've come, then plunge forward so fast that blood, air, and life force all surge to one side of my body.

Breathtaking airtime. I'm out of my seat and out of my mind.

I want to cheer the coaster on—*do it, do it, do it....*

We whip into the tunnel. Blackness, fury, and speed. Ben tries to grab me, but I shove him away, unwilling to spoil the illusion that my body is fused to the machine, that K-2 and I are one being.

Overhead in a sky full of computerized stars, Venus pulses and gleams. Constellations swirl madly as the cars power into a swoop turn.

Then I feel it, that something is different, something is wrong. K-2 lunges and lifts from the track. I am out of my seat, the airtime seems endless, the fake stars loom diabolically huge. We are too close to the top of the tunnel. Ben screams. He grabs for me, but I'm not his anymore, and the power of K-2 surges through me as I shove him away.

K-2 convulses in another neck-snapping lurch. My windpipe seems to catch on the back of my teeth. We plunge out of the tunnel into a garish blaze of red light. The night air hits my face. I feel wetness all over my sweater, my neck—I open my eyes and look over at Ben. Then the screams that I hear are too loud and too mindless, too mad—they can't be mine, can't be mine, can't be mine....

# # #

Ben stood up coming out of the tunnel—that is what must have happened. Such accidents are rare, but they happen. The police believe me, so it must be true.

His body landed on top of the Twister. His head splatted onto the midway between a shooting gallery and an elephant ear stand.

That was it—he stood up in the tunnel. But right before that, I remember him clutching my hand and the machine leaving the track, taking flight with dark passion, with malice aforethought.

K-2 wins. I am free.

So I think.

After K-2 killed Ben, I never rode it again. Oh, I visited the park and stood eyeing the coaster, listening to the screams of its passengers, watching them exit, liquid-kneed, glassy-eyed, looking stunned and fuck-struck. Once I even overheard a pretty girl gushing to her boyfriend as they got off the ride, "That's the one— that's the coaster that killed a man." She was sweaty and flushed, and I could smell her cunt as they walked past me to get in the line. I knew she was K-2's new lover.

Lately I've been restless.

I moved to New Jersey and got an apartment a few miles away from the amusement park where the Quake has just been built, 214 feet of virile machinery, two double loops, a helix to stir-fry your brains and a corkscrew to halve your IQ. I haven't ridden it yet. I am waiting. I go to the park and I watch, grinding my legs together and crossing my arms over my chest so I can squeeze my nipples. It wants me. I know that it does.

A man in my apartment complex has started asking me out. In the hallway when no one is looking, he presses himself against me. He is hard, but not hard enough—he will be no match for the coaster.

I'll see what happens. If he backs off or not. One day I'll bring him here to the park. One day we'll go for a ride.

Ménage à Machine

Gerard Daniel Houarner

"Do you see?" Denise whispered. She craned her neck to look at Sterling sitting on its steel chair in a shadowy corner of the cavernous loft. "It's me she wants." She grinned, though the robot was off and could not see her bound naked and spread-eagled on the bed, at the mercy of their mutual master, Karen.

Denise needed to savor the taste of superiority over her mechanical rival. She wanted to see the glint of suffering in the machine's visual processors; the recognition of its betrayal and abandonment in the angle of its audio speakers. The thought of Sterling isolated in metal and a cloud of electronic hissing made her almost as wet as the promise of Karen's punishment.

She imagined AI algorithms writhing in the sweet agony of jealousy, and for a moment she was tempted by Karen's perverse idea that Denise suck the bullet and virtually experience Sterling's machine state. Loaded with illegal Shanghai and Bangalore emotion-simulation programming, the robot was a popular stop on the Players' circuit in the Eidolon Palace. Riding an early-model human interface chassis with custom-designed and home-engineered add-ons, its limited portable memory and processing capacity enslaved by the command to convert sensor signals into analogs of human sensations, the Sterling default personality was an exquisite marriage of simple intellect and raw inno-cence. Denise was not certain she wanted to reduce her self to its simpler parameters.

The cinnamon scent warned her; she tensed reflex-ively. A hand grabbed her jaw and wrenched her head back. Karen's tight-lipped, flat, pale face filled her vision. A frown that made her eyes smaller, her gaze even more piercing, preceded the six sharp, strong slaps that jerked Denise's head back and forth and sent flashes of pain down her neck.

"Am I boring you?" Karen asked.

"No, Master," Denise answered, vision blurred, voice quavering.

Karen's strong fingers, warmed by the explosions of flesh smashing flesh, slid down Denise's neck, circled her breasts, pinched her nipples, long and hard. "After all our preparation, I would hate to think you were distracted."

"No, Master." Denise drew a sharp breath in as Karen's razor-edged nails dug into her nipples. Writhing uncontrollably, tugging at the wrist and ankle restraints, Denise stifled a cry.

"You must focus." Karen slipped her fingers between Denise's legs. "Pay attention. This is what you've prayed for. What you earned. Do you want it?"

"Yes." Denise thrust her hips up to meet Karen's teasing, stroking fingers.

"Tell me."

Denise did, all thoughts of Sterling banished before the rush of sweat and blood carnality. She surrendered herself to the power and love of Karen's hands and lips, the strength of her thighs and arms, the damp heat of her sex. Smothered in the dark heart of Karen's attention, Denise wept with the joy of fulfillment as her tongue probed salt-sweet flesh, her mouth gently sucked the delicate bud of her owner's pleasure.

Denise roused herself as the weight of Karen on her shoulders and chest, the taste of Karen in her mouth, the smell of cinnamon, blew away like sand from ancient ruins, exposing the bare foundations of her hungers and needs. Denise shook her head, blinked at the light from nearby dimmed halogen lamps.

"Master?" she called. Sweat sheathed her body in a gleaming patina. She shivered, tugged at the restraints. They held firm. Staring into the loft's corners, Denise picked out the scattered accessories of their everyday lives: dirty laundry overflowing plastic bins; a tiny steel kitchen with pots, pans, dishes and cups piled over the sink rim; an enormous antique oak dining table with eight high-back chairs, two leather sofas, a baroque coffee table. Electronic components covered all flat surfaces. Sterling had not been allowed to do the menial tasks he had been programmed for in quite a while.

Karen's moan broke over the faint hum of the loft's power bus, peaked with a sharp cry. Denise closed her eyes. Opened them again to track her master's panting. Her gaze passed over the nest of cables and controllers that was her antiquated computer workstation, past Karen's elegant Eidolon Palace interface suit and bullet jacks, Karen's more exotic tools and clothes displayed like hunting trophies, then came to rest on the bare corner allocated to Sterling.

Karen's cinnamon scent was soured by the odor of machine oil and the sharp ozone bite of electrical discharge. Karen's tight, severe curves curled around the smooth cartoonish lines of Sterling's tattered synthetic flesh. Her lips brushed plastic and metal, her tongue pushed through a tear in cheek flesh to probe the smooth sensor bundles beneath. A cable strung from skull to skull connected the lovers like a vine bridge swaying over a chasm.

In her rising hysteria, Denise saw a ghostly cyber-spirit form of Karen overlapping Sterling. Denise shut her eyes, shook her head, looked again. The hallucination vanished.

Sterling's visual processors glowed bluish. They

roved in their sockets, scanning Karen. Denise. In the Eidolon Palace, lurkers savored Denise's abandonment. Her gut twisted.

"Karen!" she cried out, struggling frantically. "Please— don't leave me here!"

Karen rolled her hips over the naked metal rods and braces of Sterling's skinless thigh and plugged in a new genital extension. Settling onto the robot's lap, Karen looked over her shoulder.

"Shut up!" she snapped. "You bore me."

Denise wailed as Karen commanded Sterling to lay on the floor, spread its arms and legs, lock them in position. Karen took her pleasure, again and again. Denise knew her own suffering was as much a source of Karen's satisfaction as Sterling's programmed performances. She knew, and took what joy she could from the agony of that knowledge.

"You know I want this," said Karen.

Denise answered, "Yes."

"You know you want this, too."

"Yes."

"Beg for it."

"Please…"

"Again."

She did.

Karen slid down a little in the sofa chair, raised her hips, parted her legs. "Show me how much you want to please me."

Denise kissed her way up from Karen's toes, licking the bulge of calf muscle, lingering along the inside of the thigh, breathing in her unmistakable scent before following a heavier, musky smell and a salty taste to root for the source of Karen's love. She worked her way deep into the groove, using lips and tongue and teeth, carrying Karen through familiar canyons of pleasure like a fast-running river over a rocky bed, racing toward the falls, toward surrender as complete as that of water to a precipice and gravity.

She had no choice. Karen was drifting away from her, distracted by the mysteries, promises, and challenges of Sterling's robotic nature. The only way to return to Karen's center was to put herself where Karen had focused her attention. Put herself in Sterling. Suck the bullet, jack herself into the Eidolon Palace, and allow Karen to bind her to Sterling's systems.

Before Sterling had been added to the equations of pleasure, Karen amused herself by seducing lovelorn, tube-born, corp-raised castaways. She had savored picking service laborers up from their world of menial tasks and consumption quotas, introducing them to high-resolution flesh/tech sex, integrating their reactions into her entertainment programs until they burned out and fell back to their born ranks emptier than when she had met them.

Denise had remained as long as she had in Karen's world by resisting surrendering completely to her master's will. Raised in regimented nurseries where the glories and wonders of the technological age had not supplanted her need for the touch of warm flesh, she still had to fight panic when jacked in during her corporate birth sponsor's required survey downloads. Her fears inhibited her from complete immersion in the Eidolon Palace games that led eventually to Karen's boredom. Karen had even admitted, after imprisoning Denise for a week in a latex bondage suit that controlled access to every orifice, that she thought the bond of their intimacy was based on the question of who was in truly control. Who was the master, who was the slave.

When Sterling joined their household, the balance of power shifted. The desire to add metal to the equation of flesh and virtual sex had captured Karen. Denise saw new questions forming in her master's mind: would metal break to her will or make her its slave? What would a machine add to the mix? What would it feel like, metal against flesh, gear grinding against muscle? How much farther might she travel in her quest for satiation if she paved her path with metal?

Karen pushed her away. Denise fell back, lips and tongue numb, jaws aching. She rolled herself into a ball, feeling her body with trembling hands, as Karen stood and walked to the dining table Sterling had cleared earlier. She turned to Denise and said, in a voice untouched by the passion of the service she had received, "It's time."

Denise gathered herself, looking away from Sterling

and the medical robots connected to it by a web of cables. The smell of antiseptics permeated the air as probes and blades were prepped. Whining pumps and whirring motors drowned her ragged breathing. She approached the nest of machinery, eyes downcast.

Karen guided Denise through the maze of instruments, helped her with cold hands onto the antique oak table. Fitted the gas mask over her face while robot arms reached down, positioned her, marked her body for incisions.

Karen left. Denise tried to turn her head. Unpadded grips held it firmly in place. She strained to pick up Karen's footsteps, breathing, heartbeat out of the nest noise, but could not. She yearned for Karen. She wanted to see the object of her surrender.

Missing. Like so much of herself.

Why Karen? Why this place, with that woman? Why did giving herself to Karen feel so perfect, as if every painful experience in Denise's life had been designed to lead her to a moment in which misery transformed into joyous fulfillment?

Denise closed her eyes, remembered the hard lines of her master's face the night they met, the smirk, the eyes that bore into the soul. Eyes like an eagle's singling her out from a terrible height. Karen needed her. Lonely and isolated, like Denise. But unlike Denise, magnificent in her solitary stalking. Centered. Self-absorbed.

A tremor passed through Denise. Machines squeaked and beeped in protest. She opened her eyes, searched again for Karen. Avoiding Sterling standing nearby, she followed the dance of shiny silver and matte black instruments above her.

As wires were threaded through needles next to her ear, she let her thoughts drift from needs and power, hunger and yearning. She thought instead of what was happening to her now. Karen had said surgery would be required. Her specifications were lengthy and complex. Illegal. Filled with experimental upgrades and dangerous add-ons designed and manufactured in rogue space-drum labs beyond Mars orbit or in South American and Asian jungle factories. A set of programs cobbled together by Karen trading in black cyber-markets and hacking corp databases was already in place, to be downloaded as soon as the hardware was installed.

Delicate, articulated fingers like spider limbs, unfolded along the inside edge of the mask and pried her mouth open. Gas hissed. She smelled peppermint. Felt cool fingers scrape against her teeth, tasted metal on her tongue. The wood at her back reflected body heat, seemed to yield slightly to her hips and sweaty shoulder blades.

The skin around the jack implant at the roof of her mouth tickled, just as it did when she reported to her corp sponsor and had to suck the company bullet to download. The memory sparked a moment of panic in Denise as the impact on her life rolled through her like the gas filling her lungs, her bloodstream. She would be dropped from the subsidy rolls when she failed to report in; her ID would be deleted from the universal databases; an APB would be issued. Forced into the underground world Karen crossed in and out of so easily under the protection of her class, Denise would depend on her master for survival. If caught by her sponsors, she would not survive to suffer from the blood poisoning, infections, or cancer that eventually claimed so many illegally enhanced.

Her vision narrowed, became a tunnel of light bounded by medical robots. Sterling's visage floated overhead a moment. Its opticals glinted. Light twinkled in the pits and crevices of its faceplate. A shadow fell over the robot, touching off a flicker of hope in Denise. But Karen did not appear in Denise's closing circle of consciousness.

Missing. Like so much of her own self.

Sinking, circle shrinking, darkness swallowed her.

"Come on," Karen urged, rocking her hips over Sterling. Sweat dripped from her face, splashed against the robot's chest. The corners of her mouth twitched, a shudder seized her shoulders. She licked her lips, slapped the cushioned sensor pad in Sterling's cheek.

Denise gasped with the shock of pain. Reality came into focus. She was watching Karen over her, from inside Sterling. More, there were shadow selves inside her mind, echoing thoughts and reactions, confusing her own thinking. Multiple levels of awareness and information screamed for her attention; waves of sensation assaulted her nervous system. Drowning, she fought for space, for peace.

Voices whispered instructions all around her. They shut down her perceptions, slowed the firing rate of her synapses. She looked for whoever spoke, saw only Karen looking down. The loft in the background. A figure on the dining table, bandaged, IV and life-support monitor lines hooked into flesh.

Herself. Denise. Sucking the bullet plugged into her mouth socket. Bloated and bruised body wired, shaved head studded with sockets and adaptors and signal amplifiers. Face covered by a tight-fitting latex mask stuck through with breathing tubes.

By sucking the bullet, Denise had been sucked into Karen's arena. Her brain trapped in bone and flesh, senses tied to Sterling's experiential shell, her awareness suspended in distant supercomputers and AI colonies.

"Pay attention!" Karen slapped Sterling's cheek sensor pad again. Her sweat fell on other sensing elements on the robot's chest, and Denise felt the moisture, tasted the salt.

A corona of cables dangling from skull jacks connected Karen to Sterling. The lurking Players from the Eidolon Palace. Ghosts with the right to entertainment, however and wherever they chose, guaranteed and protected by the corporations in which they held stock, for which they worked. Consumers of her relationship with Karen and Sterling.

She had no sense of the robot, except as a vast, cold universe of steel and plastic, ceramics, and fiber optics. She was shocked by the robot's impersonal regard; she had wanted, expected, hoped for a sign of the default personality behind metal, machine, and superficial interfacing protocols. But it lay cocooned, bound and asleep, sealed behind fire walls, leaving her nothing to hurt, as Karen hurt her. Nothing that would make her the center of its universe, as she had made Karen the center of hers.

"That's better," said Karen. "There you are, you little thing. Let's see how you taste."

A primal big bang of perceptions peeled away translucent layers of the universe, and her mind. Karen's distinctive scent mingled with the childhood memory of lunch in the corphanage cafeteria, lost and isolated in a herd of squealing preadolescents, sucking on the metal spoon she had used to savor a faintly sweetened pudding dessert. Karen's eyes, a mix of blues and greens, brought back the bright, pulsing hues of her childhood. The subliminal messages in wall ads and elevator music. Dreams whispered from therapeutic playback pillows. Frenetic schooling by virtual corporate spokesmen. Karen's weight pressing down on Sterling's chest sensors mimicked the crushing burden of emotional deprivation she and the other corp children carried, the yearning for fulfillment constantly denied, the eagerness to have what was beyond reach.

The Eidolon Palace's was more complex than any

she had ever experienced. It enveloped her, penetrated her. Exploded inside of her, made her world over. Memories: her first steps out of the corphanage bubbled out of the maelstrom. She remembered being released to pursue in the corp-created world the appetites that had been carefully piqued and frustrated in her corp-created childhood. The terror of a new world, of change and the rush of choices and stimulation, came back to echo and shadow and permeate with aftertastes and ghost sensations the receding chaos and wonder of a new creation.

She was disappointed, as she had been in the aftermath of her release. No matter how many products and services her corp credit bought, her purchases never quite satisfied her inner need. She feared that now, floating like a tadpole in a crowded pond, the enormous eye of the object of her desire staring at her, everything she had surrendered, everything she had chased, would not be enough. She would still be empty. Disappointed. Again. Pain without pleasure. Unsatisfied sucking the bullet.

Time stretched. Creation unfolded. Denise became more than herself, more of herself.

Vision shattered, fragmented, scattered in a dozen different directions.

She looked down at Sterling, up at Karen, at Sterling and Karen from her body on the table, at the entire loft from the dozen remote cameras planted in corners and along track lights and hidden in vents and behind mirrors and equipment. Each shard of vision was over-laid with out-of-synch multiple images from the same point of view. Rotating, tumbling in a three-dimensional kaleidoscope.

The voices in her mind laughed, muttered.

She smelled cinnamon on a warm draft of air, and sweet-scented oil, and the musty breath of Karen's sex.

"That's it," Karen whispered. "Let me feel it...."

Karen moved up and down on Sterling, kissing pressure pads, licking probes, sucking on minute sensor pods dotting the robot's body like goose bumps. Denise moaned as pleasure, like a signal amplified, repeated, multiplied, flooded her mind and drove her to the brink of madness. Just as consciousness began to fade, the torrent relented. Whispering shadow voices reinforced her sanity, explained how machines and programs controlled the flow of sensation rushing from her to Karen and back, reassured her she would survive, told her to relax and enjoy. She hung on, focusing on Karen, on the intimacy they were sharing, the bond they were building.

The bond was founded on a bridge built from clit to clit by Sterling's stainless-steel cock. Sheathed with sophisticated sensing equipment, bristling with mechanical stimulators, its thrusting and recoiling motions coordinated by a hundred tiny motors, Sterling's sex connected the pumping of Karen's vagina to Denise's gyrating hips through cables and tight beam transmissions. Brain to brain, from Karen's wired body to

Denise's bullet-sucking mouth, the rhythms of sex traveled back and forth, volume rising, frequency shifting higher.

Denise watched her meat body convulse as her mind floated between bodies, looping from Karen's grunting ecstasy to Sterling's stoic servicing to her own disembodied, cascading orgasms.

"It's not enough," Karen said, stroking Denise's flesh arm.

The loft smelled of sex with an ozone bite. Two technicians in latex bodysuits, tight leather harnesses, and electronically enhanced goggle-eyed masks worked over open access panels on Sterling's body.

"Please, don't—" Denise began.

"You know it's not enough," Karen said as she walked. Her passing made the intravenous line, and nearly pulled them out of Denise's arm.

"Please don't make me."

"You want to."

"Yes, but I can't."

"You can. You must."

"But my body…" She looked to Sterling. The monitors tracking her physical functions beeped and spiked. Shivering, her heart racing, she was still caught in the mechanical rhythms of robot sex, filtered through the Eidolon Palace's exotic point of view.

Karen faced away from Denise and toyed absently with a tangle of cables at the foot of a battered, portable military-grade communication link. "You have to give it up. Surrender everything. Give yourself completely to me. Put yourself utterly in my power. You know you want to. You know you must. You have no choice."

"Please, I'm afraid."

"Of course you are."

"It wasn't what I thought, what I hoped, might happen."

"You didn't go far enough."

"We were in Sterling, in the Eidolon Palace."

"Not far enough."

"How far?"

"Ask how deep. That's how far inside me you will be, in the Eidolon Palace."

"But we were just there!" Denise wailed in frustration.

Karen turned to face Denise. "You were still tied to your flesh. You were only sucking the bullet. You have to go to the next level and—"

"But, I don't want to die—"

"You want to stay with me."

"Yes."

"You want to be with me, in my heart, in my mind."

"Yes."

"You know you belong to me."

"Yes."

"Then you'll do as I say, or I'll send you away."

"Yes."

"Say it."

"What."

"You know."

"…Yes, I'll…"

"What."

"I'll bite the bullet."

A burst of light signaled creation. Again.

Denise woke, the pleasures of her last performance reverberating in the world coming up around her.

Voices whispered. Giggled. She overheard snatches of conversation, and the electronic whine of AI speech, and people moving through a strange, cramped space that was not Karen's loft or her old room or the orphanage or any of the places in which she had worked. A phrase, followed by laughter, sifted through the background rumble.

…tech snuff…

Karen, Denise called out.

Yes.

Bright white light coalesced into colors, shapes.

What's happening?

Everything.

I need you.

I am here.

No. No, you're not.

Pieces of memory drifted into her awareness, categorized by three-dimensional icons. Labeled. Discrete, contained in tiny time-controlled segments.

The room took shape. Interactive pods squeezed next

to each other along a rising series of widening, circular balconies. A round theater above a pit stage. Medical. Operations had once been performed in this place, on living meat by living meat, before an audience of meat students and faculty. A long time ago. Facility abandoned, now hijacked and hot-wired for Players who could tolerate transmission interference from Eidolon Palace lines.

The experience of machine sexuality.

Information streamed into her awareness, unwanted. Technical specs, power spikes, line drops, emergency rerouting routines, encryption programs, an endless bombardment of processes and data describing her environment and herself without actually showing them in a way she could comprehend.

Pay attention.

The data storm dissipated; the physical world came into focus, gained depth and resolution. Two humanoid robots sitting on a steel-framed, silk-cushioned bed. Who are you? Denise asked. And when she realized she had not actually spoken, she asked, where am I?

In me.

You're not Karen.

I will do, until the real thing comes along.

An AI mimic, Denise realized.

The mimic continued: You have been loaded into one of a matched pair of soft-shell fashion test robots, each equipped with twin sensor rigs, one directed outward, the other internal, for a full-sensation spectrum.

The Eidolon Palace's fuzzy, confusing environment receded into the background. The robot's rich soup of input pumped into her awareness, choking her with its view of reality.

Yes.

Nodes of memory opened before the word, as if it were a key allowing her to remember a paradise from which she had fallen, to which she could never return. Shunning the past, she reached to taste the present. She cried out: Karen, that's you, I know, I can hear it in your…voice.

But her heart did not beat faster. Her skin did not flush. No, of course not. Her body was elsewhere, it was—

The other robot reached over, stroked the mop of delicate sensory fibers attached to her skull. Denise came, white-hot and pulsing, like a string of molten pearls. Polished. Contained.

Remote.

Denise's mind drifted from the pleasure, a cold crystal snowflake falling from a gray sky. She perceived Karen in the other robot as a shadow trapped in metal and plastic. Tracing communication lines through sewer servers and black-hole relays, Denise returned to the loft, to Sterling's robot form, its mechanical embrace, its web of wire and cable containing Karen's plugged-in flesh. She perceived Karen's feedback loop, the Players superimposed on her path.

Scanning the rest of the loft, she did not see her body.

Nor could she find links to a site holding her form. Turning her attention to her own feedback loop, she tracked it back to the fashion test robot and its supporting hardware hidden outside the operating theater.

Karen, what's happened to me?

You bit the bullet, Karen answered, as if from a distance, her voice slurred and accented with the weight of all the Players riding her signal.

Denise reached for a memory. The day she was let out of the corphanage to play in snow rose like a misty curtain around her. She exited the memory, reached for another. Loneliness pierced her as she sat in a bar, frustrated by the media others immersed themselves in, her hunger unsatisfied, the emptiness nurtured by corphanage upbringing gnawing at her spirit. She fled the bitter memory, ran into another icon.

Recoiled.

Came again, as Karen tweaked Denise's robot nipple, ran a moist, rubbery tongue along her shoulder and neck.

Players crowded around Denise, urging her to take action, touch Karen's robot, raise the output of sensation. Play.

But the memory of her biting the bullet, surrendering her body and allowing Karen to bind her in programs and algorithms and databases, echoed like thunder through her. She had not stayed long enough in the memory icon to experience her death again, but specific images remained, like afterimages of blinding lightning: needles, brain scans, neuron firing analyses, memory imprints, recognition-pattern imaging. Cutting-edge experimental processes developed through secret collaborations between Earth-based corporate labs and independent, off-world colonies dedicated to merging the machine with the human. Forgetting how to breathe, how to make her heart beat. Imploding in an all-consuming flash of Flesh rendered. Separated from the rhythms of natural life.

She was dead, and alive in the universe of the machine. Reborn. Created in the image her master desired.

I didn't want—

Yes. This is what you wanted. To belong to me. Your files are mine, to open and close whenever I need them. You have my attention, completely, whenever I access you.

Karen, no...

Your service pleases me. Fills me, as I've always wanted to be filled.

Thank you. Thank you so much.

Denise struggled with thoughts, words, as the frenzy of sexual pleasure increased. She put her hand on Karen's thigh, felt a vibration, came, rode the ecstasy to higher pleasure, coming again as Karen responded to her touch, moved to her, licked Denise's lips, thrust her tongue into Denise's mouth, linking them, merging their feedback loops, adding layers of resonance, depth and information to the pleasure.

But I can't remember, I can't feel—

Yes, you can feel, my sweet thing.

Probes emerged from all over Karen's robot, nuzzling Denise, uncovering sockets hidden under the pseudo flesh, thrusting into the holes, penetrating deep into Denise. She fought, tried to pull back, but Karen anticipated her moves, and their wrestling flowed with erotic power. A hundred hard links connected them. Sensation moved freely along the bonds of their intimacy, back and forth, pleasure building in strength and intensity.

You see, Karen said. Others echoed her words.

Denise saw the endless stimulation, the pleasure curve rising exponentially, limited only by the capacity of her robot's hardware and her personality software. She saw the Palace's Players, their sink lines dipping into the currents of sensory data, their nets trawling the feedback loop. She caught glimpses of experiential ghosts: previous times she had been called up by Karen to perform in cruder robots, with less-sophisticated sensor rigs and programs. Lingering images, not yet written over in the liquid medium in which she was stored, haunting her present. Warning her of repetitions yet to come.

She grazed Sterling's fire wall, realized she had become a reflection of that stunted personality. Another shadow in Karen's mirror. Another prisoner of Karen's appetite.

She was at the bottom of an enormous well, performing a ballet of the senses over and over for her master's pleasure. At her master's pleasure. In the center of Karen's attention, for as long as her program was engaged. She understood, as the dance swept her up in the growing violence of the Eidolon Palace's hunger for sensation, that nothing could touch her. She had nothing left in which to receive and hold anyone's attention. The flesh of her body responded to the simplest touch.

In her search for intimacy, someone to fill her life with meaning and make her complete, the capacity to be fulfilled had shriveled and died. She wanted to mourn, but had no eyes to shed tears. And no one in the sex loop had time or reason to listen to her words.

Karen thrust herself with relentless passion into every slot, jack, receptor in Denise's robot. Denise came again, with more orgasms flocking, ready to soar. Reason disintegrated in the up-welling of pleasure. Circuits and memory gave way to the demands of pleasure. But no matter how much she lost, how much she felt, she held on to the certainty that nothing could truly touch her. She was missing too many parts of herself.

And she missed the scent of cinnamon.

Rough, Trade

Cecilia Tan

Call it the weather (which was a steady millennial rain), call it the post-project blues (or burnout, more like), call it whatever, but for weeks I'd been home, restless but without the energy to do much, no interest in dinner with friends or concerts or much of anything. This is the life of a technolinguist, I told myself. A few months of neuron-burning, sleepless, intensity, interfacing and trying to keep up with a project, and then a few months of dullness and checking my bank balance. Cleaning my office. Playing video games. Every night I sank into bed with the vibrator and thought nothing more of it.

At least, that was the way it was for the first week or

so. And then it began to sink in that maybe I really ought to go out and get laid. Such an expression, "get laid," but apropos—I wanted to be laid down, pressed flat under another human being's body—cruelly literal but true. It had been a couple of years since I'd had time to maintain or look for a regular relationship. I mean, even I can admit that I'm not the most fun to be around when I'm talking like a machine and I can't tell any-more whether the blue in the sky is real or optic-nerve burnout. I didn't think of what other complications might have kept me unattached, of course not—I'm into cognitive intelligence, not psychology.

It sank in one night when I was, literally, twiddling my thumbs and thinking about the motor mechanism of habitual motion. I looked at the liquid-silver display morphing the seconds on my wall. Only nine P.M. I could suit up, head down to The Market and try my luck. As soon as I thought of it, energy came to me and I ran to the bedroom to brush my hair and make myself presentable.

Communications is my business, it's true. The communion between human and machine becomes more intertwined every day. We need it now; our economies and political outcomes and resource allocation and transportation—computers handle it all, and humans need to work harder and harder to keep up. Yeah so anyway, I was muttering to myself all the way there to make sure I remembered how to actually talk to people. Please, thanks, how you doing? The rush of air around my helmet meant I could hear myself only subvocally.

At The Market, the music never stops, but in some parts of the club it's louder than others. I like the loud part, which is also the darkest part, usually. But if I was going to meet anyone, that was a sucky place to wait. Just in case, I made myself an Illumiprint card that read: "I just want somebody to treat me rough, fuck me silly, and keep my safety the top priority" in glowing green letters when stroked. The card was in the back pocket of my jeans. I caught a glimpse of myself in the mirrored side of the bar's cash register. Disaster, probably, I told myself. I hadn't been able to decide butch or femme, and ended up in just a T-shirt and jeans, my riding boots unglamorously scuffed. But well, I actually rode a two-wheeler, unlike most of the posers in here. Well, whatever. I checked my signals to make sure they were in place: the black ribbon around my throat pegged me officially as a bottom, the red one looking for sex. To me the red one was redundant—what was the point if they didn't fuck you? But some people swore No Sex, so you had to know somehow. I always said those people should have worn a Band-Aid or surgical mask or something, but the system wasn't exactly designed by semantic experts. Before my time, you know.

Bill, the one bartender I knew, was too busy to talk. There wasn't anyone else there I recognized. No matter how little time has gone by between when you last visited a place and the current time, if it feels like a long time has gone by, you can be sure there has been some disconcerting piece of renovation done since the last time. The reverse is also true: that the renovation itself can make you feel like you haven't been there in forever. I struck a pose near a new-looking holographic fountain and waited.

The waiting's the boring part, so I won't tell you much about it other than that my thoughts were high on the statistical list of what 90 percent of the other people in that place were thinking: What if I don't meet anyone? What if I meet some psycho? What if I embarrass myself? what if s/he wants to get serious? Just because I know the stats doesn't make me any less common in that respect. Anyway, to cut to the chase.

When "he" came along, I was almost convinced that I should give up and leave. He had his hair cut short, peach-fuzz short, and somehow the way that it revealed the hardness of his head was sexy, like he was one giant erection. He walked up to me, flicked his eyes toward my ribbons, and said, "Does that say it all?"

I palmed the card to him and he looked at it, chuckled to himself. "I don't know…"

"Don't know what?" I burst out. "What do you want me to do?" He had dark eyes, dark skin, but I couldn't guess where he was from. He couldn't have been any older than me.

He rummaged in his leather jacket for a second and jutted his chin toward the back of the bar. I turned to take a step in that direction but didn't want to take my eyes off him.

His hand on my shoulder propelled me into the men's room. (It was somehow less objectionable, even in this day and age, for a woman to be caught in the men's room than the other way around.) He pushed me into a stall, sat me down on the lid of the toilet, and told me to push my jeans down.

I did. Underneath I was wearing a G-string because I liked how it sawed at my clit. He propped my heels against his hips and spread my knees. From his inner pocket he took something small and plastic with wires that ended in small pads—my mind was already giving me two descriptions for it: the common me would have seen it as an old-time transistor radio with headphones, the technolinguist me wondered what the electrodes were for and whether he was going to read my brain waves here in this muffled-dance-floor-scuffed-paint-sex-club bathroom stall. He squirted a small bit of jelly onto my clit from a tube and stuck the pads on either side of it. Then he pressed one small plastic piece against my clit while he held the other in his hand.

The plastic piece began to vibrate and my hips jumped. A weak vibration compared to what I had at home, but enough to make my breath quicken at first.

He stared down at me with his dark eyes—patiently, it seemed—yet I wondered if I saw a hint of anger there. He moved the vibrator in a circle and I moaned and thrust myself against it harder.

"Does it always take you this long?" he said after a while. I wondered how much battery power he had.

"No, not always," I said, my teeth a little gritted. "It's just—"

His eyes went back to the little box in his hand. "If you don't peg these meters, I'm not taking you home. Understand?"

I nodded. I was aroused, of that there was no doubt, and I felt wetness drip down my open cunt to my ass. I looked back up at that hard cock of a head and wished he were doing it already.

"Are you holding back?" he asked then.

"No! No, I swear. It's just…I've been using a vibrator every night this week, and it's got me a little desensitized.…"

He snorted and went back to watching the meters. I was dying to have a look at the readings. My hips shook and my teeth ground but I was no closer to coming. Damn it! Why would I have to get one of these types? Why'd he have to pick the one test I might not pass today? I squeezed my eyes shut, trying to will myself to come. I imagined him inside me, thrusting in, no mercy, no stopping, and yet in complete control.…

I whimpered out loud and broke my own reverie. He was looking down at my face now, a little bit of pity and a little bit of anger on his. "I don't—" he began.

You know I'm desperate when I interrupt, one method of verbal interface that always annoys me when other people do it to me. "Please, sir, just a little longer. I…I want you so much. I wish you could just fuck me, stick your hard cock in me, sir, please, anything, sir, please.…" I stopped myself before I said anything else stupid. I'd called him "sir," hadn't I. Inside I cursed myself for manifesting old, stupid habits, things I thought I was done with.

But if I was really done with them, I wouldn't be cruising a place like this for rough sex, for sex without mercy, would I?

His look mutated to a catlike bemusement, a little hungry, a little distant. "What are you really looking for?"

"Nothing, just a good fuck, dammit, even if I have to beg to get it, understand?"

"Oh, I understand," he said, and began to shake the vibrator with his hand. "Peg these meters for me, sweetie. Come on, do it for me, honey."

The come started at the tip of my clit like fire, and ran over the skin of my cunt like live acid, shaking me and making me howl. But it was all on the surface, and my vag was gasping like a fish. That's what I get for abusing that stupid vibrator.

He ripped the device from me and I gasped even though it didn't hurt. He was smiling. "It was good enough," he said. "Pull up your pants and follow me."

At his loft the back of my mind noticed things like his Ikaru rig and charts of hard copy on the wall. The thought went through my mind—he's some kind of project technologist, too, maybe a hardware engineer. We "soft"-ware types, cogno/comm types like me especially, we're almost more like guinea pigs than we are like scientists. But I wasn't really thinking about talking shop with this guy, I was following him behind a paper screen to a low futon bed, where he pushed me down and, one hand on the back of my neck, started undressing himself with the other. He stepped back to finish and when he stood completely naked in front of me, it seemed somehow that in nakedness there is power, and my clothes denoted me the poor, weak one. (No, I can never shut off the symbology filter, so just get used to it.) He leaned down to me, one hand tugging the thin ribbons around my neck while the other slipped inside my jeans, down into the wet place, and I prayed silently to myself that he would put his fingers in me—he did. One, then two, the knuckles widening me as he maneuvered the second one in, and my eyes closed and my mouth opened like I was giving thanks to the saints.

Then his hand was at my throat and that little question (what if I go home with a psycho?) flitted by, but he was growling in my ear "You like that? Is this what you like?" and me answering "yes yes yes…"

The hand at my throat threw me back and he tugged my jeans down around my ankles. He stood with his knees touching mine and indicated his bobbing cock with his hands. "Sit up."

I did.

"Come here and breathe on me."

I knew what he meant, and I opened my mouth

around the helmeted head of his cock. He was good and thick, heavy with veins and angry red.

"Go on," he prompted. But I hesitated. I've never been good at sucking cock, and given this guy's penchant for tests and shit, I worried what he'd do (or not do) if I weren't good.

"Come on. If you want it, you better." I hesitated a second longer. Then he pulled my head forward by the hair until my tongue made contact.

So then I sucked him, trying hard to please him. But by the same token, I was worried that he'd come and then what would I do?... I varied what I did, slurping him up and twisting my neck so he could dig into the soft flesh of my cheek with the tip when he thrusted, nibbling the edges and flicking my tongue, until, finally, he said "Enough. Get your fucking boots off."

I got the fucking boots off, or non-fucking boots, in this case, and my pants, and my G-string, and he pulled the T-shirt over my head and laid me back on the bed. "I'd tie you," he said, "but that makes it harder to fuck." I love that word, fuck, when it refers to what it really means. It's an old word, older than modern English, even older than England itself, and yet it always sounds so current, so now. As in, fuck me now.

He slid on a form-fit condom and it made his cock appear even bigger. Then I realized it had leads of some kind and he snaked them out and stuck them to my clit. Hardware technologist? I thought again. Or did he buy this stuff somewhere? I don't keep up on new sex toy technologies. But then he was inside me, the first thrust pushing for an awkward moment against me until it slid in. Suddenly I was clinging to him with all my limbs. His whole body was hard and rigid with well-toned muscle, in motion it felt like it rippled, as I imagined his cock rippling inside me. Maybe it was. Who knows what his doodad could do. His thingama-jig. His apparatus. But that makes it sound like I'm referring to his anatomy, not to his device. See?

I was losing myself in the sensation, almost not-believing that I actually found what I was looking for. His thrusts got harder. My hands roamed over his shaven head. He slowed down and made each one long and deep. I clawed at his back as if I could push him deeper.

A little bit later, as he held himself above me with his arms, going in with short jerks, he said "Do you go there often?"

My breath was short. It seemed an odd time for a verbal exchange, but I participated. "Aren't you supposed to ask that before you take me home?"

He ground in a hard, painful way that I like. "Answer me."

"I used to, I guess." I said, realizing I still think of myself as a regular even though none of the old crowd is there anymore, and I'd been there, what, once, twice this year? Only when I've been desperate. And before that there was Sasha. "You?"

He shrugged and switched to grinding his hips in a

circle. "Not that often. Not enough women there. I mean, worth meeting."

I tensed, the relationship question surfacing briefly as I read the potential implications of his words. But he was on to his next question already. "Rough you up, fuck you, but safely, huh?"

I nodded, my breath coming in time with his strokes.

"Why'd you call me 'sir' back in the bar? I don't see any discipline chain on you." He moved his head, a redundancy in the communication as he made a false show of looking for my hidden/nonexistent chain.

I tried to shrug, but it came out like a spasm. "Don't know. Just feeling you out, I guess."

"Good. Because I don't need no stray pets around here—you know what I mean? I can't take care of a slave. Too much responsibility."

"Oh, yeah," I agreed, "too much. I'm not into that kind of thing anyway," I said. But I knew from the tone of my voice and the way he looked at me that the lie was obvious. "I mean, not anymore," I amended.

He shut his eyes suddenly and doubled his pace. "Good," he said again. "Long's we understand…each other."

And then he began to come. I knew it not just from the way he clenched and strained in his throat, but because the sensation was channeled through his condom-device (which I'd forgotten about) into me. And in a millisecond, I was coming, too. Right from the center, deep rooted in me, the orgasm squeezed my guts and then exploded outward through my bones.

He disengaged and peeled off the gadget, let it fall on the floor as he slumped next to me. "That's how I make sure my partner always gets off," he said. "The anxiety of worrying about it was enough to keep me from cruising, before. I mean, there's only so much...bah, you know what I mean."

I did. For a lover, a girlfriend, a wife, you could take your time and figure out her favorite things and invest more emotional energy in her orgasm. But with a one-night trick? "Thoughtful of you," I answered, unable to move a muscle other than my mouth, or so it seemed.

"Nah, just practical." He sat up then and I was amazed that he could. He was looking at me and I realized this was an honest-to-God postcoital chat.

"So," I said, against my better judgment, "why do you think a slave's too much to handle?"

"Tried once," he said, his face impassive. "Fucked it up. You?"

"Tried once," I said. "Was the one who got fucked up."

We both nodded like: That's what I thought.

"Well, anyway," he said. "You want something to eat? Drink?"

I propped myself on an elbow. "Nah, got to get back to work."

"You do?"

I shrugged. I didn't really have to start the next

project until next week. But I didn't have anything better to do, and I didn't want...something. "I'm in software," I explained. "It's never finished."

"Hardware neither," he answered, but got up from the bed. He fished for something in his discarded jeans. "Here, my card. Give me a call in a couple of weeks if you want to do this again. Don't bother with The Market. Buncha sleazeballs there."

"Yeah." I took the card and watched his shadow on the other side of the screen.

"Shower?"

"Yeah, okay." We got into the spray not looking at each other. I did not scrub his back and he did not scrub mine. I got dressed and felt very tired. I slipped his card into my back pocket.

"Hey," he said as I shrugged on my jacket. "What's your name?"

I opened my mouth, but nothing came out. Names meant things, depending on what you meant by "name." In the owner-slave world, it meant something specific. He didn't mean it that way, but I couldn't seem to answer it any other way. "Don't have one," I said, then, cursing myself (and Sasha) as I did. "If I did, I wouldn't be here."

He looked at me sideways and wrapped a towel around his waist. "I thought you were over all that shit."

"Nope," I said. "Never said that."

"Okay then." He took a step forward, his nipples standing out against his hard chest. "I'll give you a name to use with me." But that's all, his eyes said. "If," he added, "you think you really will call me."

"I don't know." I bit my lip.

He held up his hands. "Hey, you're the one playing the game, not me."

He was right. I was the one insisting on this stupid thing. I could just tell him my real name and we could be friends and that would be that. He might even know me from the nets. "Lucin," I said then, "not short for Lucinda."

He smiled. "Terence. Not long for Terry." We shook hands which felt ridiculous. "But I was going to call you something like Cocksucker."

We both blushed and laughed a little to hear it out loud. "You're being sarcastic, right?"

"Not exactly," he said, shifting from one foot to the other. "I mean, you did."

"Yeah, but I suck at sucking."

"Not me you didn't."

"Really?"

"Yes. All right, Cock Worshiper."

"That's closer," I said.

"Cock Martyr," he went on. "Cock Saint."

"Now you're pushing it."

"So are you," he said, still smiling. But his hand reached for me and even though I stepped back, his long, hard fingers still clutched my lapel. "I just want to give you something appropriate, you know." His voice softened with practiced menace, and I had one brief moment of curiosity about what he must have been like as a Master, flashes wondering what went wrong, before I put it out of my mind to listen to what he said. "Something that would tell you for sure what I think of you, who you are, what's expected, and what the limit is." It was embarrassing to hear him explain the things I already knew, and not be able to tell him that I knew but that it didn't help, that I was still brain-damaged when it came to certain issues. "So I thought Cocksucker might fit. If it doesn't, you can walk out of here and name yourself, or find someone else who'll do it for you." He let go of me with a self-righteous shrug. "I'm just looking for a good screw from time to time."

I held up my hands in apology, not surrender. "You're right. I'm jerking you around. I'm sorry. It was such a terribly nice good screw, too."

"So get out of here, why don't you?" He was smiling again and his eyes looked sleepy. "Quit angsting and get some rest."

"Thanks."

"Don't mention it."

I had to walk back to The Market to pick up my two-wheeler, and then there was the ride home in dark wind and deserted streets. For once the only chatter I could hear was from a loose valve; even street signs seemed mute. I didn't have to decide whether I would call him again yet. Next time I emerged from a project, maybe. Maybe next time.

Sustenance
Nancy Kilpatrick

It's always hungry for my body. In the months I've been
down here, not one revolution of the planet has taken
place when IT hasn't fed on me. There are no windows
in this gray cell I'm locked in. Natural light cannot get
through, but I know when it's night. That's when I'm
tired. That's when IT comes for me.

I feel like the Marquis de Sade, writing this endless
journal diabolique on toilet paper. With a stolen ball-
point. I hide both under the mattress. I'm not writing
with the hope that this will ever be read, more to
preserve whatever sanity I may have left. All that keeps
me sane is the pleasure I derive from my own hand,
fingers that know my body so well, when to caress

softly, when to be firm, when to be violent. When to drive me from my tortured mind and into the hot and human inferno that blazes through me nightly, when IT finally leaves me alone.

I hear scratching on the wall of the next cell—gouging, really—as if a primitive metal tool drills at the cement holding the cold gray bricks in place. One day enough sealer will be chiseled away and the brick will loosen sufficiently to either push out or pull inward and then...

And then all hope will be crushed. The driller will not have found a route out of this prison, but only a large peephole to another cell. To me. Confined as much or even more than whoever is dismantling the wrong wall.

I used to call out. Every day. But either my voice didn't carry, or else the tormented mind on the other side heard the sounds as life remembered. Or imagined I am outside this prison, my cries carried on air waves in the clean sunshine of a free world. A world free of metal monsters. I doubt I'll ever see that world again.

I don't bother calling now when I hear the noise. Iron rodents chewing through building materials. Hope digging frantically toward freedom. Toward annihilation.

Another meal has come and gone. Eating is a mundane activity. They feed me protein, meat, plenty of it; to keep up my strength, no doubt. To make me last longer. It keeps me energized enough to touch myself in the darkness and revive my spirits.

I was brought here one hot summer night when I'd

had too much white wine and was feeling maudlin enough to wander foolishly down an alley off a side street. I remember seeing the man—or what I thought of then as a man—lingering ahead in the shadows. This time my affair with Alan was over for good. I felt reckless. Sentimentally vulnerable. Drunk.

Foolishly, I proceeded. As I passed, something snagged me from the darkness. Clamping metal fingers around my forearm, a metal plate over my mouth. I kicked and screamed, or at least I think I did, but the mechanical world surrounded me, and folded in on me, encasing me as if in a metal box, airtight, black as a black hole, soundproof. Within, cords of steel ripped off my clothing. I felt the cold iron slide over my nipples, snapping tight, until my head fell back, until I could hardly stand, squeezing, pinching, until I became weak and those vises held me up by the nipples while other cords slid up my thighs.

Cool iron entered me—my vagina, my anus, my mouth—larger than any penis, harder, like pistons, ramming in and out, forcing me beyond the terror, to stimulation, to excitation, until my juices slicked the metal, smoothing out this demented ride. I came many times, too many times, like some slut who had no inhibitions, who opened to anyone, anywhere, who walked around hot and wet, waiting, just waiting and wanting and… And then…

I awoke in this stark box, slightly bigger, blazing with light so bright it kills any tones of color that might exist. Empty white everywhere—the bed, the floor and walls, the toilet, the metal chair and table.

A robot matron in nurse's whites came first. She wouldn't answer questions but, like a computer, made sounds, little beeps, and, over days, made a steady demand that the medical history chart and menu card be ticked off. At first I refused. She wouldn't give in; neither would I. But charred meat was slipped through the small opening in the door—meat only, except for a glass of orange juice, on a time schedule that seems to be about twice each night. I'm human, not as strong as she is. I got hungry. I gave in.

Eventually I filled out the menu card—the only one—but since then still nothing arrives but meat. At least the cut is choice and cooked medium, not too bloody, not too "done," the way I like it, although I was never much of a meat eater. There's something to survival of the fittest. The other reason I capitulated was the feeling of devastating weakness that hit from the first time IT began to feed.

The ritual is the same nightly. The lights are dimmed until blackness swallows the room and everything in it. I hear metal slide against metal as the door is unbolted from the outside. Through thick darkness I can just barely make out a form gliding into the room, bringing with it brittle cold. More than seeing, I sense IT wafting toward me like a gust of arctic air. The air seems to form ice crystals as though molecular movement has slowed. At first I could not identify the unpleasant odor. Now I recognize the stench. Metal. The biting scent of metal. The inanimate overwhelming the animate.

The thing that comes for me has many red eyes that glow like dozens of taillights on a pitch-black highway. I back up against the wall to the next cell, which stops me dead, and cringe there. Something about those glowing crimson coals—the way they throb, or pulse, or blink—reminds me of flies swarming over spoiled meat.... I can't remember more.

The eyes, the stark smell, the bone-splitting cold overwhelm me as it grasps me in its dead-chill embrace and enters me. Its parts become greater than the sum of my whole. I am fucked in every orifice, squeezed in its impossible grip. And, despite my resolve, IT brings me to crisp orgasm, again and again, until I am spent, frozen, in a way that it can never be. That's all I know until suddenly the lights are blinding and I'm prone on the floor, my insides raw, defrosting, the brassy taste coating my mouth. My stomach full of its cold, inhuman cum. There is always a stainless-steel pitcher and glass on the table. When I sit up, I'm dizzy and nauseous, so eventually I sip water and pat wetness against my seared labia, my torn anus, my wounded nipples. My fingers always touch blood.

IT comes once in what feels like a twenty-four hour cycle. After the first session, I felt so weak my body seemed to have only air inside, a balloon on the verge of becoming deflated. I knew I was dying and made a decision to eat the meat and drink the juice and exercise and do whatever I could to help myself. When I filled out the menu card, I stole the pen. I don't know what I'll do when it runs out of ink.

The worst part is the loneliness. There are moments when I disappear. Not physically, but I go somewhere inside and a lot of time passes and when I return to this prison I don't know where I've been, only that it's better than here. I find that frightening.

I've always been what they call an extrovert—being with people recharges me. That's one of the problems Alan and I had. He's an introvert. Insisted on being alone more than our relationship could sustain. The sex was great—at the beginning. But his moods kept him away from me, and I went to bed starving while he digested porn videos. I felt resentful. We should have been acting out what he saw on the videos. But that's all over, and now I wish I was more like him. Not needing actual sex. Not needing what this monster does to me, for as much as I loathe it, I love it. IT keeps me going.

Since my first week of captivity in this "laboratory," the robot nurse has come back only four times, to take my blood pressure, blood samples, check my heart and other vital organs. She still does nothing but beep, but now that my initial confused terror has subsided, at least I can observe her. She's rod-thin, gunmetal, all efficiency, focused on her duties because she was built to fulfill one function only. I talk to her, ask her questions, but she never responds, of course, and her red lights won't meet my eye. I kicked over the chair once when her back was turned. She jerked. She began beeping in earnest. So, I know she can hear. It was a small victory.

The iron-willed monster that fucks me is another story. Nightly HE—I don't know why, but I've started thinking of IT as male, perhaps because of all the penetration—comes in the same way, does the same things to me. I can't stay conscious. I've tried, but the sex is so extreme, and so sustained, and so many orgasms take me over the edge of humanity into a realm where only a machine can function…it's impossible. Once I talked to HIM—IT—as IT was fucking me, to plead really, but the room went subzero and I heard a hiss like air being let out of a radiator.

That's all I remember.

Not so long ago, I would have said there was nothing worse than the horror of being raped nightly. I was wrong. A new feeling has developed that terrifies me. Anticipation. When I hear the metal scraping and feel the chill sliding in as the door opens—this is hard to write—I find I'm looking forward to HIM—IT—somehow. IT relieves the soul-crushing boredom, even for a little while, and I know I'll be dead to this isolated world for precious minutes as it drives me beyond my own limits. This is all so twisted and masochistic that I don't want to think about it. I worry about my sanity.

The only other distraction to endless time under white glare is the drilling. The hours I'm awake the noise is incessant, but I welcome it. I imagine someone like myself on the other side. I've even named her— Lisa. Lisa is more determined than I am. Inspiring. So much so that for the last week I've been using the spoon they send in with the pre-cut meat to dig from my side. Something in the sound of both of us trying, struggling, has renewed my hope, even though I know deep down that in the end we'll only find each other and not a way out. But it's something to do. Something to look forward to. Something more positive than welcoming IT. And she is human.

Something has happened that frightens me. Food doesn't come anymore. At least three twenty-four-hour periods have gone by and, nothing. Not the robot nurse, not the food. Just IT.

I've been alone with the scrapings. If I hadn't given back the spoon, I'd help. I don't want to damage my pen and there's nothing else I can use. Lisa's efforts lift the weight of despair pressing in on me, and yet that's stupid. Lisa will get through, and soon. I can feel it. Unless she starves to death first. Or I do. And then what? But I feed the insane plans within me. Together we can find a way out of here, I'm convinced of it. We can fight IT off—two are certainly stronger than one. At least one of us can stay awake when HE—IT—feeds and that might lead to a way of killing IT. Maybe she has more tools. With her for company, I would sacrifice my pen and put it to better use—it could be a weapon. At the very least, together we can dig through the wall to the outside and...

A small chink falls through on my side. I run to the wall. The hole is the size of an iris. I peer through and it is dark. Then bright light. She must be looking at me as I am looking at her. I press my lips to the hole. "I can't help you. Keep digging, Lisa," I say, my voice scratchy like nails on tin, then realize that Lisa may not be her name. She may not even be female. "Keep digging," I repeat, and feel compelled to add "Lisa," sure she'll understand when I explain.

I am so excited, I can't keep still. Despite my resolve, I use the other end of my pen to try to loosen some of the mortar from my side. I work for a long time, building up a sweat, shattering the plastic, feeling weak from hunger and long-term dissipation, but I finally pry out a small chunk and feel extremely proud of myself.

I carry on as long as I can until I drop from exhaustion. "I'm going to take a nap," I say into the hole, now forehead size and shape. Lisa looks through again at the same time as I do. I back away to let light in, but the brick is so dense, she's all shadows and my eyes are blurring anyway. "I'll be back," I assure her. "Sleep will make me stronger."

I dream of her, soft skin, porous, lungs breathing, warmth, wetness inside as my tongue slides into her, as she writhes and squirms beneath me, responsive. Alive.

When I awake, the hole is the size of a human head. I push my face against it and call "Hello!" There is no response from the other side. I feel panicked. Maybe she's asleep. Or, dead, the gloomy part of me thinks. No, I refuse to accept that.

The hole is large enough that I can pick up the metal chair and use the leg as a hammer. It's awkward, but better than nothing. I pound at an angle and large chunks of weakened cement come away from the edges. After a long time, I have a space big enough to get my head and shoulders through.

The room on the other side is just like mine. On the bed, back to me, is a form under the blanket. "Wake up!" I call out. "Please. Lisa, don't leave me." She does not stir. The dread crawling up my body deflates me. I cannot bear the idea that I am completely alone here.

I crawl to my bed and jot these notes before IT comes.

Sounds wake me. I feel delirious. Light-headed. Beyond hunger. Sick from despair. I look across at the hole. It is now large enough to crawl through. I hear familiar noises. They coalesce into the hopeful sound of someone breaking through the wall. Lisa!

I rush to the opening and look through. It's so dark, but I think I see legs. Yes, she is female. I knew it! I feel overwhelmed with joy and sadness. Great tears gush out of me along with a string of anguished wails. She stops working. She must have bent down, because the hole is obscured; I stand up and step back from the wall so she can get through.

Whatever happens, I think, I will not be alone.

There's some comfort in that. No, for me that is all comfort.

Cement dust sprinkles from the opening. I reach out to help her but freeze. Something is familiar, but my mind just will not make the connection. She lifts her face as she emerges from the womb and glares at me. Blank red eyes, piercing, blinking. Dead silver skin. Robotlike efficiency. Nurse's whites. Fierce inhuman hunger. Pincer raised like a metal clamp, like a weapon.

I have learned to accept my situation, as de Sade would recommend. My acceptance gives me energy. And I find I have all I need.

Now that my quarters have doubled in size and, thanks to Lisa, there are two new pens and extra rolls of toilet paper, I have more room for my writings, which I no longer hide.

Thank God Lisa is still with me, although she sits in the corner most of the time, immobile, silent. Deactivated, she is not the lively companion I envisioned. Still, I value her company. There's someone to talk to. I've taken over her room, and she's in mine. A change is as good as a rest, I tell her patiently, but she only stares at me, her once-brilliantly-lit red eyes now dim like rotting raspberries; she stares at me as though I'm crazy.

Time has lost its grip on me, which is another benefit to having a friend. But Lisa is so unlike me, I fear for her at times. When IT comes, when IT takes her, she is so passive. IT takes both of us at the same time, and this three-way joining allows me to observe what is happening, and that allows me to stay conscious. Alan was right: watching the sex act is far better than being involved in it, for watching IT fuck Lisa, I find, stimulates me more than I could have imagined, so that as IT fucks me, I am taken to greater and greater heights, like the peak of a glacier, where I freeze into eternity. I wonder if watching IT fuck me stimulates Lisa in the same way.

Sometimes I get mad and tell Lisa she should be more active and enjoy herself more. I don't think she ever has orgasms, but then she's not really as strong as I am, either physically or emotionally, and I've had to accept her limitations as well as my strengths. Nor is she the tower of optimism and energy I imagined. Still, if she hadn't dug through the tunnel, we wouldn't be together. HE wouldn't be satisfied. And, after all, we are here to sate HIM. I understand now. Lisa taught me that. WE look forward to HIS visits.

The lights are dimming. Metal scrapes against metal. My nipples harden, and my juices begin to flow. Giving and receiving are sacred responsibilities. The nadir of our days, the apex of our nights. I must hurry and assume a position where I can be fucked and watch Lisa being fucked at the same time. So we can all enjoy this sustenance.

Trainslapper

Marc Levinthal

When the time came, she put the Disremembering on the boy Henry, who was nearly a man.

She left him, in accordance with the Way, in the city, on a busy street corner. As she turned and stepped away quickly, eyes brimmed with tears, she prayed to the All that he would have the wits to survive, and to find his way back, to remember just enough.

Let him remember the light, she prayed.

If he remembers the light....

It smelled like rain in there, like rust, like the sea. He could see the moon between the tracks, half-hidden by luminous clouds boiling around it, stirred by high breezes.

He lay on his back, tucked up under a girder on the bridge south of Shit's Creek below Colvin Avenue. There was about two feet between him and the railroad ties in front of his face.

He inhaled deeply, exhaled. A rumble was starting up under his body. An electric buzz started in his balls and radiated outward toward his stomach, his pelvis, his thighs. A low roar was building.

There was angel light coming, and three microtonal bursts like the howl of a beast from another dimension, trapped in the thick night air. Pistons heaved, wheels pounded the tracks, shrieking metal on metal. He shuddered as several tons of steel banged and clacked over him, his erection bulging against tight jeans.

He shook in a rhythm with the pounding and shrieking, his shudders matching those of the vibrating bridge —building, undulating, he was nearly convulsing now, as shadows and light from above raced across his sweaty face, rictus grin. His body was covered with sweat by now, lubricated, greased like the axles and bearings that shook there, pounded, inches from his face....

Henry felt the power coming in, rolling pulses through the steel beam under his back—the power to move him up and out, the power in the light that strobed through the tracks, saturating all, moving all with it.... The electric buzz grew as he arched his hips forward, grinding the bulge in his pants upward, toward the locomotive and the shifting, growing light, building the angel light...

...and with one final spasm, he ejaculated, as the

last car rolled away, the cacophony diminishing, fading into the nocturnal ambience. The fine rush hung there in his spine, nerve buzzes diminishing slowly, slow denouement as if they were the tendrils of some rare fragrance unraveling....

The angel light had remained, for just a little while, and he basked in its brilliance until it faded, until sleep came.

In the morning, he climbed down to the bottom of the bridge. He took his pants off and removed his underwear, wiped himself off with them, and tossed them away. He put his pants back on and climbed back up the hill to his lean-to.

His shelter was back up in the trees, far enough in to be hidden, but close enough to the tracks to have a good view.

Something small smacked him in the head. He spotted an acorn rolling down the slope.

"Hey! Trainslapper!" A snotty-looking boy, about ten, peered through the branches. "Freak!"

He heard giggling and multiple small bodies scrambling for safety.

"Fuck you! Punks!"

All the neighborhood kids called him "Trainslapper." His real name was Henry, but they'd all seen him staring at the trains and slapping himself in the head, and that was it. He'd tried to tell them "Henry," but they'd laugh and run.

Henry dug the blue three-ring binder out of his knapsack and walked up the dirt path that rose behind the shopping mall. He headed for the gas station on the corner so that he could clean up, as best as he could.

The library was just down the street from the Mobil station, on Delaware Road. Henry liked this one—a modern split-level affair with lots of books in it, lots of train books. He liked to read about the old ones, the steam locomotives especially.

He walked in the front door, up the stairs past the old lady at the front desk. She glared at him coldly, but she was always nice enough to him. Always let him stay as long as he wanted to and helped him if he had a question. Henry guessed she just didn't approve of his untidy beard and matted hair, his wrinkled clothes.

The section on trains had a few books that he hadn't seen yet, one on the history of railroads. He pulled it off the shelf, opened it, his pulse racing as he took in the pictures. He looked up, stared into space, imagining, as the eighteenth-century inventors had, a network of trackless highways with their steam cars racing, white clouds billowing from the smokestacks.

Henry grabbed a few more books off the shelf and went to sit at one of the study tables in the middle of the room. He opened up the *History of Railroads* book and began leafing through it again.

"Railroads."

He looked up. He thought he'd heard someone say

"railroads," but then he heard stuff sometimes, and there wasn't always somebody there saying it. He put his nose down into the book again.

"Been on one."

This time he noticed this weird, skinny young woman down at the far end of the table. She looks kind of like Olive Oyl, he thought. Kinda dirty, too. Huh. She wasn't looking at Henry, she was looking at a *Highlights* magazine for children, the kind commonly found at a dentist's office.

He started to read again, a chapter about Sadi Carnot in France in the 1820s.

"A TRAIN."

Henry looked at her. Now he was sure she'd said it.

"Hey," he said, louder than he should have, "You been on a train? Wanna talk about it?"

The woman looked at him, stuck her tongue out, made a disgusted face. Then she was back to "Goofus and Gallant."

"Good. 'Cause I'm trying to read here." He gave himself a light slap on the face, as if to punctuate.

The next night, he didn't go anywhere near the tracks, just listened to the unearthly tones and traced the glow of the angel light. He knew it wouldn't linger even a little bit if he went to the tracks, but it was beautiful just the same.

He saw that the glow came from a doorway, long ago, long before he could really remember. Henry saw

his own hands, tiny, clutching a small toy steam locomotive. The door was just slightly ajar and the light
poured down. And someone, someone was talking in
the glow, telling him about a wonderful place where he
belonged, where things didn't work the same way,
where you walked for a day while a hundred years
could go by like a row of freight cars over in this world,
where kids didn't call you "Trainslapper" and doctors
didn't call you "schizophrenic" and give you Clozaril to
make you gray, stop the voices, and stop caring about
the trains....

And the voice was very much like an angel's.

*She found the Mage in an alley, coughing bloody drool
onto his filthy rags. The woman roused him enough to
walk him down into the subway, past the attendant
drowsing in the predawn. They made their way back,
across and away from the tracks, into the secret place,
into the glow, into the Vault of the Thousand Candles.*

*She laid him down on soft skins, and began to
prepare him for his death, for the ancient rituals of
passage.*

*He murmured and twitched to his Voices as she
sewed shut first his eyes, then his mouth, using such
precision and tenderness that he felt nothing through
his delirium.*

*When the time came, the woman straddled him,
kneading his sex until it became hard enough to put
inside her.*

She took the Mage's seed as he passed, forever, to another realm, there in the angel light, as the trains rumbled behind her, behind the walls.

Henry walked down Delaware Road in the morning, munching on a honey bun and sipping on a cup of coffee he'd just bought with his coins from panhandling.

He was about to walk up the stairs of the library when he noticed the sound of a sick engine, close to him on the street, realizing that he'd been hearing it for a while without really paying attention. He turned and saw the weird woman sitting behind the wheel of a decrepit '78 Mercury station wagon. It was filled with junk: clothing, newspapers, paper bags containing various inscrutable contents, a thermos, cardboard boxes holding glass jars. He watched a cockroach flit behind a sneaker. There were two dirty cats sleeping on top of the heap, with about a quarter-inch of clearance to the roof. There was barely enough room for her to steer and work the pedals.

It dawned on Henry that she'd been following him all the way down the street. He looked at the car, looked up the stairs, looked back and forth a couple of times, and smacked himself on the chin. The woman just stared straight ahead, forming words with her mouth. Finally he just plodded up the stairs.

He stayed until early afternoon, memorizing sections of one book or another desultorily. He pored over pictures of steam engines, cowcatchers, and various caboose interiors. Sometimes he opened the binder and took some notes. Sometimes, when he was sure nobody was looking, he'd touch and rub himself under the table as he looked at the pictures.

Finally, as the shadows began to lengthen in the silent room, Henry picked up his binder, stood up, and walked up past the old lady librarian. "Good-bye," he said to her as he passed.

She glanced up, then back down at the stack of books in front of her.

Henry opened the heavy glass door and saw the Mercury, still idling in front of the library. He speculated about whether or not the young lady had been driving around the block, or had actually been parked in front of the library all of this time, starting the engine occasionally. It seemed unlikely that she'd sat for the entire time with the car idling. He wondered about how she paid for the gas; she didn't strike him as being very employable.

He went up past the car, moving warily down the sidewalk as if he were holding a pit bull at bay.

"Ride," she said, out of nowhere, not looking at him.

Maybe she wasn't really speaking to him, Henry thought. "What?" he managed to grunt.

"Want one?" Now she did glance at him for a second, expectantly.

Henry peered into the station wagon, speculating. "Well, where the hell am I gonna sit?"

She turned to the passenger side, and deftly, miraculously began to move and fit clutter into the area where the backseat was buried. The two cats shifted, mewling complaints and licking themselves.

Henry edged around the front of the car, tried to open the door, which stuck. She had to give it a kick from the inside, then it popped open with a jolt. He climbed in, moving newspapers and cardboard aside, pushing space for his feet to go into.

He didn't say anything for a while, and she just drove.

"Y'know," he said, after a bit, "you never did ask me where I wanted a ride to." Punctuating "to" with a smack to his chin. "And I don't know who you are, either." Waiting for her to speak. "My name is Henry."

"You like the trains," she said.

"Well, lady, I love the trains," he said, looking at her sideways, them back to the road, which the woman was navigating precariously. "Trains have magic. The locomotive *moves*. You might say it is a window to other modes of thought, other states of consciousness. You might say the endless track is a conduit to parallel times, other dimensions. You might say."

She was mumbling to herself again.

Henry gripped the seat as she turned a corner too fast, almost lifting onto two wheels, tires squealing. He looked at her sideways again. "You ever seen Popeye? You know, the cartoon?"

The mumbling stopped; she twitched a look at him.

"My name—my name is Audrey." She ignored the Popeye question. "Pookah and Felix are the cats."

"Well, I'm pleased to meet you, Audrey, and if you don't mind me asking again from another direction— just where the hell are we goin'?"

"Trains." Mumbling.

"Mweeah?" asked Felix.

The train museum was at the bottom of a big hill at the edge of Mendelsohn Park. The locomotives on display dated from as far back as the 1860s.

Luckily for the odd pair, admission was free. Henry gaped at the collection around him.

"Shit!" he exclaimed. "Excuse me, lady. I didn't know this was even here."

Audrey smiled at him quickly. Then the smile was gone. "I'm sorry I stuck my tongue out at you," she said. "I didn't know."

Henry squinted at her, overwhelmed by the museum, and by the idea of her stringing so many words together at the same time. He looked away, then squinted at her again. "You didn't know what?"

She twitched her head, birdlike, focusing on different spots in the air. "That you were a nice man."

"How would you know if I'm a nice man or not?"

"You are *a nice." "You are a nice man."*

She was twitching her head, her mouth wasn't moving.

She hadn't said anything. It was *them.*

Henry's little voices were back.

"Oh shit," he said, under his breath, and smacked himself on the ear.

A group of kids on a field trip marched by, double-file. They were being herded away from the two of them by their teacher, a slight black woman in her late thirties. She shot a wary glance at Henry.

"What's wrong?" Audrey asked.

"Nothing. 'Sokay."

"They're talkin'." She grinned.

"Who's talkin'? Whatayou know about it?"

"We're talkin' to ya, Henry. Talkin'. Tooya."

"I got voices. You gotta have 'em."

"Gotta?"

"Or you can't get back and forth right."

"Forthright."

Henry's voices shut up right then; it was a short episode. Sometimes it went on like that for days. It looked to Henry like Audrey did indeed have voices, too, now that he thought about it. Didn't look like hers ever shut up, or that she thought it was a particular problem.

He leaned against a tree, closed his eyes and took a few deep breaths. He felt her hand touching his, tentatively. Henry looked up at her. "Cats gonna be all right back there?"

Audrey nodded. "Window's cracked. They got food, too."

He'd seen her pour out some water for them from an old plastic bottle.

"Well, hell, then let's go look at the trains, I guess."

# # #

They ambled around the old steamers for a while, Audrey interested, Henry lit up from the inside with his fanatic glow most of the time, describing this or that feature on one or another of the great machines.

Finally the sun began to slow-dive, low in the orange sky, and it was time to go. They made their way back up the hill and began the struggle to open the driver-side door, the two cats cheering them on the whole time. After about a minute they succeeded, and climbed in.

They drove, mostly in silence, until it occurred to Henry that she was driving him to the wooded section of Colvin Avenue without him having told her where he lived.

"How do you know where to go?" he asked.

She blushed. "Know where you live." She looked out the window. "Seen you for a long time."

"You been spying on me?" He couldn't believe it.

"Not spying. Looking. I—wanted to be sure."

"Sure?"

"About the trains." She faced him. "About the Light."

Henry turned beet-red and started boxing his own ears. He seemed about to implode, go super-nova with embarrassment and shame.

"Henry! Stop! Wait. Please!" She tried to grab at his arms to make him stop hitting himself.

Finally she succeeded.

By then, the voices were all over him.

"I gotta go. They're back."

"Back to the shack." "back to the track to the backto."

Audrey looked sad. But like she understood.

She started to speak, but he cut in, waving his hands around. "I'm not really like other people. I'm sorry, Audrey, but it's like... My place doesn't exist—here. It's somewhere else, where the—the trains—" Smacking himself on the cheek. "Where—I can't even tell you about them. About the trains. I can't tell you." Slap.

Then he was out of the car, running. Back through the trees, back to the shack.

"Back to the track to the."

By the time he reached the tracks, he was frantic. The only way they were going to leave him alone was if he took them where they wanted to go, where he wanted to be. Henry knew that the big freight was going to be rolling through anytime now, and that he had to get under the track now, had to get into that place, down into the angel light.

He scrambled down the hill and climbed up under the bridge, right under the track, and waited, sweat starting to pour down his face, excitement building, the energy rolling up his spine.

"Into the light Henry." "Angel angel light."

He felt his erection pulsing against his belly, tightening, sending tender shivers through him.

Then—to his amazement—Audrey was there, sliding over on top of him, unzipping his fly, her tiny frame close against him. He felt her warmth as she slid herself down over his shaft, took him inside her, moved him into her. Together they began to slow-vibrate, two parts of one machine, each informing the other, one raising the other's energy higher, building, drawing in the force of the mighty machine that rolled over their heads, lost in the white noise and roar of the steel wheels, frequency rising, grinding together faster, the stripes of moving light binding with them, transporting them down into themselves and out of the world…into a hyperpulse of energy, infusing them, permeating everything as they came together, as the Dopplered whine of the train whistle shone out loud, panchromatic over them, singing the angel light.

And then he Remembered, remembered the door, remembered the lady, and—some old place that was so very hard to get to.…

Audrey held him, her arms tight around his neck, held him between her legs as the last train car rumbled over them, and the light caressed them, and bloomed.

"It takes two to make the Light stay," she whispered into his ear.

There was a power in the pattern of her life, the routine, which sustained her even in the midst of so much squalor and pain. The cycle of day into night into day soothed her, as she soothed the others she'd find.

She lived the way she did because she had to; her mind didn't operate in the same manner as those who dwelt fully in this plane.

The Bright Ones, who were once called the Faerie, often fell victim to the physical laws of this place; their minds, their physiologies were somehow different. They'd fall into themselves, forgetting. Half in and half out, her people always hung on the fringes, in the shadows of tall buildings, in catacombs beneath the cities.

The ancient code, the Way, demanded that those who began to forget must be allowed to forget, and that those who began to remember could be aided in their search for the truth, but could never be told the truth.

Those rare Bright Ones who were born into the world of men must suffer the Disremembering, until such a time as fate decided which world they really belonged to.

Few were allowed to take liberties with the law.

She was one of these few: she was a Finder.

She watched the city people by day, and looked for others of her kind: the sick, the lost. Sometimes, she'd bring them back with her for healing, for counsel, before blessing them, leaving them to continue their wanderings. In the evenings, she'd return to her retreat, to the Vault of the Thousand Candles, a between place, always filled with the Moving Brightness, the angel light, down in the bowels of the subway.

Though the centuries, she'd kept this rhythm, and had found comfort in it. But on the day she found the Old Mage, the rhythm changed forever.

# # #

As they lay together, Henry saw that it was true: the light had stayed. He peered up between the tracks and saw the Light, hanging in the air—liquefied moonglow, and in it, smaller lights, flitting back and forth, each with the form of a tiny human. As he watched, one of them hovered down between the tracks, sat on one of the ties.

"You!" Henry said, and recognized the imp immediately. It smiled a toothy grin at him, tipped its head.

It was one of his Voices.

"We hadda do that," it said. *"Haddado that—you couldn't see—see?"* It flew back to join its mates.

And he looked into Audrey's eyes, saw that she had changed: her ears were slanted back and slightly pointed, her face fuller, familiar yet alien, strong and wild. Her eyes were almond-shaped, deep blue. She kissed his mouth with full crimson lips, and then, smiling sweetly, raised his hands up to follow the curve of her breasts. She stretched, arching her back and twisting arms like a cobra, gave him one last squeeze and slowly eased her bottom up off him. She rolled over and took his hand, tugging at him to come out from under the tracks.

What he saw when they emerged was more a garden than a patch of woods. The track still ran through the middle of it, though the bridge was different, ornate and filigreed. He looked away from the tracks and saw a wide dirt path leading away through the riotous flora.

Henry noticed that the traffic noise from the street

was absent. Instead he heard the cries of strange birds, then silence. Then from far down the path he heard the deep, contented growls of large cats, the clinking of belled harnesses, and the wheels of a large carriage approaching.

He gazed through the crystal light at the variety of flowers and trees possessed of the same wild, alien beauty Audrey now had, and was struck with the certainty that he *knew* this place. This was the place the Lady—his mother—had spoken of, always, in her stories.

This was *his* place to find, and Audrey had helped him, in one of the many ways, to find it. Just as the Lady had for so many of their people.

And he knew that one day, as he traveled this land—maybe if he followed these tracks—he'd find a door, and that door would lead to the sad, beautiful room filled with light, and the rumbling of trains.

Brush Your Cares Away
or:
In Between the Sheets,
In Between the Molars

Bill Brent

Hiya, M. Christian and friends:

Just checking in right now—decided to hook myself up to your *Eros ex Machina* trip today for whatever part of it works. I dropped some fantastic acid a while ago, and now I'm up in my private little loft space, see? No one goes here, 'cept me...and whom I see fit to let in on a particular day, hear? Today it's just me and my cuuuute li'l electric toothbrush.

Eros ex Machina. Not so alien a concept. We are all sexual. We are all little heartbeat machines. And just like any good machine, I know when it's time to take care of myself. Depress the off-switch. Nap-time.

But then, at some point, I must emerge from my

nap-time. Pass along whatever sacred, secret truths that some poor schmuck is always trying to make a buck off of borrowing from me. I sure don't know what those secrets are. But, as the heavens know, M. Christian is one of those rare and gifted, inspirational individuals who always, shall we say, manages to give more than he gets? He is certainly no schmuck.

So it is with the grrrreatest of pleasure that I share with you today the secret truths I have been shown by the Ordenta Corporation.

The Ordenta Corporation manufactures exactly one product—the Ordenta. Its alleged purpose is to clean your teeth. Don't be fooled.

"What keeps all these people smiling?" pose the ads. "Ordenta!" Ahh, but if they only knew what was going on behind this special little device. The unique one that won't be confined by so limiting a label as "electric toothbrush." The name "Ordenta" stands alone, unsupported by adjectives and nouns, as proof of its very timeless, utilitarian invincibility.

I was given this little gift by my very sexy dentist (okay, so I paid for it—at the low, low price of just $79.95) because I was suffering from periodontal disease. Not very sexy. But, after a year, my teeth and gums have never been better, so I'm sold on the Ordenta.

Ordenta.

Reorganize the letters a bit, and it becomes *"aden-*

tro." Spanish for "inside." A clue? Most definitely. Come, let's see what's inside....

"Use me as a toothbrush," it states, just a bit too officiously on the package.

"Use me...."

As if. Sure, you could also use it on a nipple, a succulent clit, an angrily flared crown of swelling, captive dickbulb perhaps lashed to the mattress. But would you? Could you?

Sometimes I think that the greatest absurdity of human existence is our need to put each item into its appropriate category, department, box, drawer. All assignment of proportion to things.

When the potential of the sensual realm is infinite....

But let's start with the teeth, shall we?

One miraculous feature of this lovely device-that-refuses-to-be-called-just-a-lowly-electric-toothbrush is that it gets the damn things clean. I never feel ready to get it on until my teeth are clean. Clean teeth are *very* sexy, don't you think?

Fast-forward back to the loft. I've cleaned my teeth, I feel sexy. The cool and sticky feel of the 0.4 percent Stable Stannous Fluoride Gel on my cock is a delight, as always. I pick up the Ordenta, and with that ritual glimmering gesture, I foreshadow all that is to come.

The whirring of the little engine, repetitive massaging of little infinite universes all exploding in on each other and blossoming outward into an electric orgasm of paralytic ecstatic friggin' ecstasy. Prayer.

I really do like the whirring engine, but basically, it's a cheap job. I mean, it's great as far as the dental market, but it's pretty lightweight as far as the pro-vibro stuff goes. In other words, this ain't no Hitachi Magic Wand. Then again, maybe it's all in how you examine (or de-examine) lust. Here goes:

Whirrrrrrr.........

The dick is hard. The handle feels good in my palm. I've put on the special "braces" attachment. Forgot to mention that—this thing has about four different tips, but you can't really tell the difference on the flesh.

Grasping my cock firmly at its base, I slowly move it toward the Ordenta. I flinch momentarily, always worried that I'll be shocked at the roughness of the bristles. I'm not. But my cock has amnesia. It feels good, moving up and down the veins of my shaft, a bit ticklish around the crown of my cock, *very* ticklish across the piss slit and down the dickhead.

Now I put it first on the right nipple, then on the more sensitive left one. It makes me laugh because the centrifugal force of the device always grabs my nipple and sends it spinning around the tip, over and over. Wind-up nipples? It feels good, but it looks pretty fucking silly. Especially when I'm stoned on acid. I'm glad no one can see me right now. I think about the time that Mom walked in on me whaling away on my pole when I was sixteen. Very close call.

And I think about how we're all basically looking for the same exact thing.

All trying to find mother Nature, mother Comfort, mother Superior, mother MOTHER a place to let go of your cheap flesh long enough to enjoy it and purrrrr like this little engine little dental machine goes for a while puuuuuuuuuurrrrrrrrrrrrrrrr....

But where oh wherrrrrrrrrrr did we learn to eroticize the sound of our own million little whirring engines? All so independent? So self-contained? All still need, still feed on mother's milk. Electric juice. Animal or mechanical, we all need fuel.

Engines open me up to where our possibilities extend. Next. Little electric tongues, little muscles, little cocks, little cunts. Engines have been pushing the envelope for a long time now, and that envelope is sealed with bodily fluids. *Eros ex Machina* is about the pelvic thrust, that evolutionary push to the next frigging good step.

The little machine, it feels so good upon the earlobe ...secretly, that's the best spot. I know you'd rather hear a story about how great it feels on my dick, and how it made me squirt five times, but truthfully, the Ordenta gives me eargasms, not cockgasms. I love the little motor, whirring so close to my ear's inner shell. Inside, my head is vibrating with sound...my own little engine.... My brain is in flames. Ohhhhh...moan...whirrrrr... purrrr.... Little dental Ordenta engines pillowing me to one feathery climax higher than the last. On little engines our loftiest (sleaziest) thoughts and wishes reach their express delivery potential...love....

# # #

Now I am in the bathroom with the Ordenta, chewing on its bristles, and somehow *that* feels erotic, too. Those sexy teeth. Chewing on the bristles...how *human* that is, an animal urge...always the fleshly attempt to convert the mechanical into the more beastly, eh?

Did I forget to mention how good the damn thing feels when applied to its RIGHTEOUS purpose? Indeed, it is the finest dental instrument I have seen. Like a good lover, the Ordenta is gentle yet insistent.

It's about...what it all comes down to is this.... We can appreciate anything in its truly finest, most elemental components, only by chewing up its bristles—reducing it to its measliest bits.

Which will always be impossible.

We don't really *want* to know how things are constructed, we just want them to work. Examination is just a means to an end. What we want is the comfort of reliability—yes, damn it, we're cheap sluts—we'll even settle for the *promise* of comfort. Which is the tease that the electronic umbilical cord holds out to us, seemingly infinite. But we're a small planet, and our power supply only remains infinite as long as our ingenuity keeps up with new ways to harness it before it all runs out. If that should fail, then—COLLAPSE. Entropy. Orgasm. But isn't that inevitable? Things fall apart. Every story has an ending. The endless dance of constructo-destructo whirrrr. See, even the roots of those words: Constructo. Destructo. Tells you that since the Latin days, we haven't found a better way of saying it yet.

So what are we all waiting for this GODDAMNED DEMON, yes, ELECTRIC BEAST to deliver us from? What jaws of the inescapable unknown?

Demise. Now, technogeeks were the first to eroticize machines. And as every geek knows, no matter how far your passion transports you, you must still remember to hit the "save" button so that all traces of your existence here today will not be lost. But is that all that matters? I think not. I like to think I exist in some component far beyond my electronic trace.

Whirrrrrrrr.... I love the motors and engines that go humming through my life. But when I am given one, as did this dentist mine (so kind, so kind), must I respect it, worship it? Put it *only* to its *rightful* use? But why? I'm a good consumer. I *paid* for it. Is it not mine? Do I not own it now? Did I not purchase the blasted thing with mine own sweat? Mine own SWEAT, damn it? Is it not MINE yet?

Only as long as I pay the electric bill. Ownership is always conditional. And warranties always expire. No guarantee is infinite.

Still, the Ordenta is a lovely reminder that all of those nasty, painful trips to the dentist's chair couldn't have been so bad if he gave me such a nasty, delicious device!

The truth is that it's always you, baby. No matter what electronic dial, or device, or little comforting whirrrrrrr we can hook up in that elusive attempt to hang the goods somewhere else.

You are your own engine. This is what makes you respectable. Dangerous. Beautiful. Fiery.

Revel in your own glorious luminescence. And if that is enhanced for you by strapping on some device, you sure don't need my permission to go off and enjoy yourselves, OK?

That is what the little engines have taught me. Love is within yourself. All the rest follows from that. Trust your own little internal engine. It's what keeps you ticking....

Love,
Bill

Tripping

Jack Dickson

"My name's Mac and I'm a tripper."

A ripple of applause, punctuated by low "Hey, Mac"s.

In his pocket, strength-seeking fingers rubbed along metal. "It's been two years since my last trip." The ripple surged into a wave.

"Did eighteen months in rehab. Almost got sent down, but…" His voice cracked. Mac swallowed. "…ten weeks tomorrow I've had it—ten weeks, two journeys a day, five days a week and I've been…" Fingers rubbed harder at the talisman in his pocket. "…fine, so far."

Applause crashed over his head and broke around him. Someone stood up. Then someone else. He was surrounded by a storm of clapping, supportive hands.

Mac's face reddened. In his pocket, wetness flowed freely from ripped fingers. His legs began to buckle. With a slight nod of his head, he sat before he fell down.

After the meeting, he tossed the usual dollar into the usual box and took a coffee from the table. Eric, his sponsor, had noticed the bleeding, asked if everything was okay.

Mac had smiled the practiced smile and taken the offered handkerchief which now bound his gashed fingers. Sipping scalding instant, he scanned the room. He recognized few faces: addicts came and went like the seasons. His eyes lingered on a figure leaning against the back wall.

Late twenties, maybe thirty. Gangly. Long limbs encased in loose-fitting nylon. Cropped hair. More facial piercings than Mac had seen in a while. Wild eyes bounced off his, then darted around the room. Could be a skim-freak—definitely pale enough—or an acid-casual: AA handled every kick in the book...and some that weren't.

Mac remembered his first time at a meeting. What was it Eric said about helping yourself by helping others? He took another sip of the coffee and strolled over. "Hey, there!"

Cropped head flicked up.

Mac extended his bandaged hand. "Rennie MacIntosh—call me Mac."

Callused, work-gnarled fingers gripped his. "Chev."

Tension pulsed from the man's knuckles into his own. "Unusual name…"

Wild eyes glinted, lit up from inside. "Short for Chevrolet…" Fingers tightened, pressing into the bandage. "One of the greatest achievements of twentieth-century combustion engineering…" He tried to pull away. Couldn't.

"…pure power…"

The coffee cup fell to the floor. Mac wanted to pick it up. Couldn't. He dragged his eyes from blazing irises and stared down at their linked hands. Blood from the cuts was oozing through the handkerchief, dripping onto hard, rough skin.

"…pure energy…"

Mac wrenched his fingers free. "Sorry…got to go." He walked unsteadily from the room. Outside, it took every shred of strength he possessed to go straight home.

In front, the stream of cars slowed to a surly crawl.

Mac focused on a nodding toy dog in the back window of the vehicle in front. The pink/white of a makeshift crash barrier flashed on the periphery of his vision. Under his hand, the plastic-coated knob of the gearshift quivered. Ten weeks of nothing, and now…?

…the car was too warm. He wound down the window, inhaling what passed for morning air on the freeway. And other smells.

Gasoline.

Oil.

The nodding dog lurched. Mac pressed his foot to the accelerator and inched forward. The approaching whine of the emergency services changed pitch. He wound the window down completely. Underneath gas and oil, something else. Not so much a smell as a taste.

He shifted into neutral, eyes moving from the nodding dog to the asbestos roofs of the warehouses which lined the left side of the freeway. Mouth open, he drew the odor onto his tongue and rolled it around. The siren dropped a semitone and sped past. Mac closed his eyes.

Furious honking from behind.

Eyelids shot open. He shifted gears, closing the gap between himself and the nodding dog.

Out of the corner of his eyes, chrome glinted through early morning smog. Like a wink, the gleaming shard invited his gaze. Mac stared straight ahead. Fingers tightened over the gearshift's vibrating knob. His right eyelid began to twitch. The leatherette under his back and ass was hot and damp.

Seconds dragged by, stretching into minutes that could have been hours. His stiffening cock ticked its way up the inside of his thigh.

"Fuckin' trippers, eh? No consideration for other people!"

Whiplash tingled down his neck. Mac stared through the open window at the back of the man leaning on his hood. Behind, other drivers had left their vehicles and were standing around, in loose groups bemoaning the inconvenience.

The man switched his gaze from the coned area of the freeway and scowled at him. "They're sayin' it's an illness now—can ya believe it? Some crap about cadmium-contaminated breast-milk! Fuckin' sick, all right—sick fucks, if ya ask me!" No one had. Mac stared at the scene to his right.

Two bemused drivers, shaken but uninjured. Three vehicles. Two at opposite sides of the road, hoods and radiators crumpled by impact with a road sign and a wall, respectively. The third was upside down, wheels still kicking like the useless legs of some shelled invertebrate. Rainbow liquid bled from a perforated gas tank and shimmered blue/pink in the cop car's revolving light. The trail snaked across tarmac, then split, trying to connect with each of its injured companions.

"Why do they do it, eh?" The face turned, blared into his.

Mac flinched. He knew the driver didn't really want answers. Which was just as well, because he didn't have any.

A single roar punctured his thoughts. The head of his cock nudged the buckle of the safely belt. Mac released the gearshift, unbuckled and scrambled out of the car. More drivers were moving toward the pink/white crash barrier.

Mac peered beyond two firemen holding chain saws to the source of the roar.

Blood-spidered hands gripped the shattered roof frame. A paramedic was attempting to apply a gauze pad to the gaping wound in a bare, blood-freckled shoulder. Two uniformed figures tried unsuccessfully to grab flailing legs which pumped and kicked like pistons.

The roar subsided into an agonized moan.

Mac felt the sound deep in his guts. His skin prickled as chain saws buzzed into life, hacking at already damaged bodywork and ripping the man from the arms of his metal lover.

The moan became a series of sobs, rising over the screech of disintegrating vehicle. Mac thought of the sound a ship made when breaking up in a storm. He stared at a sheen of gasoline which slicked pale, scarred skin. "There's the culprit! If I had ten minutes with one of them, one of those drivers, I'd—"

Mac screened out the end of the rant. Not a driver— not anyone who entered and left the vehicle at the beginning or end of each journey.

Not even a journey—not in the conventional sense.

A trip.

He followed the procession to the back of a waiting ambulance. The sobs were almost inaudible now, the sheened, naked limbs writhing less. Mac's eyes traveled down onto tarmac, and the remnants of a blood trail trickling its way into the iridescent pool at his feet.

Seconds before the cops managed to bundle the now-limp figure into the back of the ambulance, he glimpsed the face.

Under multi-pierced eyebrows, tears sparkled in Chev's bruising eyes. The smooth forehead was peppered with crushed glass, tiny punctures weeping red.

The pain of defeat trembled in Mac's guts.

The ambulance doors slammed shut. Tremors beneath his feet told him the wrecking-crew had arrived to dispose of the debris. Voice at his side: "Lock 'em up an' throw away the key, that's what I'd do!"

Shaking, Mac returned to his car.

He stared at the white-coated night nurse. "No, I'm not a relative, just a—" Friend? Acquaintance? Fellow sufferer? Brother-beneath-the-skin? Having rehearsed this speech all day, Mac cleared his throat and made way for the half-lie. "…er, but I was there at the…accident. I work with people like Chev."

"Well, you can't see him!" Harassed frown. "But at least we've got a name now—he's still unconscious, and his ID tag won't scan!"

Mac instinctively rubbed the titanium identification plate behind his own ear: the authorities had no idea that when they'd instituted mandatory tagging, they were giving a generation their first taste of body modification. And lust for metal. "He okay?"

"Apart from the coma?" A deeper frown. "Mainly superficial stuff—we'll patch him up, keep him here for a day or so…." Eyes flicked over his shoulder.

Mac followed her gaze to the two cops lounging against a Pepsi dispenser.

"Then he's not our problem anymore."

"If I can't see him, tell him Mac was here—and tell him I'll be back." The metal amulet was warm in his pocket.

He knew he should go to a meeting. Or phone Eric. Crawling on his stomach through mud and petro-chemicals, Mac listened to the distant barking of the wreckers' guard dogs.

Just once.

Just this once. It was a lie, and he knew it. There was no "just once." When the metal got back into your blood, you were a goner. Mac inhaled the stench of oil and grease and stared at the twisted heap. Security lights illuminated tall piles of kinked fenders and accordioned radiator grills. He crept forward, hands slipping in pools of sump oil.

Trips…lots of different trips.

He'd known a chick who could get wet only in new cars. The cops caught her in a Hyundai dealership at four in the morning, wouldn't believe she was only there to breathe in the smell. Couple of years later, GM and Ford caught on, started bottling the stuff to sniff in the comfort of your own home. Too late for Lisa: a six-to-ten for attempted auto larceny had turned her on to other pleasures.

Mac raised himself onto all fours, skirting a tower of buckled steering columns. Grease-monkeys, chrome-chasers, rust-ranchers: lots of different trips. Some got it up for interiors, others exteriors. Some didn't even drive...

...garage cases, sneaking down just to look and wank, once a week.

Mac edged past a pile of crankshafts. He thought about Chev's naked legs as the cops had dragged him from the wreckage, and the steel knee-pins which had twinkled in the sunlight. The man had at least two pounds of metal in him already. A total body tripper.

In the security lights' blind spot, Mac stood up and scanned the recent-arrivals' area, searching for the caved-in roof of a Peugeot 260.

And found it. The metal skeleton had been crumpled further by the wreckers' claws. Mac hoped the inside would be intact.

He laughed aloud.

The dogs barked once, then fell silent.

His own detachment surprised him. Two years ago, he'd been unable to pass a parking lot without getting hard. These days, he was driving one of the things, ten times a week, no sweat....

...Once a tripper, always a tripper?

Oily mud squelched under his feet. He walked over to the vehicle. The engine had been removed—Mac knew that. But if his instinct was right, there was life inside. He stuck his head through a jagged space, groping in the darkness. Fingers contacted with metal.

Cold metal.

Cold, hard metal.

The denuded hand brake was at an almost ninety-degree angle. Mac's balls tightened as he fumbled toward the shattered dashboard.

Dry. Crystalline. He raised shaking fingers to his lips and tasted...

...saltiness. Not blood-saltiness, though he could smell there was plenty of that around. Another more intimate, equally vital body fluid.

Mac's guts turned over. Licking dried spunk from his fingers, he closed his eyes.

Skinned metal rubbed his thigh.

His cock started to stretch inside his pants. Mac groaned, leaning back farther. He inhaled the smell of two spent life forces.

One drilled from deep in the ground.

The other fucked from deep in a man's balls.

Before he knew what he was doing, his pants were down and cold metal was pressing against his hole. Mac gripped the edge of the roof frame and began to gyrate. His fingers slipped a couple of times as he circled the hand brake, teasing himself. Readjusting his hold, he swung back, raising his legs and planting his feet on the dashboard. Crushed safety glass crunched under his boots. He hung there, suspended, then began to bear down.

His thighs spasmed uncontrollably. Mac stared through the shattered windshield into darkness as the hand brake pushed past his sphincter.

He hovered there, the first inch of hard, solid steel inside his ass. Mac savored the invasion, the way the muscle clenched around the cold shaft. He could feel the beveled finger indentations, feel his sphincter tighten around the first...then second...third...

...at the fourth finger-grip, Mac's right hand released the roof frame and grabbed his cock.

He was out of condition. The muscles in his left arm screamed as he used his feet to lever himself back up the hand brake...

...then down again. He closed his eyes, inhaling the freeway smell of blood and gas and sweat and spunk. Mac fucked himself harder and faster, jacking his cock as the steel shaft buried and reburied itself in his ass.

The car moved beneath him, grating and grinding. Mac blinked back another saltiness as the pain in his left arm became almost unbearable. His cock was agony, his balls knitting together....

He howled when he came, splattering the dashboard with another layer of milky liquid. And the wreckers' dogs howled with him.

He'd forgotten how easy it was, how plausible he could be. A phone call to Eric had resulted in their meeting for a drink. It had taken imagination to divert his sponsor's attention...

...and only seconds to slip the official ID from the pocket of Eric's jacket into his own.

Mac flipped the stolen wallet open at one of the two cops who flanked the door to Chev's hospital room. He watched sleep-deprived eyes register the Official Counselor's symbol, then blink him forward. Inside, the rhythmic bleep of a heart-monitoring device punched holes in a wall of silence. Mac stared at the inert figure.

Chev's pale face was almost gray against the white sheets.

Mac strode across the room and sat on the edge of the bed.

Beneath metal porcupines, eyes were closed. Mac counted the eyebrow piercings: six in each. Tiny slats running from left-to-right in one, right-to-left in the other. He was pleased the medics had at least learned not to try to remove the metal. His own nipples and foreskin were a mass of numb scar tissue, after eighteen months in rehab, the doctors believing out-of-body meant out-of-mind.

He studied the lip piercings at each side of Chev's mouth. Mac shivered at this tripper's alliance with the trip. Nothing hidden, nothing shrouded in shame—like something parents thought their kids would grow out of.

He glanced at the door, then beyond to a uniformed sleeve which was just visible through the Plexiglas panel. Now tripping was a Code One Offense. There would be no rehab-alternative for Chev...

He stared down at the unconscious figure.

...not that rehab would do any good.

During his own therapy, his caseworker had shown him endless pictures of naked women, naked men, naked children, rutting animals. After a year of trying to will himself hard, Mac had finally succeeded....

If only the medics had realized it was the '56 T-Bird behind the well-muscled black guy which was responsible for his eventual erection. He laid a damp palm on Chev's glass-pocked forehead.

Eyebrows darted toward hairline. Eyelids sprang open. "Hey! What ya...?" Panicked pupils darting. Shoulders and chest straining up from the bed. Then eyebrows V-ing in suspicious recognition.

Mac withdrew his palm. "Keep quiet—the longer you're unconscious, the longer the cops gotta leave you here."

The pale body sank back onto paler sheets. Heart monitor stuttered, then resumed its tracking.

Mac stood up, moving round to the other side of the bed, blocking any view of Chev from the door's Plexiglas panel.

"What you want?" The suspicion remained.

Mac's guts turned over. "Listen, I can—"

"What's it to you, man? What do you care?" Mouth scowled.

Adrenaline shot through his veins. Chev was right: what was it to him? He had a new life now, a normal future of nine-to-five with a nice pension at the end—a future filled with meetings and Eric's ever-reliable, unquestioning support. He stroked the chain of stitchclips in Chev's right shoulder. "Let me help you."

"Save your sermons, man—I don't need your help...."

"You've not got a lot of choice—me or the cops."

The lip piercings curled into a sneer. "I'll take my chances, thanks!" Chev twisted away.

Mac's cock was throbbing against the fly of his pants. He focused on the jagged metal teeth surrounding the gash just above Chev's left buttock. "I can get you out of here. I can get you a car. I can show you a couple of tricks...."

Chev turned his head.

Mac stared into glittering eyes. "...you need an alternator connected to the transmission—that'll cut out the engine when you reach the desired speed—and an extra gas tank, maybe two...." He was dizzy, light-headed as blood fled from his brain and rushed to his already-swollen cock.

"That works?" Chev's eyes shone. "I mean, I've heard guys talk about..."

"I almost scored, but I was alone.." Mac frowned. "That was my mistake—yours, too. It's got to be a—"

The head shook slowly. "I'm strictly a two-way man."

"Let me be there—what you got to lose?"

Chev pushed himself up and leaned on an elbow.

Mac stared at the bulge which was tenting the sheet just above Chev's groin and pressed home the advantage. "You can't do it without me." Bandaged hand groped for bandaged hand. Mac lowered his head and kissed steel sutures.

A low moan. Bloody fingers squeezed his.

# # #

Mac's brain was working so fast he could hardly speak. He'd lain awake all night, then called in sick as soon as the switchboard was manned.

Oh, he was sick all right—a sick fuck, just like they'd always said.

Getting the car was easy—hell, he owned one, didn't he? Body-Shop Johnny was surprised to see him. And curious. Two thousand dollars had considerably diminished both responses. Mac had left the list of modifications, with strict instructions the car be ready by midnight.

Getting Chev past his cop guard and out of the hospital wasn't going to be quite that easy.

Mac smiled at the night nurse. "Sorry to be so late tonight." He sat the small carryall blatantly on the counter.

She returned the smile this time. "Five minutes, then—the doctor'll be round at ten."

Mac nodded benignly. "Ah, good—I hoped to have a word with his consultant!" He smiled and walked on. The cops barely acknowledged his presence as he opened the door and slipped inside.

Chev lay on his back, the sheet lowered to waist level.

Mac could see the shoulder wound was healing nicely: more skin bonding with more metal. He sat on the side of the bed, between Chev and the door. His voice was low. "Disposable slippers, surgical mask, and cap are in the bag. Don't say anything. Just follow me."

He spent the next ten minutes moving furniture and exploring metal-meshed flesh with his tongue.

If the doctor thought it strange the segregation screen was in place around the bed, he made no initial comment...

...and no further comment, after one swift blow rendered him unconscious.

Luckily, the surgical greens were a good fit.

Luckily, two cops and a receptionist only registered an addiction counselor and a doctor leaving the room.

Mac knew luck had little to do with it.

The metal was in their blood.

Body-Shop Johnny's workmanship was as reliable as ever. Mac closed the hood. On the other side of the car, Chev was tearing off the baggy green shift and pants. Mac stared at the scarred, bruised body then dragged his eyes beyond.

He'd driven to a long-abandoned feeder road—close enough to smell other vehicles, distant enough to avoid detection. It had taken all his concentration to stop Chev grabbing the controls and tripping right then and there. A quarter of a mile away, the city's main freeway streamed with motor life. Mac turned.

Chev was inches away, his damage-modified body-work strong and glistening in the headlights.

Mac's balls were sweating. He forced himself to look. Even in semidarkness, he could see the darker hollows in Chev's thighs, where gearshifts and steering columns had impacted over the years. Titanium winked at him from the tibia pins. Mac groaned, wanting to fall to his knees and nuzzle the implants. His eyes came to rest on the wiry V of hair between bruised thighs and the half-hard member nestling there. Mac stretched out one hand, touching the shoulder wound. The other met the smooth metal of the car's vibrating hood.

Fingers on his cheek told him Chev was doing the same.

Three skins.

Three hearts.

A frisson of expectation glimmered over his body. He withdrew his hands and began to undress. Jacket, pants, shirt and shoes fell away. He felt Chev's eyes on him. Mac stood naked, body hair erect as heady exhaust emissions surged into his nostrils.

A three-way. He'd waited a lifetime for this.

Chev was leaning over now, both hands clamped against pulsing metal. Lip piercings contacted with the hood in scraping kisses.

Mac moved behind Chev's body and edged between splayed thighs. Vibrations resonated up through the fleshy conductor into his own tissue. Fingers resting on titanium sutures, his cock brushed Chev's ass, the sensitive head a second contact with the power source.

Chev moaned more loudly, face pressed side-on to the hood. Metal porcupines shivered against each other. The moan lowered in pitch, became a hum which hovered in unison with the life force beneath the metal skin. Mac heard the tone, felt it deep in his guts. His cock trembled, his asshole spasmed in rhythm with the timbre. He opened his mouth and let the note escape into the night.

Chev pressed back against him, hard asscheeks pulsating with the sound.

Mac allowed his cock to stroke Chev's quivering pucker, then wrenched himself away and pulled open the driver's door.

Body-Shop Johnny had done a good job.

He fingered the straps of the double body-harness —reinforced polymer silica. No chain saw could cut through that. A voice in his ear: "Let's do it—do it now!"

Mac glanced past a cropped head to the road in front.

Chev was facing him, suspended just above the driver's seat. One leg brushed his.

Mac's thighs spanned the root of the hand brake. He could feel engine tremors shooting up through the vibrating stick and into his tight balls. He stared at their two cocks, stiff with expectation, then at the projectile which stuck up between them.

Chev's breath on his forehead, Mac shifted into first.

The car roared its annoyance.

Mac pressed a bare foot to the gas, increasing the sound. He raised his face to Chev's, fingers gripping the metal shaft between their legs. Another hand on his.

The lip piercings were inches away from Mac's mouth. Metal curled into a smile. Cock pulsing, Mac leaned forward and tasted adrenaline. Ten fingers tightened on the hand brake. Beneath, the car was barely held in check.

Two hands began to pull as two mouths continued to kiss. On the periphery of sensation, Mac felt the double alternator kick in. The harnesses left them both a free arm. He encircled Chev's hard, scarred waist, drawing the man closer to the quivering shaft.

The engine was screaming now, begging for release. Mac yanked the hand brake up another inch. Chev's mouth gnawed at his; he longed to gnaw back, but knew he had to concentrate, pace the act. The passion itself would last nanoseconds, if they were lucky. Anticipation was all.

Mac had made this trip in his head so many times. He didn't need to check the instruments to know the speedometer was about to hit ninety. His eyes flicked open.

Chev stared back, pupils swollen.

Mac noticed the irises for the first time: a ring of iridescent petrol-blue, all but eclipsed by the oily depths of ever-expanding pupil. Strapped between the front seats of a vehicle he had owned less than three months, staring into the eyes of a man he had known less than forty-eight hours, Mac felt complete. Almost.

Above Chev's eyes, twelve shards of metal quivered. Then V-ed. A harsh laugh. "Enough shit—let's trip!"

The smell of burning fossil fuels and sweat hot in his nostrils, Mac threw back his head and released the hand brake.

# # #

They were discovered two weeks later, by a couple in a Winnebago who had taken the wrong exit. According to the medical examiner's report, the heat of the post-impact inferno—caused mainly by the extra three gas tanks—had fused what was eventually identified as the bodies of the two male passengers with the surrounding metalwork of the vehicle.

Separation for the purposes of interment was not deemed feasible.

Wearing Her
Don't-Talk-to-Me Face

Maxim Jakubowski

The machine stopped.

My heart skipped a beat as the screen went dead, the colors of writhing flesh, sweat, and leaking secretions disappearing in an instant from the glass surface, while their transmuted mental images lingered on inside my head a moment longer.

I looked around me, searching for answers.

Had my foot somehow slipped, the carpet been moved, disturbing the tangle of the wires, interrupting the vital electrical connection? I didn't think so. I had been sitting there, quietly, trousers down to my ankles, the only movement in evidence the rhythmic up-and-down of my hand over the hard velvet softness of my cock.

Now detumescing.

Bad timing. The coffee-colored stud was about to pierce Jackie's anal aperture, always the pornographic moment which affected me most and invariably triggered the inevitable relief and unstoppable flood of pleasure to course like molten lava through my own body. Both men had already brutally serviced the young woman's genitals, and the hard-core tape was now winding through to its final stage of sexual humiliation.

This particular film was no different from any other. The roving reporter with his ever-active video camera had approached this girl in a large, teeming railway station, sweet-talked her into joining him and two friends in the rented apartment they happened to have close by. Something about auditioning her for a part as a dancer in a rock video. She said she was eighteen and came from South London.

The men's unctuous patter was unconvincing, and Jackie seemed aware of the fact. But then it was either that or a boring afternoon up in Southgate with her girlfriend, trawling the bars or burger joints where all the men were kids and pimply with few exceptions. They had served her a martini and flattered her no end, although she knew all too well her breasts were too small. She had stripped down to her panties and white leggings. Then, what the hell, she had allowed Ben, the one with the purring camera, to slide the thin material down and unveil her pubes. They had marveled at the fact she was partly shaven down there. Made her feel wet to be the object of the strong and lustful gaze of three men. Like being onstage. Her eyes were gray, or maybe blue. The technical qualities of the videotape were just about average and the only color that felt right was the pallor of her skin. She looked very young. Hair light brown, slightly on the auburn side, with a delicate fringe, thin but pulpy lips, a small nose, just like an overgrown schoolgirl. Which she must have been until very recently.

The combination of innocence and potential sluttishness that got to me every time.

To my heart, my mind, my cock.

Over the years, I had seen most of the so-called classics of porn, from *Deep Throat* to the 1990s pretentiousness of Michael Ninn's poor-man's special effects or the sheer mechanical and joyless vulgarity of so many others; they had all, in their day, given me a rise and a cheap thrill.

But the amateur tapes, where the women were no longer on first-name terms with corrective surgery or silicone implants, were now my stamping ground. These were women I could recognize, women who could break my heart in a thousand ways as they went about their life in the world of sex, flinching when the come spread over their faces and into their hair, moaning with pain as their tormentors impaled and stretched them to unknown limits, tears coming to their eyes as the shame mingled with the pleasure and the horror and the silent eye of the nearby camera captured it all in inglorious color.

Jackie was one of those.

As she submitted herself impassively to the formulaic gang bang, I could touch myself to the music of her sadness and orchestrate my crescendo to the sound of her small voice moaning under the attack of the unholy-sized cocks battering her insides. Holding back for the best moment. When, I knew, they would turn her over, position her knees down on the carpet, facing the leather couch where one of the men would sit, thighs apart, his jutting cock still slick from her inner juices, ready for her mouth, while the other would crouch over the rise of her arse, and position himself, ready to break down her tight, final barrier.

And the VCR malfunctioned.

Leaving me high and dry. Unrequited.

I pulled my trousers up, knowing all too well what a figure of ridicule I must look like to some invisible, and hopefully nonexistent observer. Crawled my way across the dark gray carpet toward the machine with its red and green winking lights. It was still on. I pushed the PLAY button. Somehow the remote-control gizmo had gone walkabout a fortnight earlier. There was a click inside the VCR's guts, then a whirr and the sound of the video rewinding at high speed. Maybe there was something wrong with the tape. I'd bought it in some back-street shop in the Frankfurt red-light zone on a business trip the week before. There was never any guarantee with these sorts of dodgy purchases. I suppose I'd been lucky customs hadn't asked to examine my luggage on the way back.

Click again as the tape completed its rewind. Maybe it was just some ordinary glitch, I reckoned. I was never that good with bloody machines, always scared stiff the computers would eat up my best stuff forever. I extended my finger gingerly. PLAY.

I retreated to the comfort and softness of the settee as the tape began unrolling again. First the ads for American 1-800 lines. I undid my belt, stroked my cock gently through the thin fabric of my boxers. The clumsily letraset credits followed, right on schedule. I relaxed. Good, I didn't mind seeing this one again from the beginning; there was something about young Jackie's face and voice that made the anticipation of her defilement so fucking exciting.

The man behind the camera greeted his two arriving studs as they walked past the barrier. Cameron, the sweet-faced black one, and Valentino, the tall half-caste with the high forehead. The Victoria Station crowds milled around them, an occasional, curious glance towards the camera. The men joked among themselves. Soon Jackie would be seen moving across the concourse and would catch their attention, and quickly become the object of their seduction.

My cock rose to half-mast in anticipation. All ready.

A woman's shape detached itself from the busy background of the railway station, still out of focus but approaching the camera and the trio. The colors appeared wrong. I remembered Jackie wearing a short woolen dress with red and white stripes, above her white leggings. This woman seemed taller somehow and wore a white, short-sleeved top and a flowing skirt of rainbow colors. I squinted at the screen while my hand still distractedly went about its business of arousal.

The camera captured the approaching young woman in the very center of the picture. This was not Jackie. No way.

My hand interrupted its mechanical movement.

Eddie.

No.

This wasn't possible. She hadn't been on the tape when I had watched its first half earlier. I would have noticed. I caught my breath. She walked along the station, under the giant clock, wearing her little-girl-lost and don't-talk-to-me face, with long purposeful strides, then came to a halt by the news agents, looked around a few times, as if she were waiting for someone who wasn't yet there. I thought that once it had been me she had waited for in this very place, before that fateful weekend in Eastbourne. Strange I hadn't noticed this part of the tape first time around. Soon, the camera would move away from her and Jackie would come into the shot and the so-called piece of porn cinema vérité would resume. The voices of the men were commenting on the tall, dark-eyed blonde. Speculating. The camera approached her as they did.

"Waiting for someone, love?" the cameraman asked Eddie.

This was ridiculous, I thought.

But the videotape in the machine had been there all the time. It hadn't been switched, just rewound somehow.

Impossible.

She answered them:

"I'm expecting a friend, but I don't think he's going to turn up, the bastard."

It was Eddie's voice. I could have recognized it in the dark.

Jackie had said the same. Almost. But the friend she was awaiting had been a she, and Jackie hadn't said "bastard."

"Why are you filming me?" Eddie asked.

"He's always doing that," Valentino said. "Loves beautiful girls. We're impresarios. Looking for dancers for a video shot. You're really tall," he added. "You must be a great dancer."

"Not really," Eddie answered, visibly intrigued by the men's attentions.

Dread surrounded me. My cock had shriveled back to its normal size, or even less.

I knew what was about to come.

The men kept on chatting her up. All about the video. How it could lead to a part in some independent movie. The apartment nearby their producer had left at their disposal. How she looked really good. How they were so sure she could win through a short audition. She was such a natural in front of the camera, already, anyway. They had spun the same sweet words to Jackie, and she had followed them to the fuck pad and its mirrored walls.

My stomach knotted up in pain as the rigmarole unraveled with its fixed inevitability. I felt like shouting out to them, "No, Eddie, don't listen to them, don't believe a word they say. They're just pornographers who want to get you into a porno loop that other men can wank, too, to their heart's desire. Don't. Please, don't!"

I rushed over to the VCR machine and tried to switch it off.

No go. The controls would not respond any longer.

Blood rose to my brain. I could no longer hear the familiar dialogue as I witnessed Eddie following the men out of the station. There was an editing cut here. Next, she was sitting on a couch between the two studs sipping a Coke and rum. Jackie, I recalled, had taken a sweet martini.

I slumped back, powerless, my drooping cock against my thigh, too depressed to pull my underwear up as the film unrolled at a leisurely pace.

Still complimenting her on her grace and beauty, they asked her to stand. Yes, definitely a dancer's posture, they remarked in unison. Requested her to take her top off. Dancers have to wear these skimpy outfits, you see. Her nipples would be visible. Had to see her shape. She proceeded slowly.

More admiration. Wonderful small boobs, great in a dancer, they explained. The cameraman asked to touch them. Twisted one nipple, then another. Whistled, as the two others watched on. So sensitive.

Eddie now only wore her black knickers.

"Turn around, love, so I can film you."

The camera glided around her, alighted on her rear.

"Great arse," one of them said.

"Really great," another commented.

Eddie held her hands up to her breasts shyly.

"So demure."

"So natural."

"Let's see the rest," one of them asked.

She hesitated. A bit late at this stage, I reckoned. You bitch, why did you follow them to the flat? Three men, you should know what to expect!

She bent to slip the final piece of underwear off. The camera moved to her rear and caught the indiscreet crack of her arse as she stepped out of the garment. The camera revolved again and filmed her pubic area.

"Wonderful," they said.

"A real blonde."

"So curly."

I felt sick, watching the obscene spectacle develop.

I suppose I could had left the room without watching the ensuing festivities, but my body had slumped back into the deepness of the chair and I knew I was incapable of moving away, my eyes glued to the television screen, watching the wondrous whiteness of Eddie's beauty, the shocking intimacy of her flesh, the secrets of her anatomy that had once been mine and that I had betrayed so badly as the two studs and the roving silver-tongued cameraman urged her on to infamy and I wretched over and over until there was nothing left to be sick with and the emptiness sunk into the sheer depths of me with the whole weight of the sky.

The cameraman pointed out how hard her beauty had made his two friends and beckoned her to caress their rampant cocks through the material of the leather trousers they both sported.

"They're nice and hard, hey? Wouldn't you just like to taste them, girl?"

"Yes," Eddie mumbled.

My lost Eddie.

They were both impossibly long and thick, as she serviced them, her lips stretching to accommodate their respective bulks, crouched between the two standing men, sucking on one cock while jerking the other off with her hand. This went on forever, the camera lens detailing the suction, the friction, and the surrounding humidity as she labored on relentlessly, even once attempting to take both together into her mouth, encouraged all the time by the roving cameraman.

Finally, the filming narrator moved the camera away from her busy mouth and lowered it to her crotch, where he slipped a finger inside her.

"You're so wet," he remarked. "Wouldn't you like Cameron to lick you there? He's very good, you know."

"Yes, please," Eddie asked.

They allowed her to spread out on the couch and the black guy began licking away at her cunt, while she continued to service the other's cock at the opposite end.

She moaned.

She groaned.

Sounds that were all so sickeningly familiar and nostalgic to me.

Another eternity of depravity.

"Isn't it fun? What would you like now?" the filmmaker asked Eddie.

She looked down toward the black guy chewing and nibbling delicately at her sex and swollen lower lips, his oversize trunk of a cock dangling between his legs as he knelt below her on the couch.

"I want him…inside me."

Eddie, how could you? How can you?

"I thought you would. Come on, Cameron, do what the lady says."

He placed himself astride her and inserted his cock into her. It looked as if she couldn't take him. But she did. All of him. Still sucking avidly on Valentino's bulging member.

I was sick again. The bile rose from the very deep abysses of my soul. Yellow spittle lingered on my tongue. I closed my eyes as the tape continued unspooling inside the VCR and all over the large television screen.

But I couldn't do anything about the sound.

Having earlier relished Jackie's voluntary ordeal, I already knew the scenario all too well. In truth, not a particularly original one, as hard-core tapes went. One man would succeed another, fucking her so hard she would scream. Then each would sodomize her in turn, before the classic double-penetration sequence as they sandwiched her between them. Eyes still in darkness, I heard it all. The cries, the vulgar encouragement, the slapping of balls against her backside, the shouted obscenities, the sweat running down her body, the way she would say "Jesus, Jesus, Jesus" when the pleasure or the pain submerged her, the gurgling, the secretions, the sighs, the sounds that pinned me down, powerless. Unable to protect her, to save her, to love her any longer as she accepted all this inhuman punishment on my behalf. After all, I was the one who had bought the illegal tape, hadn't I?

Surely, it must come to an end soon? After all this thrusting, this fucking, this royal screwing of Eddie, they would have to ejaculate. The obligatory final come scene as they would disengage from her openings and spill their seed over her face theatrically.

I listened on as they pumped away inside her.

The voice of the cameraman rose over the physical action.

"You're good, Eddie. You're really good. What do you want from my boys now? Do you want to swallow their nice, juicy come?"

"That would be nice," she answered.

Christ!

"OK, let's do it now, guys. I'll soon be out of film, and I've got to go to the bathroom, anyway."

"You can pee all over me," Eddie said.

I howled like a madman. Enough! I just couldn't take any more of this. No. Please. No, Eddie. Eddie who had once upon a time told me such sweet things and kissed me as if tomorrow would never come. Eddie who...

The pain was becoming unbearable as I sat there so helpless, overcome by deadly nausea and guilt. My hand gripped a cushion and, without thinking, I hurled it at the VCR. My aim was true; the cushion struck the machine with a dull thud and the obscene sounds ceased. I opened my eyes.

The machine had stopped.

I didn't care if I'd destroyed the damn thing forever.

I heaved a sigh of relief.

Outside the drawn curtains, night was falling and the sky was darkening.

I think I sat there for another two hours. Thinking. Sobbing. Wishing. Imagining all the million scenarios of what could have been had Eddie and I not parted ways in such a stupid fashion all those years back and I had begun my fall into infamy. My left foot was numb with cramp. I moved it carefully. The videotape's illustrated box lay flattened underneath my heel. I gingerly picked it up. *Benny Margate Presents London Babes, Vol. 4.* Jackie and her toothy smile no longer adorned the front of the box. It was now Eddie. Of course. I even recognized the photograph. It's one of the few I had taken. We had just made love for hours. The hotel in Brighton. She was all flushed and blushed even further when I had suggested taking a Polaroid. When we separated, she had insisted I return all the photographs. I turned the box around. "Featuring the fantastic Edwina, the most amazing beginner we have ever come across."

I dropped the video's box onto the carpet and glanced at the machine. The red light was still on. Damn, what the hell had I done with the remote? It must be somewhere. I rose and leaned over to switch off the VCR.

It wouldn't.

I tried a few times.

The light stayed on.

Thought I'd take the tape out. Maybe it would switch off then.

I pressed the EJECT button.

A click. But instead of the tape being disgorged by the machine, I just heard it begin to rewind inside. Damn. I sure didn't wish to view the heartbreaking tape all over again. Even if by some unholy miracle of science Jackie had returned.

I tried every button and knob on the VCR. To no avail. The film kept on rewinding. Then began again. The 1-800 numbers advertising. The credits. I was determined not to be kept in thrall to the damn thing again, so I closed my eyes and stuck my fingers in my ears as the credits faded. The utter silence of outer space surrounded me momentarily as I isolated myself inside my artificial cocoon.

Peace.

But then, slowly but surely, the sounds from outside began filtering through. First, an indistinct blur of distant noises. A muted din. Lots of voices, steps, even the sound of a train pulling into a station. I shouldn't be hearing any of this, I thought, my fingers dug deep inside my ears. But the sounds just kept on growing and growing outside of me. I pulled my fingers away, and the crescendo continued. An announcement of a delay on the loudspeaker. I opened my eyes.

I was standing on the main concourse of Victoria Station and three men were walking toward me, one of them holding a camera whose red light was blinking.

Of course, I knew exactly where I was. I looked up at the big clock hanging from the elevated rafters. Then back at my watch. Eddie was already a quarter of an hour late. Typical of women, I knew, but not Eddie. She was always so punctual. In another five minutes, the Eastbourne train would depart and our first weekend together would vanish up in smoke. Damn. The three men moved nearer.

"Waiting for someone, mate?" the guy with the camera asked me.

I accepted the familiarity of the scene calmly.

"I don't think she's coming now," I said. "I always knew, somehow, it would never last. Shit!"

They sympathized, asked me back to this flat a producer friend of theirs had nearby. Said I had an interesting face. They were seeking distinctive faces to cast in some indie movie. Sounded interesting.

Cut.

I'm sitting on this slippery leather couch in this poncy flat with mirrored walls. I'm sipping a Pepsi-Cola with no ice and Cameron and Valentino are on either side of me. I don't know how, but the conversation has moved on to the tricky subject of cock size. The cameraman says:

"They say men with big noses usually have large cocks, don't they, guys?"

Cameron and Valentino nod.

"Come on," one of them suggests. "Let's see."

I know I've seen this movie before, and I have to follow the script; I rise from the couch and loosen my belt.

"Not bad," the cameraman remarks, the lens focusing on my freed penis. "You might as well take your shirt off, you know. Don't you think men always look a bit stupid when it just dangles there?"

I obey.

I know my part in the charade.

I've seen porno movies before.

I have to suck their cocks. Cameron's gigantic member stretches my lips but tastes musky. The odor of Valentino's crotch is mildly unpleasant, but I overcome the feeling and lick his dark, heavy balls dutifully, crouching on the carpet as, behind me, Cameron rims my arsehole and spits into his palms to lubricate his jutting cock. It hurts when he attempts to penetrate me, but he dribbles some more saliva into my rear aperture and forces his way in. It hurts like hell.

"See," the cameraman remarks. "It's all so easy. For a beginner, you're really good, you know."

As Cameron digs deep into my rear, I realize I've never seen gay porn films before. Now, I don't know what comes next. It's a bit unsettling. What's the climax supposed to be? You can't have a double-penetration sequence. Or can you? I shudder briefly at the thought.

Valentino moves away as the filmmaker pulls the camera away from my stuffed rear and focuses the lens on my face. I must be squirming with discomfort. Feel as if I need a shit. Is this normal?

"Be a good boy. Look straight into the camera, will you?"

I raise my head slightly to follow his command.

Peer deep into the lens.

First I see the reflection of my face, shaken by the repeated, metronomic thrusts in my rear. At last, the pain begins to fade and gentle, rising waves of pleasure start to move in concentric circles away from my crotch. I keep on watching my image on the shiny mirror of the protruding lens fixing me in its web.

As the pleasure increases, my grimacing face disappears from the surface of the lens and I see behind it. I squint to see better.

There's a room beyond. On an old settee, a familiar woman with wild hair is sitting, her skirt raised to her waist, legs apart, fingers twitching mechanically in and out of her cunt. Her mouth is open wide and I think I can lip-read what she is saying. "Yes. Jesus. Yes. Jesus. Jesus."

Suddenly I feel Cameron disengage from my bowels, but within a second or so, Valentino has taken his place, digging even deeper into my ravaged innards.

Eddie, jerking off on her settee, slows down the compulsive movement of her hands, trying to delay her climax. I want to call out to her, but something inside tells me she has switched off the sound. "Come," I want to tell her. "Don't wait."

But she does wait.

One hand abandons her genitals and picks up the video box. I peer deep inside the lens purring just an inch away from my nose. Try to make out the writing on the tape's box. She stretches her arm and I decipher the title quickly. *Bennie Margate Presents London Snuff, Vol. 4.*

As she drops the box to the carpet, she brandishes the remote and fast-forwards. The pain in my rear becomes quite excruciating and everything blurs in front of my eyes. It doesn't take long.

Finally everything slows down.

Eddie has two fingers inside her and thrusts her pelvis forward wildly, inviting her climax at last.

The cameraman approaches the slick blade to my throat.

Behind me, one of the studs is still digging deep in my bowels, while the other lies underneath me sucking on my hard cock, his teeth grazing the skin, as if he were about to bite.

The blade penetrates my skin.

Outside the machine, Eddie comes at last.

Doesn't she look wonderful right now?

Useful Pieces

Stephen Dedman

When I was a teenager, and arguably more human, I always wanted to meet a nymphomaniac who actually liked me. And so here I am, thirty years later subjective (a century and a half Earth time), lying on my stomach on the bed while Veronica, a UNASA psych, rubs her tiny breasts against my back, tickling me with her nipples (yes, we do have nerve endings, but we also have a sensitivity control), and my expensive flesh (flesh?) is willing, it always is, but the bedroom ceiling is tiled, little white hexagons that make me as uneasy as Hell for reasons I don't understand.

I shut my eyes, turn down the gain on the nerves, and try to watch a little Lo-V on my implant. A comedian, telling the old joke about the naut who burnt himself screwing a toaster, whatever that is. I change channels. The UNASA stations are having a twenty-cent horror-movie festival. *The Andromeda Strain. Jaws. Alien* (with a real cat, yet; must be the original). *Starship Troopers. Independence Day. Earth vs. the Flying Saucers. The Birds. The Thing. The Green Slime.* All interspersed with recruitment ads. Carrying humanity to the stars, my overpriced foot!

I change channels. An award ceremony, lots of nauts and UNASA brass. I change channels again, quickly. Another comedian—no, an historian. She's talking about the way the Biodiversity Treaty was rewritten in 2012 to ensure the survival of the maximum number of human genes at whatever cost. Go forth and multiply. Lots of stuff about the peaceful uses of outer space; lots of pictures of riots, and some old natural, barely alive, in a robe and a funny white hat. I always thought that treaty had something to do with animals, but maybe they were already extinct by then.

I never really studied history. It wouldn't have done a damn for my career prospects, and besides, nothing between the dinosaur-killer and *Voyager I* seemed remotely relevant: only political historians study the Apollo program. For us, history began when *Viking I* was looking for life on Mars and causing endemic headaches on Earth. Veronica's nipples are rubbing against my asscheeks now as she kisses my back, working down inexorably. I change channels.

There's two dozen stations of skin, the same number there was when I last left Earth, five het-only for the religious fanatics, six unclassifiable, all but the classics channel fully holo and interactive. Beautiful women, beautiful men, beautiful hermaphrodites, beautiful body parts made in beautiful molds, beautiful machines. Brown skin, pink, white, black, green, paint, tattoos, stripes, spots, jewelry, hair, no hair, dark eyes, green eyes, old-fashioned round eyes, metal eyes, no eyes, no faces. Nipples of every shade, two four zero arms, meter-long cocks, half-meter tongues, cunts and asses and mouths and cleavages you could dock a starship with, sweat and lube and saliva and cum and tears and wax, arousal and ejaculation and afterglow and bruises and welts and scars and dialogue. They try, I'll give them that, but there is nothing new for them to show: body-painting and strap-ons and piercings and prosthetics are literally prehistoric, and I have it on good authority that even the dinosaurs were into anal sex, though not double penetration. Of course, no one's sure how the stegosaurs and spinosaurs and the other species with ripsaws on their backs managed to fuck, quadruped-style, without disemboweling their partners; personally, I think they relied on a high male—female ratio, high sperm motility, and one-night stands, like black widows. I remember before I became a naut, when I couldn't turn my testosterone on and off like a tap, seeing women who I thought I'd die for a chance to fuck, women I would've fucked even if they were wrapped in razorwire. Ah, youth.

One show catches my attention for a few seconds: a magnificent redhead teasing a man between her perfect breasts. Used to be my favorite fantasy many years ago, but pornpeople are as artificial as I am, all silicon prosthetics and hydraulics and biofeedback implants, if it's not just computer animation. They try to disguise it with a medieval or twenty-cent setting, like nearly all the porn nowadays, as though there was something erotic about dirt and dying young. I switch to interact mode, make her breasts smaller, her nipples more erect, her eyes more blue, her hair more blonde, but it doesn't work. I change channels again.

I guess there's no accounting for fantasies. I used to fantasize about being a naut, used to fantasize about having a permanently hard cock as long as my forearm, and like I said, I used to fantasize about having a friendly, uncomplicated relationship with a sex addict like Veronica, even if that's not what I expected her to look like. And all those fucking fantasies all came true, though by the time I met Veronica I was already married, fairly happily, too, but you can probably figure out what happened to that. Jessie, my wife, didn't like the idea of my joining the project, and I couldn't expect her to wait seven years for me to get back. Actually, I did expect it, which shows what sort of idiot I was, and I was divorced by radio. Apparently, leaving Earth counts as desertion. It took nearly a month for the decree to cross the distance, and I don't remember if she waited for a reply. I do remember Melas, the ExMule pilot, laughing until I hit him. Penelope Melas was nearly brain-dead anyway, and some men might've gone this far to avoid her.

But maybe Melas chose wisely, at that. The girl he married was a slow, awkward teenager, awestruck by the glamorous naut. The woman who met him when we were released from quarantine was twenty-four and sophisticated, with a nice line in banter and a spectacular real body—and I say that with the benefit of hindsight. By the time we landed, all the female nurses had to handle us with cattle prods and stunwhips: anything with breasts looked beautiful to us. Did I mention razorwire? I could bite through the stuff now, floss with it. I wonder what the female naut crews are like when they come home.

Fleischer told me once there was a reason why all nauts are het and the crews aren't mixed; something to do with eroticizing the ship, but I don't remember the rest.

I turn off the Lo-V (I guess that makes it mutual) and look over my shoulder at Veronica, who's licked her way down my spine down to one of the few parts of me that's still mostly flesh rather than plastic. She's small, dark, with eyebrows that meet and pubic hair up to her navel: sort of primitive, almost animal, and she likes to act the part. I used to dream of blondes with tits like planets: Veronica won't go anywhere where topless or nude is de rigueur. But then, neither will I. You can't hide the scars. We spend most of my R&R

time on Earth fucking in rooms like this one, and we get on okay.

She looks up and smiles at me carnivorously, and I remember Jessie, claiming she was divorcing me because we couldn't have children "naturally." Naturally? I kept thinking of women dying in childbirth in mud huts, surrounded by goats and rats and mammoths. Naturally? The tourships bring back horror stories of people acting "naturally." Nature shredded their lungs with vacuum, it boiled their blood, it stopped hearts with a lousy three gs, it picassoed their skin with radiations—with light, godfuckit, with the wavelengths I use to read by—and nature didn't give a fuck. I suppose there's not much "natural" about me, but none of those things worry me. We do most of our trip at three or four gs: anything else would be uneconomical. Of course, we can't exactly colonize—our gonads are in little jars at Cape Reagan—but I never have to be short of breath, or bleary-eyed, or ticklish, or impotent.

"Where are you, love?" Veronica whispers, then, when I don't answer, "What can I do to help?" I shrug. Where the fuck am I, really? In a hotel room? At an awards ceremony on the Lo-V? In a little jar at Cape Reagan? On the ship? Still on Procyon II? Which part of me is really me?

I roll over and reach into the nightstand, and we choose an erection from the collection and Veronica helps me plug it in, expertly fondling my balls while she does it. The hydraulics engage and it swells to its full quarter-meter, and Veronica lowers herself onto it slowly.

She says that one day she's going to learn that *Kama Sutra* trick of rotating on a cock; I retort that I'll make it easier for her by getting one with a built-in turntable. I retract my nails and slowly slide a finger up her ass, grab a nipple and feel it swell, turn up the gain on the nerves in the cock, and try to concentrate on the sensations, the wonderful natural smell of her, the look on her face and the sounds she makes as she cums, again and again and again, I know it's no good trying not to think about hexagons, I have to think about—

Veronica arches her back until I can't see her face any longer, and I almost forget who I'm with. Jessie? No, Jessie and I are history.

History! Part of my mind seems to drift away from the sex. History. Biodiversity Treaty. Procyon II. *Viking I.* It feels as though I should be remembering something important…Wish to fuck I could control my memory the way I control my body.

I remember Fleischer theorizing that the "something" was merely an unknown inanimate compound. There were no Martian princesses or dinosaurs, not even a Martian passenger pigeon or pneumonic plague …but it's funny: The planet's as civilized as Antarctica or Australia, now, and those compounds have become impossible to find.

Veronica screams…

Mandaglione told us another story which didn't

make the history books: blobs of dirty helium on Pluto which acted as though they were alive—even aware, in the way that a flatworm or wristcomp is aware. He saw them himself, when he was a naut, swears they reproduced by fission in an almost perfect cycle.

UNASA made him a full professor after that, and tripled his salary, but they never sent him back to Pluto. Just as well, I guess; they tried to terraform the planet, and destroyed it instead. Nothing left but an afterglow that'd keep a Geiger counter happy for centuries. Someone must have goofed....

Another scream...

Then, on Procyon II, we discovered what Fleischer, our biologist, still maintains was silicon life: I know we discovered fields of tessellated hexagonal prisms, like the beehives you see in paleontology exhibits, and none of the minerals on Procyon II would form hexagonal crystals anywhere near that size naturally.

Procyon II is useless for colonization, as hot as Venus and oxygen-free, but it was rich in transuranic elements which the colony on Providence needed. I wish, now, I'd kept some of those prisms: Fleischer tried, but they exceeded our mass allowance. I don't say Fleischer's lifeforms were intelligent, or even that they were animals —but sometimes I wonder if any chemist, anywhere, could recognize life before it bit him to death.

Fuck, two hundred years ago, chemists would've dismissed me as impossible. My bloodstream, my CSF, my nervous system, my body temperature, my systolic pressure: any of these would kill a human being instantly. Sometimes I think the universe was designed to kill humans instantly...and then, I wonder what humans were designed for, and I don't enjoy the thought.

I remember Fleischer theorizing that one day they'd disconnect our legs and fingers, plug them into the pilot seat, and leave us there on an efficient diet. We wouldn't need planets at all; we'd make love to the ship, a lifelong marriage, if you can call that a life.

Fleischer always was weird. He hangs around S&M clubs, the star attraction 'cause he can disconnect his nerves and take so much punishment. Human space are us—we're wiping all the others out, soon there'll be nothing off Earth except human-built machines fucking more human-built machines, a mechanical danse macabre forever and ever amen amen.

I see Veronica's face looming above me, muttering something, a command sequence of some sort, and the world—the universe—turns red and black, it rushes in to get me, burns me alive, freezes me, flays me, as every nerve ending in my body suddenly switches to full pain setting. I try to think, to remem—

"Where are you, love?" Veronica whispers. "What can I do to help?"

I shake my head until the blackness goes away. Where the Hell am I? "Was I asleep?" The room looks different, completely different. I seem to remember dreaming....

"We were making love, and you passed out." She smiles. "Was it that good?"

I smile back. I don't know if women are changing, or whether there've always been a few xenophiles who could love freaks like us, freaks who can carry their erections in their briefcases. Veronica is still playing with mine, absentmindedly. Maybe I should leave her some of them to remember me by.

Melas has Penelope, though he'll probably divorce her before the next trip, marry another flat-chested adolescent. Fleischer has his Bacchante pack. Robertson has his religion: he's probably descended from celibates. And I have Veronica, as long as I'm on Earth, and I guess I don't mind sharing her with UNASA. Maybe I love her. Maybe I even love that natural body, that hair, those minuscule breasts. Or maybe—and I wish to hell I knew why—I just hate silicon.

Closed Circuit
Marc Laidlaw

As he stepped closer to the blue glowing video screen
to feed a dollar bill into the slot, two things happened
at once: a spark leapt from the screen, a small swirl of
charge that licked out to snap at his fingers, and the
heel of his boot came unstuck from something gummy
on the floor, making precisely the same electric sound.
He snatched back his hand instantly and jerked his
foot sideways, knowing beyond a doubt what he was
standing in. On the black linoleum floor between his
heels were several luminous blue glutinous splatters,
the largest of them smeared by his heel. That would
explain the smell. He had supposed, on entering the
booth, that it emanated from the small black wastebas-
ket lined with plastic and full of crumpled tissue paper,

415

which should have been labeled "Biohazard" considering all the viruses and infectious agents it probably contained. And yet, that was sheer paranoia, for wasn't this blackened little booth truly a safe haven? Images of lust and fulfillment reigned here in supreme solipsism, with no possibility of human contact or viral transmission, no real exchange at all apart from the one-way relationships between his wallet and the money slot, the video screen and his starving eyes, his testes and the interior of a wadded Kleenex provided at no extra charge by a sturdy metal dispenser mounted on the wall.

The seedier establishments, awkwardly, furnished no such amenities, as he had discovered while shopping for a comfortable venue. He wondered how many tourists had wandered into those other places, purchased a handful of tokens, and plunked them into the closed-circuit video screens, only to find themselves caught in a blinding assault of hard-core images unlike anything they could have wandered into in their little hometowns (not without risking eternal pollution of their reputation anyhow), suddenly on the unexpected (but possibly still welcome) verge of losing control, but with absolutely no means of catching or containing their emissions.

What did they do? Did they wait in the booths for an hour or so, until their trousers completely dried, then hobble out stiff-legged and with crusted thighs? Did they dry their hands on their shirttails? Did they somehow, struggling out of the straps of Handicam cases, manage to change their clothes?

It was a mistake one made only once, and therefore reserved mainly for tourists. More commonly, one saw local businessmen from the financial district ducking in for a quick episode of lunchtime self-abuse, then slipping out blinking at the brilliant sky through dark glasses they had not dared to remove except when locked safely inside a private booth. (His own motivations were quite different, of course; one might even call them artistic.) Passing such civic paragons on their way out of the various low-end arcades, he always smiled to himself, smug in the knowledge that somewhere in their pockets was a dank handful of tissue or a stained handkerchief perhaps not suitable for laundering by the wife or professional dry-cleaner. Sometimes he followed them back to their offices, trailing half a block behind, amused at the way they tried to confuse their trail, in case they had been followed; circling around the stock exchange and coming in from the opposite direction so that no one might guess in which part of town they'd spent their lunch hour. You'd see them pausing casually on a corner, reaching into a pocket, discovering, as if by accident, a clump of tissue paper from deep in some pocket; they would toss it into a garbage can without looking, already hurrying away.

He preferred his own brand of tissue to the industrial varieties offered by even the best arcades, and today he had several layers of the soft linty stuff folded

and ready in a pocket of his jacket. But suddenly, straddling the gluey pool on the unmopped floor, he felt
that paper alone was less than worthless. He would
have liked to scrub the floor, the walls, the little narrow
ledge of a bench, with bleach. He withdrew into
himself like a chilled scrotum, suddenly wary of touching any surface at all. Even his heavy boots did not
seem protection enough from whatever might be hanging or dripping unseen down the invisible black walls.

The screen itself bore faint lines of cellular residue;
thicker at the tails, where the lazy arcade staff had
skimped on disinfectant and not bothered to scrape the
glass clean. It seemed to him now that the very walls
glistened with semen, some of it only minutes old
(spermatozoa still struggling in the drying pools like
would-be amphibians gasping on a prehistoric beach),
and some of it quite ancient. The sunken-eyed, foul-
bodied graybeards in rotting clothes who padded about
in the maze of halls, pockets rattling with change on
the first of every month, might have blazed the milky
primordial trails themselves in the first flush of their
youth. In those days, of course, videos were unknown.
The incipient hermits had probably contented themselves with 16 mm film loops, never appreciating the
fine resolution and high image quality of actual film
stock as compared to grainy, harsh, low-resolution
video.

The arcade still paid small tribute to the glory days
of analog pornography, but it was a faded and pathetic

paean, without even the historical interest of a sepia-toned photograph. In the most distant corner of the arcade's maze, one small booth lurked alone, its cobwebs strung with the corpses of ancient sperm like burned-out Christmas lights. Here you stood (if you bothered, for the booth was always empty), somewhat bewildered and with a certain necessary sense of irony, staring through a Plexiglas partition into another booth whose far wall was occupied by a yellowing screen which—despite the distance and the plastic barrier—bore evidence of having been used for remarkable feats of long-range target practice. And as you fed quarters into the box (exactly like those affixed to rocket ships and rocking horses stationed outside supermarkets for the entertainment of bored children), the loop of faded film would light and lurch to life, play briefly (no more than twenty-five seconds), and then dim and slow to reveal the stained yellow screen once more. A quarter at a time, it could take you all afternoon to see both part-ners satisfied.

But he never would be, for there was something almost touching about the "actors" shedding their bell-bottom trousers and paisley skirts; and he found himself more interested in trying to glimpse headlines and dates on magazines casually tossed on the motel nightstands, than in trying to participate vicariously in the arousal of these youths who were probably long since dead or otherwise assimilated.

On the wall above a bed with a crumpled chenille

spread was a cheap knockoff of W. Eugene Smith's photograph, "The Walk to Paradise Garden," showing two small children guiding each other away from the camera, out of a shadowy tunnel of hedge, and into softly glowing yet somehow blinding light. And he could never see that dreadful imitation without recalling the circumstances in which Smith had made the photograph, the first he attempted after a grenade explosion which had nearly claimed his life on a South Pacific island during World War II. Consider the superhuman effort Smith had put into extracting the finest possible print from his negative; ponder everything the picture must have signified to a man just returning from the brink of nonexistence. And then to see it up there, squandered—not even the photograph itself but a cheap, wavery motel rip-off captured by a shaky movie camera in a poorly lit room on brittle film-stock from which all but a trace of color had faded...well, the sight was not conducive to sexual fantasy. It induced yearnings for a far distant source.

He always left the 16 mm booth in a pensive mood that continued to expand and elevate, carrying his spirits with it as the day went on, leaving him feeling rather noble and proud of his restraint in having spent nothing more than money that afternoon. He typically went home in a philosophical mood and took snapshots of his children in the garden.

But now he thought of the baby, and how she always grabbed his boots from underneath the bed and, like a human puppy, invariably rammed some part of them into her mouth and proceeded to leave wet trails up and down the leather soles as she chewed and chewed in search of solace, something to soothe the teething pains. Since the baby couldn't accidentally swallow and choke on a boot, his wife did not seem terribly bothered by the (to him) disgusting practice. But he could not bear the thought of his infant daughter rubbing the boot heel against her tender gums, absorbing any stubborn infectious matter that might be swimming in the stale puddle he had trod upon accidentally. There was no foolproof way to wipe such stuff on grass or the edge of a curb as he would after stepping in dogshit; no pools of chlorine he might stamp through on his way home. He would have to contrive an excuse to disinfect the boots, risking damage to the fine black leather.

Of course, the main thing was to get out of this particular booth before he stepped in the goo again. He would find another more to his liking, cleaner. He had learned one should always smell a booth before entering. You could tell a lot by sniffing the dark cubicles— more than your eyes could uncover.

He shoved his money back into his pocket and reached for the doorknob, which he knew to be of brass with a simple rickety lock, the same sort on the door of his bathroom at home. You could open it from the outside by sticking a pin into it. If he were locked in, he need only hammer and howl until someone came and let him out, although why that image should cross his mind was unclear. Perhaps it was because he could not find the knob immediately. He had closed the door behind himself a moment before, and he still had a distinct impression of the cold, sweaty metal pressing the palm of his squeezing hand. But when he reached with that hand to recapture the sensation, he felt nothing. He shrank from touching the door itself, or any of the walls, although none could have been more than a foot or two away from him. Overhead, instead of a ceiling, was a mesh of slack chicken wire, hardly even tacked down; above that was plumbing and conduit, all painted black. One could hardly call this a cage.

And yet, now it was not the dread of whatever deathless microorganisms might be living on the walls that kept him from groping for the elusive knob. It was the idea that if he reached out farther, he would still feel nothing. Certainly, except for the blue screen, he could see nothing. If not for that light, he might have fooled himself into thinking he'd closed his eyes, or had them sealed for him by some unknown force. He turned to the screen as to a beacon, a hearth. And with little shuffling steps, careful not to stray across the edges of the pool, he moved right up to the faintly rounded blueness of the glass. He raised his hands as if to warm them, but the light was devoid of warmth or frigidity or indeed any character at all. It was simply a dance of electrons against the surface of a phosphorescent pane. Something like that. Even when alive and tumbling with bodies, it was still mere thin and fragile concealment for a darkness crackling with emptiness. He could see his bones through the skin as he pressed his palms to the glass. Then they were melting, bones into flesh, flesh into glass into light. He pushed harder, into the screen, leaving the black walls around him forever untested. For some reason, he was not at all afraid. He only wished he had thought to feed the rest of his money to the machine. He wasn't going to need it where he was headed, and it would have been nice to have at least the illusion of company.

The Bachelor Machine
M. Christian

In the Pile, again—

Shoals of cubed safety glass, shimmering snow high enough to block out—or at least dazzlingly reflect—the lights of distant Austin; like the metal underpinnings of industrial dinosaurs, cranes moved ponderously, massively in some high-altitude wind high above; the heads of every evolution of servicer piled in chaotic mountains, blind sensors glistening only from Austin's far light pollution; reefs of cars, mazes of vehicles, forming avenues and alleys too tight to drive down—their mindless, picked-clean corpses (in spite?) making him walk. The phallic disappointment of an airliner fuselage crumpled at one end, smooth at the other, tilted and twisted and neatly pinched between a pile of burned, blistered capsule apartments.

Friday, *again*—

—and it was raining: a hard, driving rain that seemed more to pummel him into the mud than just fall from distant, invisible clouds—as if it resented having to come such a distance only to find Kurtis at the end of its journey.

Luckily, he'd had some advance warning, wisely taking a small amount of his Thursday money to pay for three hours of net access. In those three hours, he had discovered two more likely jobs, that the government of the Sovereign Nation of Texas had changed hands yet again, that the cure for Hep TCI was false, and that the next day—when he traditionally wore his best—it was going to pour.

It didn't say anything at all about *hammer*.

Still, he'd had some notice—enough to wrap himself from his fake California clone-leather shoes to his one-size-too-small fake European suit in a Walking Bag™. The rain was like a perpetually full bucket spilling onto his head, blinding him to everything except the hardest lights of the Pile, turning its yellow dirt into sole-sucking mud, and shoving him down just about to his knees—but, at least, he wasn't wet.

LOVE in red biolight so dark it came close to purple. Pulsing even through the static-sounding rain, glowing past its distorting pour. There may have been, at one time, something before LOVE or after LOVE but that side of the place was gone—cropped off by a cliff of compressed cars and an imprecise pyramid of refrigerators. LOVE was lopsided, tilted, twisted—barely able to glow. Whoever had made it had, despite the natural laws of the universe, made LOVE last.

Once, the front had been a plastic display of eroticism: organiform—no, *sensual* form, the exterior showed curves and dips, dimples and swells that once might have architecturally echoed the subtle contours of a woman. The door was a protruding dome, the knob a brass spiral that could have been a nipple. The front was a play of gentle slopes and heavy overhangs with a kind of frozen fleshy weight to them. Along the bottom was a fringe of brilliant pink plastic, like lips dragging on the ground—hiding, no doubt, the unit's tires, the service's ability to pick itself up and move on when a neighborhood or a town tired of it.

When LOVE had run its course for them.

Once it had been a paradise of sexual form and enticing design. But it was in the Pile, now. The fleshy contours were now sad and mildewed. Like acne, vacant gaps told where smaller, pocketable, details had been wrenched free. Like cellulite, supposedly eternal plastics had sagged under industrial-strength weather and persistent gravity. The door was yellowed and streaked, clouded till it revealed nothing at all of LOVE's interior—a tawdry shawl for a very old, and unwanted, edifice.

As Kurtis stepped up, the door opened pneumatically, a fasting gasp and an irritating grating of mud and sand caught in some mechanism—that put LOVE as far away as dry on that rainy day. The foyer had once been plush and decorative: an attempt to recall the elegance and promise of a historical bordello. Red velvet, antique prints of ladies in daring positions and tantalizing postures. Tassels and gold ropes. A vase of brilliant roses. Now, though, it was all covered with a thick coat of yellow dust, the floor and hardened mud inches deep. The roses were plastic and out of focus from dust and spiderwebs. The once—red-velvet walls and the once-thick shag looked like they'd been in the stateroom of a lady of dubious repute on the *Titantic* —*after* it had sunk and been on the bottom for years.

The main room was mostly lost to soft—but deep— shadows. Unzipping his bag calmly, Kurtis climbed out, and folded it carefully so that the dry inner lining wouldn't touch anything in the place and put it down on a red velvet chair—with only three legs, propped against a built-in couch, and covering a low hill of disposable sunjoy syringes.

One door. Padded leather gutted by an impressionist series of slashes, yellowed stuffing puffing out like geometric fungus. Over the door was a red indicator. As Kurtis glanced up, it flickered, pulsed, then lit: AVAILABLE.

The room beyond was dark and smelled of hot plastic, ozone, and mildew. There was one window—a porthole that leaked in a grainy light from the Pile's hard industrial lights filtering through the storm. It splashed a crisp oval on the bed, showing a plastic ankle and the top of a red-spangled pump.

"Hello there, sugar," said tones that had once been melting butter, scintillating sugar, a purring kitten from the top of the bed, lost to shadows—but had since evolved through countless breakdowns, missed upgrades, and general disuse into a scratching, wheezing of sounds that could, or could not, have been actual words.

"Um, er, ah—hello?" Kurtis said, looking up and around for the lights, thinking that he might have to do some banging around to get them to work.

"Hello there, sugar."

The ceiling was high. Too high to reach, even if he wanted to risk climbing the stances of the high four-poster bed that took up most of the room.

"H-h-hello, ssssssugar...."

A heavy click, and a thud that Kurtis felt through his fake shoes—a sound exactly like someone giving one of the plastic walls a hefty smack, then: "Looking for love, honey?"

A chime, like glass heated too fast. The first flash of light showed the room, like a flash of lightning: bed with satin canopy, chair—toppled and broken, table—listing, bric-a-brac (small lamp in the shape of a stretching deco nymph, glass jar of some unnamable liquid) frozen, glued, to its tilted surface), and painting of an overly developed woman reclining on a flowered sofa.

"Um, er, yeah—" Kurtis said, feigning innocence but,

because the smell of the place—mildew and ozone from frying electronics—was making him faintly nauseous didn't do a very good job of it.

Another chime. Another blast of pure white light from the biolights overhead. She moved from her "sultry" and "provocative" position on the bed, moving forward till she was sitting on the edge, looking over her next client: "Are you a virgin, by any—*hummm* —chance?"

"Um, I guess you could say so. I mean I haven't done it with a...um, before...." Kurtis felt stupid and hot with embarrassment. He said the words with the conviction of an underpaid actor; then, thinking of which, he smiled at the tilted truth of that and laughed a bit to himself.

"You are in good hands, sweetie. Very good hands," she said, moving with misfiring, hesitant steps off the bed and out of the shadows as the lights surged one last time before dropping down to their designed "intimate bedroom" glow—that made the room look like it was at the bottom of a crimson-watered lake.

Her face was plastic, a pink and rouged mask and moved with glacial expressions in response to motors under the stiffening and cracking skin. Her eyes were glass or some kind of clear material, and when they moved they jerked from one seen object to another: Kurtis's face, his body, his crotch.

Her hair had slipped to one side; once-golden curls now faded white way beyond Gretta Garbo—she was half-bald. Her mouth didn't move when she talked: instead it hung, half-open, showing a bright red sheet of spongy plastic tongue.

She was tall, a fact that always surprised Kurtis—no matter how many Fridays, times he saw her. For some reason always initially he expected her to be smaller, less threatening in her misfiring and stuttering movements. Maybe it was his memory that was misfiring more—and it was only in his faulty retrospect that she was diminutive, with larger, deeper eyes.

Her body was leggy, and exaggerated—as if her designers had realized their true opportunity and instead of trying to artifice a real person they instead realized a broad icon. If she were flesh and blood instead of polymnemonic alloys, resin composited, fiber threads, and biosmart circuits she would be a hopeless victim of gravity. Instead she was firm and shaped in ways that no flesh woman could be. She was a Vargas, a playing card, a calendar, a T-shirt.

Her breasts were almost bare, hardly hidden by her shift. They were—he admitted to himself, carefully keeping his eyes from her face and its malfunctioning rigor—more than just quite nice. Plastic, yes, used and abused by God-knew-how-many clients since it had been given its own unique semblance of life by a division of Lovelife, Inc. some twenty-five years previous.

Kurtis took off his coat, hoping that the rest of her wasn't misfiring as badly as her voice, and draped it carefully on the bag.

"Oh, you're a handsome one—" she purred, her voice not quite coming from her mouth, as she stepped up close to him.

Close, his eyes locked on her imperfections, her broken parts. The smell of mildew and fried circuits was powerful, scraping the inside of his sinuses. The world became a walk uphill. It wasn't just another day, just another Friday. Instead, he faced too many hours till the end of it. It was almost like a physical pain, an ache in his belly and back at the thought of going through the minutes, maybe even the hour to get to the end of it.

It wasn't just her, because despite her misfiring and deteriorated condition, because what was rolling heavy and mean through his mind wasn't just the work for that afternoon—it was everything. His life. His age. His income. His shoes.

His shoes. In the space of the moment the feelings took to roll through him, he looked over at his coat and then down at the shoes still on his feet. Fake. Not cheap, but still fake. He was proud of his shoes, proud that he looked nice on Fridays.

He looked at her, saw her for being what she was—broken. Once she was new, state-of-the-art. People came from all over to indulge themselves with her.

Now though it was raining outside. Her carpets were caked with the yellow mud of the Pile and she knew, perfectly, that the future wouldn't bring anything but more and more—deeper mud on her once-fine carpets.

And Fridays. The one thing that perhaps made her circuits warm was Fridays. Fridays and Kurtis.

Somewhere through that, Kurtis felt some of the weight lift. Much of it was still there, but then it was replaced with a wry sense of warmth, a glow of self-satisfaction. How bad could it fucking be, he thought. At least I don't have just someone like me to look forward to.

Her eyes, shining glass buttons, looked straight at him and right then, he felt like she was looking up at him, and not down.

"Very fine," she said, her voice fading like its volume was decreasing. "Has anyone told you that you're very handsome?"

"No, not really" he said, with a firm touch that was totally opposed to his usual role.

"Well more people should," she said, "because I sure think it's true." She was wearing a simple shift, a once-white synthetic silk gown that draped tight over her large, perfectly conical breasts and fell, stopping just above her feet. As she walked, they swung, heavy and firmer than any real woman's ever could and her nipples, on an electronic cue, hardened under the soft, but stained, torn, *used* fabric.

Her movements were haltingly fluid, an action he never could have envisioned till he saw her—it was as if her normal ballet of getting up off the bed and walking over to him was given an internal quake of misfiring motors: a dancer with a muscular stammer.

"You know," she said, in a smiling tone that was totally beyond her normal banter, "I know this is business, and all, but at least it is a business I enjoy."

Oh, for God's sake, Kurtis thought. *Just get on with it.* What he said, though, was slightly acidic. "Me, too, hon. I mean it."

"Flatterer," she said, trying to smile. Her frozen lower jaw buzzed, then clicked together savagely, making Kurtis's cock freeze in his pants. "Should charge extra for that—" Now her jaw was working better, synching its action with her voice.

She was next to him, standing too close. Her hand, middle finger slightly hesitant as, he guessed, its motors were going, flattened and rested gently on his chest. "I specialize in first-timers, you know—" she said, following the script again. "There's nothing to be afraid of. We're going to have fun, hon—*lots* of fun."

"Thank you, ma'am," Kurtis said, looking down at her, feeling an icy tone in his words.

"Like I said, honey—the pleasure's going to be mine as well." Her hand dropped, brushing the front of his pants, pausing over the lack of a bulge. "Nervous?"

"Well, yeah, kind of—" Kurtis touched her hand, trying to gently move her hand away from his crotch, get her away from his failure.

"There's nothing to be ashamed of, sweetheart," she said, taking his hand and pulling him gently toward the bed.

It was dusty, dirty. Somehow seemingly to have

collected a thicker coat since the last time he'd been on it. His shoes. "Wait a minute," he said, maybe a little too firmly, and went back over to the Walking Bag™. Shoes. Pants. They all went on the plastic. In his socks, underwear, and shirt, he went back to the bed. Investment protected.

Her head was down slightly, as if she'd diverted her glassy plastic eyes from his step beyond the fourth wall of their routine. Sitting back down on the bed, she seemed to look at him: the shy virgin and not Kurtis from countless Fridays. "It's all right to be shy, even scared. It's the same for many people—there's nothing to be ashamed of. Believe me, I understand." The words were smooth and kind, even though her voice was hard and crackling. "I'm here to help you, to make you feel good. That's what this is all about—having fun and feeling good. I want you to be comfortable, to relax. I won't do anything that's going to hurt you. If I do, you just say so and I'll stop right away."

"Thank you," he said, looking at her eyes for some reason. Glistening plastic.

"Do you like the way I look? Do you like to look at me?" She arched her back, showing her artificial breasts to their ancient-designer perfection. Nipples like fingertips, harder, redder than any human woman's. One foot was cocked up near her lap and he noticed that the skin there was cracked, split—showing a braid of amber fibres and the dull shine of a polycarbon-alloy shin.

"Yes." Her skin was not quite human, the luster

having been removed after thousands of men's hands had touched her, fucked her. Even cutting-edge technology becomes dull and lackluster after having been ...used for too long. That middle finger again, hesitated and clicked as she moved her hand up his leg, inching toward his cock. The lie was sharp and impatient on his lips.

"Would you like to see my breasts?" Her head was tilted down gently. She looked up at him with a coy and almost-slightly-shy expression.

"Yes, I would," he said, surprised by the softness in his words. There had been innocence in her voice—buzzing and clicking—that had pushed away the industrial reality of her form.

With a too-feminine gesture, she slipped the straps of her gown off then brought her hands together—holding the weight of her breasts. Reaching down, she took one of his and put it on the almost too-warm slope of her left one. Many hands, many fucks, but the texture was just about right, a hairbreadth from being a real woman's.

"I like my breasts. I think they're pretty. Do you like them, too?"

"Yes—yes, I do," he said. The sun had moved and the rain had stopped. A hard beam of sunlight landed on her face and, for a moment, he watched the dust motes from the stuffy room drift past her clear eyes.

She took one hand away, leaving his on the swell of her breast. Under his thumb, resting there unconsciously or accidentally, he felt her nipple harden even more, grow even hotter.

Her hand was on his crotch, slowly stroking his cock. Distantly, he realized he was getting hard.

"It's okay—it really is. It's all right to get excited, to feel the way you do—"

Come on, just get it over with! he thought, feeling a flush of irritated anger.

"—you just have to relax and do what feels good." She was stroking his cock—very hard—deftly, with the accuracy of a lathe, with a piece of factory-floor machinery, but with the programmed skill of a world-class courtesan. "Now, then, doesn't this feel good?"

"It does," he said sharply, irritated with himself that his hand was stroking her breast, teasing and circling the nipple with his finger. He was tempted to pinch it, to squeeze too hard...but didn't. Partially because he needed the work, but also because he suspected she wouldn't, or couldn't, complain.

His cock was out and rockhard. It felt like it was happening to someone else, someone with a body just like his own but a million miles away. That same person had lifted her breast and was enjoying the weight of it. That same person had his lips an inch or two away from a plastic, artificial nipple.

"You want to suck? Please—go right—*hummmmmm*—ahead. I like that."

He kissed it. Expecting dust, oil, stale plastic, Kurtis was surprised by faint salt. Trying to think about the subtle technology required for the parlor trick, he lost his train of thought as she stroked his cock with deft gestures.

"I remember this one boy. He must have slipped out of his house to come—was kind of scared at the time, you know? He was so nervous but so sweet. I remember he had this faint little mustache, like rust on his upper lip. Pale face, with lots of freckles. He could have been older, I suppose, but I think he was young. That I was his first.

"He was so scared. At first I thought it was because of me, you know—some people have had a real hard time putting what I am aside. Others, of course, got off on it. I thought that he was that, scared of getting caught in the gears. But he was just shy—scared of women. I tried the usual things to try and get him relaxed but he was just too frightened. But he didn't leave, see?

"So I talked to him. I put him in that chair"—broken and leaning, dimmed by the dust—"and I just talked to him. I told him that it was okay to feel what he was, that loving women, or men for that matter, is nothing to be frightened or ashamed of. I offered myself, holding his hand and speaking softly, but I also told him that if he didn't want to then we wouldn't. We just talked. When my time was up and he had to go, he gave me a hug and cried a little bit."

His cock was hard. He was surprised by how much it ached, throbbed. *Damn,* he thought, *fucking good programming!* As she'd spoken, going beyond her usual lines, he'd licked and kissed her nipple, feeling its almost-perfect texture on his lips and with his tongue.

With a gentle hand on his chest, she pushed and guided him down onto the bed. Distantly, something told him he should be taking his shirt off—so he stopped her with a cold expression on his face, got up, and folded it neatly on top of his other clothes. Standing tall and rigid he—walked—back to the bed.

Again she pushed him down. He let himself be, with a bit of strength in his spine, a little protest.

Her mouth may have been malfunctioning but the skill with which she...pressure, wetness, texture, the play of all of that, the soft weight of her large breasts on his lap. Getting up, he'd started to droop, with the action of folding his coat, he'd gone completely limp—remembering what he was doing there—and when he'd laid down he'd actually shrunk.

He was hard again. Misfiring aside, she was cutting edge, state-of-the-art once. Her program was still fine, her skill...adept.

Up on his knees, watching with grim interest as her plastic head slid up and down on the shaft of his cock, he felt his eyes waver, his heart pound. Sliding down, he lay back and closed his eyes—lost to the swirling action or her artificial tongue, her plastic teeth, her foam-and-Perspex throat, the complex series of molecules designed to give him the best sensation with superb lubrication. His groin ached, his cock was beyond throbbing and had—quickly, damned quickly—rocketed up to that wonderful agony, that good hurt of balls pressurized from her action on his shaft and head. His breathing was rocky and quick. Kurtis found himself mumbling things, whispering and grunting half-words and fragments of sounds as she grew more and more rough, more and more intense.

Fucking soon….

Before he was even aware of it, she was slowing, easing back. Her actions became gentler, softer—the pressure in his balls was there, dangerously so, but it wasn't a cliff he was running off, but rather a hill he could roll down. Then it was a cool wash on his cock and balls and his heart was thudding regularly. Then the ache dropped down to a slow throb. He was still hard, but coming was so near to…well, coming.

"I remember this one time," she said, plastic smile at his budding cock. "A guy brought his girlfriend to me. Said that she wanted to try it with girls. Oh, my—you wouldn't believe the times I've told guys about women, and being with them. But I hadn't, you see—just stories to get them off. I had the knowledge, you know, but not really the"—her chuckle sounded as if something had broken down deep inside of her, something grating—"experience. At first I was, you know, not sure about this. Like, maybe, the girl wasn't into this at all, that she just had this pushy boyfriend.

"But her eyes. She liked looking at me. Liked touching me. I kept it simple that time, just some kissing and letting her feel my breasts, my pussy. I could tell she wanted more, but I kept seeing him, looking at us. There was something in his eyes I didn't like, something that kept coming between seeing us having fun and us not needing him."

Getting up, she slipped off the rest of her dress. The skin around her stomach was wrinkled, as if something in her internal workings had slipped down and was almost pressing out of her plastic skin. Her thighs, too, looked like the skin was about to break and as she moved, climbing with sudden bursts of misfiring hesitancy onto him, he could see flashes of optical circuits through the stretched plastic.

Kurtis closed his eyes, tried to think about money through his aching cock, and leaned back.

"Later—" He felt his cock touch her lips. Cool. Not cold at least. Some thermal function not quite working. Wet, though. Very. He felt her lips part gently as she held herself over his cock. Straining, he felt himself move gently against them, sliding on the slippery fluid of her cunt "—I saw her again. She came to me when he was out of town. She was more than interested but was so scared. I was parked at this mining town, you see— one of those Latter-day Saints enclaves, you know? They didn't like me being there but at least they were able to look the other way—clink, clank, clunk, right? Sex with a piece of equipment is better than sex with a person." Sadness? So many years of giving pleasure, only to end up in the Pile? "She came back. I saw her a lot. Once a week for a while. She was so enthusiastic, like she was starving. Then her unit was sold off to the Amazon Reclamation Project, and I never saw her again."

Her weight was on him and his cock, his pulsing shaft and shimmering head, eased up inside of her wet warmth—at least her inside heat was working. She swallowed him up inside her, pushing herself down on top of him to get as much of his cock into her as she could. As she did her own words broke and fragmented —turning into soft grunts and vowels. With her head tilted back, her too-perfect-for flesh breasts hanging big and soft in front of him, she brought her feet up next to him and pulled herself up softly, as if enjoying the action of his cock sliding out as much as she had feeling it slide in.

"She gave me a rose. She paid for a full hour just to run in and give me a rose. It was a fake one, and she was so ashamed of that. Couldn't find a real one, she said. I thought it was perfect, though—and told her so. Just perfect."

She started to move up and down on his cock, pumping herself up and down him and in and out. Kurtis' body shook, quaked from the meticulous action of her pulling herself up and down. His balls, again, throbbed with release—a fine, ecstatic ache.

Damn, he found himself thinking, *she's fucking good….*

"An old man came to me once. He'd taken PassOn™ —had something incurable, he said, didn't want to feel the pain. I didn't know what to do—" Sadness? Thinking of him? Knowing that she wouldn't have any more like him? Now, old and obsolete, so it was just Kurtis every Friday? Just Kurtis, so she could feel like she was needed, wanted again. The programmers had been too good, too skilled. She liked what she did, but now was too old—except for Kurtis every Friday. "—so we kissed and I held him.

"Then he talked. He told me all of the horrible things he'd thought or done. I don't really know if they were all that bad, I don't know those kinds of things, but he certainly did. He cried as I held him. Finally he said he wanted to go feeling good and empty—and he couldn't tell anyone else he loved the things he told me. He wanted to tell the truth for once, to let it all out to someone who would still love him afterward."

Her movements were clear and crisp, but there was something else, a kind of shiver as she brought herself up and brought herself down. As she talked, her voice laced with fewer and fewer buzzes, clicks, whirs and hums, she moaned and groaned more and more from her actions, from the feeling of him inside her. Her hands went to her breasts and stroked and felt their shape before landing on her nipples. Taking them between thumb and forefingers, she pulled them, hard— much harder than he ever would have—turning their round beauty into stressed cones. Her voice, still speaking, became rough and ragged—chopped with hard vowels from their fuck.

"We made love, the old man and I. When we were done he didn't have that much time. He kissed me and left. Later I found out that he'd died out on the street, two steps from my door. The funeral was big. Many people came, and I guess they cried. I know I would have, watching him go into the ground—if I could."

Kurtis felt her thighs slap down into his own, felt her cunt—expertly constructed—envelop and constrict around his cock. He felt her internals massage and work him, milking the come out of his body. Leaning forward, she let go of her nipples and dropped down to drape them, heavy and hot, in his face. Something rough and feeling almost broken rested in his chest, but he didn't care. He heard something deep inside her grate and squeak with a sudden lack of lubrication. He would have cared—been even frightened—but he was too far gone, too far beyond the edge. The hill was far beyond him and the edge of the cliff was coming up fast—

He exploded. Wet and organic fireworks as he jetted into her synthetic cunt. His body jerked and shook with the power of his orgasm, the rocket that went from his balls, up his shaft and out the head. Stars. Light-headedness, the closeness to God and death—the usual clichés of a powerful, mind-altering come. But for Kurtis, they might have been hoary, but they were also incredibly good, fine, brilliant.

Feeling somewhere else, somewhere distant and fuzzy, she cleaned him up neatly with a washcloth and helped him to his feet. Quiet, silent, she rubbed his back and he tried to form thoughts that would lead to the action of putting on his pants, shoes, shirt, and coat. Finally enough of his brain was behaving itself to allow him to actually turn intent into action—and he did.

"What do I owe you?" Eyebrows designed to show lust, artificial lips created for sensation and beauty, looked sad and old. Eyes designed for seeing and for showing interest looked cold and remote. Her voice was hollow, stilled: "Two hundred?"

"Three," Kurtis said, more from reflex. Rather than look in her eyes, at the glass, he carefully noticed a bit of wayward fluff on his pants, brushed it off.

"I—I don't think—" the device sighed, a heavy, vast sound as if it came from some great bellow hidden in the depths of the her body. "Three, then."

Kurtis collected his three hundred, swiping his card through an ornate terminal she produced, then left— trying too hard not to look back, not to think too much as he did.

It was raining again. With an embarrassed shock, he realized, standing in it, feeling it dot his face with chilled drops, that he hadn't put on his bag, that it was still folded neatly over his arm.

Stepping into the protection of an overhang caused by the twisted metal corpse of an Aeroflot delivery van that had somehow been shoved slightly off the vast wall of crushed vehicles, he struggled and fought with the bag till it was on.

Then he took out his debtcard and cleared the credits she'd paid him for his attention, to feel as if she was wanted again—returned it all. Every cent. Not quite, but almost, he thought *Thanks for those who didn't get to say so.* The words might not have been there, in his mind, but the feelings were. Then he pulled up the hood on his bag, zipped it, and walked away—till next week.

Design/Engineering Team

Kim Addonizio is the author of two books of poetry, *The Philosopher's Club* and *Jimmy & Rita*. Her fiction has appeared in a number of publications, including *Frighten the Horses*, *The Gettysburg Review*, and *Penthouse*, and in the anthologies *Chick-Lit*, *Dick for a Day*, *Hard Love*, and *Microfictions*.

Bill Brent is the founder and editor of *Black Sheets*, a humorous zine about sex and popular culture. Two of his stories have appeared in *Best American Erotica 1997* and *The Factsheet Five Zine Reader*. For a free catalog write to PO Box 31155—CM, San Francisco CA 94131. Include an age statement, please.

447

Pamela Briggs's fiction has appeared in *Young Blood*, *The Brood of Sycorax*, *The Urbanite*, *Daughters of Nyx*, and her chapbook *Tooth & Nail: Two Stories*. She and her older sister spent many nights playing with a tape recorder. Not in the way you're thinking, though.

Leatherdyke, social critic, and professional troublemaker **Pat Califia** is the author of two short story collections, *Macho Sluts* and *Melting Point*, a novel, *Doc and Fluff*, and a book of poetry, *Diesel Fuel*. She has also edited the anthology *Doing It For Daddy*. She is working on a novel, *The Code*, about a master-slave relationship between a gay man and a woman. She lives in San Francisco with two cats, a very fancy sewing machine, dozens of whips, a PowerMac, and her longtime companion, a Panasonic Panabrator. Recently diagnosed with fibromyalgia, she believes that multiple orgasms are the best analgesic.

Renée M. Charles lives in the Midwest in a big pink Queen Anne house filled with books and cats. Her work has appeared in *Selling Venus*, *Genderflex*, *The Revised Worlds of Women*, *Blood Kiss*, *Fetish Fantastic*, *Vampirica Erotica*, *Dark Angels*, *Women Who Run with the Werewolves*, *Best American Erotica 1995*, and *Virgin Territory II*.

M. Christian the boss of this book ("Get back to work, you damned writers!"). Additionally, he has appeared in such publications as *Best American Erotica 1994 &*

1997, Best Gay Erotica 1996, The Mammoth Book of International Erotica, Noirotica 1 and *2, Hot Ticket, Grave Passions, Happily Ever After,* and many others. He is also the editor of the forthcoming anthology *Midsummer Night's Dreams.* He is far too intimate with far too many gadgets.

Stephen Dedman lives in Western Australia with his wife, his wife-in-law, two cats, and a computer named Uma. His first novel, *The Art of Arrow Cutting,* was published in 1997, and his short stories have appeared in *Little Deaths, Science Fiction Age, Realms of Fantasy, Issac Asimov's Science Fiction Magazine, Fantasy & Science Fiction,* and *Bones of the Children.*

Jack Dickson is a self-confessed fender bender and auto eroticist. He no longer drives, his adored Escort having taken all his money only to abscond from his garage with the first rough-fingered joy rider to penetrate its ignition. In between writing *Oddfellows, Freeform,* and "Dragon's Fire" in *SexMagik II,* Jack spends his free time cruising bus depots.

Two-time O. Henry Prize-winner **Janice Eidus** is the author of the novels *Urban Bliss* and *Faithful Rebecca,* and the short story collections *Vito Loves Geraldine* and *The Celibacy Club.* Among the many anthologies in which her stories appear are *Mondo Elvis, Dick For A Day* and *Growing Up Female.*

Amelia G is the editor in chief of *Blue Blood Magazine*. In collaboration with *Blue Blood* art director Forrest Black, she has done photography of and/or writing about both underground and pop culture for *Skin Two*, *Chic*, and others and is the editor of the anthology *Backstage Passes: An Anthology of Rock-and-Roll Erotica from the Pages of Blue Blood Magazine*. Amelia G can be contacted c/o *Blue Blood*, 2625 Piedmont Road #56332, Atlanta, GA 30324.

Paula Guran writes and produces *DarkEcho Omni Horror* (www.omnimag.com/darkecho), writes a weekly newsletter for horror writers and others, and edits-publishes *Wetbones*, a magazine of cutting-edge dark fiction. She's held a gun only once in her life, and it was a .45.

Gerard Daniel Houarner is a rehabilitation counselor at the Bronx Psychiatric Center and resides in a house filled with books, toys, comics, videos, music, five computers, and three human brings. Recent work includes a collection of short stories, *Painfreak*, and a novella in *Inside the Works*, a three-author anthology, as well as his editing of the *Going Postal* anthology for *Pirate Writings*.

Maxim Jakubowski is a British author and editor who somehow got hooked on erotica at an unhealthy early age (but don't blame his parents). He is responsible for three volumes of the *Mammoth Book of Erotica*; a collection of extreme but loving stories, *Life in the World of Women*; and a savagely violent and sexy road thriller, *It's You That I Want to Kiss*. His next novel, *Because She Thought She Loved Me*, will be less explicit, but who knows? His forty other books are judged respectable.

Kevin Killian lives in San Francisco. He is the author of *Shy* and *Bedrooms Have Windows*. His latest books include a novel, *Arctic Summer*, and *Little Men*, a book of stories.

Award-winning author **Nancy Kilpatrick** has published nine novels, two collections, and over 100 short stories. Much of her work is erotic horror. Although she confesses to an intimate relationship with every tool in her life, she is highly selective about the equipment she shares time and space with.

Marc Laidlaw is the author of the novels *The 37th Mandala, The Orchid Eater, Kalifornia, Neon Lotus,* and *Dad's Nuke*. His short stories have appeared in numerous anthologies and magazines, and he is a regular contributor to *Wired* magazine. Recently he has moved toward even greater obscurity by holing up in San Francisco and putting all his creativity into designing levels for the 3-D computer game *Quake*.

Marc Levinthal lives in Los Angeles and has written scores for the film *Valley Girl* and cartoonist Krystine

Krittre's *Anemia and Iodine* for Nickolodeon. His quintet, the Torture Chamber Ensemble, performs live music to film. Marc recently released his first CD, *Dimetrodon Collective Volume One.*. Writing collaborations (with John Mason Skipp) include "The Punchline," in *Dark Destiny II,* and "On a Big Night in Monster History" in *Dark Destiny III.* A novel is in the works.

Anita Mashman is a forty-three-year-old, 285-pound, buxom, blue-eyed brunette. When she isn't fantasizing during her commute, Anita enjoys spending time at home where she lives with a retired Marine/nude art model, three dogs, and two cats. Her stories have appeared in *Best American Erotica 1993, Libido, More Sisters in Sin, Cupido, BBW Magazine,* and *Largesse Volumes I—IV.* She is also the editor of *Gran's Great Recipies.*

Carol Queen is the author of *Real Live Nude Girl, Exhibitionism for the Shy,* and many erotic stories, and the editor of *Switch Hitters, PoMoSexuals,* and *Sex Spoken Here.* She lives in San Francisco.

Stephen Mark Rainey is a prolific author of horror/dark fantasy fiction, with over seventy short stories sold and/or published in such anthologies and magazines as *Robert Bloch's Psychos, Whitley Streiber's Aliens, The Shub-Niggurath Cycle & The Azathoth Cycle, Miskatonic University, The New Lovecraft Circle, The Earth Strikes Back, Cemetery Dance,* and more. He is the author of a collection of short stories, *Fugue Devil & Other Weird Horrors*. Mark is also well known as the editor of the award-winning *Deathrealm* magazine.

Shar Rednour is the quintessential renaissance femme dyke. Among her many fancies are her absolutely filthy zine *Starph*kr*, a quarterly that is pulp full of sex-with-stars stories; sewing fancy see-thru clothes; leading workshops at Sex Works: A San Francisco Institution; and dancing till dawn with her stud, Jackie.

Mike Resnick is the best-selling author of such novels as *Santiago*, *Ivory*, *Soothsayer*, and *The Widowmaker*. He has won three Hugos and a Nebula, plus a host of other awards. Since 1982 he has written some thirty novels and 100 short stories on his various computers, all of which he distrusts completely.

Thomas S. Roche's short stories have appeared in *Black Sheets*, *Blue Blood*, *Cupido*, and *Paramour*, and in such anthologies as *Best American Erotica 1996* and *1997*, and *The Mammoth Book of Pulp Fiction*. He edited two volumes of the *Noirotica* series and his short fiction is collected in *Dark Matter*. He lives in San Francisco.

Chadwick H. Saxelid lives in the San Francisco Bay Area with his wife, son, cat, and a *very* large video library. "Clean" is his first published narrative fiction.

D. Travers Scott is the author of *Execution, Texas: 1987* and his writing appears in several anthologies, including *Best American Gay Fiction 1997; Best Gay Erotica 1996* and *1997; Reclaiming the Heartland; PoMoSexuals; Switch Hitters; Memory Practice Pleasure: Gay Male Performance; Forbidden: Defiant Lesbian Writing; Queer-View Mirror 2;* and *Noirotica 2.* He lives in Seattle.

Simon Sheppard's work has appeared in many anthologies, including *Best American Erotica 1997; Best Gay Erotica 1996* and *1997; Bending the Landscape: Fantasy; Brothers of the Night;* and *Grave Passions.* He's not what you'd call mechanically inclined; he can barely change a tire on his motorcycle. And he's never been to Kansas.

John Shirley is the author of numerous novels and short-story collections including *Silicon Embrace, New Noir, Eclipse* trilogy, and *The Exploded Heart.* He's the lead singer of the San Francisco rock band The Panther Moderns.

Cecilia Tan lost her eyesight to a computer and her "virginity" to a fat Magic Marker (one of the scented kind). She is the author of *Black Feathers: Erotic Dreams,* a collection of erotic fantasy and sf stories, editor of *SM Visions: The Best of Circlet Press,* and the publisher of Circlet Press, the world's only book publisher specializing in erotic science fiction. She also writes political essays, rants, literary fiction, and other

stuff, some of which you can read free on her Web site:
http://www.circlet.com/pub/u/ctan/home.html

Lucy Taylor's works include the collections *Close to the Bone, The Flesh Artist,* and *Unnatural Acts and Other Stories,* and a Stoker award-winning novel, *The Safety of Unknown Cities.* Her fourth collection is called *Painted in Blood.* She lives in the hills outside Boulder, Colorado, with her seven cats.

MASQUERADE BOOKS

MASQUERADE

S. CRABB
CHATS ON OLD PEWTER
$6.95/611-1
A compendium of tales dedicated to dominant women. From domineering check-out girls to merciless flirts on the prowl, these women know what men like—and are highly skilled at reducing any man to putty in their hands.

PAT CALIFIA
SENSUOUS MAGIC
$7.95/610-3
"*Sensuous Magic* is clear, succinct and engaging.... Califia is the Dr. Ruth of the alternative sexuality set...."
—*Lambda Book Report*

Erotic pioneer Pat Califia provides this unpretentious peek behind the mask of dominant/submissive sexuality. With her trademark wit and insight, Califia demystifies "the scene" for the novice, explaining the terms and techniques behind many misunderstood sexual practices.

ANAÏS NIN AND FRIENDS
WHITE STAINS
$6.95/609-X
A lost classic of 1940s erotica returns! Written by Anaïs Nin, Virginia Admiral, Caresse Crosby, and others for a dollar per page, this breathtakingly sensual volume was printed privately and soon became an underground legend. After more than fifty years, this priceless collection of explicit but sophisticated musings is back in print—and available to the contemporary connoisseur of erotica.

DENISE HALL
JUDGMENT
$6.95/590-5
Judgment—a forbidding edifice where unfortunate young women find themselves degraded and abandoned to the wiles of their cruel masters. Callie MacGuire descends into the depths of this prison, discovering a capacity for sensual torment she never dreamed existed.

CLAIRE WILLOWS
PRESENTED IN LEATHER
$6.95/576-X
The story of poor Flora Price and the stunning punishments she suffered at the hands of her cruel captors. At the age of nineteen, Flora is whisked to the south of France, where she is imprisoned in Villa Close, an institution devoted to the ways of the lash—not to mention the paddle, the strap, the rod...

ALISON TYLER & DANTE DAVIDSON
BONDAGE ON A BUDGET
$6.95/570-0
Filled with delicious scenarios requiring no more than simple household items and a little imagination, this guide to DIY S&M will explode the myth that adventurous sex requires a dungeonful of expensive custom-made paraphernalia.

JEAN SADDLER
THE FASCINATING TYRANT
$6.95/569-7
A reprint of a classic tale from the 1930s. Jean Saddler's most famous novel, *The Fascinating Tyrant* is a riveting glimpse of sexual extravagance in which a young man discovers his penchant for flagellation and sadomasochism.

ROBERT SEWALL
THE DEVIL'S ADVOCATE
$6.95/553-6
Clara Reeves appeals to Conrad Garnett, a New York district attorney, for help in tracking down her missing sister, Rita. Clara soon finds herself being "persuaded" to accompany Conrad on his descent into a modern-day hell, where unspeakable pleasures await....

LUCY TAYLOR
UNNATURAL ACTS
$7.95/552-2
"A topnotch collection"   —*Science Fiction Chronicle*

Unnatural Acts plunges deep into the dark side of the psyche and brings to life a disturbing vision of erotic horror. Unrelenting angels and hungry gods play with souls and bodies in Taylor's murky cosmos: where heaven and hell are merely differences of perspective.

J. A. GUERRA, ED.
COME QUICKLY:
For Couples on the Go
$6.50/461-5
The increasing pace of daily life is no reason to forgo a little carnal pleasure whenever the mood strikes. Here are over sixty of the hottest fantasies around—all designed especially for modern couples on a hectic schedule.

ERICA BRONTE
LUST, INC.
$6.50/467-4
Explore the extremes of passion that lurk beneath even the most businesslike exteriors. Join in the sexy escapades of a group of professionals whose idea of office decorum is like nothing you've ever encountered!

MASQUERADE BOOKS

OLIVIA M. RAVENSWORTH
DOMESTIC SERVICE
$6.95/615-4

Though married for twenty-five years, Alan and Janet still manage to find sensual excitement in each other's arms. Sexy magazines fan the flames of their desire—so much so that Janet yearns to bring her own most private fantasy to life. She persuades Alan to hire live-in domestic help—and their home soon becomes the neighborhood's most infamous household!

THE DESIRES OF REBECCA
$6.50/532-8

Rebecca follows her passions from the simple love of the girl next door to the lechery of London's most notorious brothel, hoping for the ultimate thrill. She casts her lot with a crew of sapphic buccaneers, each of whom is more than capable of matching Rebecca's lust.

THE MISTRESS OF CASTLE ROHMENSTADT
$5.95/372-4

Lovely Katherine inherits a secluded European castle from a mysterious relative. Upon arrival she discovers, much to her delight, that the castle is a haven of sexual perversion. Before long, Katherine is truly Mistress of the house!

GERALD GREY
LONDON GIRLS
$6.50/531-X

In 1875, Samuel Brown arrives in London, determined to take the glorious city by storm. Samuel quickly distinguishes himself as one of the city's most notorious rakehells. Young Mr. Brown knows well the many ways of making a lady weak at the knees—and uses them not only to his delight, but to his enormous profit!

ATAULLAH MARDAAN
KAMA HOURI/DEVA DASI
$7.95/512-3

"Mardaan excels in crowding her pages with the sights and smells of India, and her erotic descriptions are convincingly realistic."
—Michael Perkins,
The Secret Record: Modern Erotic Literature

Kama Houri details the life of a sheltered Western woman who finds herself living within the confines of a harem. *Deva Dasi* is a tale dedicated to the sacred women of India who devoted their lives to the fulfillment of the senses.

VISCOUNT LADYWOOD
GYNECOCRACY
$9.95/511-5

Julian is sent to a private school, and discovers that his program of study has been devised by stern Mademoiselle de Chambonnard. In no time, Julian is learning the many ways of pleasure and pain—under the firm hand of this beautifully demanding headmistress.

N. T. MORLEY
THE OFFICE
$6.95/616-2

Lovely young Suzette interviews for a desirable new position on the staff of a bondage magazine. Much to her delight, Suzette is hired—and discovers that her new employer's interest in dominance and submission extends beyond the printed page. Before long, Suzette and her fellow staffers are putting in long hours—and benefitting deliciously from some very specialized on-the-job training!

THE CONTRACT
$6.95/575-1

Meet Carlton and Sarah, two true connoisseurs of discipline. Sarah is experiencing some difficulty in training her current submissive. Carlton proposes an unusual wager: if Carlton is unsuccessful in bringing Tina to a full appreciation of Sarah's domination, Carlton himself will become Sarah's devoted slave....

THE LIMOUSINE
$6.95/555-7

Brenda was enthralled with her roommate Kristi's illicit sex life: a never ending parade of men who satisfied Kristi's desire to be dominated. Brenda decides to embark on a trip into submission, beginning in the long, white limousine where Kristi first met the Master.

THE CASTLE
$6.95/530-1

Tess Roberts is held captive by a crew of disciplinarians intent on making all her dreams come true—even those she'd never admitted to herself. While anyone can arrange for a stay at the Castle, Tess proves herself one of the most gifted applicants yet....

THE PARLOR
$6.50/496-8

The mysterious John and Sarah ask Kathryn to be their slave—an idea that turns her on so much that she can't refuse! Little by little, Kathryn not only learns to serve, but comes to know the inner secrets of her keepers.

MASQUERADE BOOKS

VANESSA DURIÈS
THE TIES THAT BIND
$6.50/510-7
This best-selling account of real-life dominance and submission will keep you gasping with its vivid depictions of sensual abandon. At the hand of Masters Georges, Patrick, Pierre and others, this submissive seductress experiences pleasures she never knew existed....

M. S. VALENTINE
THE GOVERNESS
$6.95/562-X
Lovely Miss Hunnicut eagerly embarks upon a career as a governess, hoping to escape the memories of her broken engagement. Little does she know that Crawleigh Manor is far from the upstanding household it appears. Mr. Crawleigh, in particular, devotes himself to Miss Hunnicut's thorough defiling.

AMANDA WARE
BOUND TO THE PAST
$6.50/452-6
Doing research in an old Tudor mansion, Anne finds herself aroused by James, a descendant of the property's owners. Together they uncover the perverse desires of the mansion's long-dead master—desires that bind Anne inexorably to the past—not to mention the bedpost!

SACHI MIZUNO
SHINJUKU NIGHTS
$6.50/493-3
Using Tokyo's infamous red light district as his backdrop, Sachi Mizuno weaves an intricate web of sensual desire, wherein many characters are ensnared by the demands of their carnal natures.
PASSION IN TOKYO
$6.50/454-2
Tokyo—one of Asia's most historic and seductive cities. Come behind the closed doors of its citizens, and witness the many pleasures that await. Men and women from every stratum of society free themselves of all inhibitions in this tour through the libidinous East.

MARTINE GLOWINSKI
POINT OF VIEW
$6.50/433-X
The story of one woman's extraordinary erotic awakening. With the assistance of her new, unexpectedly kinky lover, she discovers and explores her exhibitionist tendencies—until there is virtually nothing she won't do before the horny audiences her man arranges. Soon she is infamous for her unabashed sexual performances!

RICHARD McGOWAN
A HARLOT OF VENUS
$6.50/425-9
A highly fanciful, epic tale of lust on Mars! Cavortia—the most famous and sought-after courtesan in the cosmopolitan city of Venus—finds love and much more during her adventures with some cosmic characters. A sexy, sci-fi fairytale.

M. ORLANDO
THE SLEEPING PALACE
$6.95/582-4
Another thrilling volume of erotic reveries from the author of *The Architecture of Desire*. *Maison Bizarre* is the scene of unspeakable erotic cruelty; the *Lust Akademie* holds captive only the most luscious students of the sensual arts; *Baden-Eros* is the luxurious retreat of one's nastiest dreams.

CHET ROTHWELL
KISS ME, KATHERINE
$5.95/410-0
Beautiful Katherine can hardly believe her luck. Not only is she married to the charming Nelson, she's free to live out all her erotic fantasies with other men. Katherine's desires are more than any one man can handle—and plenty of men wait to fulfill her extraordinary needs!

MARCO VASSI
THE STONED APOCALYPSE
$5.95/401-1/Mass market
"Marco Vassi is our champion sexual energist."   —*VLS*

During his lifetime, Marco Vassi's reputation as a champion of sexual experimentation was worldwide. Funded by his groundbreaking erotic writing, *The Stoned Apocalypse* is Vassi's autobiography; chronicling a cross-country trip on America's erotic byways, it offers a rare an stimulating glimpse of a generation's sexual imagination.
THE SALINE SOLUTION
$6.95/568-9/Mass market
"I've always read Marco's work with interest and I have the highest opinion not only of his talent but his intellectual boldness."
                                    —Norman Mailer

During the Sexual Revolution, Vassi established himself as an explorer of an uncharted sexual landscape. Through this story of one couple's brief affair and the events that lead them to desperately reassess their lives, Vassi examines the dangers of intimacy in an age of extraordinary change.

MASQUERADE BOOKS

SUBURBAN SOULS
$9.95/563-8

One of American erotica's first classics. Focusing on the May–December sexual relationship of nubile Lillian and the more experienced Jack, all three volumes of *Suburban Souls* now appear in one special edition—guaranteed to enrapture modern readers with its lurid detail.

THE MISFORTUNES OF COLETTE
$7.95/564-6

The tale of one woman's erotic suffering at the hands of the sadistic man and woman who take her in hand. Beautiful Colette is the victim of an obscene plot guaranteed to keep her in erotic servitude—first to her punishing guardian, then to the man who takes her as his wife. Passed from one lustful tormentor to another, Colette wonders whether she is destined to find her greatest pleasures in punishment!

LOVE'S ILLUSION
$6.95/549-2

Elizabeth Renard yearned for the body of rich and successful Dan Harrington. Then she discovered Harrington's secret weakness: a need to be humiliated and punished. She makes him her slave, and together they commence a thrilling journey into depravity that leaves nothing to the imagination!

NADIA
$5.95/267-1

Follow the delicious but neglected Nadia as she works to wring every drop of pleasure out of life—despite an unhappy marriage. With the help of some very eager men, Nadia soon experiences the erotic pleaures she had always dreamed of.... A classic title providing a peek into the sexual lives of another time and place.

TITIAN BERESFORD
CHIDEWELL HOUSE AND OTHER STORIES
$6.95/554-9

What keeps Cecil a virtual, if willing, prisoner of Chidewell House? One man has been sent to investigate the sexy situation—and reports back with tales of such depravity that no expense is spared in attempting Cecil's rescue. But what man would possibly desire release from the breathtakingly corrupt Elizabeth?

CINDERELLA
$6.50/500-X

Beresford triumphs again with this intoxicating tale, filled with castle dungeons and tightly corseted ladies-in-waiting, naughty viscounts and impossibly cruel masturbatrixes—nearly every conceivable method of erotic torture is explored and described in lush, vivid detail.

JUDITH BOSTON
$6.50/525-5

A bestselling chronicle of female domination. Edward would have been lucky to get the stodgy companion he thought his parents had hired for him. But an exquisite woman arrives at his door, and Edward finds—to his increasing delight—that his lewd behavior never goes unpunished by the unflinchingly severe Judith Boston.

TINY ALICE
THE GEEK
$5.95/341-4

An offbeat classic of modern erotica, *The Geek* is told from the point of view of, well, a chicken who reports on the various perversities he witnesses as part of a traveling carnival. When a gang of renegade lesbians kidnaps Chicken and his geek, all hell breaks loose. A strange but highly arousing tale, filled with outrageous erotic oddities, that finally returns to print after years of infamy.

LYN DAVENPORT
THE GUARDIAN II
$6.50/505-0

The tale of submissive Felicia Brookes continues. No sooner has Felicia come to love Rodney than she discovers that she has been sold—and must now accustom herself to the guardianship of the debauched Duke of Smithton. Surely Rodney will rescue her from the domination of this depraved stranger. *Won't he?*

GWYNETH JAMES
DREAM CRUISE
$4.95/3045-8

Angelia has it all—exciting career and breathtaking beauty. But she longs to kick up her high heels and have some fun, so she takes an island vacation and vows to leave her inhibitions behind. From the moment her plane takes off, she finds herself in one steamy encounter after another—and wishes this horny holiday would never end!

LIZBETH DUSSEAU
MEMBER OF THE CLUB
$6.95/608-1

A restless woman yearns to realize her most secret, licentious desires. There is a club that exists for the fulfillment of such fantasies—a club devoted to the pleasures of the flesh, and the gratification of every hunger. When its members call she is compelled to answer—and serve each in an endless quest for satisfaction.... A best-selling look at the workings of the ultimate sex club.

MASQUERADE BOOKS

SPANISH HOLIDAY
$4.95/185-3
Lauren didn't mean to fall in love with the enigmatic Sam, but a once-in-a-lifetime European vacation gives her all the evidence she needs that this hot, insatiable man might be the one for her....Soon, both lovers are eagerly exploring the furthest reaches of their desires.

JOCELYN JOYCE
PRIVATE LIVES
$4.95/309-0
The dirty habits of the illustrious make for a sizzling tale of French erotic life. A widow has a craving for a young busboy; he's sleeping with a rich businessman's wife; her husband is minding his sex business elsewhere!

SABINE
$4.95/3046-6
There is no one who can refuse her once she casts her spell; no lover can do anything less than give up his whole life for her. Great men and empires fall at her feet; but she is haughty, distracted, impervious. It is the eve of WW II, and Sabine must find a new lover equal to her talents and her tastes.

SARA H. FRENCH
MASTER OF TIMBERLAND
$6.95/595-6
A tale of sexual slavery at the ultimate paradise resort—where sizzling submissives serve their masters without question. One of our bestselling titles, this trek to Timberland has ignited passions the world over—and stands poised to become one of modern erotica's legendary tales.

MARY LOVE
ANGELA
$6.95/545-X
Angela's game is "look but don't touch," and she drives everyone mad with desire, dancing for their pleasure but never allowing a single caress. Soon her sensual spell is cast, and she's the only one who can break it!

MASTERING MARY SUE
$5.95/351-1
Mary Sue is a rich nymphomaniac whose husband is determined to declare her mentally incompetent and gain control of her fortune. He brings her to a castle where, to Mary Sue's delight, she is unleashed for a veritable sex-fest!

AMARANTHA KNIGHT
THE DARKER PASSIONS: FRANKENSTEIN
$6.95/617-0
The mistress of erotic horror sets her sights on Mary Shelley's darkest creation. What if you could create a living, breathing human? What shocking acts could it be taught to perform, to desire, to love? Find out what pleasures await those who play God in another breath-taking installation in the phenomenally popular Darker Passions series.

The Darker Passions: CARMILLA
$6.95/578-6
Captivated by the portrait of a beautiful woman, a young man finds himself becoming obsessed with her remarkable story. Little by little, he uncovers the many blasphemies and debaucheries with which the beauteous Laura filled her hours—even as an otherworldly presence began feasting upon her....

The Darker Passions: THE PICTURE OF DORIAN GRAY
$6.50/342-2
One woman finds her most secret desires laid bare by a portrait far more revealing than she could have imagined. Soon she benefits from a skillful masquerade, indulging her previously hidden and unusual whims.

THE DARKER PASSIONS READER
$6.50/432-1
Here are the most eerily erotic passages from the acclaimed sexual reworkings of *Dracula, Frankenstein, Dr. Jekyll & Mr. Hyde* and *The Fall of the House of Usher.*

The Darker Passions: DR. JEKYLL AND MR. HYDE
$4.95/227-1
It is a sexy story of incredible transformations. Explore the steamy possibilities of a tale where no one is quite who—or what—they seem. Victorian bedrooms explode with hidden demons!

THE PAUL LITTLE LIBRARY
TEARS OF THE INQUISITION
$6.95/612-X
Paul Little delivers a staggering account of pleasure. "There was a tickling inside her as her nervous system reminded her she was ready for sex. But before her was...the Inquisitor!" Titillating accusations ring through the chambers of the Inquisitor as men and women confess their every desire....

MASQUERADE BOOKS

CHINESE JUSTICE
$6.95/596-4
The notorious Paul Little indulges his penchant for discipline in these wild tales. *Chinese Justice* is already a classic—the story of the excruciating pleasures and delicious punishments inflicted on foreigners under the tyrannical leaders of the Boxer Rebellion.

FIT FOR A KING/BEGINNER'S LUST
$8.95/571-9/Trade paperback
Two complete novels from this master of modern lust. Voluptuous and exquisite, she is a woman *Fit for a King*—but could she withstand the fantastic force of his carnality? *Beginner's Lust* pays off handsomely for a novice in the many ways of sensuality.

SENTENCED TO SERVITUDE
$8.95/565-4/Trade paperback
A haughty young aristocrat learns what becomes of excessive pride when she is abducted and forced to submit to ordeals of sensual torment. Trained to accept her submissive state, the icy young woman soon melts under the heat of her owners, discovering a talent for love she never knew existed....

ROOMMATE'S SECRET
$8.95/557-3/Trade paperback
A woman is forced to make ends meet by the most ancient of methods. From the misery of early impoverishment to the delight of ill-gotten gains, Elda learns to rely on her considerable sensual talents.

TUTORED IN LUST
$6.95/547-6
This tale of the initiation and instruction of a carnal college co-ed and her fellow students unlocks the sex secrets of the classroom.

LOVE SLAVE/
PECULIAR PASSIONS OF MEG
$8.95/529-8/Trade paperback
What does it take to acquire a willing *Love Slave* of one's own? What are the appetites that lurk within *Meg*? The notoriously depraved Paul Little spares no lascivious detail in these two relentless tales!

CELESTE
$6.95/544-1
It's definitely all in the family for this female duo of sexual dynamics. While traveling through Europe, these two try everything and everyone on their horny holiday.

ALL THE WAY
$6.95/509-3
Two hot Little tales in one big volume! *Going All the Way* features an unhappy man who tries to purge himself of the memory of his lover with a series of quirky and uninhibited vixens. *Pushover* tells the story of a serial spanker and his celebrated exploits.

THE END OF INNOCENCE
$6.95/546-8
The early days of Women's Emancipation are the setting for this story of very independent ladies. These women were willing to go to any lengths to fight for their sexual freedom, and willing to endure any punishment in their desire for total liberation.

THE BEST OF PAUL LITTLE
$6.50/469-0
Known for his fantastic portrayals of punishment and pleasure, Little never fails to push readers over the edge of sensual excitement. His best scenes are here collected for the enjoyment of all erotic connoisseurs.

CAPTIVE MAIDENS
$5.95/440-2
Three young women find themselves powerless against the debauched landowners of 1824 England. They are banished to a sex colony, where they are subjected to unspeakable perversions.

THE PRISONER
$5.95/330-9
Judge Black has built a secret room below a penitentiary, where he sentences his female prisoners to hours of exhibition and torment while his friends watch. Judge Black's brand of rough justice keeps his captives on the brink of utter pleasure!

DOUBLE NOVEL
$6.95/86-6
The Metamorphosis of Lisette Joyaux tells the story of a young woman initiated into an incredible world world of lesbian lusts. *The Story of Monique* reveals the twisted sexual rituals that beckon the ripe and willing Monique.

SLAVE ISLAND
$5.95/441-0
A tale of ultimate sexual license from this modern masterA leisure cruise is waylaid by Lord Henry Philbrock, a sadistic genius. The ship's passengers are kidnapped and spirited to his island prison, where the women are trained to accommodate the most bizarre sexual cravings of the rich and perverted. A perennially bestselling title.

....

ALIZARIN LAKE
CLARA
$6.95/548-4
The mysterious death of a beautiful woman leads her old boyfriend on a harrowing journey of discovery. His search uncovers an unimaginably sensuous woman embarked on a quest for deeper and more unusual sensations, each more shocking than the one before!

MASQUERADE BOOKS

SEX ON DOCTOR'S ORDERS
$5.95/402-X

A tale of true devotion to mankind! Naughty Beth, a nubile young nurse, uses her considerable skills to further medical science by offering insatiable assistance in the gathering of important specimens. Soon she's involved everyone in her horny work—and no one leaves without surrendering exactly what Beth wants!

THE EROTIC ADVENTURES OF HARRY TEMPLE
$4.95/127-6

Harry Temple's memoirs chronicle his incredibly amorous adventures—from his initiation at the hands of insatiable sirens, through his stay at a house of hot repute, to his encounters with a chastity-belted nympho, and much more! A modern classic!

LUSCIDIA WALLACE
THE ICE MAIDEN
$6.95/613-8

Edward Canton has everything he wants in life, with one exception: Rebecca Esterbrook. He kidnaps her and whisks her away to his remote island compound, where she learns to shed her inhibitions with both men and women. Fully aroused for the first time in her life, she becomes a slave to his—and her—desires!

JOHN NORMAN
HUNTERS OF GOR
$6.95/592-1

Tarl Cabot ventures into the wilderness of Gor, pitting his skill against brutal outlaws and sly warriors. His life on Gor been complicated by three beautiful, very different women: Talena, Tarl's one-time queen; Elizabeth, his fearless comrade; and Verna, chief of the feral panther women. In this installment of Norman's million-selling sci-fi phenomenon, the fates of these uncommon women are finally revealed....

CAPTIVE OF GOR
$6.95/581-6

On Earth, Elinor Brinton was accustomed to having it all—wealth, beauty, and a host of men wrapped around her little finger. But Elinor's spoiled existence is a thing of the past. She is now a pleasure slave of Gor—a world whose society insists on her subservience to any man who calls her his own. And despite her headstrong past, Elinor finds herself succumbing—with pleasure—to her powerful Master....

RAIDERS OF GOR
$6.95/558-1

Tarl Cabot descends into the depths of Port Kar—the most degenerate port city of the Counter-Earth. There Cabot learns the ways of Kar, whose residents are renowned for the grip in which they hold their voluptuous slaves....

ASSASSIN OF GOR
$6.95/538-7

The chronicles of Counter-Earth continue with this examination of Gorean society. Here is the caste system of Gor: from the Assassin Kuurus, on a mission of vengeance, to Pleasure Slaves, trained in the ways of personal ecstasy.

NOMADS OF GOR
$6.95/527-1

Cabot finds his way across Gor, pledged to serve the Priest-Kings. Unfortunately for Cabot, his mission leads him to the savage Wagon People—nomads who may very well kill before revealing any secrets....

PRIEST-KINGS OF GOR
$6.95/488-7

Tarl Cabot searches for his lovely wife Talena. Does she live, or was she destroyed by the all-powerful Priest-Kings? Cabot is determined to find out—though no one who has approached the mountain stronghold of the Priest-Kings has ever returned alive....

OUTLAW OF GOR
$6.95/487-9

Tarl Cabot returns to Gor. Upon arriving, he discovers that his name, his city and the names of those he loves have become unspeakable. Once a respected Tarnsman, Cabot has become an outlaw, and must discover his new purpose on this strange planet, where even simple answers have their price....

TARNSMAN OF GOR
$6.95/486-0

This controversial series returns! Tarl Cabot is transported to Gor. He must quickly accustom himself to the ways of this world, including the caste system which exalts some as Priest-Kings or Warriors, and debases others as slaves.

SYDNEY ST. JAMES
RIVE GAUCHE
$5.95/317-1

The Latin Quarter, Paris, circa 1920. Expatriate bohemians couple wildly—before eventually abandoning their ambitions amidst the temptations waiting to be indulged in every bedroom.

BUY ANY 4 BOOKS & CHOOSE 1 ADDITIONAL BOOK, OF EQUAL OR LESSER VALUE, AS YOUR FREE GIFT

MASQUERADE BOOKS

THOMAS S. ROCHE
DARK MATTER
$6.95/484-4
"*Dark Matter* is sure to please gender outlaws, bodymod junkies, goth vampires, boys who wish they were dykes, and anybody who's not to sure where the fine line should be drawn between pleasure and pain. It's a handful."—Pat Califia

"Here is the erotica of the cumming millennium.... You will be deliciously disturbed, but never disappointed."
—Poppy Z. Brite

NOIROTICA 2: Pulp Friction
$7.95/584-0
Another volume of criminally seductive stories set in the murky terrain of the erotic and noir genres. Thomas Roche has gathered the darkest jewels from today's edgiest writers to create this provocative collection. A must for all fans of contemporary erotica.
NOIROTICA: An Anthology of Erotic Crime Stories (Ed.)
$6.95/390-2
A collection of darkly sexy tales, taking place at the crossroads of the crime and erotic genres. Here are some of today's finest writers, all of whom explore the extraordinary and arousing terrain where desire runs irrevocably afoul of the law.

DAVID MELTZER
UNDER
$6.95/290-6
The story of a 21st century sex professional living at the bottom of the social heap. After surgeries designed to increase his physical allure, corrupt government forces drive the cyber-gigolo underground, where even more bizarre cultures await....

LAURA ANTONIOU, ED.
SOME WOMEN
$7.95/573-5
Introduction by Pat Califia
"Makes the reader think about the wide range of SM experiences, beyond the glamour of fiction and fantasy, or the clever-clever prose of the perverati." —*SKIN TWO*

Over forty essays written by women actively involved in consensual dominance and submission. Professional mistresses, lifestyle leatherdykes, whipmakers, titleholders—women from every conceivable walk of life lay bare their true feelings about issues as explosive as feminism, abuse, pleasure and public image. A bestselling title, Some Women is a valuable resource for anyone interested in sexuality.

NO OTHER TRIBUTE
$7.95/603-0
Tales of women kept in bondage to their lovers by their deepest passions. Love pushes these women beyond acceptable limits, rendering them helpless to deny anything to the men and women they adore.
BY HER SUBDUED
$6.95/281-7
These tales all involve women in control—of their lives and their lovers. So much in control that they can remorselessly break rules to become powerful goddesses of those who sacrifice all to worship at their feet.

AMELIA G, ED.
BACKSTAGE PASSES: Rock n' Roll Erotica from the Pages of *Blue Blood* Magazine
$6.95/438-0
Amelia G, editor of the goth-sex journal *Blue Blood*, has brought together some of today's most irreverent writers, each of whom has outdone themselves with an edgy, antic tale of modern lust.

ROMY ROSEN
SPUNK
$6.95/492-5
Casey, a lovely model poised upon the verge of super-celebrity, falls for an insatiable young rock singer—not suspecting that his sexual appetite has led him to experiment with a dangerous new aphrodisiac. Soon, Casey becomes addicted to the drug, and her craving plunges her into a strange underworld, and into an alliance with a shadowy young man with secrets of his own....

MOLLY WEATHERFIELD
CARRIE'S STORY
$6.95/485-2
"I was stunned by how well it was written and how intensely foreign I found its sexual world.... And, since this is a world I don't frequent... I thoroughly enjoyed the National Geo tour."
—*bOING bOING*

"Hilarious and harrowing... just when you think things can't get any wilder, they do." —*Black Sheets*

Weatherfield's bestselling examination of dominance and submission. "I had been Jonathan's slave for about a year when he told me he wanted to sell me at an auction...." A rare piece of erotica, both thoughtful and hot!

MASQUERADE BOOKS

CYBERSEX CONSORTIUM
CYBERSEX: The Perv's Guide to Finding Sex on the Internet
$6.95/471-2

You've heard the objections: cyberspace is soaked with sex, mired in immorality. Okay—so where is it!? Tracking down the good stuff—the real good stuff—can waste an awful lot of expensive time, and frequently leave you high and dry. The Cybersex Consortium presents an easy-to-use guide for those intrepid adults who know what they want.

LAURA ANTONIOU
("Sara Adamson")

"Ms. Adamson creates a wonderfully diverse world of lesbian, gay, straight, bi and transgendered characters, all mixing delightfully in the melting pot of sadomasochism and planting the genre more firmly in the culture at large. I for one am cheering her on!"
—Kate Bornstein

THE MARKETPLACE
$7.95/602-2

The first title in Antoniou's thrilling Marketplace Trilogy, following the lives an lusts of those who have been deemed worthy to participate in the ultimate BDSM arena.

THE SLAVE
$7.95/601-4

The Slave covers the experience of one talented submissive who longs to join the ranks of those who have proven themselves worthy of entry into the Marketplace. But the price, while delicious, is staggeringly high....

THE TRAINER
$6.95/249-3

The Marketplace Trilogy concludes with the story of the trainers, and the desires and paths that led them to become the ultimate figures of authority.

TAMMY JO ECKHART
AMAZONS: Erotic Explorations of Ancient Myths
$7.95/534-4

The Amazon—the fierce woman warrior—appears in the traditions of many cultures, but never before has the erotic potential of this archetype been explored with such imagination. Powerful pleasures await anyone lucky enough to encounter Eckhart's spitfires.

PUNISHMENT FOR THE CRIME
$6.95/427-5

Stories that explore dominance and submission. From an encounter between two of society's most despised individuals, to the explorations of longtime friends, these tales take you where few others have ever dared....

GERI NETTICK
WITH BETH ELLIOT
MIRRORS: Portrait of a Lesbian Transsexual
$6.95/435-6

Born a male, Geri Nettick knew something just didn't fit. Even after coming to terms with her own gender dysphoria she still fought to be accepted by the lesbian feminist community to which she felt she belonged. A remarkable and inspiring true story of self-discover and acceptance.

TRISTAN TAORMINO & DAVID AARON CLARK, EDS.
RITUAL SEX
$6.95/391-0

The contributors to *Ritual Sex* know that body and soul share more common ground than society feels comfortable acknowledging. From memoirs of ecstatic revelation, to quests to reconcile sex and spirit, *Ritual Sex* provides an unprecedented look at private life.

AMARANTHA KNIGHT, ED.
DEMON SEX
$7.95/594-8

A blood-chilling descent into erotic horror. Examining the dark forces of humankind's oldest stories, the contributors to *Demon Sex* reveal the strange symbiosis of dread and desire. Stories include a streetwalker's deal with the devil; a visit with the stripper from Hell; the reemergence of an ancient Indian magic; the secrets behind an aging rocker's timeless appeal; and many more guaranteed to shatter preconceptions about modern lust.

SEDUCTIVE SPECTRES
$6.95/464-X

Tours through the erotic supernatural via the imaginations of today's best writers. Never have ghostly encounters been so alluring, thanks to otherworldly characters well-acquainted with the many pleasures of the flesh.

SEX MACABRE
$6.95/392-9

Horror tales designed for dark and sexy nights—sure to make your skin crawl, and heart beat faster.

FLESH FANTASTIC
$6.95/352-X

Humans have long toyed with the idea of "playing God": creating life from nothingness, bringing life to the inanimate. Now Amarantha Knight collects stories exploring not only the act of Creation, but the lust that follows.

MASQUERADE BOOKS

GARY BOWEN
DIARY OF A VAMPIRE
$6.95/331-7
"Gifted with a darkly sensual vision and a fresh voice, [Bowen] is a writer to watch out for."
—Cecilia Tan

Rafael, a red-blooded male with an insatiable hunger for the same, is the perfect antidote to the effete malcontents haunting bookstores today. The emergence of a bold and brilliant vision, rooted in past and present.

GRANT ANTREWS
LEGACIES
$7.95/605-7
Kathi Lawton discovers that she has inherited the troubling secret of her late mother's scandalous sexuality. In an effort to understand what motivated her mother's desires, Kathi embarks on an exploration of SM that leads her into the arms of Horace Moore, a mysterious man who seems to see into her very soul. As she begins falling for her new master, Kathi finds herself wondering just how far she'll go to prove her love.... Another moving exploration from the author of *My Darling Dominatrix*.

SUBMISSIONS
$7.95/618-9
Antrews portrays the very special elements of the dominant/submissive relationship with restraint—this time with the story of a lonely man, a winning lottery ticket, and a demanding dominatrix. Suddenly finding himself a millionaire, Kevin Donovan thinks his worries are over—until his restless soul tires of the high life. He turns to the icy Maitresse Genevieve, hoping that her ministrations will guide him to some deeper peace....

ROGUES GALLERY
$6.95/522-0
A stirring evocation of dominant/submissive love. Two doctors meet and slowly fall in love. Once Beth reveals her hidden desires to Jim, the two explore the forbidden acts that will come to define their distinctly exotic affair.

MY DARLING DOMINATRIX
$7.95/566-2
When a man and a woman fall in love, it's supposed to be simple, uncomplicated, easy—unless that woman happens to be a dominatrix. This highly praised and unpretentious love story captures the richness and depth of this very special kind of love without leering or smirking.

JEAN STINE
THRILL CITY
$6.95/411-9
Thrill City is the seat of the world's increasing depravity, and this classic novel transports you there with a vivid style you'd be hard pressed to ignore. No writer is better suited to describe the extremes of this modern Babylon.

JOHN WARREN
THE TORQUEMADA KILLER
$6.95/367-8
Detective Eva Hernandez gets her first "big case": a string of murders taking place within New York's SM community. Eva assembles the evidence, revealing a picture of a world misunderstood and under attack—and gradually comes to face her own hidden longings.

THE LOVING DOMINANT
$7.95/600-6
Everything you need to know about an infamous sexual variation, and an unspoken type of love. Warren guides readers through this rarely seen world, and offers clear-eyed advice guaranteed to enlighten any erotic explorer.

DAVID AARON CLARK
SISTER RADIANCE
$6.95/215-9
A meditation on love, sex, and death. The vicissitudes of lust and romance are examined against a backdrop of urban decay in this testament to the allure of the forbidden.

THE WET FOREVER
$6.95/117-9
The story of Janus and Madchen—a small-time hood and a beautiful sex worker on the run—examines themes of loyalty, sacrifice, redemption and obsession amidst Manhattan's sex parlors and underground S/M clubs.

MICHAEL PERKINS
EVIL COMPANIONS
$6.95/3067-9
Evil Companions has been hailed as "a frightening classic." A young couple explores the nether reaches of the erotic unconscious in a confrontation with the extremes of passion.

THE SECRET RECORD:
Modern Erotic Literature
$6.95/3039-3
Michael Perkins surveys the field with authority and unique insight. Updated and revised to include the latest trends, tastes, and developments in this misunderstood genre.

MASQUERADE BOOKS

AN ANTHOLOGY OF CLASSIC ANONYMOUS EROTIC WRITING
$6.95/140-3
Michael Perkins has collected the best passages from the world's erotic writing. "Anonymous" is one of the most infamous bylines in publishing history—and these excerpts show why!

HELEN HENLEY
ENTER WITH TRUMPETS
$6.95/197-7
Helen Henley was told that women just don't write about sex. So Henley did it alone, flying in the face of "tradition" by writing this touching tale of arousal and devotion in one couple's kinky relationship.

ALICE JOANOU
BLACK TONGUE
$6.95/258-2
"Joanou has created a series of sumptuous, brooding, dark visions of sexual obsession, and is undoubtedly a name to look out for in the future." —Redeemer

Exploring lust at its most florid and unsparing, *Black Tongue* is redolent of forbidden passions.

SAMUEL R. DELANY
THE MAD MAN
$8.99/408-9/Mass market
"Delany develops an insightful dichotomy between [his protagonist]'s two worlds: the one of cerebral philosophy and dry academia, the other of heedless, 'impersonal' obsessive sexual extremism. When these worlds finally collide...the novel achieves a surprisingly satisfying resolution...." —Publishers Weekly

Graduate student John Marr researches the life of Timothy Hasler: a philosopher whose career was cut tragically short over a decade earlier. Marr begins to find himself increasingly drawn toward shocking sexual encounters with the homeless men, until it begins to seem that Hasler's death might hold some key to his own life as a gay man in the age of AIDS.

PHILIP JOSÉ FARMER
A FEAST UNKNOWN
$6.95/276-0
"Sprawling, brawling, shocking, suspenseful, hilarious..." —Theodore Sturgeon
Lord Grandrith—armed with the belief that he is the son of Jack the Ripper—tells the story of his remarkable life. His story progresses to encompass the furthest extremes of human behavior.

FLESH
$6.95/303-1
Stagg explored the galaxies for 800 years. Upon his return, the hero Stagg is made the centerpiece of an incredible public ritual—one that will take him to the heights of ecstasy, and drag him toward the depths of hell.

TUPPY OWENS
SENSATIONS
$6.95/3081-4
Tuppy Owens takes a rare peek behind the scenes of *Sensations*—the first big-budget sex flick. Originally commissioned to appear in book form after the release of the film in 1975, *Sensations* is finally available.

DANIEL VIAN
ILLUSIONS
$6.95/3074-1
Two tales of danger and desire in Berlin on the eve of WWII. From private homes to lurid cafés, passion is exposed in stark contrast to the brutal violence of the time, as desperate people explore their darkest sexual desires.
PERSUASIONS
$4.95/183-7
"The stockings are drawn tight by the suspender belt, tight enough to be stretched to the limit just above the middle part of her thighs, tight enough so that her calves glow through the sheer silk..." A double novel, including the classics *Adagio* and *Gabriela and the General*, this volume traces lust around the globe.

LIESEL KULIG
LOVE IN WARTIME
$6.95/3044-X
Madeleine knew that the handsome SS officer was dangerous, but she was just a cabaret singer in Nazi-occupied Paris, trying to survive in a perilous time. When Josef fell in love with her, he discovered that a beautiful woman can be as dangerous as any warrior.

SOPHIE GALLEYMORE BIRD
MANEATER
$6.95/103-9
Through a bizarre act of creation, a man attains the "perfect" lover—by all appearances a beautiful, sensuous woman, but in reality something far darker. Once brought to life she will accept no mate, seeking instead the prey that will sate her hunger.

MASQUERADE BOOKS

THE ARENA
$4.95/3083-0
Preston's take on the ultimate sex club–where men go to abolish all personal limits. Only the author of *Mr. Benson* could have imagined so perfect an institution for the satisfaction of male desire.

THE HEIR•THE KING
$4.95/3048-2
The Heir, written in the lyric voice of the ancient myths, tells the story of a world where slaves and masters create a new sexual society. *The King* tells the story of a soldier who discovers his monarch's most secret desires.

THE MISSION OF ALEX KANE
GOLDEN YEARS
$4.95/3069-5
When evil threatens the plans of a group of older gay men, Kane's got the muscle to take it head on. Along the way, he wins the support—and very specialized attentions—of a cowboy plucked right out of the Old West.

DEADLY LIES
$4.95/3076-8
Politics is a dirty business and the dirt becomes deadly when a smear campaign targets gay men. Who better to clean things up than Alex Kane!

STOLEN MOMENTS
$4.95/3098-9
Houston's evolving gay community is victimized by a malicious newspaper editor who is more than willing to boost circulation by printing homophobic slander. He never counted on Alex Kane, fearless defender of gay dreams and desires.

SECRET DANGER
$4.95/111-X
Alex Kane and the faithful Danny are called to a small European country, where a group of gay tourists is being held hostage by brutal terrorists.

LETHAL SILENCE
$4.95/125-X
Chicago becomes the scene of the right-wing's most noxious plan—facilitated by unholy political alliances. Alex and Danny head to the Windy City to battle the mercenaries who would squash gay men underfoot.

MATT TOWNSEND
SOLIDLY BUILT
$6.50/416-X
The tale of the relationship between Jeff, a young photographer, and Mark, the butch electrician hired to wire Jeff's new home. For Jeff, it's love at first sight; Mark, however, has more than a few hang-ups.

JAY SHAFFER
ANIMAL HANDLERS
$4.95/264-7
In Shaffer's world, every man finally succumbs to the animal urges deep inside. And if there's any creature that promises a wild time, it's a beast who's been caged for far too long.

FULL SERVICE
$4.95/150-0
No-nonsense guys bear down hard on each other as they work their way toward release in this finely detailed assortment of fantasies.

D. V. SADERO
IN THE ALLEY
$4.95/144-6
Hardworking men bring their special skills and impressive tools to the most satisfying job of all: capturing and breaking the male animal.

SCOTT O'HARA
DO-IT-YOURSELF PISTON POLISHING
$6.50/489-5
Longtime sex-pro Scott O'Hara draws upon his acute powers of seduction to lure you into a world of hard, horny men long overdue for a tune-up.

SUTTER POWELL
EXECUTIVE PRIVILEGES
$6.50/383-X
No matter how serious or sexy a predicament his characters find themselves in, Powell conveys the sheer exuberance of their encounters with a warm humor rarely seen in contemporary gay erotica.

GARY BOWEN
WESTERN TRAILS
$6.50/477-1
Some of gay literature's brightest stars tell the sexy truth about the many ways a rugged stud found to satisfy himself—and his buddy—in the Very Wild West.

MAN HUNGRY
$5.95/374-0
A riveting collection of stories from one of gay erotica's new stars. Dipping into a variety of genres, Bowen crafts tales of lust unlike anything being published today.

ROBERT BAHR
SEX SHOW
$4.95/225-6
Luscious dancing boys. Brazen, explicit acts. Take a seat, and get very comfortable, because the curtain's going up on a very special show no discriminating appetite can afford to miss.

MASQUERADE BOOKS

MASQUERADE BOOKS

WANDERLUST:
Homoerotic Tales of Travel
$5.95/395-3

A volume dedicated to the special pleasures of faraway places—and the horny men who lie in wait for intrepid tourists. Celebrate the freedom of the open road, and the allure of men who stray from the beaten path....

THE BADBOY BOOK
OF EROTIC POETRY
$5.95/382-1

Erotic poetry has long been the problem child of the literary world—highly creative and provocative, but somehow too frank to be "art." *The Badboy Book of Erotic Poetry* restores eros to its place of honor in gay writing.

AARON TRAVIS
BIG SHOTS
$5.95/448-8

Two fierce tales in one electrifying volume. In *Beirut*, Travis tells the story of ultimate military power and erotic subjugation; *Kip*, Travis' hypersexed and sinister take on *film noir*, appears in unexpurgated form for the first time.

EXPOSED
$4.95/126-8

A unique glimpse of the horny gay male in his natural environment! Cops, college jocks, ancient Romans—even Sherlock Holmes and his loyal Watson—cruise these pages, fresh from the pen of one of our hottest authors.

IN THE BLOOD
$5.95/283-3

Early tales from this master of the genre. Includes "In the Blood"—a heart-pounding descent into sexual vampirism.

THE FLESH FABLES
$4.95/243-4

One of Travis' best collections. Includes "Blue Light," as well as other masterpieces that established him as one of gay erotica's master storytellers.

BOB VICKERY
SKIN DEEP
$4.95/265-5

So many varied beauties no one will go away unsatisfied. No tantalizing morsel of manflesh is overlooked—or left unexplored!

JR
FRENCH QUARTER NIGHTS
$5.95/337-6

Sensual snapshots of the many places where men get down and dirty—from the steamy French Quarter to the steam room at the old Everard baths.

TOM BACCHUS
RAHM
$5.95/315-5

Tom Bacchus brings to life an extraordinary assortment of characters, from the Father of Us All to the cowpoke next door, the early gay literati to rude, queercore mosh rats.

BONE
$4.95/177-2

Queer musings from the pen of one of today's hottest young talents. Tom Bacchus maps out the tricking ground of a new generation.

KEY LINCOLN
SUBMISSION HOLDS
$4.95/266-3

From tough to tender, the men between these covers stop at nothing to get what they want. These sweat-soaked tales show just how bad boys can really get.

CALDWELL/EIGHNER
QSFX2
$5.95/278-7

Other-worldly yarns from two master storytellers—Clay Caldwell and Lars Eighner. Both eroticists take a trip to the furthest reaches of the sexual imagination, sending back ten scalding sci-fi stories of male desire.

CLAY CALDWELL
SOME LIKE IT ROUGH
$6.95/544-1

"Caldwell's charm is more powerful, his nostalgia more poignant, the horniness he captures more sweetly, achingly acute than ever." —Aaron Travis

A new collection of stories from a master of gay eroticism. Here are the best of Clay Caldwell's darkest tales—thrilling explorations of dominance and submission. Hot and heavy, Some Like It Rough is filled with enough virile masters and willing slaves to satisfy the the most demanding reader.

JOCK STUDS
$6.95/472-0

Scalding tales of pumped bodies and raging libidos. Swimmers, runners, football players—whatever your sport might be, there's a man here waiting to work up a little sweat, peel off his uniform, and claim his reward for a game well-played....

ASK OL' BUDDY
$5.95/346-5

Set in the underground SM world—where men initiate one another into the secrets of the rawest sexual realm of all. And when each stud's initiation is complete, he takes part in the training of another hungry soul....

MASQUERADE BOOKS

MASQUERADE BOOKS

CHAINS
$4.95/158-6
Picking up street punks has always been risky, but here it sets off a string of events that must be read to be believed. The legendary Townsend at his grittiest.

RUN, LITTLE LEATHER BOY
$4.95/143-8
The famous tale of sexual awakening. A chronic underachiever, Wayne seems to be going nowhere fast. He finds himself drawn to the masculine intensity of a dark and mysterious sexual underground, where he soon finds many goals worth pursuing....

RUN NO MORE
$4.95/152-7
The sequel to *Run, Little Leather Boy*. This volume follows the further adventures of Townsend's leatherclad narrator as he travels every sexual byway available to the S/M male.

THE SEXUAL ADVENTURES OF SHERLOCK HOLMES
$4.95/3097-0
A scandalously sexy take on the notorious sleuth. Via the diary of Holmes' horny sidekick Watson, experience Holmes' most challenging—and arousing—adventures! An underground classic

THE GAY ADVENTURES OF CAPTAIN GOOSE
$4.95/169-1
Jerome Gander is sentenced to serve aboard a ship manned by the most hardened criminals. In no time, Gander becomes one of the most notorious rakehells Olde England had ever seen. On land or sea, Gander hunts down the Empire's hottest studs.

....

DONALD VINING
CABIN FEVER AND OTHER STORIES
$5.95/338-4
"Demonstrates the wisdom experience combined with insight and optimism can create."　　　—*Bay Area Reporter*

Eighteen blistering stories in celebration of the most intimate of male bonding, reaffirming both love and lust in modern gay life.

....

DEREK ADAMS
MILES DIAMOND AND THE CASE OF THE CRETAN APOLLO
$6.95/381-3
Hired by a wealthy man to track a cheating lover, Miles finds himself involved in ways he could never have imagined! When the jealous Callahan threatens not only Diamond but his innocent an studly assistant, Miles counters with a little undercover work—involving as many horny informants as he can get his hands on!

THE MARK OF THE WOLF
$5.95/361-9
The past comes back to haunt one well-off stud, whose desires lead him into the arms of many men—and the midst of a mystery.

MY DOUBLE LIFE
$5.95/314-7
Every man leads a double life, dividing his hours between the mundanities of the day and the pursuits of the night. Derek Adams shines a light on the wicked things men do when no one's looking.

HEAT WAVE
$4.95/159-4
Derek Adams sexy short stories are guaranteed to jump start any libido—and *Heatwave* contains his very best.

MILES DIAMOND AND THE DEMON OF DEATH
$4.95/251-5
Miles always find himself in the stickiest situations—with any stud he meets! This adventure promises another carnal carnival, as Diamond investigates a host of horny guys.

THE ADVENTURES OF MILES DIAMOND
$4.95/118-7
The debut of this popular gay gumshoe. To Diamond's delight, "The Case of the Missing Twin" is packed with randy studs. Miles sets about uncovering all as he tracks down the delectable Daniel Travis.

....

KELVIN BELIELE
IF THE SHOE FITS
$4.95/223-X
An essential volume of tales exploring a world where randy boys can't help but do what comes naturally—as often as possible! Sweaty male bodies grapple in pleasure.

....

JAMES MEDLEY
THE REVOLUTIONARY & OTHER STORIES
$6.50/417-8
Billy, the son of the station chief of the American Embassy in Guatemala, is kidnapped and held for ransom. Frightened at first, Billy gradually develops an unimaginably close relationship with Juan, the revolutionary assigned to guard him.

HUCK AND BILLY
$4.95/245-0
Young lust knows no bounds—and is often the hottest of one's life! Huck and Billy explore the desires that course through their bodies, determined to plumb the depths of passion. A thrilling look at desire between men.

MASQUERADE BOOKS

FLEDERMAUS
FLEDERFICTION: STORIES OF MEN AND TORTURE
$5.95/355-4
Fifteen blistering paeans to men and their suffering. Unafraid of exploring the furthest reaches of pain and pleasure, Fledermaus unleashes his most thrilling tales in this volume.

VICTOR TERRY
MASTERS
$6.50/418-6
Terry's butchest tales. A powerhouse volume of boot-wearing, whip-wielding, bone-crunching bruisers who've got what it takes to make a grown man grovel.
SM/SD
$6.50/406-2
Set around a South Dakota town called Prairie, these tales offer evidence that the real rough stuff can still be found where men take what they want despite all rules.
WHiPs
$4.95/254-X
Cruising for a hot man? You'd better be, because one way or another, these WHiPs—officers of the Wyoming Highway Patrol—are gonna pull you over for a little impromptu interrogation....

MAX EXANDER
DEEDS OF THE NIGHT: Tales of Eros and Passion
$5.95/348-1
MAXimum porn! Exander's a writer who's seen it all—and is more than happy to describe every glorious inch of it in pulsating detail. A whirlwind tour of the hypermasculine libido.
LEATHERSEX
$4.95/210-8
Hard-hitting tales from merciless Max. This time he focuses on the leather clad lust that draws together only the most willing and talented of tops and bottoms—for an all-out orgy of limitless surrender and control....
MANSEX
$4.95/160-8
"Mark was the classic leatherman: a huge, dark stud in chaps, with a big black moustache, hairy chest and enormous muscles. Exactly the kind of men Todd liked—strong, hunky, masculine, ready to take control...."

TOM CAFFREY
TALES FROM THE MEN'S ROOM
$5.95/364-3
Male lust at its most elemental and arousing. The Men's Room is less a place than a state of mind—one that every man finds himself in, day after day....
HITTING HOME
$4.95/222-1
Titillating and compelling, the stories in *Hitting Home* make a strong case for there being only one thing on a man's mind. Hot studs via the imagination of this new talent.

"BIG" BILL JACKSON
EIGHTH WONDER
$4.95/200-0
"Big" Bill Jackson's always the randiest guy in town—no matter what town he's in. From the bright lights and back rooms of New York to the open fields and sweaty bods of a small Southern town, "Big" Bill always manages to cause a scene!

TORSTEN BARRING
GUY TRAYNOR
$6.50/414-3
Some call Guy Traynor a theatrical genius; others say he was a madman. All anyone knows for certain is that his productions were the result of blood, sweat and outrageous erotic torture!
SHADOWMAN
$4.95/178-0
From spoiled aristocrats to randy youths sowing wild oats at the local picture show, Barring's imagination works overtime in these steamy vignettes of homolust.
PETER THORNWELL
$4.95/149-7
Follow the exploits of Peter Thornwell and his outrageously horny cohorts as he goes from misspent youth to scandalous stardom, all thanks to an insatiable libido and love for the lash. The first of Torsten Barring's popular SM novels.
THE SWITCH
$4.95/3061-X
Some of the most brutally thrilling erotica available today. Sometimes a man needs a good whipping, and *The Switch* certainly makes a case! Packed with hot studs and unrelenting passions, these stories established Barring as a writer to be watched.

BUY ANY 4 BOOKS & CHOOSE 1 ADDITIONAL BOOK, OF EQUAL OR LESSER VALUE, AS YOUR FREE GIFT

MASQUERADE BOOKS

BERT McKENZIE
FRINGE BENEFITS
$5.95/354-6
From the pen of a widely published short story writer comes a volume of highly immodest tales. Not afraid of getting down and dirty, McKenzie produces some of today's most visceral sextales.

CHRISTOPHER MORGAN
STEAM GAUGE
$6.50/473-9
This volume abounds in manly men doing what they do best—to, with, or for any hot stud who crosses their paths.
THE SPORTSMEN
$5.95/385-6
A collection of super-hot stories dedicated to the all-American athlete. These writers know just the type of guys that make up every red-blooded male's starting line-up....
MUSCLE BOUND
$4.95/3028-8
Tommy joins forces with sexy Will Rodriguez in a battle of wits and biceps at the hottest gym in town, where the weak are bound and crushed by iron-pumping gods.

SONNY FORD
REUNION IN FLORENCE
$4.95/3070-9
Follow Adrian and Tristan an a sexual odyssey that takes in all ports known to ancient man. From lustful Turks to insatiable Mamluks, these two spread pleasure throughout the classical world!

ROGER HARMAN
FIRST PERSON
$4.95/179-9
Each story takes the form of a confessional—told by men who've got plenty to confess! From the "first time ever" to firsts of different kinds....

J. A. GUERRA, ED.
SLOW BURN
$4.95/3042-3
Torsos get lean and hard, pecs widen, and stomachs ripple in these sexy stories of the power and perils of physical perfection.

DAVE KINNICK
SORRY I ASKED
$4.95/3090-3
Unexpurgated interviews with gay porn's rank and file. Get personal with the men behind (and under) the "stars," and discover the hot truth about the porn business.

SEAN MARTIN
SCRAPBOOK
$4.95/224-8
From the creator of Doc and Raider comes this hot collection of life's horniest moments—all involving studs sure to set your pulse racing!

CARO SOLES & STAN TAL, EDS.
BIZARRE DREAMS
$4.95/187-X
An anthology of voices dedicated to exploring the dark side of human fantasy. Here are the most talented practitioners of "dark fantasy," the most forbidden sexual realm of all.

MICHAEL LOWENTHAL, ED.
THE BADBOY EROTIC LIBRARY
Volume 1
$4.95/190-X
Excerpts from A Secret Life, Imre, Sins of the Cities of the Plain, Teleny and others.
THE BADBOY EROTIC LIBRARY
Volume 2
$4.95/211-6
This time, selections are taken from Mike and Me, Muscle Bound, Men at Work, Badboy Fantasies, and Slowbum.

ERIC BOYD
MIKE AND ME
$5.95/419-4
Mike joined the gym squad to bulk up on muscle. Little did he know he'd be turning on every sexy muscle jock in Minnesota! Hard bodies collide in a series of horny workouts.
MIKE AND THE MARINES
$6.50/497-6
Mike takes on America's most elite corps of studs! Join in on the never-ending sexual escapades of this singularly lustful platoon!

ANONYMOUS
A SECRET LIFE
$4.95/3017-2
Meet Master Charles: eighteen and quite innocent, until his arrival at the Sir Percival's Academy, where the lessons are supplemented with a crash course in pure sexual heat!
SINS OF THE CITIES OF THE PLAIN
$5.95/322-8
indulge yourself in the scorching memoirs of young man-about-town Jack Saul. Jack's sinful escapades grow wilder with every chapter!
IMRE
$4.95/3019-9
An extraordinary lost classic of obsession, gay erotic desire, and romance in a small European town on the eve of WWI. An early look at gay love and lust.

MASQUERADE BOOKS

THE SCARLET PANSY
$4.95/189-6
Randall Etrange travels the world in search of true love. Along the way, his journey becomes a sexual odyssey of truly epic proportions.

HARD CANDY

ELISE D'HAENE
LICKING OUR WOUNDS
$7.95/605-7
"A fresh, engagingly sarcastic and determinedly bawdy voice. D'Haene is blessed with a savvy, iconoclastic view of the world that is mordant but never mean." —*Publisher's Weekly*

Licking Our Wounds, Elise D'Haene's acclaimed debut novel, is the story of Maria, a young woman coming to terms with the complexities of life in the age of AIDS. Abandoned by her lover and faced with the deaths of her friends, Maria struggles along with the help of Peter, HIV-positive and deeply conflicted about the changes in his own life, and Christie, a lover who is full of her own ideas about truth and the meaning of life.

CHEA VILLANUEVA
BULLETPROOF BUTCHES
$7.95/560-3
"...Gutsy, hungry, and outrageous, but with a tender core... Villanueva is a writer to watch out for: she will teach us something." —Joan Nestle
One of lesbian literature's most uncompromising voices. Never afraid to address the harsh realities of working-class lesbian life, Chea Villanueva charts territory frequently overlooked in the age of "lesbian chic."

KEVIN KILLIAN
ARCTIC SUMMER
$6.95/514-X
A critically acclaimed examination of the emptiness lying beneath the rich exterior of America in the 50s. With the story of Liam Reilly—a young gay man of considerable means and numerous secrets—Killian exposes the complexities and contradictions of the American Dream.

STAN LEVENTHAL
BARBIE IN BONDAGE
$6.95/415-1
Widely regarded as one of the most clear-eyed interpreters of big city gay male life, Leventhal here provides a series of explorations of love and desire between men.

SKYDIVING ON CHRISTOPHER STREET
$6.95/287-6
"Positively addictive." —Dennis Cooper

Aside from a hateful job, a hateful apartment, a hateful world and an increasingly hateful lover, life seems, well, all right for the protagonist of Stan Leventhal's latest novel. An insightful tale of contemporary urban gay life.

MICHAEL ROWE
WRITING BELOW THE BELT: Conversations with Erotic Authors
$7.95/540-9
"An in-depth and enlightening tour of society's love/hate relationship with sex, morality, and censorship." —*James White Review*

Michael Rowe interviewed the best and brightest erotic writers and presents the collected wisdom in *Writing Below the Belt*. Includes interviews with such cult sensations as John Preston, Larry Townsend, Pat Califia, and others.

PAUL T. ROGERS
SAUL'S BOOK
$7.95/462-3
Winner of the Editors' Book Award

"A first novel of considerable power... Speaks to us all." —*New York Times Book Review*

The story of a Times Square hustler, Sinbad the Sailor, and Saul, a brilliant, self-destructive, dominating character who may be the only love Sinbad will ever know. A classic tale of desire, obsession and the wages of love.

PATRICK MOORE
IOWA
$6.95/423-2
"Full of terrific characters etched in acid-sharp prose, soaked through with just enough ambivalence to make it thoroughly romantic." —Felice Picano

The tale of one gay man's journey into adulthood, and the roads that bring him home.

LARS EIGHNER
GAY COSMOS
$6.95/236-1
An analysis of gay culture. Praised by the press, *Gay Cosmos* is an important contribution to the area of Gay and Lesbian Studies.

BUY ANY 4 BOOKS & CHOOSE 1 ADDITIONAL BOOK, OF EQUAL OR LESSER VALUE, AS YOUR FREE GIFT

MASQUERADE BOOKS

WALTER R. HOLLAND
THE MARCH
$6.95/429-1

Beginning on a hot summer night in 1980, *The March* revolves around a circle of young gay men, and the many others their lives touch. Over time, each character changes in unexpected ways; lives and loves come together and fall apart, as society itself is horribly altered by the onslaught of AIDS.

BRAD GOOCH
THE GOLDEN AGE OF PROMISCUITY
$7.95/550-6

"The next best thing to taking a time-machine trip to grovel in the glorious '70s gutter." —*San Francisco Chronicle*

"A solid, unblinking, unsentimental look at a vanished era. Gooch tells us everything we ever wanted to know about the dark and decadent gay subculture in Manhattan before AIDS altered the landscape." —*Kirkus Reviews*

RED JORDAN AROBATEAU
DIRTY PICTURES
$5.95/345-7

Dirty Pictures is the story of a lonely butch tending bar—and the femme she finally calls her own.

LUCY AND MICKEY
$6.95/311-2

"A necessary reminder to all who blissfully—some may say ignorantly—ride the wave of lesbian chic into the mainstream." —Heather Findlay

The story of Mickey—an uncompromising butch—and her long affair with Lucy, the femme she loves.

DONALD VINING
A GAY DIARY
$8.95/451-8

"*A Gay Diary* is, unquestionably, the richest historical document of gay male life in the United States that I have ever encountered...." —*Body Politic*

Vining's *Diary* portrays a vanished age and the lifestyle of a generation frequently forgotten.

FELICE PICANO
AMBIDEXTROUS
$6.95/275-2

"Makes us remember what it feels like to be a child..." —*The Advocate*

A highly acclaimed volume, and the first of the author's novelistic memoirs. Picano tells all about his formative years: home life, school face-offs, the ingenuous sophistications of his first sexual steps.

MEN WHO LOVED ME
$6.95/274-4

"Zesty...spiked with adventure and romance...a distinguished and humorous portrait of a vanished age." —*Publishers Weekly*

In 1966, Picano abandoned New York, determined to find true love in Europe. He becomes embroiled in a romance with Djanko, and lives *la dolce vita* to the fullest. Upon returning to the US, he plunges into the city's thriving gay community of the 1970s.

THE LURE
$6.95/398-8

A Book-of-the-Month-Club Selection

After witnessing a brutal murder, Noel is recruited by the police, to assist as a lure for the killer. Undercover, he moves deep into the freneticism of gay highlife in 1970s Manhattan—where he discovers his own hidden desires. A hypnotic whodunnit, enlivened with period detail.

WILLIAM TALSMAN
THE GAUDY IMAGE
$6.95/263-9

"To read *The Gaudy Image* now...it is to see first-hand the very issues of identity and positionality with which gay men were struggling in the decades before Stonewall. For what Talsman is dealing with...is the very question of how we conceive ourselves gay." —from the introduction by Michael Bronski

ROSEBUD

THE ROSEBUD READER
$5.95/319-8

Rosebud has contributed greatly to the burgeoning genre of lesbian erotica, introducing new writers and adding contemporary classics to the shelves. Here are the finest moments from Rosebud's runaway successes.

DANIELLE ENGLE
UNCENSORED FANTASIES
$6.95/572-7

In a world where so many stifle their emotions, who doesn't find themselves yearning for a little old-fashioned honesty—even if it means bearing one's own secret desires? Danielle Engle's heroines do just that—and a great deal more—in their quest for total sexual pleasure.

LESLIE CAMERON
WHISPER OF FANS
$6.50/542-5

A thrilling chronicle of love between women, written with a sure eye for sensual detail. One woman discovers herself through the sensual devotion of another.

MASQUERADE BOOKS

RACHEL PEREZ
ODD WOMEN
$6.50/526-3
These women are sexy, smart, tough—some say odd. But who cares! An assortment of Sapphic sirens proves once and for all that comely ladies come best in pairs.

RED JORDAN AROBATEAU
STREET FIGHTER
$6.95/583-2
Another blast of truth from one of today's most notorious plain-speakers. An unsentimental look at the life of a street butch—Woody, the consummate outsider, living on the fringes of San Francisco.
SATAN'S BEST
$6.95/539-5
An epic tale of life with the Outlaws—the ultimate lesbian biker gang. Angel, a lonely butch, joins the Outlaws, and finds herself loving a new breed of woman and facing a new brand of danger on the open road....
ROUGH TRADE
$6.50/470-4
Famous for her unflinching portrayal of lower-class dyke life and love, Arobateau outdoes herself with these tales of butch/femme affairs and unrelenting passions.
BOYS NIGHT OUT
$6.50/463-1
Incendiary short fiction from this lesbian literary sensation. As always, Arobateau takes a good hard look at the lives of everyday women, noting well the struggles and triumphs each experiences.

RANDY TUROFF
LUST NEVER SLEEPS
$6.50/475-5
Highly erotic, powerfully real fiction. Turoff depicts a circle of modern women connected through the bonds of love, friendship, ambition, and lust with accuracy and compassion.

K. T. BUTLER
TOOLS OF THE TRADE
$5.95/420-8
A sparkling mix of lesbian erotica and humor. An encounter with ice cream, cappuccino and chocolate cake; an affair with a complete stranger; a pair of faulty handcuffs; and more.

ALISON TYLER
THE SILVER KEY: Madame Victoria's Finishing School
$6.95/614-6
In a Victorian finishing school, a circle of randy young ladies share a diary. Molly records an explicit description of her initiation into the ways of physical love; Colette reports on a ghostly encounter; and Katherine transcribes the journey of her love affair with the wickedly wanton Eden. Each of these thrilling tales is recounted in loving detail....
COME QUICKLY: For Girls on the Go
$6.95/428-3
Here are over sixty of the hottest fantasies around. A volume designed a modern girl on a modern schedule, who still appreciates a little old-fashioned action.
VENUS ONLINE
$6.50/521-2
Lovely Alexa spends her days in a boring bank job, saving her energies for the night—when she goes online. Soon Alexa—aka Venus—finds her real and online lives colliding sexily.
DARK ROOM: An Online Adventure
$6.50/455-0
Dani, a successful photographer, can't bring herself to face the death of her lover, Kate. Determined to keep the memory of her lover alive, Dani goes online under Kate's screen alias—and begins to uncover the truth behind Kate's shocking death....
BLUE SKY SIDEWAYS & OTHER STORIES
$6.50/394-5
A variety of women, and their many breathtaking experiences with lovers, friends—and even the occasional sexy stranger.
DIAL "L" FOR LOVELESS
$5.95/386-4
Katrina Loveless—a sexy private eye talented enough to give Sam Spade a run for his money. In her first case, Katrina investigates a murder implicating a host of lovely, lusty ladies.
THE VIRGIN
$5.95/379-1
Seeking the fulfillment of her deepest sexual desires, Veronica answers a personal ad in the "Women Seeking Women" category—and discovers a whole sensual world she had only dreamed existed!

LOVECHILD

GAG
$5.95/369-4
One of the bravest young writers you'll ever encounter. These poems take on hypocrisy with uncommon energy, and announce Lovechild as a writer of unforgettable rage.

ELIZABETH OLIVER

THE SM MURDER:
Murder at Roman Hill
$5.95/353-8
Intrepid lesbian P.I.s Leslie Patrick and Robin Penny take on a really hot case: the murder of the notorious Felicia Roman. The circumstances of the crime lead them through the leatherdyke underground, where motives—and desires—run deep.

LAURA ANTONIOU, ED.

LEATHERWOMEN III:
The Clash of the Cultures
$6.95/619-7
Laura Antoniou gathers the very best of today's cutting-edge women's erotica—concentrating on multicultural stories involving characters too infrequently seen in this genre. More than fifteen of today's most daring writers make this a compelling testament to desire.

LEATHERWOMEN
$6.95/598-0
"...a great new collection of fiction by and about SM dykes."
—SKIN TWO

A groundbreaking anthology. These fantasies, from the pens of new or emerging authors, break every rule imposed on women's fantasies. The hottest stories from some of today's newest writers make this an unforgettable exploration of the female libido.

LEATHERWOMEN II
$4.95/229-9
Another volume of writing from women on the edge, sure to ignite libidinal flames in any reader. Leave taboos behind, because these Leatherwomen know no limits....

VALENTINA CILESCU

MY LADY'S PLEASURE:
Mistress with a Maid, Volume 1
$5.95/412-1
Claudia Dungarrow, a lovely, powerful professor, attempts to seduce Elizabeth Stanbridge, setting off a chain of events that eventually ruins her career. Claudia vows revenge—and makes her foes pay deliciously....

DARK VENUS:
Mistress with a Maid, Volume 2
$6.50/481-X
Claudia Dungarrow's quest for ultimate erotic dominance continues in this scalding second volume! How many maidens will fall prey to her insatiable appetite?

BODY AND SOUL:
Mistress with a Maid, Volume 3
$6.50/515-8
Dr. Claudia Dungarrow returns for yet another tour of depravity, subjugating every maiden in sight to her sexual whims. But she has yet to hold Elizabeth in submission. Will she ever?

THE ROSEBUD SUTRA
$4.95/242-6
A look at the ultimate guide to lesbian love. The Rosebud Sutra explores the secrets women keep from everyone—everyone but one another, that is...

MISTRESS MINE
$6.50/502-6
Sophia Cranleigh sits in prison, accused of authoring the "obscene" *Mistress Mine*. What she has done, however, is merely chronicle the events of her life under the hand of Mistress Malin.

AARONA GRIFFIN

LEDA AND THE HOUSE OF SPIRITS
$6.95/585-9
Two steamy novellas in one volume. Ten years into her relationship with Chrys, *Leda* decides to take a one-night vacation—at a local lesbian sex club. In the second story, lovely Lydia thinks she has her grand new home all to herself—until dreams begin to suggest that this *House of Spirits* harbors other souls, determined to do some serious partying.

PASSAGE & OTHER STORIES
$6.95/599-9
"A tale of a woman who is brave enough to follow her desire, even if it leads her into the arms of dangerous women."
—Pat Califia

Nina leads a "safe" life—until she finds herself infatuated with a woman she spots at a local café. One night, Nina follows her, only to find herself enmeshed in an maze leading to a mysterious world of pain and pleasure where women test the edges of sexuality and power.

LINDSAY WELSH

SEXUAL FANTASIES
$6.95/586-7
A volume of today's hottest lesbian erotica. A dozen sexy stories, ranging from sweet to spicy, *Sexual Fantasies* offers a look at the many desires and depravities indulged in by modern women.

ORDERING IS EASY

MC/VISA orders can be placed by calling our toll-free number
PHONE 800-375-2356/FAX 212-986-7355
HOURS M-F 9am—12am EDT Sat & Sun 12pm—8pm EDT
E-MAIL masqbks@aol.com
or mail this coupon to:
MASQUERADE DIRECT.
DEPT. BMMQ98 801 2ND AVE., NY, NY 10017

**BUY ANY FOUR BOOKS AND CHOOSE ONE ADDITIONAL BOOK,
OF EQUAL OR LESSER VALUE, AS YOUR FREE GIFT**

QTY.	TITLE	NO.	PRICE
			FREE

DEPT. BMMQ98 (please have this code available when placing your order)	SUBTOTAL
	POSTAGE AND HANDLING
We never sell, give or trade any customer's name.	TOTAL

In the U.S., please add $1.50 for the first book and 75¢ for each additional book; in Canada, add $2.00 for the first book and $1.25 for each additional book. Foreign countries: add $4.00 for the first book and $2.00 for each additional book. No C.O.D. orders. Please make all checks payable to Masquerade/Direct. Payable in U.S. currency only. NY state residents add 8.25% sales tax. Please allow 4–6 weeks for delivery. Payable in U.S. currency only.

NAME _____

ADDRESS _____

CITY_____ STATE _____ ZIP_____

TEL( ) _____

E-MAIL _____

PAYMENT: ☐ CHECK   ☐ MONEY ORDER   ☐ VISA   ☐ MC

CARD NO. _____ EXP. DATE _____